# The Cryptic Clue

Amanda Hampson grew up in rural New Zealand. She has lived in London and Sydney, and now lives in Melbourne. Writing professionally for more than twenty years, she is the author of *The Olive Sisters*, *Two for the Road*, *The French Perfumer*, *The Yellow Villa*, *Sixty Summers*, *Lovebirds*, and cosy crime novels *The Tea Ladies* and *The Cryptic Clue*.

'As cosy mysteries go, this has to be one of the best. Never underrate a tea lady!'

'One of the most entertaining and cosy audiobooks I've listened to this year. Right up there with *The Thursday Murder Club*.'

'Great plot with just the right amount of mystery, suspense and humour thrown in.'

'A powerful sense of place and time, a hint of nostalgia, wonderfully crafted characters and friendships, a soupçon of magic realism, and an intricate crime plot that brings deadly danger to one of the most delightful amateur sleuths I've read.'

'This was the cosiest of cosy crimes and I absolutely loved everything about it.'

'I would love to sit down with any of them for a tea and cake or even a shandy at the Hollywood.'

'Thank you for lifting me out of the doldrums. I picked up your book and I laughed and wept my way through it. Now I feel *so* much better.'

'A delightful and heartwarming cosy crime novel that unexpectedly brightened my life.'

'Hampson's writing is smart and so funny. Do yourself a favour and get your hands on this book.'

*The Olive Sisters*
*Two for the Road*
*The French Perfumer*
*The Yellow Villa*
*Sixty Summers*
*Lovebirds*
*The Tea Ladies*

The Cryptic Clue

A TEA LADIES Mystery

Amanda Hampson

PENGUIN

VIKING

VIKING

UK | USA | Canada | Ireland | Australia
India | New Zealand | South Africa | China

Viking is part of the Penguin Random House group of companies
whose addresses can be found at global.penguinrandomhouse.com.

Penguin
Random House
Australia

First published by Viking, 2024

Cover illustrations: magnifying glass by donskarpo/Shutterstock; hanger by DebStudio/
Shutterstock; dynamite by Timplaru Eugenia/Shutterstock; fuse by Tartila/Shutterstock
Inside front cover: teacups by Aleksandra Novakovic/Shutterstock
Cover design by Debra Billson © Penguin Random House Australia Pty Ltd
Typeset in Adobe Garamond Pro by Midland Typesetters, Australia

Printed and bound in Australia by Griffin Press, an accredited
ISO AS/NZS 14001 Environmental Management Systems printer

 A catalogue record for this
book is available from the
National Library of Australia

ISBN 978 1 76134 102 1

penguin.com.au

*We at Penguin Random House Australia acknowledge that Aboriginal and Torres Strait Islander*
*peoples are the Traditional Custodians and the first storytellers of the lands on which we live and*
*work. We honour Aboriginal and Torres Strait Islander peoples' continuous connection to Country,*
*waters, skies and communities. We celebrate Aboriginal and Torres Strait Islander stories, traditions*
*and living cultures; and we pay our respects to Elders past and present.*

*For Billie Trinder, a rising star.*

SYDNEY, 1966

# 1

# MYSTERY AT THE BELLEVUE

Hazel Bates has been keeping a close eye on the man at the corner table since they arrived at the Bellevue Hotel. He eats alone at the same table each night and looks around the dining room, his curious gaze alighting on each of the guests in turn. Occasionally he jots down something in his notebook – almost as if he doesn't realise that they can see him. When his gaze meets Hazel's, he turns his attention to his meal in an unhurried way but soon resumes his silent surveillance. Despite this interest, he keeps very much to himself. Tonight, arriving in the dining room right on time, he eats his meal slowly and methodically and leaves as soon as he's finished.

Hazel's companion on this holiday, Betty Dewsnap, sits with pen poised over her notebook. 'What do they call those people who study people?' she asks in a loud whisper.

'An anthropologist?' suggests Hazel.

'Oh goodness, that's too difficult to spell. I'll put "people-watcher" – that's just one of my observations about him. My instincts tell me he's up to something.'

'He may be watching us, but we're doing the same thing,' says Hazel.

'It's the way he watches us . . . with intent.' Betty writes that down and leans across to whisper, 'Also, he's foreign.'

This is Hazel's first holiday in more years than she can remember. With their workplaces, Empire Fashionwear and Farley Frocks, shut for holidays until mid-January, the tea ladies have an entire week at Manly Beach, which is easily reached from the city by ferry.

The guesthouse, set several streets back from the beach, was once a smart private hotel. It's a little rundown now, which is the only reason she and Betty can afford to stay here. It's clean enough but the furnishings are worn, the curtains faded, and the paintwork on the front of the house is losing its battle against the salt air. The place perpetually smells of burnt toast, but the food isn't bad, and the beach is a short walk away.

Hazel and Betty share a room, which comes with its own problems. There's so little space between the two lumpy beds that they need to coordinate getting in and out of their beds to avoid getting in a tangle. The only other furniture in the room is a dressing table with a wardrobe attached, the mirror cracked across one corner. It has a little stool with a velvet cushion, where Betty likes to sit and put her rollers in while she provides an update on her various ailments, but Hazel doesn't mind. After decades of friendship, she's used to Betty's funny ways.

That said, despite her friend's many endearing traits (and the financial necessity), Hazel would be reluctant to share a room with her again. Betty's warm generosity and enthusiasm are offset by her snoring and nocturnal flatulence, which sounds like a pistol shot and has Hazel waking in fright several times a night. If they could afford separate rooms, it would be a perfect holiday.

The waitress dumps two bowls of soup in front of them. To Hazel's dismay, it's onion, which doesn't bode well for the night ahead.

Betty continues. 'He has the exact same routine every day. Takes the early breakfast, leaves the Bellevue at exactly 7.45 am carrying a leather satchel. And he walks down towards the ferry – I watched him from the window.'

'Betty dear, please don't suggest we follow him. We're on holiday.'

'I told you, I have a gut feeling, Hazel.'

'You're probably just hungry.' Hazel nudges the plate of bread closer to Betty. 'Have a slice of bread with your soup.'

After two cloudy days threatening rain, the afternoon of the third day delivers sunshine and a brilliant blue sky. Betty hires a sun umbrella from the Bellevue (complaining bitterly about the two-shilling deposit), and they take a couple of towels down to the harbourside beach.

The shoreline is busy with families spread out on picnic rugs with umbrellas and deck chairs. When the ladies are settled on their towels and the umbrella is screwed into the sand, Betty gets out a bag of lollies, pops one in her mouth and passes them to Hazel.

'When the girl was getting the umbrella from out the back,' she says, rolling the lolly around in her mouth, 'I looked in the guest register for that fellow's name.'

'You're lucky Mrs Frazer didn't catch you,' says Hazel.

'I could hear her scolding someone in the kitchen, so you could say the opportunity presented itself. His name is Sorensen, Mr Oscar Sorensen. I knew he was foreign. A foreigner,' she repeats, relishing the word. 'I don't want to alarm you, Hazel, but he could be a spy or a secret agent.'

'It's possible, I suppose.' Hazel leans back and rests on her elbows to watch a ferry approach in the distance, its yellow and green paintwork bright against the backdrop of the sky. The view is a refreshing change from the narrow streets of Surry Hills with its familiar faces on every corner. And, apart from the sound of rustling lolly wrappers in her ear, it's very peaceful.

Betty leans over with warm butterscotch breath. 'It's always the one you suspect the least who turns out to have done it. Everyone knows that, Hazel.'

'Perhaps in an Agatha Christie mystery, but not necessarily in real life.'

'What if there was a murder at the Bellevue and I had already assembled a dossier on potential suspects? Before it even happened!'

'That would be impressive,' Hazel agrees. 'Do you have anyone in mind as the victim?'

Betty considers this for a moment. 'Bossy Boots Frazer with all her rules and regulations is top of my list. That fellow with the jug ears who borrowed the marmalade from our table without asking properly, thinks he owns the place. He'd be my second choice. And his wife with the sour face, I'm also not keen on.'

'She does have to put up with him,' Hazel points out.

'True. I notice Mr Sorensen is never at the guesthouse for afternoon tea.'

'He obviously doesn't know about the Madeira cake,' says Hazel. 'He most likely works in the city. He may even live at the Bellevue; there are a few residents. If you look back in the register, you'll probably find those residents are added at the start of every week.'

Betty snaps her notebook shut. 'I'm not convinced. There's something a little . . . sinister about him.'

Drowsy with the heat and the salt air tinged with suntan lotion, Hazel lies back on her towel and closes her eyes, hoping that Betty will do the same. But what seems like only moments later, she is abruptly woken by the glare of sunlight and opens her eyes to find Betty wrestling with the umbrella.

'Hurry up. We'll miss afternoon tea.'

Hazel knows better than to stand between Betty and cake. She gets to her feet, packs up her bag and shakes out the towels. They walk along the foreshore past the busy ferry terminal where the passengers are pouring out onto the Corso. As they step back to let the crowd pass, Hazel notices a familiar figure standing to one side, distinctive with his gold-rimmed glasses, pale linen suit and Panama hat. 'There's your suspect, Betty, over by the newsstand.'

Betty gives a little gasp. 'With his briefcase too. Let's wait and see where he goes.'

'We'll miss afternoon tea.'

Torn for a moment, Betty says, 'It's a sacrifice I'm prepared to make. This could be our national security at stake, Hazel.'

Passengers are still streaming out of the terminal and Hazel takes Betty's arm, guiding her to one side where they have a good view.

After a few minutes, a man comes striding out of the terminal and makes a beeline for Mr Sorensen, who raises his hand in greeting. In his forties, the man is tall and strong looking, with a healthy tan and thinning hair. A smart suit but no tie.

'Ooh look, no tie . . . Another foreigner, I'll wager,' says Betty.

The two men talk for a moment and it's clear even from a distance that the stranger is upset and Mr Sorensen is placating him.

After a few minutes, they leave the wharf and walk into a nearby coffee shop.

Betty turns to Hazel. 'Let's get a cup of tea.'

Despite herself, Hazel is also intrigued and gives Betty the nod.

Brushing off the last of the sand, they step inside the coffee shop. The waitress frowns at Betty, who has her arms wrapped around the sun umbrella. 'Can you leave that outside, please?'

'I paid a two-shilling deposit for it,' explains Betty, gripping it tighter.

'Well, you can't bring it in here,' insists the waitress.

'Let's just pop it in a corner,' suggests Hazel, aware they're becoming the centre of attention. She takes it from Betty's grasp and leans it in the corner nearest the door. Fortunately, the two men, now poring over some papers, are too involved with their discussion to have noticed the fuss.

While Betty examines the menu, Hazel attunes her ears to the nearby table, but the men speak in such low voices she can't hear a word. She's tempted to save the sixpence and hurry back to the guesthouse for afternoon tea, but she won't get Betty out the door without a commotion.

Having thoroughly perused the menu, Betty decides on the Devonshire tea. 'A little holiday treat, Hazel. My shout.'

Half an hour later, the meeting between Mr Sorensen and his colleague ends abruptly. They gather their papers with some urgency and pack them away. As they cross to the door, Mr Sorensen notices Hazel. He turns towards her briefly with a frown.

Betty's busy layering a scone with jam and cream and doesn't look up until the last crumb is devoured. She's dismayed to find the table empty. 'Oh no, they slipped out,' she cries. 'Well, that tells you something, Hazel. If only we could have seen what they were looking at. It could be blueprints of a government facility or plans for a bank job.'

'It is intriguing . . . but I can't see them as bank robbers.'

Betty frowns. 'I've seen the tall man somewhere. Where was it? In the papers? At the pictures? A Wanted poster? Oh, how I wish I had your memory, Hazel. It will come to me. Hopefully before it's too late.'


In the late afternoon, they lie on their beds to rest before dinner. Betty falls asleep instantly, breathing out great bursts of air like an industrial bellows. After a while, Hazel gets up and slips on her shoes. She walks down the main stairs to the ground floor. The house is quiet, apart from the distant crashing of pots in the kitchen, where preparation for dinner is underway. She continues out to the verandah along the south side of the house, shady in the afternoons, and sinks into one of the large cane armchairs. She's barely closed her eyes when the sound of footsteps alerts her to company. She opens them to find Mr Sorensen's steady gaze on her.

'Are you enjoying your holiday?' he asks with a stilted politeness.

'Very pleasant, thank you. It's Mr Sorensen, isn't it? I'm Mrs Bates.'

'I have seen you in the dining room with your friend.' He sits down in the armchair opposite. 'What is your impression of these people we dine with?'

Hazel thinks for a moment. 'Not terribly friendly, but then I'm not used to staying in guesthouses, so perhaps that's the way it is.'

'The tall man with the loud voice. I see him control his wife and the daughter with the expression on his face. A little frown. Or a shake of the head. And to silence his wife, he raises one finger,' says Mr Sorensen, demonstrating. 'This man like a tyrant in his own world, not noticing the rest of us at all. But we see him.'

Hazel, intrigued by his analysis, asks, 'What line of work are you in, Mr Sorensen?'

'It is not of great interest, I am afraid. Not a poet or a prince, simply a . . .' He pauses. '. . . a simple technician.'

Hazel's surprised to feel her ears tingle a little, a sure sign that someone is not telling the truth. His hesitation was also revealing. He needed a moment to fabricate his answer.

'And what is your line of work, Mrs Bates?'

'I work for a company called Empire Fashionwear in the city, manufacturers of women's clothes.'

'You are a seamstress? Is this the correct term?' he asks.

'It is, but no, I'm the tea lady. I deliver tea and biscuits to everyone in the building, almost thirty people, twice a day.'

'You keep the workers happy. This is a valuable profession.'

'I agree, an honourable profession. My friend, Mrs Dewsnap, is also a tea lady. She works nearby, so we see each other almost every day.'

'And now you make this holiday together.' He pauses for a moment. 'Would you and Mrs Dewsnap agree to join me in the dining room this evening?'

Hazel wonders what Betty will think of this, but there is no polite way to refuse.

'If our landlady will permit it,' he adds.

Hazel smiles. 'Oh, I'm sure you can convince her. I notice she's more charming to her male guests than her female ones.'

Mr Sorensen nods seriously. 'I will discuss the matter with her.'

*

When Hazel and Betty (forewarned) arrive in the dining room, Mr Sorensen is already seated at their table. He immediately stands and pulls out their chairs with a flourish. Betty blushes and stifles a giggle.

It's soon evident that Mr Sorensen is comfortable in the company of strangers, practised at small talk, without giving anything away about himself. Betty hangs on his every word. By the time the waitress brings the soup course (potato and chive), Betty is clearly bursting to confess. Hazel tries to think of a ruse to stop it.

'We were following you!' Betty declares, halting all conversation in the dining room.

'Not actually following—' Hazel protests, giving her a nudge under the table.

'We thought you were planning something,' Betty interrupts. 'Or might be a secret agent or spy! There are a lot of spies around at the moment, aren't there, Hazel?'

'It's spy season,' confirms Hazel, resignedly.

Betty continues. 'There are government spies and KGB spies. You wouldn't know it, but they're everywhere. Not so long ago, me and Hazel got involved with all sorts of dangerous Russians. Extremely dangerous.'

'Betty dear, I don't think Mr Sorensen needs to hear all this.'

When the waitress has collected their bowls, Mr Sorensen asks what he did to fall under suspicion. Hazel sighs inwardly as Betty dives into her purse and rifles around for her notebook. There's a moment's reprieve while plates of roast beef and Yorkshire pudding are dumped in front of them, then Betty begins to read. 'People-watcher. Foreign. Briefcase. Misses Madeira—'

'That's the cake, not the city,' Hazel clarifies. 'Betty, let's not—'

'Nail scissors . . . oh, I forgot to buy those in the end. I'll have to borrow yours, Hazel . . . Meets strange man at the wharf—'

'Did you recognise this man?' Mr Sorensen asks curtly.

Betty looks taken aback. 'Should we have?'

'No, not at all,' says Mr Sorensen.

Hazel can see he's rattled, and her tingling ears tell her this is an outright lie. 'Your dinner's getting cold, Betty dear.'

Betty puts down her notebook and spears a potato with her fork. 'So, you can see I don't miss a thing,' she concludes, less confidently.

'Does someone pay you for this spying?' he asks. His friendly manner has cooled considerably.

Betty blushes. 'Of course not . . . Oh, I hope I didn't offend you, Mr Sorensen.'

'Can I ask you to keep this information to yourself, please?' he asks. 'And not discuss with anyone at all. Especially not anyone from the press.'

Betty is clearly mortified and close to tears. Hazel puts a calming hand on hers and says, 'Of course, Mr Sorensen, it will go no further. Please accept our apologies.'

Before he can respond, the waitress appears at their table. 'Mrs Bates? Telephone call for you.' She tilts her head in the direction of the foyer.

Hazel looks up at her. 'For me? Are you sure?'

'You're the only guest called Bates, so yeah,' says the waitress and walks away.

Hazel excuses herself and hurries to the telephone. The only person who knows where they're staying is her lodger, Irene Turnbuckle, and Irene would only call here if she'd set the house on fire, and probably not even then.

Hazel picks up the phone. 'Mrs Bates speaking.'

'Mrs B? Is that you?'

'Maude?' asks Hazel, recognising her young neighbour. 'Yes, it's me.'

'When are you home?' Maude bursts into tears. 'You'll never guess what's happened.'

'I'll be home tomorrow, dear. What on earth's wrong?'

'Auntie Vera died,' she says in a muffled voice.

Hazel is perplexed as to why Maude would take the trouble to call her with this news since Auntie Vera is only an acquaintance, not a close friend. 'I'm sorry to hear that, Maude.'

'You don't understand,' says Maude.

'What's happened exactly, dear?'

'Can you come over straight after tea tomorrow? I'll be home from work then. Come at seven. Please. Don't tell them I asked . . . Sorry, I don't have another sixpence—'

The line goes dead, and Hazel slowly puts down the receiver.

Still puzzling over the call, she goes back to the dining room to find Mr Sorensen has gone, and Betty is damp-eyed with remorse.

'He was very polite. Said he had business to attend to. Couldn't even wait for dessert,' she says in a wobbly voice. 'And it's trifle tonight.'

## 2

# IRENE GETS AN INTRIGUING LETTER

Irene Turnbuckle lies on the sofa in Hazel's front room, her slippered feet on the armrest, her head on a cushion. She blows one perfect smoke ring after another and watches them float up to the ceiling. Ten in a row. Not bad. Shame there's no witnesses, but also lucky that Hazel's away. Smoking in the front room is not allowed. Smoking in bed is not allowed either. Lots of rules in this house, but Irene has the place to herself right now, so there are no rules.

The entire time Hazel's been away, Irene's been racking her brains as to where Hazel could have hidden all the booze. Not just the good whiskey, kept for special occasions, but even the gut-rot wine Hazel makes out in the washhouse: rhubarb, choko, dandelion – all foul. And Irene's never been fussy about booze. Far from it. She's been trying to put herself inside Hazel's crafty mind. It's got to be somewhere that Hazel thinks Irene will never look.

From the comfort of the sofa, Irene mentally tracks her way through the house one more time. She doesn't bother with the two upstairs bedrooms. She's already been right through Hazel's wardrobe and chest of drawers and had a good look under the bed.

Her eyes dart around the front room again. There's nowhere left to look here, unless Hazel has a secret hidey-hole behind the skirting boards. Apart from the sofa, there are two armchairs, a little card table where Hazel does her jigsaw puzzling (a pointless activity in Irene's opinion, since no money changes hands), a radiogram and a bookshelf with a set of the Encyclopaedia Britannica (she's checked inside all twenty-three of them). She's also been through every kitchen cupboard, the yard, the outside dunny and washhouse. It's not a big place and she's looked bloody everywhere. Could Hazel have taken it next door to the Mulligans? She's great mates with those two heffalumps and their noisy, snotty brats. Thinking that through, it seems a bit like cheating, something Hazel would never do. She's a good sport.

Irene has a brainwave and sits up with a start, giving herself a coughing fit. The one place Hazel knows she would never look! Of course! She flicks her cigarette butt out the window into the front garden – a lost cause anyway. On crackling knees, she hurries into the hallway and opens the understairs cupboard where the vacuum cleaner, broom, mop and bucket are kept. Peering into the dark corners, her eyes are just starting to adjust when the phone rings. Swearing under her breath, she picks up the receiver.

'What?' she asks, before remembering Hazel's instructions on telephone answering. 'Mrs Turnbuckle speaking. What d'yer want?'

'Mrs Turnbuckle, I thought I recognised your melodic tones. It's Arthur Smith – from the boarding house,' says the caller.

'Yeah? Why yer ringing me?' Irene stretches the telephone cord to its limit, working her way back to the cupboard but falling short by a few inches.

'There's some correspondence arrived for you. It was about to be carelessly discarded but I rescued it on your behalf.'

'What sorta "correspondence"?' she asks, mimicking his toffy accent.

'I'm referring to a letter, Mrs Turnbuckle.'

Apart from finding the way he talks irritating, Irene has always viewed Arthur with suspicion. Pretty much everyone in that rotten boarding house had lived in places like that most of their lives, but this bloke had a better start in life. Arthur Smith isn't much of a name, probably made up. Someone said he was a lawyer or a judge or some such thing but lost it all to bookies and booze. More fool him. If Irene can deliver umpteen cups of tea, year in, year out, to the staff of Silhouette Knitwear with a drop or two under her belt and manage the odd flutter on the side, surely Arthur can sit in a comfy chair, bang his little hammer and say guilty or not guilty. In her experience, judges were half cut or half asleep anyway. Depending on who you were or who you knew, you were going to be convicted, guilty or not. Now here he is wanting a bloody medal for keeping her letter. He's only done it because he's a snoop.

'The return address is particularly intriguing,' continues Arthur. 'Prisoner T56987 Long Bay Gaol.'

Irene abandons her efforts to reach the cupboard and gives the matter her full attention. 'That right? I might just come round and get that.'

'Mrs Turnbuckle, I can say with absolute certainty that you will not be made welcome in this establishment. However, if the fragrance of Eau de Bordello pervading the building is anything to go by, our illustrious landlady is on her way out—'

'Get to the bloody point, will yer?'

'Leave it half an hour and pop around then.'

Irene hangs up without further comment. A letter from Long Bay. No doubt who that's from, but why is he writing to her?

Upstairs, she puts on her good hat and borrows a nice pale blue cardigan from Hazel. She hasn't been back to the boarding house since Hazel bailed her out of that place a couple of months ago, and she'd like those ratbags to see she's come up in the world. Living in a proper house now, and one that Hazel keeps very clean and tidy.

Irene clears her chest, spits out the open window and puts on her lipstick. She never bothers with a mirror these days; her lips aren't where they used to be, so it doesn't really matter. She even considers putting on her one good pair of shoes, but her slippers are comfy, so it makes no sense to take them off.

The boarding house is near Central Station in a street that prides itself on being the roughest in the neighbourhood. From Irene's point of view, there're a few good things about it. There's always a beer crate in the street if you fancy a sit down in the sun with a ciggie, and there's usually someone sitting on the kerb with a bottle of something – so you couldn't complain about the social side of things. Of an evening, there's usually a brawl right out the front, so free entertainment on tap. And, apart from Arthur Smith, everybody is down to earth with no one thinking they're better than the rest.

Arthur opens the front door at her knock. Instead of asking her in or handing over the letter, he sidles out onto the front landing, forcing her back down a step. He wears his usual three-piece suit. It was probably blue at the start of its life, but is now a muddy brown and stinks of metho. Irene looks him over. Whatever he was before, he's not long for this world if he's on the metho now.

The boarding house is falling apart, bits dropping off here and there, so Irene suggests they stand in the street – wouldn't be the first time someone had been clocked by a lump of crumbling brickwork. Might put Arthur out of his misery but Irene's not ready to go yet. At least not before she reads this letter.

'Well, we haven't seen much of you since you departed this fine establishment, Mrs Turnbuckle,' says Arthur, following her out to the pavement.

Irene notices he has several teeth missing now, and the rest match his suit. 'Yeah, well, as yer said, I'm not welcome. Even though I did nothing. It was all her.'

'She's not the most diligent of landladies, but she has her good points. She was very upset by the comments your friend – Mrs Bates? – made about the health inspector when she came to collect you.'

'Mrs Bates knows what's what,' says Irene stoutly. 'She don't make idle threats.'

'Unlike your good self, who has an impressive repertoire of threats, idle or otherwise.'

Irene sighs. 'Can I have me bloody letter?'

Arthur's a good head and shoulders taller than her. He stares her down for a moment before reaching slowly into the inside pocket of his jacket. Bringing out the letter, he dangles it out of reach. 'Would you like me to read it to you?' he asks.

'I can read, mate. Just give me the thing.'

When he opens his mouth to argue the point, Irene springs up and makes a grab for the letter. A short scuffle later, it's in her possession.

'If yer wanted to read it, why didn't yers just open the bloody thing and be done with it?'

Arthur looks down his nose at her. 'Mail tampering, Mrs Turnbuckle, is a criminal offence. Much as I am curious to know what your friend in Long Bay has to say, I have no desire to join him.'

'A spell inside would do yer good – straighten yers out before that metho sees yer off. They'd give yer some clean duds for a start off.'

Irene fans the letter in front of her nose in case he didn't get the hint.

'For your information, I have been cleaning windows with methylated spirits, not imbibing it. What do you take me for?'

'I believe yers, thousands wouldn't. See yers later but probably not.'

'Not much gratitude there, Mrs Turnbuckle. Very disappointing. Don't expect me to keep your mail in the future.'

Ignoring him, Irene crosses the road and cuts down a back lane towards the little playground a couple of streets away, somewhere she can get peace and quiet. She's also curious to read this letter, the first she's ever got from Prisoner T56987.

The park, with its broken swings and slide, is empty apart from a few tearaway kids. She clears the debris of bottles off the park bench, sits down and rips open the letter. She's relieved to see it's not too long; she's not keen on reading at the best of times. She squints at the page. Fred's handwriting hasn't improved. Just as she begins, one of the kids starts running up the slippery metal slide and, next thing, they're throwing stones at each other.

'Oi!' Irene shouts. 'Keep it down, youse. I'm tryna concentrate.'

The second she takes her eyes off them, a hail of gravel rains down on her. The culprit, a freckly little runt, stands on the broken swing, grinning. The others hang around to see what happens next.

'I'll bang yer bloody heads together if yer don't watch out.' Irene gets to her feet menacingly.

The kid watches her with a defiant grin. Just as she's wondering how far to go with her threat, the sound of a distant police siren starts up. Seconds later, she has the place to herself and can read in peace.

*Irene old girl in case somethink happens to me remember that time
we went on that trip to that place and we had a drink at that
royal pub and stayed there and we walked down that road in the
dark and you said somethink about it was nice and I thought so
also if somethink happens to me you can go to that place and find
somethink I don't want it to be ~~waste~~ ~~waist~~ wasted I think you get
where I mean. Yours Fred.*

Irene concentrates hard and reads it again. It's the first time she's
really twigged to the importance of full stops. What place? What
'royal' pub? What trip? What the hell is he talking about? She can
see it's been opened and taped closed again by the prison censors,
so he's done a good job of keeping whatever it is a secret from them,
and also from her.

Fred 'Tweezers' Turnbuckle, her husband of fifty-odd years, has
been in Long Bay for five and a half years on this stretch. The bloke
she was with before him was also a crook, but not a safecracker like
Fred. That one had been more of your garden-variety crook doing
the odd hold-up and break-in, and a bit of blackmail in the lean
times. Fred was in another class altogether; he could open a security
van or a big bank safe.

Irene had thought she was stepping up a rung. Fred was well-
known and respected by everyone. He had a gift, they said. The
problem with big-time safecrackers, she soon discovered, is that
they don't work alone. The jobs he got roped into were always
put together by some bright spark with a foolproof plan scribbled
down on the back of an envelope. Behind that genius was a bunch
of no-hopers who couldn't run a chook raffle, let alone pull off a
bank heist. When they needed a safecracker, they came to the best.
So, there was Fred, with his magic fingers, sent down with the rest

of them through no fault of his own. Just trying to do what he was born to do.

Irene visits him now and then. He never has much to say for himself and never mentioned this pub in the dark in some place on some trip. She thinks back to the last time she saw him and wonders if he's going senile. He says so little he could probably get away with it for a fair while. But he does seem to be trying to make a particular point in this letter. She thinks about him not wanting 'it' to go to waste, and it strikes her that he has a bit of insurance somewhere. Something he put away without telling anyone. Fred knows how to keep his mouth shut and he's careful, so that'd be just the sort of thing he'd do. She folds up the letter with a sigh, puts it in her handbag and clips it firmly closed.

It's still on her mind the next day as she loads up her trolley for the morning tea service, scouring her memory for this place and this pub Fred's going on about. If only he had given her one proper clue, it might have triggered something. Her memory is not the best these days. Not like Hazel, who remembers everything, even tiny details that don't seem to matter at the time.

Irene pushes the trolley into the deathtrap lift that shakes and rattles the cups and saucers (and her bones) all the way to the top floor. Most of the clothing manufacturers around here have the factory in the basement or on the ground floor, but at Silhouette Knitwear, the monster knitting machines are on the top floor with ceilings as high as a church and skylights in them. The noise they make is like half-a-dozen trains idling at the station. It suits Irene because she doesn't have to bother talking to the men in grey duster coats who move back and forth along the line of machines fixing tangles and breakdowns.

She leaves a plate of biscuits on the table where they take their tea break and pours five cups of tea; the sugar they can do for themselves. She puts two fingers between her lips and gives a shrill whistle. One of the men gives her a wave. She's done here. Couldn't be easier.

Back in the lift and down to the next floor where there're four ladies in the office who do the stock control and accounts. When a new one starts in here, they always greet her like a long-lost friend but soon get the message that Irene is not here for idle chitchat or sucking up. It's strictly tea and bikkies. Preferably in silence.

The only person she does greet is the managing director, because he signs the pink slips and could have her out on her ear if he felt like it. She keeps the Tim Tams just for him. She's had a sharp eye on his secretary, a chubby little thing who has taken to wearing woolly cardies lately and reckons she's got bad circulation, even though it's January and boiling hot. The girl is six months gone – if not more – and Irene wonders how long she thinks she can hide it. First off, she couldn't face a cuppa, keen to nibble on a dry Milk Arrowroot, and now she's gone the other direction, gobbling down biscuits like they're lollies. Irene wonders if the boss knows she's up the duff, given he's the likely culprit. Either way, that girl's days here are numbered.

As soon as morning tea is out of the way, Irene makes her way to an empty office on the ground floor to use the telephone. Getting the number from the operator, she makes a call to Long Bay Gaol and registers for a visit the next weekend with Prisoner T56987. It only occurs to her now to wonder what Fred worries is going to happen to him. It must be a big threat for him to take the trouble to write a letter, let alone give her the hiding place of his secret loot, or whatever.

\*

As she walks in the front door of 5 Glade Street, it dawns on Irene that Hazel's coming back this evening. Bugger. She glances around, trying to see the place through Hazel's eyes. Not bad but could do better.

Irene tops up the bottle of whiskey from the tap and tucks it back in its hiding place in the broom cupboard. In the kitchen, she scrapes the breadcrumbs and apple peelings off the bench and throws them into the backyard for the birds. She rakes up the crumbs on the floor with her foot, lifts the corner of the mat and pushes them under.

The toaster is a problem. She flips the door down and stares at the blackened crumpet glued to the element. It was a mistake to put butter and jam on first. Now it looks like a small fried bat hanging off a powerline. Not something you'd eat – unless you had to.

She gets out a knife and pokes it in between the element and the bat.

When she comes round, she's slumped against the kitchen cupboards with her dentures in her lap and a splitting headache, thinking she's been struck by lightning.

Her hat feels hot and the smell of burnt hair hangs in the air. She tries to take the hat off, but the bloody thing's melted onto her head. Without ripping all her hair out, the hat is going nowhere. She puts her clackers in her pocket, flops over onto her knees and crawls down the hall to the broom cupboard. If there was ever a time when she needed a drink, this is it.

Still seeing double – maybe even triple – she reaches into the cupboard and grabs a whiskey bottle (there seem to be a few of them in here now) by the neck. Sitting in the hall, she leans against the wall, takes a good swig and closes her eyes.

She opens them again to blinding brightness. The hallway is filled with golden light. A host of angels hover over her; she must be at the gates of heaven. Her time has come. Relieved she's not in the burning fires of hell, she gives herself up to the afterlife, murmuring a prayer under her breath to remind Him of her devotion (better late than never). It feels good, even with a raging headache. The angels gaze down on her with worried frowns – she never expected a welcome committee this size! A confusing number of hands reach towards her, and a familiar voice says, 'You look in need of a strong cup of tea, Irene dear. Let me help you up.'

# 3

# HAZEL PAYS A VISIT NEXT DOOR

Hazel's just thankful the situation wasn't worse. Irene is still alive (although she took some convincing of that) and the house didn't burn down. She clearly gave herself a nasty shock. She's fused her hat to her hair and destroyed the toaster. While she's still in a dazed state, Hazel makes her take a cool bath, gives her a couple of aspirin and puts her to bed. There's still a couple of hours before Hazel can go over to see what's troubling Maude next door, so she sets to cleaning up the house.

Evidence of Irene's week fending for herself is everywhere. She had baked beans at the start of the week (judging by the lumpy crust in the pot), there's creamed corn in another pot and tinned spaghetti eaten straight from the can. At some point she opened a tin of sardines (which accounts for the terrible smell in the house) and ate those from the tin. Hazel leaves the pots to soak, takes the rubbish out to the backyard, and dusts and vacuums the place.

Once the house is in order, she boils herself a couple of eggs, makes toast under the grill and listens to the six o'clock news. Disheartening as it can sometimes be, she likes to keep up with current affairs. There's an item about the war in Vietnam, which is very controversial, especially now more Australian boys have been killed. There is some new problem with the construction of the Sydney Opera House. The building has been in the works for six or seven years, long ago exceeded budget and is still far from finished. Experts share their dire predictions on the effect of the country's conversion to decimal currency next month, regularly referring to a person they call 'Mrs Average Housewife', who has one husband and two children. Hazel wonders about all the other people: the Mulligans next door with seven children, for example, and the thousands of women widowed by the war and the pensioners. Always the same people that politicians seem to overlook.

After her tea, she gets the stepladder out of the washhouse and brings it inside. Positioning it under the manhole in the kitchen ceiling, she climbs up and retrieves the good Scotch. Irene might be cunning, but not as cunning as Hazel.

She pours a glass and takes it into the front room where she sits down at her little card table and her current jigsaw, the Hanging Gardens of Babylon. Although Hazel has told Irene countless times not to meddle with it, Irene can't seem to help herself. She doesn't seem to understand the basic principle that the shapes are designed to fit into one another.

Hazel uncouples the pieces twisted into place and divides them back into groups of colours and edges. Getting jigsaws finished is not important to her. This is a time and place for her to sit quietly and let her mind drift while her fingers search out the patterns of their own accord. This evening her thoughts turn to Mr Sorensen and his concern that she and Betty might have recognised the man he met off the ferry. Betty was right. The man did look vaguely familiar, but Hazel can't place him either. After Mr Sorensen's abrupt departure from dinner, she had hoped they might run into him before they left, but now they'll probably never know.

At a quarter to seven, the telephone rings. As expected, it's her daughter, Norma, ringing to check on her.

'How was your holiday, Mum? Get a tan?'

Hazel laughs. 'Let's just say a healthy glow. How are the boys?'

Norma, who lives several hours away with her husband and twin sons, goes on to regale Hazel with the boys' latest antics and a recent drama on the farm. When she married Ed and they took over his parents' property, Hazel had imagined that life in the country would be quiet and serene, but she has learned over the years that that's rarely the case for very long.

'By the way, I have to come down in a couple of weeks,' says Norma. 'A charity dinner at the Town Hall. It's a bit of an effort but I feel obliged to go, and I can stay a night with you.'

'That sounds lovely.' Hazel checks her watch. 'I better go, I had a call from Maude while I was away. She was very upset and asked me to come over after tea this evening – and not to mention she'd called me.'

'Oh dear, I hope she hasn't got herself into trouble.'

'I think she's too smart for that. Besides, the eldest of seven, I think she knows how it works,' says Hazel. 'No, it's something else. You probably don't remember Auntie Vera. She was a close friend of the Mulligans', not an actual relative. Everyone round here calls her Auntie Vera. Apparently she died a few days ago.'

'I do remember her. Very jolly and cheery, and always had humbugs for the children. She was something to do with the Catholic Church?'

'The priest's housekeeper,' says Hazel. 'She was a lovely woman, and only my age.'

'Ancient then?' quips Norma.

'Very amusing, dear. I'll let you know what happens.'

They say their goodbyes and, not wanting to be late, Hazel goes straight out through her backyard. She lets herself in the Mulligans' gate, taps on the kitchen door and calls out a hello as a courtesy – no one ever answers the door here. With so many children, people wander in and out at all times of the day and night. Privacy is for small families. The house is quieter than usual – the boys must be playing out front in the street – but the sound of Maude sobbing can be heard in the front room.

'Hazel? Is that you, my love?' shouts Mrs Mulligan. 'We're in the front parlour. Come on in. We could do with your common sense.'

Hazel picks her way along the narrow hallway past bags of clothes, beer crates, discarded shoes and a rusted bike under repair. Mrs Mulligan takes in ironing and every piece of furniture in the front room holds a stack of neatly ironed items. Each pile has an upturned beermat with the owner's name written on it. Under the front window is a big table covered in blankets and old sheets scorched from years of use and a battered old iron propped up on it. Among the organised chaos, Maude sits on the sofa, her mouth downturned, her face red and puffy.

'Is this about Auntie Vera, Maude?' asks Hazel, carefully relocating a pile of ironing to sit beside her.

'Ah, but she's been offered a wonderful opportunity and she's blind to it. Kicking up such a fuss, it's unbelievable,' says Mrs Mulligan. 'I would have thought she'd be more grateful, but there she is, more waterworks than Niagara.'

'They want me to be the new housekeeper,' says Maude, barely above a whisper.

Hazel looks at Mrs Mulligan for an explanation.

Mrs Mulligan sighs. 'Our dear Auntie Vera died, God bless her heart, and now Father Kelly needs a new housekeeper. I moved heaven and earth to have Maudie considered. We had the funeral yesterday and barely a tear. Now what do I get but tantrums and tears?'

'Oh dear, I'm so sorry to hear that,' says Hazel. 'She was a lovely woman . . . and not that old. Was she unwell?'

'She was in her sixties to be sure, like yourself, not old but not young either. They think an ulcer or some such thing. She had been complaining of pain in her guts. Probably something got tangled up in there, and then only a few days later she died.'

'But she hadn't been ill before that?' asks Hazel, curious.

'We'll have none of your detective business, Hazel. The woman's dead. No bringing her back, but now here's an opportunity for Maude.'

At Maude's fresh outbreak of tears, Mrs Mulligan has the good grace to look embarrassed by her obvious ambition. 'We loved Auntie Vera, so we did. I'll miss her more than anyone. Our Lord needed another angel at his side.' She pauses to let that sink in. 'Maudie, you'll be set up for life. Roof over your head, decent food on your plate.' She turns to Hazel to close her argument. 'She'll even get a little wage.'

'Two pounds a week! I get four and six sweeping up at the brewery!' says Maude. 'And I get evenings and weekends off.'

Mrs Mulligan gives an exasperated sigh. 'It'll keep you out of trouble. There's an hour or two for yourself of a Sunday afternoon. You can come home and help with bath night.'

'Thanks very much,' says Maude bitterly. 'I don't want to be a servant, please don't make me, Mam.'

'Goodness!' cries Mrs Mulligan. 'It's an honour and a privilege to care for His Reverence. You'll be meeting the bishop when he comes and all sorts of important people.'

Hazel ventures, 'She does seem very young for the job, and she did so well in her Leaving.'

'Ah, you're not a Catholic, Hazel. You wouldn't understand, so don't take her side. Auntie Vera was a housekeeper from when she was sixteen, same age as Maude. It's quite normal and it's a good safe life for a woman.'

'It's like being a nun, but more work and less praying,' says Maude miserably.

Mrs Mulligan huffs. 'You could do to pray a bit more. Nothing to stop you. I would have preferred you join the order, as you well know, but this is the next best thing. You're spoilt and running wild. Wearing lipstick, hitching your skirts up so everyone can see your panties and God knows what else. I know what goes on when you walk out this door, and I won't have it. You'll learn domestic and secretarial work. Just take a moment to think about it and you'll see it's a step up from the brewery.' She pauses for a moment. 'So that's settled then.'

'Please don't make me. Please, Ma,' begs Maude.

Maude has always been a most dutiful, obedient daughter; she would be the last one to rebel against her mother's decision. And while it's none of Hazel's concern, she can't stand by and let a bright girl like Maude be lost to such a dreary profession.

'Can I make a suggestion?' asks Hazel.

'If you must,' says Mrs Mulligan. 'I thought you'd be more on my side, quite honestly, given you're a sensible person.'

'What do you think about a trial period?' asks Hazel. 'Would Father Kelly consider that? Perhaps three months would be a good amount of time to see if Maude is suited to the position? And if not, then you could look at your options at that point.'

Mrs Mulligan looks stubbornly suspicious, perhaps wondering if she'll have to go through this with Maude all over again. 'I suppose she might be used to it by then.'

'Just a thought,' says Hazel. 'Something to consider anyway. A compromise.'

'It's possible,' agrees Mrs Mulligan grudgingly.

Dabbing at her eyes, Maude takes an ironed white handkerchief off a pile and blows her nose loudly.

'Good grief, Maudie! That's Mr Harrison's hankie! Control yourself, girl!'

Maude lets out a groan. 'I suppose three months might be bearable.'

Mrs Mulligan's face transforms into a wreath of smiles. She struggles out of her armchair and pulls her daughter into an unwilling embrace. 'Oooh, my treasure. I knew you would see sense. You're a good girl, Maudie. You'll see this is the best life for a girl like you. I want what's best for you, and for Father Kelly, of course. It'll be a proud day for the whole family, you'll see.'

Hazel murmurs some encouraging words, getting a nod and wan smile from Maude. It's true, Mrs Mulligan does want what's best, but her ambitions for Maude are from a different era, an earlier time when women had fewer opportunities. Hazel remembers how happy and excited Maude was with life when they walked to the train together the week before. Housekeeping might be a step up from her current job, but at least she was free to come and go at the brewery. From what Hazel had heard from Auntie Vera, the housekeeper was at the beck and call of the men of the diocese without a moment to call her own.

*

On Saturday morning, Hazel wakes to the realisation that today is the day. She's made a commitment and must follow through. Her tummy is too churned up for breakfast. So she stands at the back door and drinks her tea, gazing out into her little yard. The day looks like it will be a scorcher. Her pots of red geraniums are enjoying the summer heat but she must remember to trim the choko vine before it fruits, or it will bring the paling fence down. Noting these things normally comforts her but, today, the overwhelming task ahead is the only thing on her mind. She wonders again if it is too late for her. Should she give up on this long-held dream? No. Not just yet.

She wears her blue-and-white striped sundress and white sandals, comfortable for the hot day ahead and the twenty-minute walk from Glade Street. It's not far, along familiar back lanes and across one busy road to arrive at the Sisters of Hope Convent, which is in the grounds of St Vincent's Church.

She opens the wrought-iron gate and steps inside. To her left is the convent and school, set in large grounds with lawns and gardens surrounded by a high stone wall. To her right is the church itself, an imposing building in dark grey stone. Beyond it, tucked away behind a tall hedge of hydrangeas, is the priest's house. Maude's new home.

A young nun in a pale grey habit comes out of the convent and gives Hazel a welcoming wave as she walks towards her. When they meet, she introduces herself as Sister Ruth and shakes Hazel's hand with a firm, confident grip. Despite only the circle of her face being revealed, Hazel gets a strong impression of kindness from her brown eyes and warm smile.

Beset with nerves, Hazel struggles to make light conversation but Sister Ruth chats comfortably, easing the moment. Crossing the lawn, they walk along a covered pathway towards the main convent doors. A priest in a black gown comes out of the building towards them. In his early fifties, he's darkly handsome with a vigorous stride.

'Father Kelly,' says Sister Ruth as they approach him. 'This is Mrs Bates. She's starting on the literacy program today.'

Father Kelly nods and offers his hand. 'Ah, the literacy program,' he says in a broad Irish accent. 'Yes, it's important. Very important. Well done to you . . . Mrs Bates.'

Hazel notices he has a sticking plaster covering a wound on his left temple. 'Looks as though you've been in the wars, Father,' she says, if only to make conversation.

His hand goes to his forehead. 'Ah, this. Not looking where I'm going, walked into a door, I did.' He gives a gruff laugh.

Hazel's ears begin to tingle. The plaster is angled above his brow, not vertical as you'd expect from walking into a door, and she wonders what a priest might get up to that would result in an injury he had to lie about. He asks Sister Ruth several questions about the Mass next morning and, with an air of distraction, strides off in the direction of the church.

When he's gone, Sister Ruth says, 'He's not long from Ireland, as you can probably tell. I had trouble understanding him at first.' She chuckles and Hazel likes her already. 'He's been a breath of fresh air for this diocese,' Sister Ruth continues. 'Very forward thinking.'

'That's quite an injury on his head,' says Hazel.

Sister Ruth nods. 'He must have walked into that door at some speed!'

'I was very sorry to hear about the passing of Auntie Vera,' says Hazel, as they enter the convent and walk down a long wide hallway with dark timber floors and walls.

'You knew Auntie Vera?' asks Sister Ruth. 'Oh, of course, the Mulligans are your neighbours. It was Maude who introduced you to our programme.' She smiles at Hazel. 'It's a small world. Yes, she was very loved by our parishioners. She was the housekeeper for more than twenty years, caring for Father Kelly's predecessor, who became ill. She nursed him until he died six months ago. We were fortunate to get Father Kelly, with his energy and ideas, but unfortunate to lose our dear Auntie Vera.'

'And now Maude's taking her place, I hear,' remarks Hazel.

'It's a way to serve God. The housekeeper very much lives in the shadow of the priest, and it's a great honour to serve him. There's plenty of work to do, not just running the house but appointments and typing letters and whatnot. It's a busy, happy life for a woman.' Sister Ruth stops at one of the many doorways and opens the door. 'This is my classroom.'

Hazel glances around at the chairs sitting upside down on the desks. The room is already hot, the morning sun making bright white squares on the floor. She wonders if she's going to be required to sit at one of these desks in a child-sized chair and tries to think of an excuse to leave. But it's taken half a lifetime to get this far. To run away now would be cowardly.

Sister Ruth must have read her mind because she glances around the classroom. 'We don't have to work in here,' she says. 'The whole place is empty, apart from a few nuns. Let's find somewhere more pleasant.'

Hazel agrees with relief. Sister Ruth gathers some papers and several books. They walk down the hall and into another room that is much more to Hazel's liking: tall windows with patterned leadlights, dark polished floors and a ruby-coloured rug, a long timber table with half-a-dozen chairs each side. There are two walls with floor-to-ceiling bookshelves and a sliding ladder.

They settle at the table. Sister Ruth rests her hands lightly on the books she brought with her. 'Tell me, Mrs Bates, what do you feel when you see these books?'

Hazel feels a knot form in her chest. For a moment she doesn't trust herself to speak, reminded of a thousand humiliations over the years. She stares at the books, willing herself into a calm state of mind, and decides to be completely honest. 'Fear. Shame. Embarrassment. But also . . . curiosity. I know there is a treasure trove right here in front of me.' She looks around, her gaze sweeping the hundreds of books lining the shelves. 'I just need the key to unlock it. I've been looking for that key all my life. I'm very grateful you've agreed to help me with this problem. I'm not expecting to read the classics right away, just a letter, a newspaper or a bus timetable. I'm tired of being ashamed and pretending.'

Hazel notices Sister Ruth has tears in her eyes. Most of all, Hazel continues, she wants to read in the careless way other people do. With a single glance, the way others seem to casually read a page of print without the slightest concentration.

'Mrs Bates, let me reassure you that you are far from the only one,' says Sister Ruth gently. 'The levels of literacy in this parish are the lowest in the city. That's why we decided to work not just with our parishioners but with the wider community to raise the standard. You are our first adult student. But not the last.'

Hazel nods. 'Thank you.'

'We're going to start by working out how you see words on the page,' explains Sister Ruth. 'Word blindness comes in all different shapes and forms, so I need to find out exactly how things appear to you.'

Hazel had expected this question and explains that, while she can identify most individual letters, the *b d q* and *p* get mixed up and sometimes a bit of one word will drift across to join another word. Sister Ruth nods understandingly and makes notes as they talk.

As the morning wears on, Hazel begins to relax. She notices the shifting light in the room, the shadows falling on the table and the sound of bees in the climbing roses outside the window and feels a growing sense of possibility.

# 4

# BETTY HAS A GLIMPSE OF THE FUTURE

Betty arrived home from the holiday in a funny mood. She had loved every minute of her time with Hazel. She'd loved the luxury of the Bellevue, where they were waited on hand and foot (served, anyway), the fascinating guests and the glorious seaside. She'd loved the Madeira cake and being served afternoon tea on Royal Doulton. And she'd especially loved sharing a room with her dearest friend, like schoolgirls.

Her little flat, two rooms on the ground floor of a terrace house, seems empty and a bit lonely by comparison. She's lived here quite alone since she was widowed, without even a little pet to keep her company. She shares the entrance and the bathroom on the landing with an old lady upstairs who is more like a ghost than a neighbour. Betty only knows the old girl is still alive from the lingering smell of 'Lily-of-the-Valley' talc in the bathroom.

Feeling glum, she has the urge to ring Hazel and make sure she got home safely. But that would obviously be an excuse because they had walked from the station together. It's times like this Betty misses her husband. He was a good friend and companion for thirty-seven years. Just the two of them, no children. It's only since he died that she's become so dependent on Hazel. On the other hand, she counts herself lucky to have such a lovely friend to depend on.

She takes her nightie and a towel upstairs to the bathroom, lights the geyser and runs the bath. Soaping herself with a sponge, she ponders what this year might bring for her. Monday she'll be back to making tea at Farley Frocks. Back to meeting with Hazel and Irene (with her many unpleasant habits, pipe-smoking and tormenting Betty, just for a start) and Merl Perlman, the tea lady at Klein's Lingerie, in the laneway behind their buildings. Back to gossiping about the people they work with and bickering with each other. Hazel doesn't gossip or bicker, but much as Betty would prefer to be more like her, the temptation is irresistible.

After her bath, she sits at her dressing table and puts in her rollers, tying a pink chiffon scarf tightly around them, and slathers cold cream on her face (now horribly mottled and blotchy from the bath). She can't help wishing that something exciting could happen to lift her out of the doldrums.

Last year there had been a murder at Hazel's work and the building next door was burnt down. The tea ladies had put their heads together to solve the crimes when the police weren't interested. During that time, Betty felt more alive than she could ever remember. It was as if her brain had woken up from a long nap. Normally she was a martyr to her multiple (and very real) aches and pains, but these had miraculously disappeared while they were working on the case. (The phrase 'working on the case' always gives her a little shiver of excitement.) Now they're all back. Pins and needles from her lumbago, throbbing bunions, aching varicose veins, a touch of asthma, as well as her sinus problems. On top of that, her embarrassing tummy troubles. If it's not one thing, it's another. It's like having a dozen offspring; they're hard to keep track of and invariably doing the wrong thing.

She would never have guessed that she'd have such an aptitude for this detective work. Although, years ago, when she and Hazel worked on the switchboard at the General Post Office exchange, she had taken a great interest in other people's conversations whenever she had the time to listen in. Especially on the night shift. People have the most interesting conversations late at night, she'd discovered. Back then she accepted she was a nosy parker, but perhaps that had been her apprenticeship, a training ground for her true vocation. The crimes of last year had fallen in their laps, so to speak. It seems unlikely that it could happen again. Now it's back to the old routine, her light may be forever hidden under a bushel of tea and bikkies.

Irene and Merl are already sitting on the low wall in Zig Zag Lane when Betty arrives with her sandwiches and her little cushion. She has fish paste today. Merl always complains about the odour (in the same breath pointing out it's not actually made of fish), so Betty sits beside Irene (who doesn't care about smells) and leaves a space for Hazel when she comes.

'Have a nice holiday, did we?' asks Merl, looking at Betty over the top of her glasses. 'Got a bit of colour I see.'

'We had a lovely holiday, thank you, Merl.'

'Take all yer ailments with yers? Pack up all yer pills in yer little bag?' asks Irene, munching on her usual lunch of two Scotch Fingers. 'Or have a break from 'em?'

Betty refuses to dignify this question with an answer for a good minute, but then can't resist. 'I don't think it's very nice to mock the suffering of another, Irene.'

'Suffering, my foot,' cackles Irene. She gets out her packet of tobacco and rolls a cigarette. 'They're all psycho . . . psycha . . .'

'Psychosomatic?' suggests Betty, helpfully.

'Made up,' says Irene.

'Well, I obviously have an excellent imagination, because they're very real to me. What happened to your hat, by the way? It looks as though it's melted.'

Irene lights up her cigarette. 'Nothing wrong with yer eyesight then.'

Betty decides not to continue this conversation. She's relieved to see Hazel walking up the laneway and gives her a little welcoming wave.

'Morning, ladies,' says Hazel with a smile as she sits down.

'I hear you had a pleasant time,' says Merl, fishing for more detail.

'We did. I could make a habit of holidays,' says Hazel.

'Hazel really deserved that holiday,' says Betty. 'I hope you kept the house clean and tidy while she was away, Irene.'

'Perfectly,' says Irene.

'It wasn't too bad, apart from the toaster,' says Hazel.

Betty wonders if the toaster and Irene's melted hat are connected but it seems so unlikely she doesn't bother asking. 'We met an interesting gentleman while we were away,' she says. 'A foreigner. Very suspicious but also a gentleman.'

Irene squints at her through a cloud of smoke. 'What's that supposed to mean?'

'Educated with very nice manners. We weren't fooled by that though, were we, Hazel?'

Hazel says nothing, which usually means she doesn't agree, but doesn't feel the need to argue the point.

'What sort of foreigner?' asks Merl. 'They're not all the same, you know.'

'I realise that, thank you, Merl,' says Betty. 'Not Italian or anything like that.'

'Perhaps German or Dutch,' suggests Hazel. 'Betty did ask him where he was from, but he ducked the question and changed the subject.'

Merl looks over the top of her glasses at Betty. 'I hope you didn't tell him you were tea ladies.'

'Really, Merl, why wouldn't we?' asks Hazel with a frown. 'We're proud to be part of an honourable profession.'

At Hazel's words, Betty's chest swells with pride the way it does when she gets to her feet to sing 'God Save the Queen' at the pictures. 'We had our suspicions about him,' she says. 'That's all I can say.'

'He certainly didn't give anything away about himself,' says Hazel. 'Anyway, we'll never know what he was up to now.' She pauses. 'While we were away, I was thinking about my new year's resolutions.'

'Do I know about these resolutions?' asks Merl. Folding up her lunch wrap neatly, she puts it in her bag and gets out her knitting. A little matinee jacket in peppermint green this time; presumably there's yet another grandchild on the way.

Betty has an awful feeling that Hazel's about to divulge she's learning to read, since that was on her list of resolutions. Merl would never let her live it down.

'I'd like to re-form the Tea Ladies Guild,' says Hazel. 'I always felt it was a shame it fell apart, especially the way it did.'

Goosebumpy with excitement, Betty puts her sandwich down carefully on her lap (it wouldn't be the first time she's dropped her lunch on the ground) and gets out her notebook.

'Wasn't it someone not a million miles from here who started all the trouble in the first place?' asks Irene, tilting her head towards Merl. 'Flying the flag for them White Australia ratbags, weren't yer?'

'I beg your pardon,' huffs Merl, glancing up from her knitting. 'I don't think the blame can be laid entirely at my feet. Oh, look what you've done, made me drop a stitch.'

Betty knows for a fact that Irene's right but decides to stay out of it.

'I think we need to start with a proper structure,' continues Hazel. 'We can form a committee and vote for a chairwoman. It was thrown together last time, and that's probably one of the reasons it ended up being disbanded.'

'I second that, Hazel,' says Betty, writing it all down.

'All tea ladies would be welcome, of course,' says Hazel.

Betty writes that down too. In capital letters.

'I don't mind being involved,' says Merl. 'In whatever capacity I'm required.'

Irene gives an indifferent shrug. 'Might think about it . . . so long as Merl's not running the thing.'

The little diamantés on Merl's glasses twinkle as they do when she's annoyed, and although Irene was rather rude, Betty's glad that she made that point. Merl was a schoolteacher years ago and is always on the lookout for people to boss around. She has four daughters and sons-in-law and grandchildren (she's forever skiting about), but even with all those people to push around, it's not enough for her. If Betty had children (even one would have been nice) she'd be very kind and indulgent, not at all strict. That's how Hazel was with her Norma, and look what a delightful person she's grown up to be.

'Hazel, why don't we organise a meeting? We can let our contacts know and see who turns up,' suggests Betty. 'I'll let Effie at the fire station know, and Mrs Li, of course.'

Merl pauses knitting at the mention of Mrs Li, the tea lady she had tried to exclude, but says nothing. 'Are we going to be raising funds for anything in particular?' she asks.

'There's something more important than fundraising on the horizon right now,' says Hazel. 'You might have already heard the rumour that some firms are letting their tea ladies go in favour of a hot beverage machine—'

'A machine could never take the place of a tea lady,' interrupts Merl.

'I don't think we can ignore it,' continues Hazel. 'Sometimes cost cutting overrides common sense.'

'Robots are taking people's jobs – now they're going to take ours,' says Betty. Her eyes smart at the thought of it.

'Blubbing won't help, mate,' says Irene, giving her a prod with a sharp elbow. 'What we need is an army of tea ladies to fight 'em. I'll be in charge of weapons.'

'You can't fight robots,' says Betty. 'Even with guns.'

'A stick a dynamite chucked in the front door of any firm what hires a robot,' insists Irene gleefully. 'I'll do it meself. Won't take long for 'em to get the message.'

Merl shakes her head in disgust. 'I say we stick to fundraising. A bake stall is where our strengths lie. We're not an unruly rabble of protestors, let alone arsonists.'

Hazel gives her a firm look. 'There's something between being a rabble and giving up too easily,' she says. 'Let's start by getting the other ladies together. Strength in numbers.'

'Don't count me in your numbers. I'm happy to join up and raise funds, but not for an insurrection.' Merl puts her knitting away as if preparing to leave.

Betty spies a cake tin in Merl's bag and for a horrible moment worries she's going to flounce off without sharing her latest baking triumph. For all her faults, Merl is a wonderful cook. Betty prides herself on her scones and butterfly cakes, but no one can touch Merl when it comes to the cream sponge. Even her arrangements of tinned fruit are inspired.

Betty's relieved when Merl gets out the tin and levers off the lid with her manicured nails. 'I made some nice fresh lamingtons to celebrate your return,' she says, offering the tin so they can help themselves.

Irene gives the lamingtons a suspicious look. She removes her dentures, putting them in her pocket.

'Must you?' asks Merl, exasperated.

Getting her teeth back out, Irene opens and shuts them, speaking in a squeaky voice like a ventriloquist. 'Yer know the coconut ge*th* stuck between me gums and me clackers.'

Merl purses her lips. 'Please put them away, Irene. You can be quite revolting sometimes.'

Irene's dentures do look like they belong on an elderly horse, but Betty quickly closes her eyes and concentrates on savouring the feather-light, chocolatey, coconutty sponge melting in her mouth. She gives a sigh of pleasure. She can forgive Merl almost anything when she bakes. Disappointingly (since Betty could have squeezed in another one), Merl decides she's had enough of Irene. She snaps the lid back on the tin and walks off down the lane, shoulders square, her blue tint glowing like a beacon in the sunshine.

'Tha*th* got rid of her,' says Irene. She takes a swig out of Betty's thermos (without even asking!), swills the tea around in her mouth and puts her teeth back in. She gets a letter out of her pocket. 'Read this from me old man,' she says, handing it to Betty.

'It's quite confusing,' says Betty, when she's finished reading it. 'Do you know where all these places are?'

'Been tryna think. We used to get pretty pissed so . . . I dunno.'

'Do you think he's buried some treasure somewhere? Some loot? He's written in a sort of code,' says Betty. 'How exciting!'

'I reckon,' says Irene.

'Irene and I chatted about it over the weekend,' says Hazel. 'I gather he left out all the place names to fool the authorities, but I'm just wondering if he's forgotten himself?'

Irene's face drops. 'Hadn't thought of that. Thought he was being tricky.'

'And Irene dear, if it's something he has come by illegally—'

'That's called the "proceeds of crime",' interrupts Betty, who has been reading up at the library about legal matters. 'You'd have to give it back. Otherwise, you could be charged with receiving stolen goods.'

Irene gives her a pained look. 'When did yer get to be such a know-it-all? Yer as bad as her,' she says, nodding in the direction Merl had departed.

'I'm just stating the facts, Irene. Don't shoot the messenger.'

'Anyway, let's wait and see what he has to say when you visit,' suggests Hazel. 'Very wise not mentioning it around Merl. She'd be reporting it straight to her son-in-law. I'd keep it under your hat for the moment – what's left of it, anyway.'

Betty agrees. 'Detective Pierce would love to arrest you, Irene.'

'I reckon,' says Irene, seemingly pleased by the idea. 'Too smart for him.'

'Well, don't get too cocky, Irene,' Betty warns her. Despite the looming threat of robots, the letter has cheered her up. A mystery. A letter full of clues. The tea ladies are back in business.

# 5

# BATTLE OF THE BISCUITS

Hazel's washing up the cups and saucers in the downstairs kitchen when the telephone rings. It's only on the rare occasion she gets a call here, and it's usually an urgent request from the top floor requiring a batch of scones to be whipped up for an important visitor. She wipes her hands on her pinny and picks up the receiver.

'They want you to pop upstairs, Hazel,' says Edith Stern, secretary to the two directors of the company: Mr Karp Senior (referred to within Empire Fashionwear as Old Mr Karp) and his son, Frankie Karp (referred to by many names, none of them flattering).

'Do you know what it's about?' asks Hazel. She reaches for a tea towel to dry her hands properly. 'I was only up there half an hour ago, and no one mentioned anything.'

'You'll see soon enough,' says Edith, darkly.

'Good-oh, give me a moment and I'll be right up.'

Hazel takes a quick look in the mirror hanging behind the kitchen door. It's odd that she would be called upstairs. She's up there twice a day serving their tea and biscuits and often has a good chat with Mr Karp. Frankie is another matter. Chatting with the tea lady is not something he would waste his time with unless he wanted something. Hazel wonders if it's something that actually concerns her, thinking of the earlier conversation about the tea machine. She runs a comb through her hair and freshens her lipstick before going upstairs.

Exiting the lift, Hazel passes through the outer office, where Edith Stern sits typing at a desk-rattling speed. 'They're arguing again,' she says, without pausing. 'Every day something new.'

Hazel takes a deep breath and, with a quick courtesy knock on Mr Karp's door, steps inside. Mr Karp sits behind his mahogany desk, while Frankie stands at the window smoking a fat cigar. Seen in profile, Hazel notices Frankie's figure has crossed the line from plump to portly in the last few months. His tailor-made three-piece suit now strains at the shoulders, the waistcoat pulled taut across his belly and the buttons ready to pop.

'Hazel, thank you for coming up. Please take a seat,' says Mr Karp.

Sitting down, she glances across at Frankie. She can usually read his face like the weather. Storms ahead, by the looks.

'It goes without saying that after all you have done for this firm and, of course, for me personally – since I would not be here today without your prompt action when I had my heart attack last year – that you are one of our most valued members of staff.' Mr Karp pauses, to let that compliment sink in. 'Now we are in a situation where the firm is changing direction. We're at a crossroads. The way ahead is unclear, the future more uncertain. Frankie and I have been discussing cost-cutting and the need to prune our overheads.'

Hazel wishes he would get to the point, but it's not his way. He likes to go twice around the houses first. Everyone is well aware that Empire Fashionwear had a big shake-up last year when the British model known as The Shrimp wore a short dress to the races and threw the industry into chaos overnight. The department stores cancelled their orders and the firm seemed on the brink of collapse. It was Frankie's daughter, Pixie Karp, barely out of secretarial school, who was quick thinking enough to start making similar dresses and sell them by mail order.

Hazel knows from the company accountant, Mr Levy, that the mail order business has been very successful. But the dramatic change in the way the company does business seems to have left both Mr Karp and Frankie confused and uncertain. It's possible that Mr Karp may be ready to give up some control to a younger generation, but Frankie? Never.

Finally, Mr Karp gets to his point. 'Frankie has made a suggestion, and since it concerns you, I wanted to get your thoughts.'

Frankie sighs, gazing out the window through a cloud of cigar smoke.

'Yes?' Hazel waits for the axe to fall.

'The suggestion is that we ask staff to pay for their tea and biscuits. It wouldn't be much, say, fivepence or perhaps ten cents when the new money comes in, to cover the cost. It would obviously involve you, as you'd have to collect the money—'

'No great hardship, I'm sure,' Frankie murmurs to himself.

'I wanted to find out what you thought about the idea, Hazel. And what you think the response from the staff might be. You're better placed to know than we are.'

Hazel makes a habit of carefully considering her words before she speaks. In her mind's eye she travels up from the ground floor factory where the machinists work, to the designer's room run by the Rosenbaum sisters, to Doug Fysh in the sales office. Up to Accounts where half-a-dozen young women, commonly known as the Queen Bees, process the garment orders and payroll. She knows exactly how the staff will react, particularly Gloria Nuttell, the outspoken factory supervisor who controls production.

'Mr Karp, I understand why it might seem like a good idea, but for the sake of a few dollars a day—'

'Fifteen dollars a week,' interrupts Frankie.

Hazel nods in acknowledgment and continues. 'I think that goodwill is priceless. It's easy to lose and hard to get back. A hot beverage and a biscuit morning and afternoon reminds staff that they're important. It reminds them that you care for their wellbeing.'

'Nevertheless, providing tea and biscuits is a costly affair,' Frankie chips in. 'And they do get paid for their work.'

Hazel knows for a fact that charging staff for tea would be disastrous. No one likes something that they consider a right being snatched away from them, let alone being made to pay for it on top of that. But she's witnessed Frankie's towering rages over the years and knows better than to openly disagree with him.

'When I first came here,' she ventures, 'you might recall that the factory workers were only served broken biscuits.'

'It was standard practice everywhere,' says Frankie irritably.

Mr Karp nods. 'I recollect that you campaigned strongly to end that practice, and I admit that generated a lot of goodwill.'

Hazel nods. 'Plain biscuits only. Two each. It wasn't a big thing, but downstairs were delighted. I think it made them feel more respected by management.' She hesitates for a moment. 'You could think about getting rid of the "upstairs biscuits", which are much more expensive than the ones the other floors are served,' she continues, knowing Frankie's fondness for an Iced VoVo or three.

Frankie turns towards them, really annoyed now. 'This is a financial decision. And not one that the tea lady should be making.

I don't know why we don't have Levy up here discussing this – if we must discuss it at all. He's the accountant, after all.'

'Another thing to consider,' she says carefully. 'It may well open the door to the union coming in. They're growing stronger around here. I know that many of the staff at Klein's Lingerie have joined up.'

As usual, Mr Karp pales at the very mention of the union.

'It's a small gesture that makes a big difference,' says Hazel, in her closing argument.

'Point taken,' says Frankie. 'For the moment.' With that, he walks out, banging the door shut behind him.

Mr Karp gives Hazel a wan smile. Since that heart attack last year, he's never quite regained his strength or his confidence. 'Thank you, Hazel.' He pauses. 'Now, on another matter. Tell me, honestly, how's young Pixie going?'

'Why do you ask, Mr Karp?'

He leans forward confidingly. 'Between you and me, I'm worried there is a lot of responsibility on her shoulders. I'm concerned that because she's my granddaughter, people are giving me glowing reports and telling me what I want to hear.'

Hazel has always sympathised with Mr Karp. He started Empire Fashionwear more than twenty years ago with a single sewing machine. Back then, he knew everything about the business. Now with thirty staff over four floors, it's impossible to know exactly what's happening at every level and who to rely on for an honest appraisal.

'I don't need to tell you that last year was one of the most difficult years in our firm's history,' he says. 'The episode with the English model, and this "mini-dress" shook the industry's foundations. We've never had anything like this happen overnight before.

Is it a fad?' He shrugs, almost talking to himself now. 'None of us know. Pixie has her own ideas, but she's young and inexperienced . . . The company was established on orders from department stores in six-month cycles. Now that's less than half the business and this mail order business has taken over. But it's day-to-day – we can't forecast next year, or even next month. It all depends on the whims of thousands of fickle young women. Between you and me, Hazel, I'm worried it could all crash down on us.'

Hazel waits to see if there is more, but Mr Karp falls silent. He gives a helpless shrug.

'Pixie's smart, and being young is an advantage these days,' says Hazel. 'She and Alice work so hard. They're always here first thing in the morning and, judging by the number of dirty cups in the stockroom, work late into the night.'

Mr Karp nods. 'Hard work doesn't always pay off. She's convinced these "minis" are here to stay, but what if she's wrong? These little frocks are propping this company up, but what if Frankie's right and the bottom drops out of the market overnight?'

Hazel says nothing. She believes in Pixie, but he's right that the tide of fashion could swing in another direction very quickly. No one can predict that. And she understands his concern; it must be terrifying to think that everything you've built over two decades rests on the fragile shoulders of a nineteen-year-old with a dream. But Pixie is a very determined young woman and not to be underestimated.

Mr Karp smiles. 'Thank you, Hazel. Good to get that off my chest,' he says, leaning back in his chair. 'Forget about the silly five-pence idea. Leave everything as it is for now.'

Hazel returns his smile. She thanks him and leaves his office, closing the door softly behind her.

Edith gives her a questioning look. 'Who won?'

'It was a victory for the people,' says Hazel.

'Good for you.' Pointing towards Frankie's closed office door, Edith whispers, '*He* could cut back on his expensive dinners. Look at this.' She waves a bill in front of Hazel. 'One month of Frankie and Dottie "entertaining" at the Wentworth would feed a family for a year. Disgusting.'

Hazel puts a finger to her lips. 'Shh . . . Do be careful, Edith dear.'

Edith harrumphs, spearing the offending invoice on a spike with a dozen others. 'Oh, by the way, there was a call for you while you were in there. A personal call,' she adds with a note of disapproval.

'Oh?' Hazel can't imagine who would call her at work. 'Are you going to tell me who it was?'

'A man with an accent.' Edith picks up her stenography notebook. 'A Mr Oscar Sorensen. Ring any bells?' She waits expectantly.

Hazel, caught on the hop, murmurs, 'Oh, yes. An acquaintance.'

'A foreign gentleman acquaintance?' asks Edith. 'Well, I never . . . I told him you were in a meeting. He said he'll call back tomorrow.'

# 6

# IRENE CASTS THE FIRST STONE

Irene considers having a bath in preparation for her visit to Fred, but since it's not a Saturday, decides against it. The old hat's not looking its best after that toaster business. She still hasn't managed to get it off and has had to sleep with it on. Saves a bit of time in the morning, so that's one good thing. She squashes her good hat over the fried one and puts a hat pin through them both.

Hazel has given her the pale blue cardigan because of the scorch marks, even though they're hardly noticeable with the sleeves rolled up. Irene's been wearing it out to the pub of an evening; can't get a better talking point than an electrocution that ended happily.

Peering into the mirror, she notices her eyes look a bit sparkier than they did before the shock. Another bonus. She pats on a bit of pancake and adds a slash of lipstick. She can't remember when she went to this much trouble, but the effect is top-notch.

On the bus to the Long Bay Penitentiary, she reads the letter again. If she could remember what even one of these 'somethinks' was, then the other things he mentioned might all come back to her. Anyway, Fred will no doubt give her a hint and that will start the ball rolling. She wonders if it's jewels or cash he's stashed away. The latter would be easier, unless they're marked banknotes. She wonders why Fred didn't just ask her to come to see him and tell her in person. He's a sneaky sort. She always liked that about him. He always has an angle. It wasn't his fault the security guard got shot in the robbery. Fred was busy with the bank vault, so that was nothing to do with him. The whole lot of them are in Long Bay now, no doubt planning something big for when they get out. Still a while yet.

She doesn't like going into the gaol. It gives her a nasty feeling, like a rat in a trap, even though she's always been a visitor, never an inmate. That's why she stopped going to see him. Now she stands in the street outside, looking up at the huge wooden doors like the entry to a castle. She rolls a cigarette and smokes it slowly.

Finally, she approaches the doors and rings the bell. A small sliding window opens above her head. She flaps her hand in front of it. A moment later the door opens. The guard takes her name and checks it against a list. He gives her a funny look and she gives him a scowl in return. He scribbles something in a docket book, tears it out and gives it to her.

'Go across to the office,' he says, pointing her in the direction of a cluster of buildings.

'What for? It's a prisoner visit,' says Irene, nodding in the direction of the visitors' area.

'Do you want to come in or not?' asks the guard.

Muttering angrily, Irene takes the path towards the offices as instructed. They treat everyone like prisoners around here. She wonders who she can complain to and if she can be bothered. She knocks on the door marked 'Administration' and is let in by another guard. She shows him the note and he points her towards a reception counter. The woman behind the counter looks at the slip of paper and, without a word, gets up and goes to a filing cabinet.

'Can anyone around here speak?' asks Irene. 'What the bloody hell is going on?'

The woman returns and passes a brown paper bag over the counter to Irene, followed by a clipboard and a form. 'Sign here,' she says.

Irene flings her handbag on the counter. 'What's all this rubbish?'

'The belongings of Fred Turnbuckle. You are Mrs Turnbuckle?'

It takes a moment for this to sink in. 'He's dead?'

The woman looks at the paperwork. 'Oh, sorry. It looks like we did try to inform you at the last known address. There was no phone number, and the letter was returned.' She puts an envelope on the counter.

Irene can see it's addressed to the boarding house with 'Return to Sender' stamped on it. Bloody hopeless lot they are.

'Someone kill 'im?' she asks, turning to give the guard a furious look. 'Fred wouldn't hurt anyone. Never got into a fight. Not the violent sort. He wouldn't even eat an oyster.'

'Mr Turnbuckle died of natural causes,' explains the woman.

For no reason other than it fits the moment, Irene bangs her fist on the counter. 'Was there an autopsy? Where's his body?'

The woman picks up the phone and asks someone to come to the front office. A moment later a tall, older man in uniform appears, introduces himself and ushers Irene into another office, offering her a seat.

'I don't wanna sit down, I wanna know what the hell's going on!'

'When did you last see Mr Turnbuckle?'

Irene gives him her filthiest scowl. 'A while ago. Been busy.'

'He was diagnosed with advanced lung cancer a couple of months ago and died last weekend. We did try to contact you but without luck, and he was buried yesterday in Rookwood Cemetery, compliments of the state.'

Irene doesn't know what to say. She'd never thought of Fred dying, let alone being dead a week and no one telling her. He smoked two packs a day for years. They reckon that's a problem now. But who knows? One minute it's good for you, next thing it's not.

'Well, I'm not happy,' she says, having run out of steam. 'Not at all.'

'I imagine not. Is there anything else I can help you with?'

Irene tries to think of an unreasonable request, but all her thoughts are scrambled by this shock on top of the actual shock she got a few days ago.

'Youse have done quite enough, thank you very much,' she says. Taking the brown paper bag, she leaves the office and walks out through the giant doors of the prison.

Arriving home to Glade Street, she can hear Hazel in the kitchen and stamps down the hallway to throw the bag on the table in disgust.

Standing at the sink, Hazel glances over her shoulder. 'Is that something you've brought home for tea, Irene dear?' she asks.

'When did I ever bring anything for tea?' asks Irene crossly.

Hazel turns back to the bucket of poisonous wine she's brewed up. She scoops a cup of it and tips it into a bottle through a funnel. 'I take your point.'

'That's all that's left of Fred. He's bloody dead!'

Hazel accidentally drops the cup into the bucket and turns to look at her. 'Oh no, oh dear. I'm sorry to hear that.'

'Yer better get that cup out before it dissolves,' suggests Irene.

Hazel fishes it out. 'Would you like a glass, Irene? It's very fortifying. Choko and passionfruit.'

Irene pulls a sour face. 'Smells like the trail the dunny man leaves behind him. Tea'll do me.'

Hazel lifts the tea cosy and feels the pot. 'I'll top this up.'

Irene sits down and tips the contents of the bag onto the kitchen table: a copy of *The Call of the Wild*, a photograph of Fred and his mother when he was a kiddie and a small stone. Irene picks each item up and stares at it. 'The whole thing's bloody suspicious if yer ask me.'

Hazel brings two cups of tea to the table and sits down. 'I'm very sorry, Irene dear. I know you were still fond of Fred.'

Irene shrugs. Betty and Hazel love this soppy talk, but not her. 'D'yer reckon this could be a gold nugget?' she asks hopefully.

Hazel picks the stone up and studies it. 'I'm no expert but it looks more like a stone off the side of a road to me. From his letter, it seems he's hidden something at a location he thought you would remember. If this was valuable, I'm sure he would have pointed you in that direction.'

Irene tosses the stone out into the yard. 'Fred and his bloody stones.' She could cry with the disappointment of it all. She hasn't cried since 1932 (and that was only for a minute or two) and wonders if the electric shock has weakened her emotions. She picks up the tea towel Hazel was using and mops her face with it.

Hazel frowns but says nothing. 'Was he fond of stones?'

'Yeah, always collecting rocks and things. He liked nature. Bugger! Now I'll never know what those somethinks are. Why didn't he bloody write earlier?'

'He probably didn't expect to pass away quite so quickly. I doubt they would have stones like that in the prison yard.'

'Nah, he must've smuggled it in.'

'How would he smuggle . . . Oh . . . dear, what a thought.'

Hazel gets up and gives her hands a scrub with the carbolic soap. 'I wouldn't worry, he'd have washed it by now,' says Irene.

Hazel leans against the bench and sips her tea. 'It must be important for him to go to all that effort. More than just being fond of stones. It must be significant. I don't know why you threw it out, dear. That was a little hasty.'

Irene gets up and stands at the back door, looking into the yard. The concrete is cracked and breaking up in places; the stone could be anywhere.

'I really think you need to find it,' says Hazel.

Irene gives an annoyed harrumph and steps out into the yard. Hazel's right. That was a stupid thing to do. 'On me bloody own?' she asks.

Hazel purses her lips in that stubborn way she does. 'You threw it out there on your own, Irene dear.'

'Yoo-hoo, only me!' A chubby little hand appears over the top of the back gate, unlatching it from the inside, and a moment later Betty bursts into the yard. At the sight of Hazel and Irene, she says, 'Oh, nice to have a reception committee.'

*Timely arrival,* thinks Irene, and gives her a nice smile.

'Oh dear,' says Betty. 'Whatever it is, I want no part of it.'

Hazel explains the situation and Betty listens, giving Irene a sideways look when it comes to the part about her throwing the stone outside. They go into the kitchen, where she flicks through *The Call of the Wild* and stares at the photograph.

'No tweezers then? If he was called Fred "Tweezers" Turnbuckle

I would have thought he'd have a collection of tweezers. Didn't he use tweezers to open . . . things?'

Irene sighs. 'Course not. Tweezers was his nickname. All criminals have 'em.'

'Yes, I see what you mean. What sort of parent would call their child Tweezers? I just thought . . . Anyway, I also think the stone is an important clue, in which case, I'm prepared to assist in the investigation.' Betty gets her notebook out of her bag. 'Can you describe it in detail, please, Irene?'

'Grey stone, and a bit sandy coloured. Will yer just bloody help?'

Irene looks out at the yard in despair. She gets out her tobacco pack and rolls a ciggie to kill time while Betty rabbits on.

'Now, what we need to do . . . Please listen to me, Irene . . . You need to sit at the table and throw something else out the door.'

'I'll throw *yers* out the bloody door.'

'You also need to be nice to me. This is a proven scientific method. Please just co-operate. Also, why are you wearing two hats? We'll be calling you Irene "Two Hats" Turnbuckle if you keep that up.'

Irene unpins her good hat and puts it on the kitchen dresser.

'I think it's worth a try. We need something of a similar weight,' says Hazel.

'Oh, is this the choko and passionfruit?' asks Betty, peering into the bucket.

Hazel scoops half a cup out of the bucket and hands it to her.

Betty takes a mouthful. Her face shrivels up like she just stuck a knife in the toaster. 'It's got zing, I'll say that much.'

Irene could use some zing right now. She gets up, fills her teacup from the bucket and pours it down her throat. It tastes foul but

within a minute or two she does feel a bit brighter. She picks up a
teaspoon and throws it out the door.

'Irene, no!' cries Betty. 'Sit down in the same place . . . What
have we got, Hazel?'

Hazel opens the drawer of the kitchen dresser and puts three
reels of cotton – blue, black and white – in front of Irene. 'Sit at the
same angle and try to throw them with the same force.'

Irene does as she's told, tossing the cotton reels one after the
other out the door as the three of them watch where they land.
Betty and Hazel walk outside and stand looking at them. Irene
throws out another teaspoon, an onion and a potato sitting on the
bench, for good measure.

'Ouch! What are you doing?' cries Betty. 'Stop!'

The sun has left the yard but it's still boiling hot out there. Hazel
is crouched down, searching around the area where all the items
landed. Betty has her nose practically on the ground even though
she doesn't know what she's looking for. As far as Irene can see it's
hopeless. Then, just when they're talking about giving up, Hazel
finds the stone. While those two are busy examining it and natter-
ing on, Irene has another cup of wine. Things are looking up.

## 1

# HAZEL DISCOVERS A CODED MESSAGE

When Betty's gone home and Irene's upstairs stamping her feet and singing 'Blame it on the Bossa Nova' in a loud tuneless voice (having drunk a good pint of the new brew), Hazel can finally give the clues her full attention. She examines each item carefully, trying to imagine why these things might have been important to Fred.

The singing stops abruptly and is taken over by Irene's hacking cough and the smoke from her pipe drifting down through the floorboards. Hazel sighs. She has asked Irene so many times not to smoke in bed. She's also concerned that Irene has become chummy with Maude and recently mentioned taking the girl 'under her wing'. Not an ideal place for an impressionable young lady. Hazel had given Irene a room last year because she was ill and being evicted from the boarding house where she lived. It was never Hazel's intention that it would be a permanent arrangement, and her tolerance for Irene seems to be wearing thin. At some point, a difficult conversation will have to take place.

Hazel picks up Fred's worn copy of *The Call of the Wild* and flicks through it. After her first lesson with Sister Ruth, she feels less anxious when she picks up a book like this, without pictures. She has a set of encyclopaedias that she loves to look through, making the association of the photographs and illustrations with the words. When Norma was young, she would read out one or two entries before bed. It helped Norma's education and sharpened Hazel's memory and general knowledge. But now there's no one to read to her and she has a thirst for more knowledge.

Turning the pages of Fred's book, she wonders if the day will come when she can pick up a book and read it without having to brace herself. She recognises words, but connecting them all up in sentences with meaning is the difficulty. She pauses, noticing a tiny dot below a letter. Two pages on, there is another one and then five pages on another. They're not easy to spot and could be anywhere on the page. But Hazel suspects they are not accidental.

The light in the kitchen is not ideal. She stands and gets the magnifying glass out of the dresser drawer. It's clear from the swollen image through the magnifying glass that the dot is made in pencil, subtle but deliberate. Slowly turning the pages, she sees more and more of them. It's late now and her eyes are tired. There's something here, she's sure of it. Finding all the dots, however, will be a long job and she might need help. She tucks the book, the stone and the photograph away in the drawer, where they will be safe from Irene.

Hazel arrives at work the next morning to find Pixie Karp waiting for her in the kitchen, looking distraught. 'Pixie dear, what's happened?' asks Hazel as she puts her handbag away in the cupboard.

'Dottie's joining the firm!'

'Oh. I see.' Hazel takes her pinny down from the back of the door. 'In what role?'

Pixie's face flushes pink. 'I think my parents are trying to take over the place, and push Grandad out. She's been taking an interest in the Mod Frocks side of the business, asking me all sorts of questions. She was never interested before.'

Hazel pulls out a chair at the small table and beckons Pixie to sit down. She feels for the girl. This is her first job and she's been at everyone's beck and call. In particular, the Rosenbaum sisters, Miss Joan and Miss Ivy. In the past, they produced all the designs under Frankie's direction. They resent Pixie for reasons of their own, perhaps because she's young and has the privilege of being Mr Karp's favourite granddaughter. Frankie held the reins on the design side of the firm for years. Almost overnight, he lost his grip. It must be confusing for him that between one day and the next his daughter has gone from sorting mail and collecting his dry-cleaning to running part of the business. It's probably not surprising the Karps want to put that part of the business in the hands of someone older. But Dottie, who is Pixie's mother, is an odd choice.

'Start at the beginning,' says Hazel. Going over to close the door so they're not overheard, she's surprised to see Frankie striding down the hallway. In the entire decade she's worked here, Hazel's fairly sure Frankie has never arrived this early in the morning. Before she can warn Pixie, he's at the kitchen door.

Pixie gives her father a sullen stare. 'What?'

'Be reasonable, girl,' says Frankie. 'Dottie needs something to do. She knows about the fashion business.'

'She worked in a dress shop once,' says Pixie in a flat voice.

'Exactly. She knows the ins and outs. We've got this profitable part of the business being run by a slip of a girl, just out of school—'

'I don't know what a "slip of a girl" is, but there are three of us running this: me, Gloria and Alice,' Pixie interrupts.

'One straight out of school – all right, secretarial school – one a machinist and one a factory supervisor. None of whom know anything about running a business,' argues Frankie.

Hazel, doing her best to blend into the background, makes Pixie's tea and pours one for Frankie, adding two Iced VoVos to sweeten him up. He takes the cup and saucer without seeming to notice who gave it to him and nibbles on a biscuit.

'If she wants to join the firm, then why can't she work with you on the evening frocks and that range?' asks Pixie.

'It's bad enough for me to have to deal with the Rosenbaum sisters,' says Frankie. 'Dottie hates those two.'

'It's not my problem,' says Pixie, tears welling up in her eyes. 'She even wants to change the name from Mod Frocks to the Dottie Collection.'

'Pixie, this whole "miniskirt" business will have blown over by next season. All I'm asking is, give Dottie something to do and keep her out of my hair, will you? That's not too hard, is it?'

'We need more people wrapping up the frocks for post—' begins Pixie.

Frankie gives an exasperated sigh. 'She's not going to do that! Give her a pencil and some paper – she can knock out some designs.'

Pixie stands up, her cheeks burning. 'She doesn't know anything about designing.'

Frankie makes a sweeping gesture at the short shift Pixie's wearing. 'A child could draw these. No one will know the difference.'

Pixie stares at him in stony silence.

'Good God, just let her draw them and throw the blasted things away,' he huffs, walking out. 'It's not that difficult,' he calls over his shoulder, his heel plates tapping like Morse code as he hurries down the hallway.

Hazel glances at her watch. She still has a few minutes before the factory break. She sits down at the table opposite Pixie. 'Now, Pixie dear, you know I don't like to give advice but—'

'Please do, Mrs Bates.'

'A couple of thoughts. You need to be business-like about this . . . not emotional. Just for the moment, try to forget that Dottie is your mother.'

'Fat chance of that,' says Pixie sulkily.

'There is a time-honoured technique when an employee is foisted on you: give them jobs they won't like. Boring jobs, fiddly jobs . . . Use your imagination. I've seen this in practice many times over the years. It sorts the wheat from the chaff, as they say.'

Pixie looks interested. 'Go on.'

'It's important to be professional. Ask Mr Levy if the two of you can pop out for a sandwich at lunchtime. Your grandfather hired him for a good reason. He's not just an accountant, he has many years of experience in the rag trade, here and in Europe. Ask his advice about Mod Frocks. You and Alice and Gloria did those designs and built that side of the business. You need to make sure it can't be taken from you. Mr Levy can teach you a lot about business – if you're willing to learn, dear.'

'Of course, I am, Mrs Bates. I want to know everything.'

Hazel smiles. 'That's the spirit.' She stands up and flicks on the Zip to reboil. 'Now, this tea won't make itself and there'll be an all-out strike if I'm late to the factory.'

Pixie nods. 'Thanks, Mrs B. Thanks a lot,' she says and slips out the door.

Hazel quickly puts the trolley together, counting the items and ticking them off with her fingers as always: hot water urn, tin of Nescafé, double-handled teapot, milk, sugar, cups and saucers, teaspoons and tin of plain biscuits. The Zip shrieks. She spoons tea into the pot and fills it with boiling water. Her day has officially begun.

The factory buzzer sounds as Hazel walks through the doors. The sewing machines grind to a halt and the pop music blasting from a transistor radio is turned down. The fifteen machinists, two pressers, the cutter and Gloria Nuttell, the factory supervisor, get up and gather around the tea trolley while Hazel quickly distributes the tea and coffee, remembering who has milk and how much sugar.

'You'll never guess who was wandering around down here yesterday,' says Gloria, lighting a cigarette as she sips her black coffee.

'Let me guess, Dottie Karp?' says Hazel.

Gloria gives a throaty laugh. 'You are all seeing, all knowing, Hazel. It's frightening.'

Hazel laughs. 'What did she have to say?'

Gloria jets an angry puff of smoke. 'Dottie speak to me? That's a laugh. She just poked around like the Queen visiting the poor. She's probably thinking of redecorating the place.' Gloria points around the factory, mimicking Dottie's habit of issuing commands. 'These tatty old tables – replace them with mahogany. Wall hangings over those cobwebs. Replace all the lighting with chandeliers.'

Alice makes her way over to join them, slow and awkward with her sticks. She started here as a machinist, but turned out to have an interest in the latest fashion and a talent for design. Over the last few months, she and Pixie have not just worked closely together but become firm friends.

'Pixie says Mrs Karp is coming to work here,' says Alice.

'You know the Karps like being called Frankie and Dottie,' says Gloria. 'They think we're all one big happy family.'

Alice nods. 'Oh, I thought that was a bit of a joke by staff.'

'It is, Dottie and Frankie are a joke,' says Gloria. 'I guarantee having her around is going to cause trouble. I'm pretty sure yesterday was the first time she's ever been down here to the engine room.'

'How's the new warehouse fellow working out?' Hazel asks Gloria. 'He doesn't seem to come out for tea. I wonder, should I take it in to him?'

Gloria shrugs. 'I wouldn't bother. He brings his thermos and prefers the racing pages to our company. Fine with me.'

'He seems very helpful,' says Alice. 'He gets his wife to come in and help package up the postal orders when we're falling behind.'

'Yeah, that's true. He's not as cute as the last one, that's for sure,' Gloria says wistfully. 'But he gets the job done.'

As Hazel gathers up the cups and saucers and delivers her trolley back to the kitchen, it occurs to her how well organised the factory and mail order dispatch are now. Gloria, Alice and Pixie may be relatively inexperienced but between them, they've made it work.

She takes the lift to the top floor kitchen to prepare tea for the management.

Today, both Karps are in their respective offices and on the telephone. Old Mr Karp gives her a thank-you wave as she delivers his tea and Scotch Fingers. Frankie gives her a curt nod when she puts his tea and two more Iced VoVo biscuits in front of him.

In the outer office, Edith Stern pounds away at her typewriter, pausing only to ask, 'Did you hear the latest? Her ladyship apparently wants her own office.' Without waiting for a response, she takes a quick sip of her tea and resumes her typing.

Then it's back to the kitchen for Hazel to prepare her trolley for the middle two floors.

In Accounts on the 2nd Floor, half-a-dozen young women live in a world of their own, mostly a whirl of social engagements, and they would barely know who Dottie Karp is. But Mr Levy has already heard the news.

'She's coming in this afternoon to discuss her salary require-ments,' he tells Hazel. 'I seem to be the centre of attention today. Young Pixie wants to take me for lunch.' He raises a questioning eyebrow.

'Oh, lovely,' says Hazel. 'It's about time you two got to know each other better.'

Mr Levy nods. 'I agree. She's the future of this firm, whether people around here acknowledge it or not.'

'She's a terrific young lady, and smart. She needs a good advisor.'

'I agree, Hazel,' says Mr Levy with a wink. 'I would be honoured.'

The final stop for morning tea is the 1st Floor where Miss Ivy and Miss Joan Rosenbaum run the design department. Both stand at their long worktable, bolts of fabric in neat stacks at one end, apparently waiting for Hazel's arrival. Normally they're eager for their favourite Ginger Nuts but today it's news they're after.

'What have you heard, Hazel?' asks Miss Ivy, the moment she enters the room.

'Good morning, ladies,' says Hazel.

'Ah, here she is!' says Doug Fysh, emerging from the sales office. 'You need a bell, Hazel, like the town crier with all the gossip. "Hear ye! Hear ye!" Haw, haw haw . . .'

Miss Joan gives him a cool stare. 'I don't know what you're talking about. We never get much out of Hazel. Plays her cards close.'

All three turn to look at Hazel, who continues to pour their coffee.

'Dottie Karp,' snaps Miss Ivy.

'Listen,' says Miss Joan, turning to her sister. 'We need to be careful if she's going to be roaming around the building. She could walk in at any minute.'

Doug takes his tea and nods sagely. 'Agreed. Think of her as a hand grenade. We need to make sure no one pulls the pin or there will be bodies everywhere. We'll be up to our eyeballs in blood and gore—'

'Yes, thank you for that unnecessarily graphic detail, Mr Fysh,' interrupts Miss Joan. 'Let's hear from the voice of reason,' she says, with a nod in Hazel's direction.

Hazel considers her response. 'I'm sure she has some talents and a contribution to make, but I do agree with Miss Joan, be very careful what you say and where. Let's just keep an open mind.'

Miss Ivy gives a dramatic sigh. 'It's just one thing after another around here!'

And with that, morning tea is officially over. Hazel can take a break before doing it all again this afternoon. She arrives back in the downstairs kitchen to the phone ringing. She picks it up to hear Edith announce, 'I have Mr Sorensen on the line for you, Hazel.'

# 8
# A BUMPY START FOR THE GUILD

When Betty popped over to Hazel's yesterday, the last thing she expected was to spend the afternoon crawling around the backyard looking for a silly stone that Irene (in her usual careless way) threw out without even considering it could be important. Now here Betty is, back at Hazel's and roped into an even worse job: the surgical removal of Irene's hat – melted onto her hair! Betty wonders if the shock fried Irene's brain, like electroshock treatment, but there certainly hasn't been any improvement. It's been an uphill battle for Hazel to convince Irene this job needs doing.

Irene sits on a kitchen chair while Betty lifts the edges of the hat and Hazel carefully trims the hair to separate the two. Irene exudes an unpleasant musky smell like a little stink bug and Betty keeps her face turned as far away as possible.

'Yer done yet?' asks Irene for the umpteenth time. 'Haven't got all day, yer know. It's not a bloody problem. Matter a fact, it's bloody con ... con ...'

'Convenient?' suggests Betty.

'Handy,' says Irene. 'Saves the bother of putting it on every day.'

Hazel laughs. 'It can't be comfortable sleeping in your hat, Irene. And you'll have to wash your hair sooner or later.'

'Just hurry up, will yers?'

Typical Irene. No gratitude.

'As a matter of fact, we do need to hurry,' says Betty.

Hazel glances at her watch. 'Oh, goodness.' She quickly snips off the last strands of hair and the hat comes free. She hands it to Irene (chunks of dreadful dyed black hair stuck to it). 'I'll leave you to get rid of that, dear,' she says, and dashes upstairs to get ready.

Betty can't take her eyes off Irene's head. It looks like bushland after a big fire, all black spiky bits and bald spots.

Irene rubs her hands over her head. 'Feels like a wombat's bum,' she says cheerfully. She stands up and brushes the hair off her lap onto the floor. 'I'll just have a quick ciggie while Hazel's tarting herself up.'

While Irene stands at the back door smoking, Betty sweeps up the hair with a brush and dustpan. She's so annoyed she has to keep her lips glued tight, but when she sees Irene picking bits of hair off the hat (planning to wear it out!) Betty snatches it from her and puts it in the rubbish bin.

Irene scowls through a cloud of smoke but (surprisingly) doesn't object.

When Hazel's ready, they walk down to the Hollywood Hotel. Merl has arrived first and nabbed their favoured table in the corner. By the time they're settled, Shirley has prepared their usual shandies and arrives with them on a tray.

'Evening, Mrs B, Mrs P, Mrs T, Mrs D. How are we all this evening?' She stares at Irene. 'Must be a special occasion, Mrs T has her best hat on. Your shout tonight, love?'

Irene gives her a poisonous look. 'Very funny. For yer informa-tion, Mrs Dewsnap threw me other one in the bin.'

Shirley raises an eyebrow. 'Well done, Mrs D. Your drink's on me.' She puts a shandy in front of Betty. 'A reward for your contri-bution to the dress standards of this establishment.'

'It is an improvement,' says Merl. 'You look almost respectable in that hat.'

Irene snatches the hat off her head. 'How about now then?'

Shirley takes a step back. 'Run-in with a lawnmower, Mrs T?'

'No, clever clogs,' says Irene. 'A toaster, if you must know.'

Shirley gives a snort of laughter and chuckles all the way back to the bar.

'I think we've all heard enough about Irene and her mishaps. Let's remember we're here to discuss the Guild business,' says Merl.

'We've also invited Effie Finch. You remember her, Merl – the tea lady at the fire station,' says Betty.

Merl frowns. 'We don't want to get too many people involved at the outset. It's just going to complicate things.'

'We thought Effie would be a good addition to the core group,' says Hazel. 'And Mrs Li might pop by a bit later.'

That shuts Merl up nicely. Betty has always admired the way Hazel says the right thing at just the right time to close an argument.

Right on cue, Effie arrives, having already got herself a pint of beer at the bar. Knowing her, she'll down another couple before the evening is out. Betty wonders where she puts it all. She's thick-set and strong looking, like a wrestler, but there's not an ounce of fat on her.

'Evening, ladies!' Effie pulls up a chair and drops into it. 'What have we here? A coven of witches?'

'A cosy of tea ladies,' corrects Hazel with a smile. 'Thanks for coming along, Effie. We're hoping to work out the main committee this evening and then get in touch with other tea ladies and get started. Shirley has offered us the room upstairs for our meetings.'

'I'm going to take the minutes,' Betty reminds everyone. 'I expect that makes me the secretary. Also, I nominate Hazel as the chairwoman.'

'I second that,' says Effie.

'Me too,' says Irene.

'You have to say "I second that", otherwise it's not official, Irene,' Betty explains.

'Didn't she already second it?' asks Irene, jabbing the stem of her pipe in Effie's direction. 'Do I third it?'

Merl makes impatient tsk-tsks. 'Hazel needs to accept the nomination.'

'Thank you, ladies. I will accept the nomination for the short term – say, six months – just to get things started, and then we can have a proper election.'

Merl looks thoroughly put out; she naturally had her heart set on the position. 'I suppose it falls to me to be treasurer in that case,' she says, with a sigh.

'Actually . . . I'm sorry, Merl dear, but I would like to put forward Mrs Li as treasurer. She has a good deal of accounting experience.'

'Mrs Li?' says Merl frostily. 'I see.'

'But it would be wonderful if you could head the fundraising drive, Merl. No one can raise funds like you do,' continues Hazel.

*That's Hazel for you*, thinks Betty. Always the diplomat. There's no one better to lead the Guild than Hazel.

'All right,' says Merl. 'Provided I agree with the fundraising cause.'

Effie gives her a look. 'That's not how a committee works, as far as I know. It's a democracy. We vote. It's not up to you to decide.'

She turns to Hazel. 'I can be in charge of getting new members if you like.'

Merl purses her lips silently.

'What are you going to do, Irene?' Betty asks.

Irene gets her tobacco pouch out of her pocket. 'Nuthin' – too many busybodies for my liking.'

'Well, please don't smoke here – you know how my sinuses are,' says Betty. 'I move that no smoking be allowed at meetings!'

Hazel pats her hand comfortingly. 'No sudden moves, Betty dear. We need to have guidelines and some rules, but they need to be properly discussed and documented—'

Betty raises her hand. 'Oh, I could use one of the typewriters at work.' She glances around at the others, expecting an objection. 'I'm quite a good typist.'

'No one said yer weren't,' says Irene. 'All right. I'll do special operations.'

Merl looks over the top of her glasses at Irene. 'I doubt that break-ins will be on the agenda.'

Irene shrugs. 'I got plenty of other skills.'

'That's true,' agrees Betty. 'She does know a lot about knocking people unconscious and also kneecapping, and blackmail.'

Irene nods her confirmation at each point, but Betty picks up a look from Hazel and decides to leave it there.

'Let's always remember the tea ladies' code of conduct. We treat everyone with understanding and respect,' Hazel reminds them.

Betty notices Effie give Irene a wink and get a sly grin in return.

'I second that,' says Betty.

'Are you just going to second everything Hazel suggests?' asks Merl.

'Probably,' agrees Betty.

Mrs Li arrives. She never looks very comfortable in the pub. Betty gives up her chair and gets another. She buys a lemonade at the bar and puts it in front of Mrs Li, who gives her a nod of thanks, clearly wary around Merl. Not surprising. Merl's got some funny attitudes.

Hazel brings her up to date on the discussions so far. 'Now, as I mentioned, there's a very important issue we need to address urgently,' continues Hazel. 'You've probably all heard about this Café-bar machine by now?'

'It sounds quite swish, a café and bar combined,' says Betty.

Effie frowns. 'Never heard of it.'

Merl explains. 'It's a machine that has coffee and tea and water in a tank – separate, of course – and you press a button, and it pours out into a cup. Little paper cups you can throw away.'

Hazel gets a crumpled brochure out of her bag and flattens it out on her lap. 'Frankie had this on his desk. He threw it out, which I suppose is a good thing.'

She passes it to Betty who reads aloud: '"At last, the tea break is over . . ."' She gives a gasp at the thought and looks up at the others.

'Just get on with it, will yer?' says Irene.

'". . . thousands of Australian businesses can testify that with a Café-bar in the office, lengthy group tea breaks practically disappear . . . The Café-bar is always on duty and staff tend to have their tea when they want it and keep working while they have it."' Betty looks up. 'You can rent this machine for one dollar thirty-nine a week.'

'What's that in the old money?' asks Irene.

'Not very much,' admits Hazel. 'Not even a pound.'

'They've installed one at Darlinghurst Police Station and let the tea lady there go,' says Mrs Li. 'I suppose Surry Hills will be next, then I'll be down to only three days a week.'

Hazel nods grimly. 'There may be nothing we can do but, with the Guild, we have an opportunity to bring tea ladies together and try to hold on to our jobs.' She pauses. 'But even apart from protecting the jobs of thousands of tea ladies, I think the workers will lose something irreplaceable . . . the love and care we bring with every cup of tea.'

To Betty's embarrassment, a tiny sob escapes her throat at Hazel's words. Thankfully she finds a clean hankie tucked up her sleeve and dabs her eyes.

'Here we go with the waterworks,' grumbles Irene. 'Better than the gasworks, I s'pose.'

Ignoring her, Betty turns to Hazel. 'That was inspiring, Hazel. I second that.'

'There's a surprise,' says Merl, dryly.

When Betty reads her notes over her cornflakes the next morning, it's clear that, after the second shandy and weepy bout, her note taking was not as accurate as she might have hoped. Hazel would be very disappointed to see this tangled list; Betty's writing is almost unreadable towards the end. From now on, it's fewer drinks and more accuracy. She vows to live up to the high standard of the Guild.

She wonders if the Guild could become as well-known and respected as the Country Women's Association. Perhaps there will be mention that Betty Dewsnap was one of the founding members: a secretary of the highest calibre who embodied the values of the Guild and set the standard.

On that note, after work today she'll go to the library and find out what the role of secretary of a committee entails. She thinks about all the ladies in the office at Farley Frocks and who might let her use their typewriter, but comes up blank. They are all very fussy about their typewriters and even put little jackets over them to keep them warm at night. They wouldn't like the idea of the tea lady banging away on their precious machine. Unfortunately, it seems Betty will have to take a leaf out of Irene's book and sneak in when they've gone home for the day. It's a risk, but one she's willing to take for the good of the Guild.

# 9

## HAZEL HAS A RENDEZVOUS

When Mr Sorensen had telephoned Hazel at work asking if they could meet, he mentioned there was something he would like to discuss. She's very curious to know why he's gone to the trouble of tracking her down. Now she's getting ready, and it's hard to know what to wear. It's late afternoon and, with the lack of rain, the heat feels sticky and dusty at the same time. She decides on a navy cotton frock and sandals, to be cool and comfortable.

When she comes out of St James Station, he's waiting for her, dressed in his usual pale linen suit, open-necked shirt and Panama hat. He shakes her hand rather formally and invites her for an aperitif at a nearby hotel. She has no idea what an aperitif is but decides she'll just wait and find out.

To her surprise, they enter the mirror-lined foyer of the Australia, with its grand staircase, marble floors and stained-glass windows. A party of women in satin, silk and chiffon cocktail dresses, accompanied by men in tuxedos, pass by on their way out. Hazel glances down at her simple dress and low-heeled sandals and wonders uncomfortably what she's doing in such a place.

Upstairs, the Winter Garden bar has an air of refinement and old wealth, with a high glass-domed ceiling, thick carpets, and clusters of tables and chairs. A uniformed waiter seats them and hands Mr Sorensen a menu encased in a leather folder.

Mr Sorensen passes the menu to Hazel. 'I'm sure you are able to make your own decision,' he says.

Hazel takes the menu and stares at it for a long moment, hoping something will leap out. The pressure of having to read it makes her cheeks burn. 'I'll have a cream sherry, thank you,' she says, hoping it's on the menu.

'I will have the same,' he agrees, beckoning to the waiter.

When the waiter leaves with the order, Mr Sorensen turns to Hazel. 'I think I have made a mistake. I was told this was the best place in town and I wanted to impress you, but it's too much.' He glances around and gives a sigh. 'Too much theatre and pretence.'

Hazel laughs. 'I'm easily impressed. There was no need to go to so much trouble.'

'I am certain that is not true, Mrs Bates. I think you are impossible to impress. You are unimpressible!'

'I can't imagine why you would want to impress me, Mr Sorensen. Perhaps you could explain why we're here.'

'I wanted to make an apology to you and Mrs Dewsnap. When we met, I was under much pressure in my work. There were meetings, such as the one you mentioned, that were highly confidential. I assure you that my work is not of a criminal nature. I was impolite to leave our dinner without saying goodbye.'

'Of course, apology accepted.'

'I enjoyed our conversations at the Bellevue. I think we will agree it does not have a *belle vue* or any view at all . . .' He pauses for a moment and continues. 'You have been on my mind ever since. I sense you have many unique qualities, and I would like to get to know you better, if you would allow me that privilege.'

'I'm not sure about unique qualities,' begins Hazel, taken aback by his forthright approach. 'I suppose I don't have any objection to a . . . friendship, but I'm not sure why our brief acquaintance was enough to make you track me down.'

'I am a foreigner a long way from my home and . . . I enjoyed your company. You may think this is strange, but I would also add that your voice, the tonality of your voice, is very pleasant. Its low frequency is very soothing to my ear.'

Hazel laughs. 'That's not a compliment I've ever received before, Mr Sorensen.'

'Please, call me Oscar.'

'Of course . . . Hazel,' she says.

The waiter reappears, placing the glasses on the table with a flourish that makes both Hazel and Oscar smile.

'I'm surprised to hear that,' says Oscar. 'I noticed it before we met, overhearing the conversations with your friend – who speaks at a higher pitch in the range of ten decibels. I will explain. This is my profession. I am an engineer, a particular type of engineer. I work with interior sound, acoustics.' He glances around the room, staring up into the glass dome for a moment. 'For example, this room is of impressive design. The dramatic ceiling height makes the people feel very small. But listen to the sound and how it reverberates, echoing back and forth. The notes the pianist plays are harsh and jarring to the ear. The laughter of the guests makes a sound like a donkey standing on a cliff over a valley . . .' He stops. 'Am I boring you?'

'Far from it. Please go on.'

Oscar drinks his sherry. 'If you're sure. But let us leave this place and find somewhere more tranquil where I can formulate a better explanation.'

Hazel agrees, and as they make their way back down the graceful staircase, she finds herself more aware of the different tones of voices and the clicking of heels on the marble floor of the foyer, something she hadn't noticed earlier.

They cross the street and walk into the Botanic Gardens. The heat has thickened, and the sun has a coppery glow. As they walk towards the harbour, Oscar brings her attention to the nearby birds and the distant sounds of the city. They sit down and rest on a park bench, where they have a view towards Manly and the heads in one direction and the tall cranes and giant arching shells of the Opera House construction in the other.

'It's going to be a magnificent building,' says Hazel. 'When it's finally finished.'

Oscar nods. 'It is extraordinary. A design of genius and a miracle of engineering. I hear people compare the design to the sails of a ship, or segments of an orange.'

'I thought it looked like a stack of soup bowls on the draining board,' says Hazel.

Oscar throws back his head and laughs. 'I see that now.' He gazes at the construction for a moment. 'The sound inside this building will be the most important element.'

They fall into a comfortable silence. The low sun sparkles on the water and the shadows around them lengthen. Hazel notices the distant whistle of the ferry, the call of birds. Children's laughter and a violin in the distance, stopping and starting again. The more she listens the more she hears.

'Now we hear everything in proportion,' says Oscar quietly.

Hazel turns to him. 'I have a rather odd question for you.'

He rubs his hands together in anticipation. 'These are my favourite kind.'

'I normally don't tell anyone about this. Only my daughter and Betty, Mrs Dewsnap, know about it. I thought . . . with your expertise, you might have some insight.'

'You make me very intrigued now.'

Hazel takes a deep breath. 'I have what you might call . . . magical ears.'

Oscar seems to take this in his stride, so she continues. 'I've had this . . . sensation for as long as I can remember. It took me a long time to identify exactly what was happening. I still don't know why, but when someone is lying the rims of my ears sort of tingle. Sometimes it's just a slight tingling and other times quite uncomfortable, more like a hot prickling. It's not completely reliable—'

'How can you be sure it's not reliable?' interrupts Oscar. 'Do you have a scientific methodology?'

Hazel laughs. 'Far from it. They have let me down. Someone close to me had been deceiving me from the moment we met. I trusted him completely and . . . well, it doesn't matter now. But I lost confidence in my gift for a while.'

Oscar gives her a long look. 'I'm sorry to hear that. Can we make a test of it?'

'I suppose so,' agrees Hazel.

Oscar nods. 'I am ready for a question.'

Hazel sees an opportunity to ask an impertinent question. 'Are you married?'

If he is surprised by her directness, he gives no sign of it. 'Yes, I am.'

'Do you have children?'

'No, I don't,' he replies.

Hazel tries to think of one more thing she'd like to know about him while she has the chance. 'Where are you from exactly?'

'Sønderborg.'

'So, you are not married, you do have children and you are from Sønderborg, which I happen to know has a famous castle.'

'Very impressive,' says Oscar. 'And accurate. My wife died many years ago, and my children are no longer children but independent adults.'

Hazel smiles. 'I wondered, as an acoustics expert, if you had any idea of how this works.'

Oscar ponders the question seriously for a few minutes. 'This is not exactly my field, the "tingling" of ears. My expertise is physics and mathematics, not human behaviour, but this phenomenon is of great interest to me. So let us hypothesise that you have higher powers of observation and are sharper than the average person. You subconsciously notice distinct signs; this might be in the person's posture or a change of tone, or something in their eyes. It could be a person holding back information or offering too much. All that information is processed in a millisecond and taps into a mechanism of sorts – a receiving device. Your ears give you a simple signal, a form of vibration that tells you all is not as it seems. The weakness in the model could be if you over-ride the system. In other words, you unconsciously "block" your ears to the incoming vibrations because the wish to trust this person is so strong. Also, perhaps the individual is very skilled at deception and these factors combine to work against your instincts.'

Hazel nods. 'That makes sense. I have noticed that if someone is evasive, I often don't pick up on that, so I've learned over the years to ask direct questions.'

Oscar nods enthusiastically. 'I think this is the same for any natural gift. It requires understanding and adjustment. You had this ability as a child?'

'Yes. I used to wonder why people bothered telling lies.' Hazel laughs. 'I soon discovered that pointing them out got me into trouble and learned to stay quiet.'

'And this is how you became involved in the detective business?'

Hazel smiles. 'That's more wishful thinking on Betty's part. It was something we got involved with by accident, and now we're back to being ordinary tea ladies.'

Oscar smiles at her. 'Anything but ordinary, I would say.'

There's no tingling of Hazel's ears. Her cheeks feel a little flushed. But that's something quite different.

# 10

# IRENE GETS A TIP-OFF

Irene walks into the Thatched Pig to find the boozy legal eagle, Arthur Smith, sitting up at the bar. He must be well away, because he looks happy to see her.

'Ah, Mrs Turnbuckle of the terrifying smile. It's like looking into the jaws of hell.'

Irene scowls at him. 'Sent back me letter from the gaol, did yer?'

'I'm not responsible for the redirection of your mail. Particularly given the lack of gratitude I experienced on the previous occasion.'

'Yeah, well . . . me hubby carked it and they popped him into Rookwood without me even getting to say ta-ta. Happy now?'

Arthur considers this for a moment. 'I wouldn't say happy . . . your news has brought on an existential sadness related to my own mortality.' He picks up his glass and takes a sip. 'Ah, the sun just came out again. Now, to what do we owe the pleasure of your company today?'

Irene stares at his drink, a cocktail with an olive on a toothpick. 'In the money, are yers, Metho Man?'

'You can be very tiresome, Mrs Turnbuckle. As I explained previously, the meths was for the windows and not on my drinks menu,' he says.

Irene nods at his glass. 'Where're yer gettin' the money for them fancy things?'

He taps the side of his nose with one finger. 'We're all in the money right now.'

Irene glances around the bar for likely scoundrels. 'Yer owe me, mate. Re the letter business. Missed me old man's funeral.'

'I can see you as the black widow, wreaking vengeance on those who failed you administratively. The postal service, my good self – despite being an innocent bystander.' He sighs and takes a sip of his cocktail. 'What do I need to do to redeem myself in your eyes, dear Mrs Turnbuckle?'

'Need a tip-off. I'm a bit short at the minute.'

'A whisker under five foot by my estimation,' he says, looking her up and down.

Irene glances around the bar again. 'Hilarious. Come on, gimme.'

'Have a quiet word with Big G,' he says, nodding towards a meaty bald fellow sitting at a corner table with another man. 'As a respected member of the criminal fraternity, I'm sure you're already acquainted with him.'

Irene squints across the room. 'Oh, yeah. Him. All right.'

'Is that it? A wave of indifference.'

'Put a bloody sock in it, will yer?' says Irene. She moves along the bar and asks the barmaid for a shandy.

'Ladies aren't allowed in here unaccompanied,' says the girl tartly.

Irene tips her head in Arthur's direction.

The barmaid glances along the bar doubtfully. 'You're here with the judge?'

'Me mate Arthur,' says Irene, keeping one eye on Big G.

Once the frothing glass of gold is in front of her, Irene rolls a ciggie, parks it on her lip and takes her drink over to Big G. The table is covered in full ashtrays and empty beer glasses.

'Either of yers got a light?' she asks, looking from one to the other.

Big G tosses her a matchbook. 'Do I know you?'

'Mrs Turnbuckle. We met a couple times. Yer'd know me hubby Tweezers . . . just passed, sadly,' she says, throwing in a quivering lip.

Big G gestures towards an empty chair. Irene sits down and puts her drink on the table.

'Yeah, I heard,' says Big G. He turns to his mate, who has had every bone in his face broken at some point, leaving his dial all wonky. 'Know him?'

The mate nods. 'One of the greats.'

Big G gives a sigh. 'The good ones die young.'

'Or get locked up,' adds Irene.

'So, what can I do for you?' he asks, with a flash of his gold front tooth.

Irene wouldn't mind one of them herself – if she had teeth. 'Don't suppose yer remember any of his last jobs, do yer?' she asks.

Big G doesn't miss a beat. 'You reckon he's left you a little something?'

'Dunno. He went down for the bank job but there was a couple of others before that. Maybe a jeweller's, or I thought there might be a safe deposit box somewhere.'

'Funny you should ask that today,' says Big G. 'You're not the only one.'

'What d'yer mean?' asks Irene.

Big G considers the matter. 'You're the widow, so by rights anything should go to you. You wanna watch yourself but. The other party is a copper.'

'A cop was asking about Fred . . . Tweezers?'

'Making enquiries, he said. Either on behalf of Her Majesty or possibly he has a new hobby.'

'New hobby?' asks Irene.

'Treasure hunting,' says Big G. 'So you better be quick about it.'

'Do yer know him? Was he from around here?' asks Irene.

'Detective Pierce. Was in the CIB but he's at the local cop shop these days. Got kicked downstairs for being a naughty boy.'

Irene thinks about that for a minute. It's a bloody worry if Pierce has got himself involved.

'On another matter . . .' she ventures. 'Tryna get a bit together to bury the old man. Yer got anything going? Quick cash?'

Big G gives her a hard stare, his eyes flat as a goat's. He takes a long drag on his cigarette, holding his breath while he stubs it out in the ashtray. 'I have a few items you might be able to shift. Normally it's cash up front. But in memory of Tweezers, I'll spot you for a month. I don't want the stuff back, mind. No excuses. Just cash. Got it?'

Irene nods, curious to know what these items might be. 'Got it.'

Big G jabs a thumb in the direction of his mate. 'Onions here will take you out the back and give you the product.'

Irene thanks Big G and follows Onions out to the parking area behind the pub. He walks over to a maroon Pontiac that takes up two parking spaces and fishes around in his pocket for the keys.

'Yer like onions, then?' asks Irene, by way of friendly chat.

He pauses to think. 'Not really,' he says, finally.

'Why yer called Onions then?'

He gives her a look of pity. 'I make people's eyes water,' he says, unlocking the boot.

'Jeez, yer could fit a family of six in there, if yer packed 'em tightly,' says Irene, leaning forward to see what's in the cartons.

'How many?' asks Onions, opening one to show her the contents.

Irene grins. She's in luck. A lot of bloody luck. 'I'll take a dozen.'

Irene sneaks in through Hazel's back gate and hides the box of goodies behind the outdoor dunny. Her plan is to smuggle the tiny transistor radios, barely bigger than a man's hand, upstairs three at a time tucked in her undies. The elastic has seen better days and they jiggle a bit, but she pulls her cardie tight and holds them in place as far as the stairs, where she fishes them out and hurries upstairs to hide them under her bed.

Hazel's parked herself at the kitchen table reading Fred's book with a magnifying glass. She's either going blind or hearing the call of the wild herself. Either way, she's making Irene's operation difficult. She's not a business type and is guaranteed not to approve of this money-making effort.

As Irene ferries the last three transistors through the danger zone, Hazel asks (without bothering to look), 'What are you up to, Irene dear?'

Irene's been so caught up in calculating how much she'll get for these little fellas, it only now crosses her mind that if Hazel catches her storing stolen goods in her house, she might just kick her out. She feels one of the transistors break loose from the waistband and slip down the side of her undies. Wouldn't do for it to fall out the leg hole right now. She pulls her cardie tighter. 'More to the point, what are yers up to?' Irene asks.

Hazel puts down the magnifying glass and sits back in her chair. 'I think Fred has left you a message in this book.'

'What's it say?' asks Irene, keeping a firm grip on her cardie.

'I don't know yet. He's left a pencil dot under some of the letters. I'm writing down all those letters. It's a bit of a jigsaw. If you miss a letter or two, it doesn't make sense. It's time consuming.' Hazel takes a good look at Irene. 'Are you all right, Irene dear? Is it your tummy that's making you run in and out to the lavatory?'

'Yeah. Might have a bit of a lie-down.'

Irene edges out the door. As she gets to the foot of the stairs, one of the transistors breaks loose and falls on the wooden floor with a bang. 'I'm fine!' she shouts. Snatching it up, she pulls out the other two and gallops up the stairs as fast as her rickety old knees will take her. Once she has the radios safely tucked away, she opens the window, props herself up on the bed and packs her pipe. She gets out her flask and takes a swig, lights the pipe and puffs at it until it takes. Now she can think straight.

According to Onions, the radios are worth seven quid each in the shops. They're the latest thing, a pocket transistor. You'd need a bloody big pocket, though, and seven quid is a bloody lot of money. Big G wants three quid from her for twelve transistors, leaving her with four quid for each one. She reckons she can flog them at five quid for a quick sale and that will leave her . . . twenty . . . eighteen . . . Arithmetic is not her strong point. She has another swig of her flask but the sums are no clearer. Hazel's the one for adding things up, but not this time. Point is, sell them at a profit. No need to complicate it. Now the question is where to flog them.

*

At lunchtime Irene gets to the wall in the laneway early in the hope that Betty will be there alone. She's in luck. She sits down and gives Betty a friendly smile.

'What do you want, Irene?' asks Betty.

'Yer got a telly?' Irene's gasping for a smoke but that will only get Betty off track, moaning about her sinuses.

'No, and I don't want a "hot" one, thank you very much.' Betty glances down the lane, looking out for Hazel, while she unwraps her sandwiches.

'Radiogram?' enquires Irene. 'Record player?'

'What's all this about?'

'Just nice to have a bit of music around the place, in't? Or listen to the cricket or the races?'

'Oh, good. Here comes Hazel.' All smiles now, Betty flaps her hand as if she thinks Hazel won't be able to find them without her help.

'Well, think about it,' suggests Irene. She has one of the transistors tucked in the pocket of her pinny but it's too late to bring it out now.

'I've already thought about it. If I want to watch the telly, I can stand outside Gibson's Electrical and watch it for nothing. I don't have room for radiograms and whatnot. Also, I'm not in the market for stolen goods. Ever.'

Irene takes out her tobacco and rolls a ciggie. She might have known Betty would be too high and mighty.

Hazel sits down and she and Betty have their usual chitchat about absolutely bloody nothing for a good ten minutes.

'How's the code-breakin' going, Hazel?' asks Irene, when she can get a word in edgeways.

Betty gets all pink and excited. 'Oh, what code are we talking about?'

'I've been working on the book Fred left,' explains Hazel.

While she goes into a long explanation about it (which Irene has already heard), Irene suddenly remembers what Big G told her about Pierce, Merl's money-grubbing son-in-law.

'Where's Merl today?' she asks.

'She has a dental appointment,' says Betty. 'She told us that yesterday.'

Hazel gives Irene a curious look. 'Why do you ask?'

'Well, somehow bloody Pierce has got his nose into it. He's been asking around about the jobs Fred did before he went away.'

'Well, that doesn't make any sense,' says Betty. 'Detective Pierce can just look up the files. I expect there's a whole filing cabinet dedicated to Fred's crimes.'

Irene shakes her head. 'Ones he didn't get caught for, yer goose.'

'Irene dear, while it would be interesting to solve this mystery, stolen goods would have to be turned over to the police in any case.'

'Yer reckon Pierce is going to hand the stuff over?' asks Irene. She takes a swig from her flask. 'I reckon he's not asking officially, but on the sly.'

'I agree with Hazel,' says Betty, 'but Irene's right too. If Pierce is involved, it must be something big. It would be so much better if we could find whatever it is and hand it in. There might be a reward, for example.'

'I reckon it's gonna be cash. Bloody lotta cash. Else why would he bother?'

'It's possible,' says Hazel. 'Let me finish decoding the book and see what we find.'

# 11

# THE DOODLEBUG DROPS

Midway through Hazel's morning tea preparations for the factory, there's a phone call from upstairs.

'Morning, Hazel,' says Edith Stern. 'I've been asked – or "told" might be a better word – to inform you that Dottie would like to see you in her office.'

'Dottie's office?' The Zip shrieks and Hazel leans over to switch it off. 'I didn't know she had one.'

'She decided the old sales office next to Mr Fysh will suit her,' says Edith. 'She moved in overnight. She's like a one-woman army advancing on us while we sleep.'

Hazel laughs. 'Can you let her know I'll be there on my round in about an hour?'

'I've already told her that, but she wants to see you *urgently*, apparently.'

Hazel glances at her watch. 'She'll just have to wait until after the factory break.'

Hanging up, she quickly finishes stocking her trolley and manages to arrive in the factory as the buzzer goes. She greets the machinists, pours the tea and coffee, and hands around the biscuits.

Gloria, Pixie and Alice are in a huddle in Gloria's alcove. It's surprising how these three have become so tight. Gloria started in the factory more than a decade ago, when she was fifteen, and has risen to become the supervisor. Alice is clever and well-educated but the effects of polio have left her with few work choices. And Pixie is the potential heir to Empire Fashionwear. Perhaps it's their different backgrounds that make them such a good team.

Hazel wheels her trolley over. 'Morning, ladies!'

'Morning, Mrs Bates,' says Pixie, who is wearing quite the shortest dress Hazel has ever seen.

'Have you seen Dottie yet?' asks Gloria.

'I have been summoned,' says Hazel, handing out tea and coffee. 'Why does she want to see me, do you know?'

Gloria perches on the edge of her workbench, coffee in one hand, cigarette in the other. 'According to Dougie, she's cooking up some big society fashion event.'

'I imagine she has a lot of contacts,' says Hazel, intrigued to hear that Doug Fysh is reporting back to Gloria.

'We just thought you might know more,' says Gloria. 'And if it involves us at all.'

'I can't help you there, I'm afraid,' says Hazel.

'I talked to Mr Levy, as you suggested, Mrs Bates,' says Pixie. 'He thought there was a possibility of making Mod Frocks a subsidiary of Empire. I think Grandad might agree to it, but my parents probably not.'

Hazel nods. 'Mr Karp has the utmost respect for Mr Levy's opinions. Let's see how he goes.'

Gloria exhales a puff of smoke. 'If Dottie and Frankie find out, they'll shout him down and take over themselves. Levy's a good egg though. He knows what he's doing. Let's just get on with what we're doing and see what happens.'

'I hope we're not doing it all for nothing, that's all,' says Pixie. 'Anyway, my mother is already interfering. We were planning a fashion parade in Mark Foy's Ladieswear but she's taken that over and we've been left out. Now we're planning our own parade.' She fans half-a-dozen pages of designs across Gloria's desk. 'What do you think of these, Mrs B?'

'Gingham! I've never seen it used in a dress,' says Hazel.

Gloria grins. 'Only in curtains and tablecloths.'

Alice points out the features. 'This is what Mary Quant is doing now. In all different colours. The pockets can be in the same print but a contrasting colour. They're cheap as chips to make.'

'I'm sure these will be popular with or without the fashion parade,' Hazel assures them. 'They're very striking and pretty.'

Pixie turns to Alice. 'Show her the winter designs coming up.'

Alice opens a folder and puts one page after another down on the desk. The designs are beautifully drawn, the models very thin with long legs and large eyes, like the magazine clipping taped above Gloria's desk of the British model Twiggy, with her blank face and grey eyes ringed with thick black lashes.

Hazel, looking at Alice's drawings, doesn't quite know what to say. If the mini-dress caused an uproar, these could start a revolution. Every outfit involves trousers. Some specify men's pinstripe suiting, some have neckties and suit jackets. Where will women be able to wear these? she wonders. Certainly not to work, and any upmarket restaurant would turn them away at the door. But if these catch on, women will be wearing the pants, and plenty of men will not be happy about it.

'What do you think, Mrs Bates?' asks Alice quietly.

Hazel looks around at their faces, touched that they care what she thinks. 'Fabulous,' she says. 'Just fabulous.'

When Hazel arrives at the top floor, Edith asks, 'Have you seen her?'

'Seen who, Edith dear?' Hazel hands her a cup of tea and a Milk Coffee.

'Quite the wit this morning, aren't we?' Dipping her biscuit in her tea, Edith glances up at Hazel and says in a low voice, 'She's been up here four times this morning, harassing Mr Karp. Oh, blast!' She fishes the soggy biscuit out of her tea with a teaspoon. 'My nerves are in shreds.' She nods towards Frankie's office door. 'Of course, his nibs isn't in yet. It's just a matter of time before she takes over his office and kicks him downstairs.'

They fall silent at the ping of the lift arriving and, a moment later, Dottie herself appears in white high heels, wearing a matching skirt and jacket in pale blue shantung, complete with three rows of pearls that are no doubt the real thing.

'Hazel, there you are. I asked you to come up and see me first thing.'

'I'm here now, Mrs Karp—'

'Dottie, please. You know I like to be Dottie. Mrs Karp sounds so stuffy and old-fashioned. Besides, we're all family here, aren't we?' She flicks on a radiant smile.

'How can I help, Dottie?' Hazel pours a cup of black tea and hands it to her. Dottie doesn't eat biscuits.

'We're putting Empire on the fashion circuit. Society pages. No dreary afternoon teas. Swish cocktail party. Twenty, twenty-five people. Hors d'oeuvres. A cellist. Mozart, or maybe something brighter . . . Strauss.' She punctuates each sentence with a quick sip of her tea as if she's dictating a telegram.

'All sounds very nice,' says Hazel.

'Appetisers. Smoked salmon. That sort of thing. Get back to me with a menu to approve.' She glances at her watch. 'Now I must see Mr Karp.'

'You'll need a caterer for that event,' says Hazel. 'Mrs Stern can organise it for you.'

Dottie stares at Hazel with blank surprise. 'I see. You have a perfectly good kitchen here. Two kitchens, in fact. You can cook. A few bits and bobs. Wouldn't be too difficult.'

Hazel employs a tactic she has used many times with Frankie (who also has a habit of pointing out that things are not difficult): silence accompanied by an apologetic smile. She's not going to be pushed around by Dottie.

'I have the number of a caterer,' says Edith, breaking the silence. 'I'll get the menus for you today.'

Dottie, still looking offended, agrees. 'Hardly *difficult*,' she repeats in an injured tone. She turns her attention to Edith. 'A cellist. Or violin. Something stringed but not screechy.'

The lift pings again and a moment later Frankie appears, head down, thoughts clearly elsewhere. The sight of his wife positioned between him and his office gives him a start.

'Morning, ladies.' He continues his path into his office, glancing over his shoulder to see if his wife is following him. She is. She steps into his office behind him and closes the door.

Edith shakes her head in disbelief. 'Piece of work,' she whispers. 'Watch your back, Hazel.' She gives a heartfelt sigh. 'I couldn't have another bikkie, could I?'

'In all these years, I don't ever recall you asking for an extra biscuit, Edith.'

'That's me, unpredictable—' She pauses at the sound of Frankie's raised voice. In unspoken agreement, the two women lean towards the door, shamelessly eavesdropping.

'All right, all right, Dot! Yes, it's old-fashioned but that's what people here like. Tea and biscuits, served with a smile. Do your fashion thing. Caviar . . . whatever. I don't care . . . Get the decorators in, if you absolutely must, but don't upset the apple cart, or I should say the tea trolley. That will really piss the workers off.'

Hazel and Edith Stern both strain to hear Dottie's response, but she takes the precaution of keeping her voice down. A moment later the door opens, and she clips past to the lift without a word.

Edith raises a single eyebrow that speaks volumes.

Hazel takes Mr Karp's tea and Scotch Fingers in. He glances up from his paperwork and thanks her distractedly. He looks worried and worn but Hazel knows if he wants to talk he will say so.

In the next office, Frankie sits in his luxurious padded leather chair, smoking a cigar. His desk holds an array of gold accessories: a cigarette lighter in the shape of a naked woman, a holder for his various fountain pens, and an embossed leather blotter. He always strikes Hazel as the king on his throne and she wonders if he fears being overthrown by his ambitious queen. She puts his cup of tea and a plate with three Iced VoVos on his desk.

'Hazel,' he begins in a weary voice. 'The catering business. Can you do what Dottie wants? Please. Do it for Frankie.'

'I would like to help, of course. But the fact is that I am a tea lady, not a caterer. I don't have the expertise or the resources to cater for twenty-five guests.'

He nibbles at a biscuit. 'I'm serious. She could make a lot of trouble for you, and for Frankie. She's a force to be reckoned with. We need to keep her distracted . . .'

It occurs to Hazel that when Frankie is the voice of reason, they really do have a problem. 'I have an idea,' she says.

'Doesn't everyone?' he asks with a groan. 'Go on, what is it?'

On the 2nd Floor, Hazel delivers tea to the Queen Bees in Accounts, then pops straight into Mr Levy's office with his sweet black coffee.

'Hazel, you look like a woman of purpose today,' says Mr Levy, immaculately attired as usual in a dark grey suit with a pink rosebud in his buttonhole.

'Not just today,' agrees Hazel with a smile.

'I understand the doodlebug has landed,' he says, sipping his coffee. 'Quiet at first, then . . .' He mimes a bomb falling and makes the sound of an explosion as it hits his desk.

'She could bring a lot of new business in for the firm,' begins Hazel.

'But at what cost? What's on your mind, Hazel?'

Hazel closes the door quietly. 'It would be important for her to understand the financial side of the firm, wouldn't it? Profit and loss, margins, budgeting, stock control, that sort of thing?'

Mr Levy looks wary. 'To what purpose?'

'Slow things down a little, just for a week or two.'

'And what would change in that week or two?' he asks.

Hazel shrugs. 'People would be more settled . . . and paperwork would be in place.'

Mr Levy rubs his face pensively. 'I had a discussion with Pixie about that. But it's one thing me pulling the strings and another getting into the thick of it, and taking on Frankie and Dottie.'

Hazel nods. Neither has forgotten that last year Frankie had forced Mr Levy into early retirement against his and Mr Karp's wishes. That had ended in disaster and Mr Levy regained his position, but it was an indication that old Mr Karp's powers of resistance were waning.

'It would be a tragedy if those young women lost control of the enterprise they've worked so hard to create,' Hazel says quietly.

Mr Levy nods. 'I agree. Leave it with me, Hazel. We need to be very clever about this. I'll have a quiet word to Mr Karp. On the other business . . . yes, I suppose I could try to keep her occupied while we get things settled.'

'Lovely. Would you like an extra bikkie today?'

Mr Levy gives her a wink. 'Why not?'

Down on the 1st Floor, Miss Ivy and Miss Joan have yards of fabrics and brown paper patterns spread out on their long work-tables. The two dressmaker's dummies are wrapped in swathes of fabric and Miss Ivy sits at the old-fashioned sewing machine the sisters use to make sample garments. Tasked with the creation of a range of evening wear, cocktail frocks and debutante dresses, they are surrounded by tulle, velvet, satin and silk; the fabrics lovingly draped with diamanté trim and beaded lace.

While Hazel doesn't pretend to know anything about profit margins and the complexities of bookkeeping, it doesn't seem possible that these gowns, with their expensive fabric and time-consuming construction, can support a company this size. Downstairs they're turning out a couple of hundred Mod Frocks a day. Up here, the sisters float about on a chiffon cloud of luxury and time. Their creations are priced at five times more than the little cotton dresses and are sold in guineas, adding a shilling to every pound, which is apparently something that appeals to the wealthy. Hazel wonders how that will translate to the new currency.

Today the sisters are all smiles. Miss Joan is working on new designs. 'Dottie wants a luxury lingerie range,' she explains. 'We'll do an entire trousseau for the bride-to-be.'

'Dottie has been busy,' says Hazel, passing over Miss Joan's coffee and two Ginger Nut biscuits, which the Rosenbaums claim they can't live without.

'Tea's up!' Doug Fysh cries, emerging from his office. 'What do you think about all these nighties and panties, Hazel?'

Hazel pours his tea and hands it to him. 'I think they're useful.'

'Haw . . . haw . . . haw . . . These aren't the useful sort. They won't keep you warm on a winter's night. They're for taking off.'

'There's no need to be coarse about it, Mr Fysh,' says Miss Ivy. 'They'll be modest and elegant.'

'Who's going to model them? The Queen Bees?' he asks with a grin.

'Dottie's bringing in professional models,' says Miss Joan coldly.

'We'll have a full house for that showing. You'll have to put bromide in the buyers' tea, Hazel . . . haw . . . haw . . . haw.' Chortling, Doug takes his tea back to his office.

Hazel asks if Dottie is here, hoping to avoid a second run-in with her today.

'Oh no, she's gone for the day,' says Miss Joan. 'She has meetings.'

'You should see her office, Hazel,' says Miss Ivy, nodding in its direction.

There had once been three sales staff on this floor but now there's only one and the spare office used to store bolts of fabric for the designers to experiment with. Hazel peeks inside and finds it lavishly furnished with a polished timber desk, antique armchair, several tall lamps and an expensive-looking Persian rug. Dottie's clearly here to stay and Hazel wonders what else is to come.

Stepping out into the lane at the end of the day, Hazel breathes a sigh of relief, such is the tension in the building. As she heads towards Lisbon Street, she notices a familiar figure in a dark suit walking towards her.

'Mrs Bates, I thought you finished about now. I was hoping to catch you.'

'Detective Dibble! How lovely to see you, dear.'

'And you too. Are you in a rush, or do you have time for a cup of tea?'

'I could do with a cuppa, to be honest,' Hazel replies.

They wander up to the teashop on Lisbon Street and find a table near the window. The place is nothing fancy. Formica and cracked lino, the tea in heavy white mugs, but it's cosy and clean.

'I almost didn't recognise you,' says Hazel. 'You look taller . . . or there's something different.'

Dibble grins. 'That's what I was coming to tell you. I got promoted. I passed my detective exams and applied to Special Branch. With the case we worked on last year on my record, well . . . I was accepted. So I'm out of Surry Hills and playing with the big boys.'

'I'm so happy for you, very well deserved. Having said that, I'm not really sure what Special Branch does.'

Dibble gives a modest shrug. 'You know, just national security, that sort of thing. Intelligence.'

Hazel laughs. 'That does sound important.'

'I've only just started, so I'm not involved in these espionage cases or anything like that. I do a lot of paper shuffling, investigating trade unionists . . .'

'Ah yes, the great communist threat. Is it real, or imagined?' asks Hazel, half joking.

Dibble chuckles. 'Depends who you talk to. Mainly we keep tabs on subversives and, of course, homosexuals.'

Hazel raises a questioning eyebrow. 'How do you feel about that?'

He shrugs. 'My personal philosophy is live and let live – not as if they are a threat to the nation, is it? Some of my colleagues see them as fair game, not me.' He grins. 'I'm keen to crack something really big, you know – national security at stake.'

Hazel takes a sip of her tea: weak and lacking flavour.

'What about you and the tea ladies, Mrs Bates? How is everyone?'

'We're well enough, but right now we're worried about the automatic tea-making machines that seem to be catching on. I think it's going to cost us our jobs, sooner or later.'

Dibble frowns. 'There's more to the job than just serving up tea and bikkies. I've had a go on that machine, it's not the same thing at all.'

'I'm glad you appreciate that,' says Hazel with a smile.

'Well, if that falls over, there might be a new career as a private detective waiting for you.'

Hazel laughs. 'I'm very happy as a tea lady, perhaps with a bit of snooping on the side.' She takes the lid off the teapot and peers inside. 'As I suspected, one of those new tea bags floating around in there.'

Dibble laughs. 'See what I mean?'

# 12

# BETTY SOLVES A MYSTERY

Betty hurries into the cinema for the five o'clock matinee, arriving just as the lights dim and the National Anthem begins. She sings 'God Save the Queen' with gusto, hitting the top note perfectly (to her great satisfaction). Before the feature is the Movietone News and a round-up of current affairs, which, quite honestly, she could do without. Images of the terrible war in Vietnam flash across the screen, followed by scenes of violence and bombs exploding in Northern Ireland. All very distressing.

Closer to home is an update on a very public squabble over the construction of the Sydney Opera House. The new Minister for Public Works, Mr Hughes (looking like a movie villain with his slicked-back hair and widow's peak), is interviewed in front of the enormous construction. He has nothing but criticism for the efforts of the architect, pouring scorn on the design, the engineering and, most of all, the cost: thirty million pounds and still nowhere near finished. He labels the architect, Jørn Utzon, an 'impractical dreamer'. The newsreader (who seems to hold the same opinion) describes the building as an 'expensive piece of culture'. Then an opinionated advertising chap condemns it as a place 'for hoity-toity people with minks and diamonds, not what ordinary people want'.

Mr Utzon himself appears on the screen and Betty recognises him immediately as the man Mr Sorensen met at the ferry. There's no mistaking the distinctive weathered, handsome face and heavy half-moon brows. He looks tired but presents himself well and seems a more intelligent and believable character than the Hughes fellow or the advertising man. Betty can see the strain in his face. Poor man. So clever and everyone against him.

Before she can get worked up about the unfairness of it all, the feature starts. She lays her handkerchief on her chest to catch the inevitable tears and sits back as the orchestral music swells and the harsh world outside slips away. She's seen this film three times already and is quickly transported to a smoggy London twilight where Mary Poppins sits on a cloud powdering her nose.

As soon as the film is over, Betty rushes straight round to Hazel's. 'It's only me!' she cries, choosing to arrive through the front door, expecting that Hazel will be at work on her jigsaw. But the front room is empty. She heads through to the kitchen to find Hazel reading Fred's book with a magnifying glass.

'How was Miss Poppins this evening?' asks Hazel, still immersed in the book.

'Just the same,' says Betty, sitting down to join her. 'Cheerful as ever. But I solved a mystery with no effort whatsoever while I was there.'

Hazel glances up. 'Oh, yes?'

'Mr Sorensen's friend . . . He's that . . . Born . . . Jorn . . . Hurtson . . . the architect fellow.'

'The Opera House architect? Of course, the Danish fellow,' says Hazel, giving Betty her full attention. 'That explains a lot. Oscar must be involved with the construction. He's an acoustics engineer. It was right there in front of me.' She gives a little laugh and looks down at the book again. 'I expect people with televisions are more familiar with Mr Utzon.'

'He is quite distinctive looking and very dashing, I might add,' says Betty, quietly noting that Hazel and Mr Sorensen are on first-name terms now. She'd love to ask Hazel about her assignation but knows better than to invade her friend's privacy.

'It's very controversial now. Everyone has an opinion, so it's no wonder he's keeping a low profile,' suggests Betty. She watches Hazel laboriously tracing along the lines, pausing occasionally to peer through the magnifying glass. 'Can I help with this, Hazel? You've been working on it for days.'

Hazel sits back in her chair and stretches her arms above her head. 'That would be wonderful, Betty dear.' She hands Betty the magnifying glass and points to a word on the page. 'See, there is a pencil dot under the letter *a* – you have to be quite scrupulous. It's been very slow because the marks are so faint it's easy to miss one. They're even harder to see in this light.' She pushes a piece of paper across the table. 'Here's what I have so far.'

Betty reads Hazel's round looping handwriting: *Don't tell no one I kept something for later its not easy but I will try to help you find it remember we went there on the train after the bookie job and . . .*

'Good luck with Irene not telling anyone.' Betty snorts. 'Where is madam anyway?'

'Irene is up to no good, I suspect,' says Hazel.

'I agree. The other day she was asking me if I had a telly or a radiogram and also if I liked listening to music.'

'Exactly. It's not like her to take such an interest.' Hazel gets up and drags her chair over to the pantry cupboard. Climbing up on it, she brings out a bottle of good whiskey. 'This has been up here for a week and Irene still hasn't found it. Busy elsewhere.'

It occurs to Betty that if Irene is selling stolen goods (it wouldn't be the first time), she could get Hazel into trouble. Such ingratitude! Hazel has been the soul of kindness. Typical Irene. Never thinks of anyone but herself.

'Let's not worry about Irene just now,' says Hazel, pouring them drinks and sitting back down at the table. 'If, as she said, Detective Pierce is on the same trail, why would that be?'

'I don't like to be cynical,' says Betty, 'but I'm sure he would be after cash, or possibly jewels he could get rid of fairly easily. That wouldn't help us, but what if there was a reward? That would be a shot in the arm for the Guild! Although Irene won't like that.'

Hazel stares at Fred's book. 'Right now, it's the puzzle that interests me most.'

'You do love a good puzzle,' agrees Betty.

'It would be helpful if we could trace the jobs Fred was involved in during his heyday. That was probably the mid-fifties until 1961 when he went inside.'

Betty has goosebumps prickling all over her body. 'I can be the operative in the field!' she says. 'I'll go to the library and search the newspapers for various robberies.'

'Newspapers are only half the story. There could be unreported crimes that are more difficult to find, if not impossible. For example, an SP bookie – and they have a lot of cash –is not going to report a robbery.'

'Fred does mention a bookie job,' says Betty.

'But not necessarily in relation to what he's left behind. It's more related to this location. So, while it would be good to know about unsolved crimes, it's not the whole story.' Hazel drums her fingers on the table, thinking hard. 'Mrs Li might be able to help,' she says finally.

Betty tips her glass to Hazel's. 'Leave it to me.'

Knowing that Mrs Li finishes work at Surry Hills Police Station at 4 pm, Betty hurries over after work and waits across the street. It's a boiling hot afternoon and even under the shade of a tree Betty feels as though she's melting. She wonders if people can actually melt or if they just spontaneously combust. Thinking about the prospect of combusting gives her that funny feeling she gets when a dizzy spell is coming on. The heat seems to swim in layers around her. She is pulled back from the verge of fainting by the sight of a familiar figure in a black coat leaving the panel-beating workshop further along the street.

'Irene!' calls Betty, making herself even hotter by waving. 'Irene!'

Irene glances over her shoulder and hurries off in the opposite direction. Much as Betty would like to follow her, she has a more important task to attend to. She checks her watch. Five minutes past four. She looks up to see Detective Pierce and his offsider come sauntering out of the police station. Standing on the street (seemingly oblivious to the blistering heat), Pierce takes a pack of cigarettes out of his suit pocket, shakes one out and offers it to his mate. They light up and stand there talking, occasionally glancing up and down the street in a disinterested way. The detective in Betty wonders why they need to come out on the street to smoke and chat. It's like a furnace out here. Surely it's cooler in the office. Unless they don't want to be overheard.

The two men are still there when Mrs Li comes out a few minutes later carrying a shopping bag. Neither seem to notice as she slips past behind them and continues down the street.

Detective Pierce probably wouldn't remember Betty, but she doesn't want him to know she is acquainted with Mrs Li, so she waits until he's looking the other way before hurrying after her. Once around the corner, Betty calls Mrs Li's name and the woman stops and waits for Betty to catch up. Mopping her face with a hankie, Betty explains breathlessly that Hazel wants to set up a meeting with her. This evening if possible.

Mrs Li frowns. 'What's this about?'

'It's to do with the Guild,' says Betty, who hasn't really thought this out.

'Mrs Bates spoke to me about being the treasurer of the Guild. Aren't we meeting tomorrow?' Mrs Li pauses. 'Or is this something different?'

Not wanting to overstep her authorisation level, Betty improvises. 'It's secret Guild business. It's sort of a branch of the Guild but . . . secret.'

'I don't understand,' says Mrs Li. 'Why is it secret?'

'Um . . . well, that's a secret too,' says Betty, wishing Mrs Li wasn't being so difficult.

'All right, when and where?' Mrs Li says resignedly.

'We can meet at the Hollywood,' says Betty.

Mrs Li shakes her head. 'Too many cops in the front bar. They don't know you, but they do know me.'

'Oh, of course. We could go to Hazel's, I suppose . . .'

Mrs Li digs around in her bag, finds a piece of paper and makes a note. 'Come to this address at 7 pm. I'll be there.'


The address is in Dixon Street, the heart of Chinatown. Despite this district being adjacent to the Haymarket, where Betty regularly shops, she's never set foot in this foreign-looking place and is both nervous and excited at the prospect. She walks beside Hazel and Irene, looking right and left, fascinated by the shops with roast chickens strung up by their necks in windows, the shop signs all in foreign script and the thousand different smells in the air.

They find the address, a shop that sells medicines and herbs, and step inside. The building is deeper than it looks from the outside. There's a row of kitchen chairs along one wall with several people seated there. On the opposite wall is a long counter with shelving behind it. There are dozens, if not hundreds, of jars full of interesting-looking dried things of all shapes and colours, and timber cabinets with drawers. Three men work behind the counter, moving quickly and silently, placing leaves and twigs onto large sheets of paper laid out on the counter.

Betty gets a shiver of excitement. It's like being transported to Shanghai or Singapore, places she could never hope to visit. She stands watching the men work, absolutely enthralled, until Mrs Li comes out of a back room and beckons them in.

They duck their heads under a little curtain that hangs over the doorway and find themselves in a small, dimly lit room with an ornate circular table surrounded by six chairs. Effie's there as well, even though Betty hadn't invited her.

'I hope you don't mind me inviting Effie along,' begins Mrs Li. 'Mrs Dewsnap did explain that this is a secret operation—'

'Effie is more than welcome,' interrupts Hazel. 'Thank you both for coming. I'm sorry for the intrigue, but when I explain, you will see the necessity.'

'Now I'd like to say something,' says Irene, waving her pipe around.

Betty gets out her notebook. 'Should we have an order of business?'

'Never mind that,' says Irene. 'All these people getting in on the act—'

'Irene dear, we've already had this conversation,' says Hazel patiently. 'At this stage, we need help. Especially if, as you say, there are other interested parties.'

'Also, Irene,' says Betty, 'didn't I see you this afternoon in Bourke Street? What were you up to?'

Irene scowls at her. 'Go on then,' she tells Hazel.

'Irene's husband, Fred, the well-known safecracker known as "Tweezers", died recently,' explains Hazel. 'A few weeks before, he wrote to say he'd hidden something away and didn't want it to "go to waste" and wanted to point Irene in the right direction. He's left several clues but we're a bit stuck. It may be related to a crime. We just don't know. But it seems that Detective Pierce is also on the same trail, either officially or off his own bat.'

'He could be looking to solve an old crime,' says Effie. 'I reckon he'd still be trying to make it back into the CIB. He's got Buckley's but that won't stop him trying.'

'He might be doing the right thing,' says Mrs Li doubtfully. 'But now you mention it, he and his crooked sidekick have had their heads together a lot recently. So, unlikely.'

'Let's say that Pierce got wind of the fact that Fred left something behind,' continues Hazel. 'We don't know how—'

'He'd have plenty of informants inside Long Bay,' says Mrs Li.

Hazel nods. 'Pierce likely knows what it is, maybe cash or the contents of a safe deposit box or jewellery.'

'He'd be very interested in untraceable cash,' says Mrs Li.

'If it came with a reward, it would be simple enough to split it with a willing party,' suggests Effie.

Betty puts her hand up. 'It would be better for us if it was a reward. The Guild could use it wisely.'

'So could I,' mutters Irene.

'The fact that he's asking around makes me think it could be cash or jewels from an unreported crime,' says Hazel.

She gets out *The Call of the Wild*, Fred's letter to Irene, the photograph and the stone. 'We have a few different clues. There's Fred's original letter, a coded communication in this book, which we're working on, and this stone. The photograph . . . I'm not sure about the photo. I suspect it's a memento and not related.'

Effie grins. 'This tea ladies business is more interesting than I would've guessed.'

Mrs Li also seems intrigued. 'They almost never lock the case file cabinets, so it shouldn't be too difficult for me to find out if Pierce has a file on Fred Turnbuckle. I can also look at unsolved cases.'

'Please be careful, Mrs Li,' says Hazel.

'I will, but don't forget, they're not aware my English is proficient.' Mrs Li offers a rare smile. 'Let alone that I can speed-read.'

# 13

# A SURPRISE OUTING FOR HAZEL

Hazel arrives at the Hollywood before the others and picks up a key from Shirley. The rooms above the pub are accessed through a side door directly off the street and not easily noticed, so she waits outside for Betty. Before long, her friend comes puffing down the hill, waving in case Hazel hasn't seen her.

'Perfect timing,' says Hazel.

Betty takes a handkerchief from her handbag and pats her face all over. She stares at the orange stains on her hankie. 'I think it's a mistake to wear powder in this weather.'

Hazel opens the door and gestures for Betty to step inside. 'Hopefully a little cooler in here, dear.'

They enter a small foyer and walk up the curved staircase. Half-a-dozen small rooms lead off the upstairs hallway. These had been let out for some time, but Shirley found it too much trouble. Now they're empty and neglected, still littered with the discarded belongings of past residents.

The main room is the size of a large living room with an adjoining kitchen. A couple of tables have been pushed together with a variety of mismatched chairs. They find enough cups and saucers in the kitchen and, compliments of Shirley, a kettle and a teapot. Betty has brought along tea and milk and a tin of shortbread, still warm from the oven.

Having been shut up, the room is stifling. With some effort, they manage to get the windows open and allow some fresh, if not cool, air inside, then Betty dashes downstairs to make sure the others find the place.

The inaugural meeting is attended by eight tea ladies including Betty, Merl, Mrs Li and Effie, as well as Betty's friend Violet, who was a cleaning lady but recently secured a position as a tea lady at Imperial Slacks. There are also two Italian ladies from the Herald office (one of whom doesn't speak English). Irene has decided to stay downstairs in the bar and Hazel did not try to dissuade her.

When everyone is settled with a cup of tea and a shortbread, Hazel opens the meeting, introducing Mrs Li as treasurer, Betty as secretary and herself as temporary chairwoman. Betty announces that she has brought an exercise book dedicated to the purpose, Violet seconds that and the Guild is up and running.

Hazel starts the proceedings with the suggestion that they estab-lish a charter and purpose. 'For example, the Guild is open to tea ladies of all nationalities—'

'What about tea men?' interrupts Violet. 'All nationalities and sexes.'

'That's a good point,' agrees Betty, making a note.

'Who ever heard of a tea man?' scoffs Merl. 'I suggest we strike that from the record.'

'Yes, you're probably right,' says Betty, crossing it out.

'We don't want the minutes to be a hodgepodge of silly sugges-tions,' continues Merl.

'And who decides what's silly?' asks Violet in a belligerent tone.

'I suggest we stay with "ladies" for the moment,' says Hazel. 'Should a tea man wish to join sometime in the future, we'll worry about it then.' Everyone seems amenable to that idea, and she moves on to their purpose. 'Prior to this meeting, some of us discussed the Guild raising funds for women and children in need,' says Hazel. 'But I think our first priority has to be protecting the livelihoods of tea ladies—'

'What about men in need?' interrupts Violet.

'There are quite a number of organisations that support men,' says Hazel, starting to wonder if they will get anything past Violet.

Betty raises her hand. 'The Freemasons, for example. Also the Australia Club and the Ku Klux Klan—'

'We get the picture,' says Merl impatiently. 'Let's move on.'

'Shall I write those down?' Betty asks, pen poised.

Merl heaves a sigh. 'Of course not. You're just confusing everyone, as per usual.'

'Let's briefly discuss our fundraising cause first, then we'll get on to the more urgent business,' continues Hazel. 'We've done a little research on the new orphanage being built at the Sisters of Hope convent. I believe they're planning to accommodate around twenty-five children of varying ages. We haven't made a formal approach, but it's been suggested that we could sponsor the kiddies' beds.'

There are murmurs of approval from the group and Mrs Li takes over. 'I've looked into it and a steel-framed single bed with a mattress, pillow and blanket will cost fifteen dollars.'

'It sounds so much more in the new money,' says Betty, shaking her head.

'Everything's going to be more expensive,' says Merl.

'Shopkeepers are taking advantage. You'll see it everywhere. The cost of living is going sky-high.'

Mrs Li tactfully ignores this comment. 'Do you know when the building will be completed, Hazel?'

'They've only just begun the excavations, so we have plenty of time.' Hazel looks around. 'Any objections to establishing that as our first fundraiser?'

'We have to say "All those in favour say aye",' says Betty. 'I read about it at the library.'

'Would you like to do that, Betty?' asks Hazel.

Betty reads carefully from her notebook. 'All those in favour, say aye.'

Everyone, apart from the Italian ladies (one busy translating for the other), say aye.

'All those against, say nay,' continues Betty, glancing around the silent room.

'Good. Now, on to the more urgent business,' says Hazel. 'It seems that our livelihoods are under threat from this new machine – the Café-bar. Every day we're hearing about another casualty. The role of tea lady may end up a distant memory if we don't act quickly. The question is, what can we do?'

'I've got dirt on a couple of stuffed shirts in the government,' offers Irene, appearing in the doorway with a drink in one hand, cigarette in the other. 'We could get that machine thingy banned.'

'We could sabotage them machines,' suggests Violet. 'Put a spanner in the works.'

'I second that,' says Irene, nodding.

Hazel looks around hopefully for other suggestions. Everyone looks stumped. None of them have ever had to fight for their jobs before, and it seems no one knows where to start.

'Strike,' says Effie, finally. 'We need to strike. Not just a few of us – all of us.'

'To strike legally we'd need a union,' says Mrs Li. 'It would be very difficult for us to form a union. There's a lot of legal administration and cost. It would be almost impossible to collect the fees with tea ladies spread out everywhere. Then there's a financial risk.'

'We could join a union that already exists,' suggests Hazel. 'Let's look into that possibility.'

Betty notes that down. 'So, cross out the bit about the stuffed shirts?'

'I think you're all overreacting,' says Merl, puffing out her chest. 'The purpose of the Guild is to do good works, fundraising for the less fortunate. Not going around causing trouble like a bunch of unrefined rabble rousers. There might be a few tea ladies who lose their jobs, but—'

'We need to speak out for those tea ladies, for all tea ladies,' says Hazel. 'Thousands of older women, many, like myself, who are war widows, will lose what little income we have. If we need to be unrefined, so be it. It's important to get attention to our cause and make the workers realise what they're about to lose before it's too late.'

'We've got to bring along every bloody tea lady we can lay our hands on,' says Effie. 'We need numbers. The workers need to see what it's like not getting a cuppa and a smile.'

'We're taken for granted and it could go against us now,' says Betty.

Hazel nods. 'Let's set a date for our next meeting, and I suggest that we each aim to bring five new members along.'

A murmur goes around the room and the meeting is adjourned.

*

On Saturday afternoon, Mrs Mulligan invites Hazel to accompany her to the presbytery to instruct Maude on the finer points of housekeeping. The girl has lived her whole life squashed into the little house in Glade Street, sharing a bed with three of her siblings, and surrounded by loving chaos, and Hazel wonders how Maude is managing living in a strange house with a priest.

'We're a bit rough and ready at home,' Mrs Mulligan explains as they walk down to St Vincent's. 'She needs to make a perfect cup of tea, not with the leaves floating about like she does. She's got my recipes for toad-in-the-hole and savoury mince and a good lamb stew, but she needs to be ready for any occasion. You can help her with the baking side of things.'

'Of course,' murmurs Hazel.

'I'll tell you, Hazel,' continues Mrs Mulligan, 'I'm a mite worried the girl could pretend to be cack-handed and make a mess of the job so she doesn't have to do it. The shame would kill me if she got the boot. I would keel over on the spot and never get up. I could never hold my head up in Mass again. I would be *condemned* to a life of shame.'

Hazel smiles to herself at this biblical prediction. 'I'm sure Maude knows that, dear. I wouldn't worry too much.'

'Anyway, she listens to you. Between the two of us we'll knock her into shape and put the fear of God into her – I'll do that part, with you being a heathen and all. You can teach her that currant cake. It'll be a good one for the tins in case of unexpected visitors. And scones, of course – always useful.'

Nearing the church, they see Father Kelly and two other priests, all three wearing black suits and dog collars, striding purposefully towards them. Father Kelly, deep in conversation, doesn't seem to notice them until Mrs Mulligan plants herself in his path.

'Father Kelly, good day to you! We're just off to the presbytery to get young Maudie sorted out.'

'Ah, Mrs Mulligan, that's very kind of you,' he replies. 'She's a lovely girl, very quiet.'

To Hazel, the two other priests seem impatient at the interruption, but Mrs Mulligan doesn't notice and offers her hand to each of them. 'I'm Mrs Mulligan, the mother of Father Kelly's housekeeper,' she tells them, nodding and smiling.

The younger priest, curly-haired and thickset, introduces himself as Brother Riley and the other, taller one, with dark stubbled jaw and a penetrating gaze, as Brother O'Connell.

'Visiting from Queensland,' says Father Kelly.

Hazel's ears tell her that at least one of these men is lying, but which one and why?

After a few minutes of polite small talk, Father Kelly bids them a courteous good day, and the three men walk off as if they can't wait to get away.

'That was rather odd, don't you think?'

Mrs Mulligan gives a sigh. 'Don't be so suspicious of things, Hazel. This detective business has gone to your head.'

Inside the grounds of St Vincent's, the presbytery is surrounded by a dense border of blue hydrangeas hiding it away from the world. It could have been a pretty house, with its pointy roof and arched entry over the front porch, but grey speckled concrete walls give the place a gloomy feel.

Maude opens the door to them. The sad resignation beneath her smile worries Hazel more than the crying had. She lets them into a cool, dark hallway smelling of furniture polish.

'Father Kelly and the others are out. I can show you around if you like.'

'We don't want to intrude on His Reverence,' says Mrs Mulligan, as if the rooms are inhabited by him even when he's away. 'But let's see your room, Maudie.'

They follow Maude to the back of the house, through the generous-sized kitchen and down a short hallway. She opens the door to a small room with an awning window, too high to see out. There's just enough room for a single bed and a chest of drawers, spartan as a nun's cell. Maude has put two blue hydrangea blossoms in a jam-jar on the dresser, and the little effort to make the room more homely breaks Hazel's heart. This is a box room, not a bedroom. There must be three or four bedrooms in this house, so it seems odd she's been put in here.

'Was this Auntie Vera's room, Maude dear?' asks Hazel, puzzled.

'No. With Brother Riley and Brother O'Connell staying, they need all the bedrooms.'

'Oh, you don't need more than this!' says Mrs Mulligan. 'Very comfortable and all to yourself, what more could you ask for?'

Maude's eyes fill with tears. 'I've never slept in a bed on my own before. I'm not used to it.'

'We don't all get to enjoy these grand luxuries. Be grateful.' Mrs Mulligan turns away and walks back to the kitchen.

Hazel and Maude follow to find her standing in the middle of the kitchen, hands on hips, gazing around like a general sizing up a battlefield. For the next two hours, Hazel and Mrs Mulligan educate Maude in the art of tea making, scone baking, silver polishing, table setting and more skills than she could possibly grasp in one session.

'Does Father Kelly want you to lay out his vestments for Mass?' asks Mrs Mulligan. 'Did he mention that at all? We better get some expert advice about that. It needs to be done a special way, everything in the right order.'

'Do I have to lay out his clothes?' asks Maude. 'I don't want to. It's too . . . personal.'

'You're living in a house with himself,' argues Mrs Mulligan. 'That's personal. Your job is to care for him. You need to show some initiative, girl.'

'It's not like I'm going to get a promotion, is it?'

'What an attitude,' says Mrs Mulligan with disgust.

'I'm not comfortable here, Mam. I don't like these Brothers. They think I'm a servant, getting me to bring this and that.'

'Spare me days! They've got important church business to discuss!'

Maude scowls. 'They're up till all hours talking and they drink—'

'That's what Catholics do – we enjoy a drink, of course we do, especially the Irish. Are they not allowed a drink now and then? If God doesn't mind them having the odd tipple, I don't see why you should.'

'How do you know God doesn't mind?' argues Maude.

In an effort to get the conversation back on track, Hazel asks, 'Couldn't Maude ask Father Kelly if he wants her to lay out his vestments?'

'I suppose so,' Mrs Mulligan agrees unhappily. 'It's a crying shame that Auntie Vera couldn't show you all this before she died.'

'So inconsiderate,' agrees Maude.

Mrs Mulligan is not amused. 'None of your cheek, thank you, Missy.'

It's becoming clear to Hazel that Mrs Mulligan wants Maude to shine so she can bathe in the light of Father Kelly's praise, and that of the parish. A realisation that makes Hazel even more determined to help Maude escape this life of martyrdom and enjoy her youth while she can. There has to be a way to get her out of this situation and save everyone's pride at the same time.

By five o'clock, Mrs Mulligan's enthusiasm for housekeeping has waned. As they say their goodbyes, Maude leans in the doorway, drooping like a wilted flower.

Hazel says quietly, 'Remember I'm here every Saturday morning. I'll come at quarter to nine and we can have a chat.'

Halfway down the path, she turns to give Maude a wave, but the door is closed.

Oscar Sorensen telephones on Sunday morning to invite Hazel on a surprise outing. While she enjoyed his company on the previous occasion, Hazel still doesn't know what to make of his interest or his persistence. It's going to be another warm day and, knowing he likes to walk, Hazel wears her most comfortable shoes, a light sundress and a wide-brimmed straw hat.

Oscar waits outside St James Station wearing his usual outfit but carries his jacket as a concession to the heat. 'I hope you're going to enjoy my little surprise,' he says, offering his arm. 'I think it will be an interesting experience for you.'

With only a moment of hesitation, Hazel takes his arm. She had vowed never to get involved with another man, and yet here she is on the arm of a man who, increasingly, seems to have a romantic interest in her. She reminds herself for the umpteenth time to be cautious, and observant.

As they walk down Macquarie Street towards Bennelong Point, the giant construction of the Opera House looms ahead. Two large cranes hang above the curved sails and the base of the building is surrounded by various construction sheds and equipment. The site is quiet today. The workers who live onsite sit outside their caravans, smoking and drinking from bottles of beer behind the high chain-link fence.

'I wonder why we're here,' says Oscar with a mischievous smile.

Hazel laughs. 'Could it be because the man you met off the ferry was the famous Mr Utzon and one of your countrymen?'

'I knew you would guess it. On that day we needed to have a private discussion far away from the government people at the site and also the people working on the project who may report back to the enemies of Jørn. I hope this completes my apology.'

'Of course. I should add that, despite Betty's claims, we were not actually following you. Just curious.'

Oscar laughs. 'Jørn and I, we are old friends. He invited me to come all the way across the world, to work with him on this . . .' He pauses, lifting his gaze to the great curving sails above them. 'This palace of music and theatre. The interior sound is my area, a very difficult task and therefore extremely interesting to me.'

The main gates are guarded by a man who sits smoking inside a small booth. Oscar shows him a pass and the man hands them two white safety helmets and opens the gate.

As they walk towards the building, Hazel gazes around with a sense of awe at the scale of the most famous construction in the country – perhaps even the world – right now.

Oscar points out the hundreds of crates of tiles, shipped from Sweden, that will clad the framework of shells. He explains there are two textures to reflect light differently: shiny 'ice' tiles and matt 'snow' tiles. Then he leads her up a long concrete ramp towards the two shells, like half-built cathedrals placed side by side wrapped in scaffolding, onto another ramp and into the cavernous heart of the building.

As they walk through to the other side, which overlooks the harbour and the bridge, Oscar points out aspects of interest and explains how the building will appear when complete.

'I can almost hear the music,' says Hazel, gazing around at the sky and sea, the ferries chugging past, the yachts large and small, and the enormous white cruise ship moored at Circular Quay.

'What is this music you hear?' asks Oscar.

'I don't know anything about opera, but I imagine an orchestra, some beautiful classical music . . . Mozart, perhaps?'

Oscar nods. 'Mozart would be perfect.' He turns to look back at the building. 'I have wondered if this building was to be called something different, perhaps there would not be the anger and criticism of the building. What I read in the newspapers is that people who don't like opera are angry. They don't want to pay for an opera house or be reminded of something they don't understand.' He turns to her with a perplexed expression. 'But this is a place for all music and performance.'

Hazel agrees. 'I understand it's mainly funded by the lottery, so the financial complaints don't make much sense. I think it's more what opera represents – something only for the educated, wealthy and elite.' With a sweep of her hand, she gestures around the foreshore. 'For people who live here on the water. But, let's face it, there will always be people who are angry about change. Any change.'

Oscar nods. 'It is a symbol of change, and of the future.' He shades his eyes from the sun reflecting off the water and turns to watch a figure walking through the building. 'Ah, here is someone I would like you to meet.'

They follow the man down the stairs to where a dozen or more temporary sheds have been built, and then into a large office where

Oscar introduces her to Mr Utzon himself. He greets her with a wide smile, shakes her hand and offers tea.

'Are you sure you have time?' asks Hazel. 'You have your work cut out for you here.'

Mr Utzon laughs a warm and hearty laugh. 'We can take one moment for tea. I apologise for the untidy state of the place. Last night someone broke into the office.'

'Was anything stolen?' asks Oscar with a frown.

'It's difficult to say.' Mr Utzon looks over the long table covered in dozens of rolls of paper. 'These have been mixed up. Normally everything sits in a particular order. So I think that some plans have been taken.'

'Have you reported it to the police?' asks Oscar.

Mr Utzon shrugs. 'I suspect the police are too busy to chase the thief of a piece of paper. I will have someone check it all tomorrow.'

Hazel notices some of the rolls have fallen on the floor and she picks them up. As she places them next to the others, something bright under the table catches her eye. She takes out her hankie and picks the lolly wrapper up carefully by its corner. 'It's moments like these you need . . .' she begins before realising this famous line would mean nothing to the Danes. 'Are you a Mintie man, Mr Utzon?'

He shakes his head. 'I have not seen this before.'

Hazel asks for an envelope, slips the wrapper inside and hands it to him. 'If there are plans missing, I suggest you give this to the police. It may be nothing, but . . .'

The two men exchange glances and Oscar smiles.

Mr Utzon gestures to a couple of chairs and puts on the kettle. 'Oscar, my friend, I need your eyes for some minutes, if you have the time.'

Oscar nods and Mr Utzon gets out a dozen or more pages from his briefcase. He hands them to Oscar, who reads quickly and silently. When he's finished, Oscar asks Hazel if she minds them discussing the matter in Danish.

'Of course not,' she says.

Mr Utzon hands out mugs of tea. While the two men sit and talk quietly, Hazel wanders around the office, fascinated to be at the heart of the operation. She glances at the maps, schedules and engineering drawings pinned to the walls. One that captures her interest is an old map showing the railway lines running from St James and Wynyard stations down to the quay. Looking closely, she notices that there are additional lines marked in red ending at the construction site and wonders about their significance.

The men fall into a grim silence. After a moment, Mr Utzon gets up and walks over to join Hazel. 'I apologise for making you wait, Mrs Bates. You have found something of interest?'

'I wondered what these red lines were. A new station at the Opera House?'

Mr Utzon peers at the map. 'No, these are old tunnels built for future stations but never used.'

'Oh yes,' says Hazel. 'I remember now, there was a bomb shelter built in one under Hyde Park during the war.'

'Yes, someone told me this. The tunnels are very deep. They might have been useful for us, but there is no access from our site, only from the other end at St James.'

'I'm often in St James Station,' says Hazel. 'I didn't realise.'

'Next time you visit, you might notice a green door on the lower level. It does not call attention to itself, but behind this door is a hidden world,' says Mr Utzon with a smile.

'We better go,' says Oscar, standing. 'I need more time to think about our discussion. I'll telephone you this evening, Jørn, and we will talk again.'

The two men hug briefly and Mr Utzon, in his charming way, thanks Hazel for visiting.

As she steps out into the construction site, Hazel looks around at all the work still to be done and wonders how the architect manages the overwhelming pressure of tasks and responsibility.

Oscar suggests they walk back to the city and have a drink, and Hazel agrees. They find a quiet table in a small hotel and Oscar brings a couple of whiskeys from the bar.

Hazel lifts her glass to his. 'To the Opera House.'

'To the Opera House,' he agrees with a smile, but it's clear he's troubled by the conversation with Mr Utzon.

After a moment he says, 'The document he gave me is what I think is called an ultimatum. The government wants to take away his authority and he will be an employee on the project. So he does have a very important decision to make.'

'Ultimatums never end well in my experience,' says Hazel sympathetically.

'I agree with you. It will be disastrous for the building and for Jørn. I don't think his pride will allow him to accept it. As well, they have him in a corner. They held the money they owe him and now he cannot pay his staff.'

Hazel takes a sip of her drink. 'Pride may not be a good reason, but there is also dignity and integrity to consider.'

Oscar nods. 'Dignity and integrity. You're right, these two things are important. I will bring these matters of the heart into our conversation this evening. Whatever decision he makes, it is important for him to protect his brilliant mind. And his talent.'

'And if he decides to leave the project, what will happen with your involvement?'

'This I do not know. It is less important right now.' He smiles. 'I wonder if, next time we meet, we could be more lighthearted. Do you dance?'

'It's been a very long time, but I think I could manage a waltz or foxtrot.'

'Good,' says Oscar, raising his glass to her. 'We will make it a date.'

# 14

# IRENE PULLS A CLEVER SWIFTIE

Sitting at Hazel's kitchen table, Irene takes another sip of celery wine and pulls a face. 'I reckon they make better wine than this in the clink, out of potato peelings and whatnot.'

'You don't have to drink it,' says Betty. 'It's not my favourite, I must admit, but it's all I could find. I think it's making my tinnitus worse.'

'It's those bloody cicadas, yer twit.'

Betty puts her hands over her ears and takes them away several times. 'Oh yes, I see what you mean.'

'I coulda been a doctor.' Irene grins. 'I don't wanna hear about yer other ailments, mind.'

'Irene, I hope you won't take this the wrong way but, honestly, I have to tell you that your dentures—'

'What about 'em?'

'They need a clean.' Betty's face turns bright red. 'I say this as a friend.'

'That right?' Irene pops her dentures out and takes a good look. 'What's wrong with 'em?'

'They should be white, not brown. It's all the nicotine.'

Irene holds them up to the light. She can see what Betty's saying but doesn't give her the satisfaction of admitting it. She pops them back where they belong. Now they taste funny.

'Anyway, it's probably none of my business.' Betty looks at her watch for the tenth time. 'I hope Hazel's all right.'

'She's out with her bloke, probably havin—'

'We don't need to speculate about Hazel's private life, thank you,' says Betty. 'Let's discuss your private life instead. I'd like to know exactly what you're up to. What's your devious plan?'

'Dunno what yer on about.' Irene puts on her best innocent face.

'All of a sudden, I notice people are listening to the races on those little transistor radios. Even our awful factory manager, who you probably know.' Betty leans towards Irene. 'The detective in me suspects they're stolen.'

'No, no, no . . . I got a dozen of 'em cheap and sold 'em off. All gone now.' Irene takes another sip of wine and decides it's her last. 'Stick the kettle on, will yer?'

Betty gets up and puts the kettle on the stove. 'What did you pay for them?'

Irene can't resist the opportunity to gloat. 'I'm paying three quid each. I had to buy batteries, or people don't believe the bloody things work, so that was a shilling.'

'So, you paid three pounds and one shilling. That's quite a lot of money. What did you sell them for in the new dollars?'

'Six dollars and twenty cents, so I doubled me money.'

'Irene, you sold them for what you paid for them.'

'What're yer talking about?'

The kettle whistles. Irene tries to think how she came to that price. Her thoughts are all jumbled up now with Betty trying to confuse her. Why did these silly dollars and cents have to get in the way?

'Hang on, write it down, Betty. Me 'rithmetic's buggered.'

Betty fills the teapot and puts it on the table. 'I don't need to write it down. If you wanted to double your money, you should have sold them for twelve or thirteen dollars. Who did you get them from, anyway?'

'You know that fella they call Big G hangs around the Thatched Pig?'

'Oh, him . . . the one with the gold front tooth? Well, he's a crook, so they were stolen.'

'He's a bloody entreper . . . pre . . .'

'Entrepreneur?' suggests Betty.

'Businessman. He buys . . . discontinued lines and flogs them.' Irene's fibs are running out of steam now that Betty's stolen her profit.

'Discontinued? What phooey . . . Those little transistors are the latest thing. Shame on you, Irene, and I'll bet you hid them right here in Hazel's house.'

Irene sips her tea gloomily. 'I can't believe I didn't make a profit with all that bloody work.'

Betty gives her a slightly sympathetic look. 'I'm going to write down all the pounds and pence and dollars and cents for you, and you need to learn them.'

'Aw, they'll likely change their minds and go back to the old money. I'm not doing the new money. Waste of bloody time.'

'That's not going to happen. And you would be seventy-eight dollars better off right now if you'd done it properly in the first place.'

Seventy-eight dollars. Irene had plans to go to the trots on Friday night and turn her earnings into winnings. 'I already spent some of the money,' she says, thinking aloud.

'Well, don't think you're going to borrow money off me to make up your ill-gotten gains,' sniffs Betty. She glances at her watch again. 'It's almost nine. I better go.'

The front door opens and closes and a moment later Hazel appears in the kitchen. 'Anything left in that pot?' she asks, sitting down at the table.

Betty jumps up to get another cup. 'You look very happy.'

'I had a lovely time with Mr Sorensen and a tour of the Opera . . .' She pauses, looking at Irene. 'Is everything all right?'

Irene searches for an excuse for her glum mood and recalls one of Betty's favourites. 'Just me hormones.'

'You haven't been arrested, have you?' asks Hazel.

'Not yet she hasn't. Otherwise you'd be called to the police station to pay bail!'

To Irene's great annoyance, Betty then starts blubbering.

'What is it, Betty dear?' asks Hazel, patting the silly old chook's hand.

'I'm just scared Irene's going to bring the police in here and you'll get into trouble,' she sniffles.

'Is this about the transistors?' asks Hazel. 'I thought you'd got rid of them all?'

'How'd yer know about them?' asks Irene, wondering if Hazel's been snooping in her room.

'I assumed they were stolen goods and decided it would be better to wait until they were all gone before I broached the subject with you.' Hazel pauses. She has a certain look on her face and Irene can guess what's coming. 'Irene dear, I'm afraid that's the last straw. There's a whole list of things, which I have brought up with you many times and won't go into again—'

Betty puts her hand up. 'I will! Smoking your dangerous pipe in bed. All that dreadful coughing and spitting. Drinking Hazel's good whiskey straight from the bottle – that's disgusting – and frying yourself with the toaster, which I notice you didn't even offer to replace! Not paying a penny of rent—'

'All right, all right,' says Hazel, holding up her hand. 'I think that about covers it.'

'I could go on!' insists Betty. 'There's the drunken singing at night—'

'I got the bloody picture, thanks very much,' says Irene, wishing Betty would buzz off home.

'I think it's due time that you found somewhere else to live, Irene dear,' continues Hazel. 'It's not urgent – you can have a week or two – but I've given it a lot of thought and my decision is final.'

Irene has no memory of singing, but spitting and smoking are two of her favourite activities. She's not giving them up for anyone. 'Fine. I'll be right on the street. In the gutter with the other down-and-outs.'

Betty gets all pink and angry. 'Don't make Hazel feel guilty for putting a roof over your head, Irene.'

'How about for taking it away?' asks Irene. Sick of the whole discussion, she goes out into the backyard with its screeching cicadas and yeasty stink of the brewery, and rolls herself a smoke. It's too hot to sleep. She might as well sit out here and think. What she needs right now is money. Which brings her back to Fred's bloody letter. She needs to work out that code herself and get her hands on the loot. Pay back Big G and then she'll be right.

Happy with that plan, she clears her chest and hoicks into a pot of geraniums. She has another thought and goes into the washhouse. She pokes around in the cupboard and finds exactly what she's after. This'll show Betty what's what.

When Betty's gone home and Hazel's upstairs, Irene creeps into the kitchen and gets Fred's book out of the drawer. Hazel has a piece of paper stuck in it at page 20. She hasn't got very far, been too busy chasing that foreign fella around town. Irene stares at the page. Hazel's writing is like a five-year-old's, all neat and round:

> *Don't tell no one I kept something for later its not easy but I will try to help you find it remember we went there on the train after the bookie job and had that champagne at the . . .*

Typical Fred. Either he says bloody nothing or takes forever to get to the point. All she wants to know is what it is and where it is.

She goes upstairs to her room, grumbling under her breath even though there's no one to hear it. Locking the door, she gets her savings sock out from under the mattress. The contents are in pounds. She tries to think how much she needs to pay off Big G in the new dollars. If only she had written that down at the start.

Using Betty's list of new money, it takes her as much time to work it all out on a scrap of paper as it did to sell the stupid transistors. It turns out to be exactly what Betty said. And now she's five quid short of what she owes Big G.

Irene sets off to work an hour early with a plan in mind. Breakfast is a ciggie and a swig or two from her flask on the way. Zig Zag Lane is empty at this hour. It's not even seven o'clock. The factory workers in each of the places backing the laneway won't turn up for another half an hour. She stops at the back door to Farley Frocks, where Betty works, and has a quick shifty up and down the lane. The door has a barrel lock and a padlock for extra security. She selects a long thin pick from a few she's brought along and a minute later is inside the dark building.

She legs it as fast as her cranky knees allow into the factory. She finds the manager's office, only because he has a sign on the door. He's a round little fellow not much taller than her, but he obviously has an eye for the ladies with nudie calendars and pin-up girls stuck up all over the place. Good luck, mate.

She looks around for his transistor. It only now crosses her mind that he might have taken it home. His office is a bloody disgrace, bits of material and boxes everywhere, paper piled up on his desk. The only light comes from a grubby window onto the laneway. She strikes a match and looks through his desk, tossing the papers onto the floor.

Just as she's about to give up, she spies the radio up on the high shelf above his desk. What a stupid place to keep it! He'd need a ladder to get up there himself. Without thinking twice, she climbs on his office chair. As she leans towards the shelf, the chair has other ideas and spins in the opposite direction. With nothing to hang on to, arms windmilling, she topples off and lands on the floor with a thump. There's a suspicious cracking sound that might be the chair or could be her ribs. She takes a (painful) breath and struggles to her feet before doubling over with pain. No time to think about that now. Swearing furiously, she hauls herself onto the desk and manages to get onto her knees and stretch high enough to grab the transistor down from the shelf. Shame she didn't think of that plan earlier.

Before she leaves, she checks her hat is still in place and both slippers on. No point in leaving a trail of evidence. She tucks the transistor into her pinny pocket and scurries towards the back door, nursing her painful ribs. Seconds from freedom, she hears voices in the laneway. She steps back, opens the nearest door and ducks inside. She stands in the dark, listening to the stream of ladies gasbagging as they pass by on their way to the factory.

A moment later, the door opens. A fluorescent light flickers on overhead and Betty stands in the doorway. She stares at Irene for a second, gives a little squawk like a kicked cat and screws her eyes tightly shut.

Irene slips past her out the door. Holding her ribs and taking short sharp breaths, she dashes across the lane to Silhouette Knitwear. Standing in her kitchen looking at the sink full of dirty dishes she left behind, she breathes a sigh of relief. Even that hurts.

She sloshes the cups around in the sink while she works out the next stage of her cunning plan. She needs to trick that grub into coming to her about his missing transistor; if she goes to him it'll be a dead giveaway. On the other hand, Big G must be getting impatient for his money, and the last thing she wants is Onions making her eyes water. She'll have to give it a day or two and put herself in the manager's way.

She doesn't join the others for lunch (avoiding Betty until she calms down) and instead hangs around the back door, casually rolling one smoke after another. Eventually the little fella comes out the door opposite. Irene acknowledges him with a raised eyebrow and glances down the lane, pretending she's got more important things on her mind.

Out of the corner of her eye, she sees him coming towards her and braces herself for accusations. 'Gotta light?' he asks, pulling a cigarette out from behind his ear.

She hands him her smoke. He lights up, puffing away like a loco getting up speed.

'Don't s'pose you've got any more of those little radios, have ya?'

'What, yer want one for each ear, do yers?' Irene cackles.

'One of those little bitches in the factory nicked it. I sometimes take it home, but when I'm going to the pub after work, I put it up out of reach.'

Two of the machinists come tripping out the door chattering. He gives them a filthy stare that sets them off laughing. 'Probably those two troublemakers,' he says. 'Been getting the cricket and everything on that thing. Magic. Bloody magic.'

'They're hard to get.' Irene pops her dentures in and out to show she's thinking extra hard. 'That's the latest model, yer know.'

The manager shakes his head. By the look on his dial, anyone'd think someone died.

'I might be able to wrangle one for yer, since yer desperate,' says Irene. 'Probably a bit more. They was a special deal, them ones.'

He brightens up. 'How much?'

'Last I heard, around fifteen dollars.'

He looks as bamboozled as she is. 'That sounds like a lot.'

'Yeah, well, that's what's confusing,' she says. To further befuddle him, she adds, 'It's around four pounds five shillings and fivepence halfpenny. Or, as yer a punter, let's call it four guineas, one shilling and fivepence halfpenny.'

He blinks rapidly, trying to do the calculation. 'Oh, so a quid and a bit more than before?' He nods his head while he thinks (a dead giveaway). 'D'ya reckon you'd be able to get your hands on one?'

'Do me best for yer, mate,' says Irene, mentally rubbing her hands together at her own brilliance. 'But mate, don't tell no one, right? I can't do it for everyone.'

The manager nods, his face serious as a little boy scout. Bloody ding dong he is.

# 15

# HAZEL TRIES TO GET TO THE BOTTOM OF THINGS

Hazel's train of thought is broken by the sound of the front door slamming, followed by a beery smoky smell that often precedes Irene's arrival.

A moment later, Irene's breathing fumes over Hazel's shoulder, looking at the puzzle. 'That thingy wa*th* pink la*th* time I looked,' she slurs, before dropping onto the sofa with a grunt of pain.

'That's because this is the Hanging Gardens, Irene dear. The Taj Mahal was last year.' Hazel glances over at Irene slumped on the sofa. 'You haven't left your teeth at the pub by any chance, have you? Or did you go out without them?'

Irene pulls her dentures out of her pocket and clicks them in time to her words (a habit she's adopted since it got a rise out of Merl). 'Whaddayah take me for?'

Hazel stares at her teeth. 'Irene, why are your dentures blue?'

'*Tho*aked them with a Blue bag,' she says, examining them. 'Thought they'd go white.'

'Hmm . . . Blue bags are meant for washing, not for human consumption.'

'What'*th* yer point?' Irene winces, holding her ribs as she wriggles around trying to get comfy on the sofa.

'Have you hurt yourself? You seem to be in pain.'

'Nah, box a birds . . .' Irene pauses and adds in her sly voice, '. . . but now yer mention it, I do have a bit a pain.'

'Then you should see the doctor. You know I'm not going to change my mind. Even apart from all the things I mentioned, there's trouble brewing at work, and I'll probably need to get a paying boarder in soon.'

'How much yer chargin'? I might con*th*ider it.'

Hazel thinks of a figure and doubles it. 'I'd say about twelve dollars a week.'

'What? Yer expecting royalty? Yer can get a room at the Au*th*-tralia for that!'

Hazel shrugs. Turning her attention back to the jigsaw puzzle, she hears the wet click of Irene's dentures being reinstated and braces herself for further debate. But it seems that Irene has accepted the inevitable.

'Fred got to the point yet?' asks Irene, slurring her words. 'Would've been a bloody sight easier if he had left a map.'

'I know what you're saying, but it must have been quite a slow process to write the message. Although I suppose he had nothing much else to do.' Hazel looks over at her. 'Irene, he mentions taking the train somewhere.'

Irene stares at the ceiling. 'In a locker at the station, d'yer reckon?'

'I don't think he would suggest taking the train if it was in a locker,' says Hazel. 'Are you sure you can't remember ever taking a trip with Fred out of town?'

'We was on and off for years. Maybe we went somewhere once or twice.'

Irene falls silent for so long, Hazel glances over to see if she's gone to sleep, but she's deep in thought, a rare activity.

'Now yer mention it. I seem to recollect going to the Blue Mountains once. Yonks ago. He said champagne – could be the honeymoon, I s'pose. I didn't think of it before.'

Hazel hadn't mentioned the champagne, so Irene has clearly had her nose in the kitchen drawer. 'Well, he's hidden whatever it is somewhere that you went together. And he's counting on you remembering it.'

'All right . . . That business in the letter about that road and that royal pub or whatever . . . I'm tryna recollect. It's all kind of hazy.'

The phone rings and Hazel gets up to answer it. A woman's voice on the other end says, 'Mrs Bates, your order will be ready tomorrow evening. Usual time.'

'Thank you,' says Hazel. 'I'll be there.'

'Who was that?' Irene asks, as Hazel sits down at the card table.

'Mrs Li. She wants to meet tomorrow evening.'

Irene grunts her agreement and wanders off down the hall. 'I'll have a bit of a think in the bog,' she calls over her shoulder.

It occurs to Hazel that Irene's habit of smoking in the lavatory was another one for the list.


Hazel arrives in the factory to find Gloria, Pixie and Alice looking over some new drawings and so deep in discussion they barely notice her handing out their morning tea.

'I think we need something really different for the summer range because too many other places are doing similar designs,' says Alice.

'Copying ours,' says Gloria, leaning over the drawing with a cigarette on her lip.

Alice brushes ash off the drawing and continues. 'I thought we could make small alterations to our basic patterns that won't change the price or need another pattern made.' She points out the features in her drawing. 'This is the peter pan collar we used last season, but much longer and pointier. And with our cap sleeves, I thought we could add stiffening, so they stand out more like epaulets.'

'I like those collars,' agrees Pixie. 'We could also do them in contrasting colours.'

Alice agrees enthusiastically. 'And contrasting patterns. We could do spots with stripes, or stripes with a floral print. Have you seen the new Op Art look?' She shuffles through her magazines and opens one at a double-page photograph of models lounging about in starkly patterned black-and-white frocks.

Gloria pulls a face. 'Hard on the eyes. For the machinists, I mean.'

'I love it!' says Pixie. 'I think we should go shorter. Instead of six inches above the knee, let's make them eight.'

'It's risky,' says Gloria. 'We don't want to alarm upstairs or have stores getting in a tizz 'cause they're too "way out".'

'Girls are taking our frocks up anyway,' Pixie points out.

Gloria raises an eyebrow. 'Bet the blokes are enjoying that. Eight inches above the knee, you can't wear stockings, so that knocks out wearing them to the office. And what happens in winter? You'd freeze yer bum off.'

'There's something new coming out,' says Alice, flipping through her magazines. 'They're called panty-tights. It's sort of like stockings attached to undies in the same colour. You don't need a girdle.'

Hazel, who should really be getting along, nevertheless leans in to see the photograph of a young woman sitting on a desk, shimmering nylon stockings disappearing up her skirt. No suspenders in sight.

'They're also making them in different colours and patterns for winter,' says Alice. 'I don't know how we get hold of them. They're in the British mags, but I haven't seen them anywhere here.'

'Probably the tariffs would make them too expensive here,' says Gloria. She thinks about it for a moment. 'Hang on . . . do tariffs apply to stockings?'

'Be good to find out,' says Alice.

When the buzzer goes for the end of morning tea, Hazel quickly gathers up the cups and saucers and loads her trolley.

Pixie holds the door open for her. 'What do you think about these panty-tights, Mrs Bates?' she asks, as they walk down the hall.

'Wonderful,' says Hazel. 'Let's face it, no one likes wearing a girdle, let alone corsets. I expect if men had to wear them, these new things would have been invented years ago. You know, Mr Fysh has a bit of time on his hands at the moment. He knows a lot about importing goods. He might be just the person to help find these new stockings.'

'All right, I'll speak to him,' says Pixie. She stands at the door of the kitchen while Hazel unloads the cups and saucers from the trolley, as if she wants to say more.

'How are things at home, dear?' asks Hazel.

'Terrible. My parents argue about work things all the time now.'

Reading between the lines, Hazel can't help but wonder if the tea lady role may be one of the things they're arguing about.

'What do you think has made her want to be involved here?' asks Hazel.

Pixie thinks about it for a while. 'Maybe turning forty she realised she hasn't done anything with her life, apart from have me, and I turned out to be a disappointment.'

Hazel glances up from the sink. 'I'm sure that's not true.'

'It is, I promise. I didn't want to be a debutante or meet the sons of her friends. She was engaged at my age. The truth is, I don't ever want to get married and be someone's servant.'

'It's not compulsory,' says Hazel. 'There are plenty of other things women can do with their lives.'

Pixie nods. 'I think business is something I could be good at. When Mod Frocks started to take off last year, even though she thinks the frocks are silly and childish, I think she was jealous. That's what started all this. I don't agree with the way she wants to do things, but I just don't know what I can do.'

Hazel turns from the washing up to look over at Pixie. When she started here six months ago, she was a tongue-tied schoolgirl. The Rosenbaum sisters complained about her being scatty and unreliable. The Pixie of today is a million miles from that awkward young woman.

'You need to be smart about it, Pixie dear. Try to tackle the problem from a different direction.'

Pixie nods, unconvinced.

'I can recommend washing up for thinking about problems. There's something about having your hands in hot water that focuses the mind.'

Pixie laughs. 'All right. Let me have a go then.' She walks over and stands next to Hazel at the sink. 'What do you do?'

Hazel, stunned for a moment, asks, 'Have you never washed dishes before?'

Pixie shakes her head. 'We have a housekeeper.'

'Well, all part of your education then.' Hazel hands her the dish-scrubber. 'A useful skill that will last a lifetime. You wash, I'll dry.'

## 16

# BETTY'S SUSPICIONS ARE PROVEN RIGHT

As she walks through Chinatown a little late for the meeting (only because she needed a Bex and a lie-down after work), Betty wonders if the herbalist might have something to help with her current ailments. Her nerves are in shreds. She's had a niggling headache all day. The word neuralgia pops into her head. Where did she hear it and has she got it? On top of everything else, this morning she was hallucinating. It might have been a migraine; she's heard those can make you see things that aren't there – in this case Irene Turnbuckle with a terrifying set of blue dentures.

Betty is a little nervous walking here on her own but feels quite worldly as she enters the familiar shop and gives the men behind the counter a little wave, like a regular (even though they ignore her). She goes into the meeting room where Mrs Li, Hazel and Irene are already seated around the table with cups of tea. She apologises for being late and Hazel says they've only just sat down, so not to worry.

Betty settles herself and gets out her notebook. 'Effie sends apologies,' she tells them and then writes it down. 'She has a rehearsal for *The Pirates of Penzance*. She's the Pirate King apparently.'

'Yo ho ho,' says Irene, getting out her flask and taking a swig.

Mrs Li begins. 'It wasn't too difficult to find these old robberies, as it turned out. Our friend Detective Pierce knows everyone in the Criminal Investigations Branch and Armed Hold-ups, and he's had files sent down to Surry Hills. They were sitting on his desk. Every one of them has Fred on the list of suspects.'

'So that means Pierce is officially on the job?' asks Hazel.

Mrs Li shrugs. 'He'd be keen to get back in the CIB but, to be honest, it means nothing. They're all crooked up there anyway. I'm sure he's in it for himself.'

'So why's he going after Fred now the poor bloke's dead?' asks Irene.

Mrs Li considers this for a moment. 'I would say almost definitely that someone who was inside with Fred is trying to get some leverage and offered up the information.'

'It probably doesn't matter how he knows at this point,' agrees Hazel. 'Is it worth us pursuing if he's after it?'

'It's me bloody inheritance!' says Irene.

While Betty agrees with Hazel, it will be hard to convince Irene that the proceeds of a robbery are not her right. Also, this treasure hunt is the most exciting thing that's happened all year, so Betty has no intention of letting it drop.

Mrs Li refers to her paperwork. 'There are three robberies that might be of interest, two of which have some reward attached to them, and all three are unsolved. Around five thousand pounds were stolen from the Bank of New South Wales back in 1961. They convicted one of the robbers but never found the money.'

'Who was the bloke they got?' asks Irene.

Mrs Li looks at her notes. 'Tommy Thompson.'

Betty raises her hand. 'He could have dobbed on Tweezers!'

Betty's always had the impression that Mrs Li thinks she's a bit of a dill. Now, obviously recognising a hard-boiled detective when she sees one, Mrs Li gives her an approving nod.

'Possible. What else yer got?' asks Irene.

'All right, the next one is an armed hold-up of a pawn shop,' continues Mrs Li. 'They stole cash, jewellery, golf clubs, a record collection and twenty Tupperware containers.'

'The thief must have had a lot of leftovers to need all that Tupperware,' says Betty, thinking aloud.

'Tupperware?!' spits Irene. 'Tweezers was a *safecracker*. Why've they got him down for that one? What else?'

Mrs Li raises an eyebrow at Irene's tone but continues. 'There was a robbery from a safe in a private home in Hunters Hill. The contents were cash of about two thousand pounds and family jewels. There's a detailed description of a necklace made up of diamonds and emeralds, valued at seven thousand pounds. Two gold bracelets inset with rubies worth three thousand pounds. And a diamond ring, valued at seven thousand pounds. There's a reward posted of five hundred pounds.'

Irene licks her lips. 'What about in the new money?' She changes her mind and adds, 'I'm not doing the new money, I'm sticking with the old.'

'A thousand dollars,' says Betty.

'Sounds even better,' says Irene. 'That's got Tweezers stamped all over it. Coulda done that on his own, but probably with a mate.'

'Hunters Hill does sound likely, but the bank robbery does as well,' says Hazel. 'If he worked with a colleague, they would go their separate ways until the heat died down.'

'And he'd have a nest egg,' suggests Mrs Li. 'That robbery took place on January fifth 1960.'

'Yep,' confirms Irene. 'He got nabbed in the June of that year.'

'So what do we do now?' asks Betty.

Hazel gets out Fred's letter, the stone and her own notes and puts them on the table. 'We have a number of clues. He talks about a road and a pub, and in the dark, which makes you think it's out of the city. Irene mentioned that she and Fred went to the Blue Mountains at some point long ago.' She turns to Irene. 'Do you remember going to a pub?'

Irene curls her lip. 'It's not much of a trip if yer remember it.'

'I think we can assume there was a pub involved,' says Hazel. 'I wonder what he means by a "royal" pub.'

'There's the Kings Arms near Katoomba,' offers Effie.

Irene nods. 'Rings a bell or two.'

'Good, we're making progress.' Hazel puts the stone on the table. 'This could have come from an unsealed road nearby. It must be significant.' She picks up a piece of paper. 'Finding the code in his book is a slow job and I haven't had much time recently. I'll try to get this finished this week and we can meet again.'

Betty reads her notes aloud: 'Golf clubs, record collection . . . I wonder what sort of music, must be important . . . jazz? . . . egg . . . Oh, that was a nest egg, not an actual egg – that would be confusing . . . jewels . . . Kings Arms . . . stone . . . train . . .' She looks up to see Mrs Li's gaze on her. 'Why don't I copy down that list of jewellery items,' she adds quickly.

'You can have the list,' says Mrs Li. 'We need to be careful not to discuss the matter outside this room. I'm sure Pierce is after the goods himself, but he could double dip and get a member of the public involved, someone who can claim a reward—'

'Merl, for example,' suggests Betty.

Irene gives a rude snort. 'While Pierce palms the two thousand quid in cash.'

Hazel looks around the table. 'Eyes open, lips sealed.'

'Oh! That could be our motto,' says Betty. 'I'll make a note.'

When the meeting is over, Irene gets up from the table with her hand clamped over her ribs. She winces with pain and Betty can now see her teeth are bright blue.

'It *was* you!' Betty cries, struggling out of her seat. 'Why were you in my kitchen?'

'Dunno what yer talking about,' says Irene, limping out the door.

Betty follows her out through the herbalist shop and into the street. 'You were there, hiding in the dark. Did you take my good teapot? The Royal Doulton?'

'Course not.' Irene picks up speed, hobbling off down the street. 'Yer imaginin' things. See a shrink,' she calls over her shoulder.

Betty turns to Mrs Li and Hazel, who have followed her out. 'I'm not. I thought I was, but I'm definitely not!'

'There's no doubt Irene's up to something,' Hazel agrees.

As she and Hazel walk towards home, Betty explains. 'She was hiding in my kitchen when we opened up for the day. You can't stop Irene with a locked door. She was in there, standing in the dark. She gave me that guilty smile, you know the one, and her teeth were blue – I'm not even going to ask why – and she was lopsided.'

'She's hurt her ribs. I wonder if she's broken something,' says Hazel. 'It's not like her to show she's in pain.'

Switching on her detective mind, Betty thinks back to yesterday morning's activities. 'When I served the tea in the factory, the manager was arguing with one of the machinists . . . they're always teasing him and playing tricks on him.' She turns to Hazel. 'He was accusing her of hiding his precious transistor. The one *Irene* sold him.'

'You think she broke in to steal it back?' asks Hazel.

'Yes, I do, because she sold them too cheaply, didn't bother to work it out. She's not much of a businesswoman. He told me he'd hidden it on a shelf above his desk – out of reach!'

'She might have climbed up and fallen, do you think?'

'That's exactly what I think,' says Betty. 'She flogged him a stolen transistor and then took it back. And now she's going to flog it to someone else for a better price. You have to admit, I'm good at this, Hazel.'

'You are. But here's the twist – Irene doesn't need to find another customer. She's got a ready-made one right there in the factory manager.'

Betty agrees. It's the perfect crime. She feels a glow of pride that she, Margaret Penelope Dewsnap, could outwit the notoriously wily Irene Turnbuckle.

## 17

# HAZEL JOINS THE DEBATE

Hazel arrives home to find Irene sitting at the kitchen table smoking her pipe. Now it's agreed that she's leaving, Irene doesn't bother with Hazel's rules at all.

'What's happened to that bird next door?' Irene asks, inclining her head towards the Mulligans'. 'Friendly little thing, haven't seen her for weeks. I was giving her a few helpful tips. She been sent off somewhere?' She jiggles her eyebrows meaningfully.

Hazel would be interested to know what sort of tips Irene's given Maude; not baking ones, that's for certain.

'She has been sent off, not because she's in the family way if that's what you're implying. Since you attend St Vincent's, you probably know that Auntie Vera died, and Maude is Father Kelly's new housekeeper.'

Irene nods, puffing thoughtfully on her pipe. 'Kelly's all right. One of the better ones. He takes my confession. Not bad looking for a priest.'

Hazel can't imagine what sort of confessions Father Kelly might have heard from Irene. 'Mrs Mulligan thinks it will keep Maude out of trouble,' she continues. 'Give her a home and income. They could use more room next door but I'm not so sure . . .'

'Yeah, well, I'll tell yer something about that. Yer can look after his Reverence like a baby, but when he dies, those ladies are out on their ears. No home, no family, no money. They end up out there in the Little Sisters of the Poor, that home run by the nuns. Yer go out there to die.' Irene nods at next door. 'Cruel sending a kid into that life.'

'I agree,' says Hazel. 'They're going to try it for three months. Hopefully there's a way to get Maude out of it somehow.'

'Be an all right job for a mature lady like meself, but . . . I'd be a temptation for the priest,' says Irene, with a cackle. 'Don't mind a man in robes, or even a kilt if he's got the legs for it.'

Hazel can't help admiring Irene's self-confidence, inflated as it is, but turns her attention to other business. 'Now, Irene dear, how are you going finding accommodation?'

'Waiting for a bed with the Little Sisters meself.' Irene gives a sly smile. 'Just kiddin'. Got a room in a little attic in Lisbon Street, actually.'

'I see. What number Lisbon Street?' asks Hazel.

'Five fifty-five, as a matter a fact. Move in on the weekend.'

'Irene, you are not going to live in a brothel. There must be somewhere else with a clean room to rent.'

'Nuthin' wrong with it. It's free, for a start off. Just a bit a cleaning here and there.'

'Well, I can't stop you,' says Hazel. 'Living in an illegal estab-lishment . . . it's not exactly a stable home. But it's your choice. Now, have you seen the doctor about your ribs? They could easily be broken.'

'Nah, she'll be right. Just slept the wrong way.' Irene gets her flask out of her pocket and takes a quick swig. She squeezes her eyes shut and gives herself a shake.

'Is this injury anything to do with the factory manager at Farley's and the transistor you sold him?'

'Where'd yer get that idea?' says Irene, pretending outrage.

'Of course, you're right, dear. It seemed too preposterous that you would steal it and sell it back to him at a higher price. I knew that couldn't be right.'

'Course I wouldn't,' she mutters. 'Whaddayah take me for?'

Irene's lying, of course, but Hazel has said her piece and drops the subject. She makes them both sardines on toast for dinner and has an early night.

Each time Hazel has met with Oscar, the late summer afternoons have put on a good show. Golden light and long evening shadows, accompanied by the last calls of birds in the Botanic Gardens and flying foxes dotting the twilight sky. This evening promises to be more of the same and she's looking forward to it. But when she comes out of the station, Hazel can see that Oscar is in a sombre mood.

'Hazel, I wanted to take you dancing this evening but . . . I wonder if we can save this activity for another time.'

'Of course,' she agrees, with a mix of disappointment and relief. 'Why don't we walk instead? We don't need to talk but I'm happy to listen.'

Oscar nods. She takes his arm and they meander across Hyde Park, past the cathedral and into the Botanic Gardens in silence. They settle on the park bench overlooking the Opera House site where they sat the first evening.

'Jørn has decided to resign from the project,' Oscar tells her. 'His only alternative is to give up all control. He can't work this way. I understand this. Perhaps he has no choice.' He pauses thoughtfully. 'He has a meeting with the press tomorrow morning. He believes that if he brings the problem to public attention, things will change.' He pauses. 'I'm not sure this is true.'

It's the first time Hazel has seen Oscar's confidence at such a low ebb. 'If Mr Hughes accepts his resignation, won't Jørn lose any option for negotiation? Do you think you can talk him out of it? Or is it too late?'

'I agree with you. I think this plan will not work against this minister. It will make Jørn appear as a prima donna and then Mr Hughes can show himself as the man of reason and sense.' Oscar stares at the distant sails of the Opera House for a long moment. 'I think it will be a disaster. For him and for the people of Australia. Not just now but for years to come. I wish I knew what else to suggest.'

Hazel puts a comforting hand on his shoulder. 'It seems that Mr Hughes has Jørn cornered. Perhaps there is nothing more you can do. You've given it your best.'

Oscar turns to her with a sorrowful smile. 'The decision is for him to make. I will respect whatever that decision may be. But I can see now that the facts are lost in gossip and speculation. The public does not have the true story. There was an article in the newspaper this morning . . . you probably saw it?'

Each time they meet, Hazel has promised herself that she will tell Oscar her secret before she's forced to confess. The longer she holds back, the more difficult it seems. There may never be a better opportunity than now. She takes a steadying breath. 'I don't read the newspaper, to be honest, Oscar. I have something called word blindness. So reading is . . . well, it's difficult for me.'

'I understand. It's very common,' he says with a shrug. 'You may know there is a new term for this condition: dyslexia. There is debate whether this condition exists, but I know it does. Even the most brilliant mind can suffer this problem. A brilliant mind like the world famous architect Jørn Utzon.'

Hazel stares at him, not sure if he is playing an elaborate joke, but her ears tell her it's the truth.

Smiling, he takes her hand and kisses it. 'He is also a left-hand person like you.'

Hazel pulls away, laughing in disbelief. 'Are you teasing me?'

'I am not. Why do you think I spend many hours reading long difficult documents? This is not my job as the acoustic consultant. His English is good, but it would take him days to read a document of thirty pages. Another brilliant man, Albert Einstein, also had dyslexia. You have good company.'

'Well, I never. I don't know what to say.'

'You can say this with pride: "I have dyslexia. Many brilliant people have this condition, and Hazel Bates is one of them."'

Hazel laughs, then finds herself oddly tearful and Oscar pulls her into a warm embrace. She holds his solid body tightly in her arms and, when their lips meet, it feels like the most natural thing in the world.

# 18

# IRENE'S ON THE MOVE

Irene arrives in the laneway for lunch to find Betty alone, sitting on her little cushion. As she sits down, she can't resist murmuring, 'Dibber-dobber.'

'I beg your pardon?' asks Betty, turning bright pink.

Irene gets out her packet of Tally-Ho, licks a rolling paper and parks it on her lip till she's ready for it. 'I said, how're yer doing? Trouble with yer hearing now, is it?'

'I have twenty-twenty hearing and I heard perfectly well what you said, but I'm going to let it pass because I also heard you *gave* the manager a new transistor. Alert the press: Irene Turnbuckle does the decent thing!'

'Yeah, I'm a bloody saint,' says Irene, still not happy that Hazel putting the guilts on her has left her five quid short.

'That's a bit of a stretch. You better hope he doesn't notice it's the same one.'

Irene pauses to concentrate on rolling her smoke. 'Dunno what yer talking about.'

They both turn to watch Merl march up the laneway towards

them with a bulging shopping bag. Irene hears a muffled burp from Betty's rear end.

'Is that one of them whoopee cushions?' asks Irene. 'I always wanted one of 'em when I was a kid.'

'Very funny, Irene. It's the very thought of the sugar in that tin in Merl's bag. Ooooh, what do you think she's brought today?'

'Yer'll just have to wait and see,' says Irene.

Merl arrives, dusts off the spot where she plans to sit and plonks herself down on the wall. A moment later, Hazel arrives and takes her place next to Betty.

'Did I hear you're moving out of Hazel's place?' asks Merl, glancing across at Irene as she unpacks her sandwich.

'Nothing wrong with anyone's hearing round here,' says Irene.

'Just taking a friendly interest,' says Merl. 'Where are you off to?'

Irene gives her a sideways look. 'Why d'yer need to know?'

Merl sighs. 'I obviously don't *need* to know—'

'That's what I thought,' says Irene.

Hazel's chuckling away to herself. 'The conversation's off to a spirited start today, ladies. Now, Irene, I keep meaning to ask how that young lass at your work is getting on?'

'She popped the bun out and is back at work with tits like watermelons,' says Irene. 'Only gone a week. Bit a whispering behind her back but she gets on with her business.'

'The poor dear,' says Hazel. 'Good luck to her. You could put some tincture of sage in her tea, help stop the milk.'

'I'm not a bloody nursemaid,' says Irene.

Betty giggles. 'Thought you were a saint, Irene. Are you worried about your reputation improving?'

'These girls just don't learn,' says Merl. 'She's not the first and not the last.'

Five minutes in and Irene's had it with her already. 'That's very poetic, Merl. Yer make that up or get it from one of yer favourite poets like . . . Rembrandt or one of them Greek philos . . . plos—'

'Philosophers?' suggests Betty.

'Blokes,' continues Irene, also fed up with Betty finishing her sentences.

'Very droll,' says Merl. 'I'm going to assume you know Rembrandt is a painter.'

'Assume what yer like . . .' Irene's working up another witticism when she's cut short by Hazel changing the subject again.

'Dottie has definitely got my job in her sights,' Hazel says with a sigh. 'As well as arguing with Frankie, another one of those brochures turned up. Edith Stern intercepted it.'

'One turned up at our place too. I picked it up from the mail,' says Merl. 'Fancy referring to the tea break as a "business interruption" – disgraceful. As if workers are just machines that need lubricating now and then. Anyway, they won't let me go, the place would fall apart. And they rely on my baking skills.'

'Hazel does those things, and Dottie's still trying to get rid of her,' says Betty.

'I'm not taking it personally – though perhaps I should – but I think she wants to be a new broom,' says Hazel.

'Better watch she doesn't sweep yers out the door,' says Irene, wondering if her job is also at risk. They wouldn't dare.

'She doesn't realise that all the friendships between the girls in the factory are made during the tea breaks when it's quiet and they can chat,' says Hazel. 'There are so many factory jobs around now and not enough workers . . . it's those friendships that keep them there. Dottie comes from a wealthy family, so I suppose you can't expect her to understand the workers.'

'What concerns me is that if Empire get rid of you and put in one of these machines, it will be like the fall of Europe. One by one everyone will go,' says Merl. 'You need to work harder to make yourself indispensable.'

'Thank you for that advice, Merl dear. We are all at risk, so we need to get as many tea ladies to the next meeting as we possibly can,' says Hazel. 'That's our best hope now.'

Merl mutters to herself as she gets the tin out of her bag and announces she's made a poppyseed cake. For obvious reasons, this is Irene's least favourite cake and while everyone's attention is on the cake, she pops her dentures out and into her pocket.

As Merl hands out the slices wrapped in greaseproof paper, her beady eye falls on Irene. 'I understand Mr Turnbuckle passed away recently. I'm sorry to hear that.'

'Where'd yer hear it?' asks Irene.

'Detective Pierce was over for Sunday lunch, and he mentioned it.'

'What'*th* it to him?' Irene asks.

'No need to bite my head off. He just mentioned it in passing.' Merl pauses a moment. 'Were you in touch with him at all?'

'None of yer bee*th*wa*th*. Yer putting me off me cake.'

'Good grief, put your teeth back in – you're putting the rest of us off.' Merl screws her face up in disgust as if she's never seen a set of gums before.

To Irene's relief, Hazel comes to the rescue with compliments about the cake and puts the old battle-axe off the scent for the moment. Merl nosing around means something's worth chasing. They need to get on and find it.

*

Irene squashes as much of her stuff as she can into a borrowed suitcase and carries it around to her new home in Lisbon Street. Five fifty-five is a three-storey mansion in a row of mansions, most of which have seen better days. Her new home is the smartest in the row, painted white with red roses in the front garden. On the wrought iron fence, a sign in fancy writing reads: 'Miss Palmer's Secretarial School'. (The girls pick up plenty of skills here, but shorthand's not one of them.) It's a classy establishment, in Irene's opinion.

Miss Palmer herself answers the door. She doesn't look like a madam, at least nothing like the ones Irene's met in the past. This one looks like a smart secretary, nicely made up, wearing tight-fitting slacks with her hair in a beehive.

She looks Irene up and down, stopping to stare at the slippers that, apart from a couple of holes cut out for her bunions, are in good shape. By the look on Her Ladyship's face, though, she's suddenly less than keen to let Irene live in her attic.

'I was told you were a tea lady. You're not quite what I imagined,' she says.

Irene nods. 'We come in all shapes and sizes.'

Still not happy, Miss Palmer steps back and beckons her inside.

The hallway reeks of flowery perfume and is decorated like a palace with a dust-collecting chandelier, dark-blue carpet so thick it bounces underfoot and silver wallpaper covered in peacocks and other strange-looking birds. Irene nods her approval as she follows Miss Palmer's trim little figure up three flights of stairs, through a small door and then up another narrow flight into an attic room with a single bed, a cupboard and a bench with a gas ring on it for cooking. This will suit Irene just fine.

'Leave your bag here and come back downstairs,' Miss Palmer instructs her.

Irene does as she's told and follows her new boss down to the third-floor landing.

'So, as I explained on the telephone,' Miss Palmer says. 'I need the main areas and the bedrooms cleaned every day, vacuumed and dusted. The bathrooms on each landing must be immaculate. No need to change the beds. We have someone on duty during opening hours to do that and all the linen is sent out.' As she speaks, she points here and there with her bright red fingernails. 'The girls arrive here at 4 pm, we open for clients at 5 pm and we close at 4 am. You'll be here on your own during the day.'

Irene keeps nodding, working out that she'll have to start the cleaning before she goes to work and finish it when she gets back. Small price to pay to live free of charge in such a luxurious abode.

'Where's me lav?' Irene asks, having spent some time working out the politest term for the dunny.

Miss Palmer sniffs at the thought of Irene's bodily functions. 'There's a chamber pot under the bed you can use at night and empty in the morning. There's an outside lavatory and washhouse in the backyard for your use. I can't stress strongly enough that you can never *ever* be seen anywhere in the house during operating hours. I'll show you a back stair you can use from now on. Any other questions?'

'Not that I can think of right now, thank you kindly,' says Irene, keen to be on her best behaviour.

'Remember that discretion is vital in this house. We have clients from every walk of life, and strict confidentiality is the mainstay of our business. Anything you accidentally see or hear remains within these walls. Do I make myself clear?'

'Yes, Miss Palmer,' says Irene, secretly gleeful at the thought of the shenanigans right here on her doorstep. She's already wondering how to get a good squiz at these clients, and what she might do with the information. Never mind bloody Tweezers and his loot, she's landed herself at the business end of a rainbow.

She follows Miss Palmer down a narrow winding staircase to the ground floor kitchen, where she's shown a cupboard with all the cleaning items for the job and given the keys to the back door.

The backyard is like every other one in the area: bins, washhouse, clothesline and dunny with a locked back gate. The clients come in through a separate entrance off the laneway to a side door of the house, hidden from prying eyes by a high wall. Irene has to admire the way Miss Palmer has set it all up.

For the rest of the day, Irene trudges back and forth between Hazel's place and Lisbon Street with the rest of her bits and pieces: treasures she's collected over her lifetime, photos, letters, the wigs she never wears (might one day), the remains of her old hat (recovered from the bin), her good shoes (and her mother's before her), her winter coat and not forgetting her empty savings sock, since she's paid Big G off with every penny she had and a couple of quid borrowed from the petty cash tin at work.

Lugging all this stuff over, it crosses her mind that she doesn't know anything much about cleaning. She's seen Hazel bashing around with the vacuum cleaner. Seems easy enough once you know how to turn the thing on, but she wonders if there's more to it. Hazel has a feather duster and sometimes wipes things down with a cloth. Furniture polish, that's another thing. She has no doubt the neat and tidy Miss Palmer will have everything needed in the cupboard; all Irene needs to do is work out how little she can get away with.

# 19

# HAZEL GETS SUSPICIOUS

Hazel's house feels strangely empty without Irene. The only things she's left behind are the odour of stale smoke and a trail of litter. Hazel's lesson with Sister Ruth has been put off for this week, so she spends the morning getting her house in order, starting with Irene's bedroom, which has clearly not been cleaned since Irene moved in. Hazel boils up the copper and, leaving the sheets to soak, sets to work on the dust and cobwebs. It's a perfect drying day and by lunchtime the sheets are high on the prop line, dancing in the breeze.

In the afternoon she does some baking and takes it around to the presbytery. Maude answers the door looking tired and pale with shadows under her eyes, as if she hasn't been sleeping at all. She glances over her shoulder into the dark house. 'They're all asleep.'

Hazel beckons her outside and they walk towards the street. She gets the tin out of her shopping bag. 'I've made some Anzac biscuits for you. How's it all going, dear?'

'Thank you, Mrs B. I'm all right,' says Maude, taking the cake tin. 'It's a bit lonely but . . . I'll get used to it, I suppose. I like the flowers and birds and everything in the garden. And the nuns are nice, especially Sister Ruth. I just want to be at home with everyone.'

Hazel nods. 'I know. You've already been here over a month, only two to go and then we'll find some way of getting you out of here.'

Maude looks downcast. 'I don't think Mam will let that happen. I know it's an important job and I don't want to let her down or anything. I need to pray more and be more devout and dedicated. God will help me get used to it.'

'Is that what you really want?'

Maude prises the cake tin open. 'I don't know. It seems like the right thing to do.' She takes a biscuit out, smells it and takes a bite, closing her eyes in bliss.

'Are you sleeping all right? You look tired.'

'They're up half the night talking and drinking and keeping me awake. And wanting food. They're very fussy about their clothes, especially Father Kelly. Making me go to the drycleaners in the city every other day. Must cost a fortune, but I suppose the diocese pays for it.' She shrugs. 'Maybe they just want me out of the house.'

'Father Kelly mentioned Brother Riley and Brother O'Connell were visiting from Queensland.'

'Hmm . . . They have the thickest paddy accents. They might be down from Queensland, but they're not long out of Ireland.'

'Did he mention how long they're staying, or why they're here?'

Maude narrows her eyes at Hazel. 'Are you a little bit suspicious, Mrs B?'

Hazel hesitates. She doesn't want to worry Maude, but at the same time she should be on her guard. 'I'm not sure, dear. I just can't put my finger on it.'

Maude glances around. 'I think he might be going a bit doolally – you know, soft in the head. Senile.'

Hazel almost laughs. 'I'm sure he's too young for that. What makes you think so?'

'He's just forgetful. He's asking me about parishioners that he knows perfectly well. Auntie Vera used to help him with his sermons, so he's lost without her. I sort of understand it. He must have been depending on her for everything.' Maude grimaces. 'It's probably sacrilege to say it, but that's what I think. He can't do anything for himself and I don't know how to do it, so he gets grumpy.'

'Grumpy?' asks Hazel. 'I always got the impression he was constantly cheerful.'

'Outside the presbytery he puts on a good show. But in the house, no. He's a different person. It seems to me that he's too lazy to do some things. Auntie Vera must have done everything. Now he can't be bothered, got more important things to do.'

'Like what?'

Maude shrugs. 'Well, he asked me to find his past sermons, so he doesn't have to write new ones. Says he's too busy to have after-noon tea with parishioners. You know they sold off the land at the back of the convent to pay for the orphanage? Well, I heard him talking to Brother Riley about it – he's the short one. Something about the bank being difficult. Brother Riley was telling him to put his foot down and all that. The other two boss Father Kelly around all the time. Anyway, I'm flat out keeping them all fed. They never lift a finger for themselves.'

'I hope they don't all drink as much tea as Father Kelly,' says Hazel.

'No, they all drink coffee. At least it only takes a minute to make. Easier than tea.'

Hazel frowns. 'I remember Auntie Vera telling me that Father Kelly drinks a dozen cups of tea a day.'

Maude stares at her, perplexed. 'I didn't know that. He's never said.'

'That's extraordinary. I wonder if it was that whack on the head. Or perhaps the shock of losing Auntie Vera has affected his mind.'

Maude shrugs and pops another biscuit in her mouth. 'Something has.'

Watching Maude walk slowly back into the house, the cake tin tucked under her arm, Hazel has a feeling of unease. Something is not right here, and she needs to make it a priority to find out what.

Hazel had been expecting to see Oscar on Sunday, but he called to say that he had to go up to the Utzons' home in Palm Beach to talk to Jørn and would likely be there most of the day. He apologises but Hazel insists she completely understands.

With the day to herself, she takes her shopping bag down to the market and buys five pounds of ripe purple plums. She spends the afternoon sterilising her wine-making equipment while the smell of the crushed plums boiling in sugar syrup fills the house. At five, she pops next door to the Mulligans' to help with bath night, something she's done regularly for years, ever since Mrs Mulligan reached proportions that made it difficult for her to manage.

Hazel enjoys wrangling the six Mulligan children, scrubbing their bony little bodies clean of a week's worth of grime and seeing them transformed, pink and shiny in their threadbare pyjamas with hair slicked flat or wrapped in a rag if there's a lice infestation. With Norma and her grandsons living so far away, she's more than happy to do it. Once it's done, she has a quick glass of sherry with

Mrs Mulligan and arrives back home to the delicious smell of sweet plums filling the house and the phone ringing.

'Hi, Mum,' says Norma in a weary voice.

'You sound tired, Norma dear,' says Hazel. 'Everything all right?'

'Been on my knees praying for rain all week. Hasn't helped. We had to get a water delivery and feed in for the cattle.'

'We've got rain coming this week,' Hazel assures her. 'We'll blow it out your way. How are the boys?'

'Harry got the strap this week for not finishing his homework—'

'Oh, Norma, you know I don't agree with teachers hurting children like that. He's just a little boy.'

'Everyone gets the strap sooner or later. Barrie got it the week before for tipping out his school milk because it went lumpy in the heat.'

Hazel sighs. 'It's ridiculous, teaching children to hit people, let alone for such . . . trivial crimes. What about bringing the boys up for the Easter Show? A nice treat for them. Irene's gone now, so I have plenty of room for you.'

'I'll see how we go closer to Easter, but the boys would love that. How are things at work?'

Hazel explains about the Café-bar and Dottie's takeover plans and Norma, as always, is sympathetic and kind. She knows how much Hazel's job means to her.

'It crossed my mind just now that I might be out of a job by Easter,' says Hazel.

'I hope not. But even if you are, something better will turn up.' Norma pauses. 'I know it wouldn't be your first choice, but don't forget there's always a home for you here with us, Mum.'

'Thank you, dear. I'm a city girl, but it's good to know.'

*

When Hazel arrives at the top floor on Monday morning, Edith Stern inclines her head towards Mr Karp's office, where Dottie's voice can be heard rising and falling in an unstoppable tide of words.

'What's the topic?' Hazel asks.

'She's got a bee in her bonnet about this Carla Zampatti,' Edith explains in a low voice. At Hazel's quizzical expression, she adds, 'Italian.'

'I gather that, but who is she?'

'Fashion designer. She's in the society pages all the time – which you'd know if you ever read the papers, Hazel. Dottie met her at one of her fancy parties and now she's obsessed with her. She's just used the word "sophisticated" at least a dozen times.'

'Does that mean she wants to add another new range?'

Edith shakes her head. 'She wants to reinvent the whole company – new name, new everything. Out with the old, in with the new. That probably means us.' Edith looks grim. 'On top of that, there's a man coming in to demonstrate the Café-bar next week.'

'I see,' says Hazel. 'So it's still on the horizon.'

Edith gets up and beckons to Hazel to follow her out into the hallway. 'I was listening on the intercom, so I got the full story. She wants me to make the upstairs tea and have one of these bar things installed on the 2nd Floor for Accounts. The Rosenbaums get a kettle to make their own tea, and there's another Café-bar in the factory.'

'But surely the factory staff can't all make their tea at the same time.'

'She says tea breaks can be phased out,' explains Edith. 'First the breaks will be in shifts, then they'll disappear altogether. It's more "productive", apparently. They'll do it quietly, so it doesn't attract any attention.'

'What do Frankie and Mr Karp think about it?' asks Hazel.

'Frankie is no match for her, Hazel, we all know that. She's a bulldozer.' Edith pauses. 'Old Mr Karp sounds like he's fighting for his life – she's got her eye on his chair. Her only real opposition is Mr Levy. He's arguing with facts and figures. She doesn't like that.'

Hazel sighs. 'No, I can't see her being impressed with that approach.'

'And let's not forget, Mr Levy is an employee like us. He's putting up a good fight, but it could cost him his job if he doesn't watch out.'

'Well,' says Hazel, managing a smile. 'I think Mr Levy has an extra biscuit coming his way today.'

To Hazel's surprise, at the next Guild meeting there are twenty additional tea ladies of varying ages – more women than chairs. Merl's cream sponge wouldn't have gone far, but no one has come empty-handed and the table is crammed with plates of home-made cakes and biscuits. There are not enough cups and saucers, but the women quickly organise tea shifts, with the cups washed up in between. The minutes are read by Betty and almost comprehensible. Mrs Li, as treasurer, gives a report on the funds raised (twenty-three dollars) by the cupcake stall at the church fete organised by Merl. Hazel apologises for not attending.

'Forget about yer cupcakes,' says Irene. 'We've gotta work out what to do about these bloody machines before we all get the boot.'

Murmurs of 'hear hear' buzz around the room.

'I know no one cares about us really, but—' begins Betty.

'They'll care when we're gone,' says Violet.

There's a murmur of agreement and several hands go up: someone suggests writing a letter to the newspaper, another woman penning a letter to Prime Minister Holt.

'Bugger all that, those blokes are not gonna help us,' says Irene, standing up to her full five feet in slippers. 'I say we go on strike.' She grins as a round of applause and a hearty cheer goes up.

Mrs Li raises her hand. 'I have to agree with Irene. We have a limited time to get attention. I don't think we have much to lose. Once we all start being laid off, it's too late.'

A tall, middle-aged woman with short grey hair and a noble face stands up. 'My name is Eileen Weston. I'd like to say something, if I may. This issue is going to impact the lives of hundreds, if not thousands, of women – nobody knows how many tea ladies there are. But it's a wider issue. It's an encroachment on workers' rights, the right to have breaks. The bosses want workers chained to their desks because capitalism relies on constantly increasing productivity. It's a hungry animal that eats everything in its path. I'm a member of the Missos – Miscellaneous Workers' Union. The members are people like us: workers, cleaners, drivers, caretakers. I'm prepared to ask for the support of the union.'

Watching the serious expressions of the women in the room, Hazel has the sense she's witnessing the beginnings of something extraordinary.

Eileen continues. 'Keep in mind, we might need to strike for more than a day. It could be a week or a month. It just depends how long employers want to hold out. Especially if the Employers' Union gets involved. We'll also need to be seen. We'll have to stage a demonstration and get the cause in front of the public.'

Nervous chatter fills the room. Hazel waits, giving everyone time to settle, before she asks, 'Who is prepared to stop work?'

'Not for a month,' someone calls out. 'Me hubby would put paid to that.'

Another woman says her husband is part of the metalworkers' stop work action. 'We can't afford to both be on strike,' she says and promptly leaves the meeting. Several other women take the opportunity to follow her out.

When the chatter has died down, Hazel, realising an open-ended strike is not viable, asks who's prepared to be involved in a one-day strike and a protest meeting to test the waters. Gradually the hands go up. 'All right. We need to spread the word and meet here again in a week's time to discuss the plan in detail.'

## 20

# BETTY HAS A DREAM

Betty's not the slightest bit surprised that Irene's now living in a notorious brothel in Lisbon Street, because Irene has no sense of propriety. What is shocking is that she's responsible for cleaning the place. Good luck with that!

Surely that stuck-up Miss Palmer (Betty often sees her at the post office collecting mysterious parcels) would take one look at Irene and glean that hygiene is not her strong point? Or is there more to this job of Irene's? Could she and the Palmer woman be up to something? They're a very unlikely team, with Miss Palmer looking like a managing director's secretary or even a lady managing director (if there is such a thing) and Irene more like something the cat dragged in. No one would suspect them of working together, so perhaps there's something in it.

Shaking off the tangled threads of her own suspicions, Betty turns her attention to more important matters. Now that she has a list of the stolen jewels, she considers going around the pawnbrokers' shops. There are hundreds of them tucked here and there, and most of them dealing in stolen goods. But that's the first place

Detective Pierce would look, so it's probably pointless. Also, it's only an assumption that this is the robbery Fred was talking about and he's hidden these jewels somewhere dark and distant. That's how detectives work, and Betty accepts it's all part of the job, but she draws the line at having to go to all the pawnbrokers.

One thing is clear. Betty has never known Irene to leave the city, so a trip to the Blue Mountains, or anywhere distant for that matter, would have to be memorable. It's only Irene's terrible memory that's standing between them and a quick resolution to this case.

As Betty walks over to Hazel's place, braving the fierce heat, she delights in the knowledge that Irene, with her stinky pipe and barbed comments, will not be there. She finds Hazel at the kitchen table labouring over Fred's book. She can only imagine how difficult this job must be for her friend – like trying to make sense of Morse code or semaphore messages.

'This is a nice surprise, dear,' says Hazel, glancing up.

'I was sitting at home and then I thought two heads are better than one,' says Betty.

'Well, it's kind of you to come over to share that thought with me.'

Betty laughs. 'I mean with Tweezers' book, silly. Let's get it finished together.'

Hazel leans back in her chair with a sigh. 'You must have read my mind. It's turned into such a task, and my problem identifying certain letters makes it more time consuming. Irene has been no help at all.' She gets up from the table and goes to the fridge. 'I've got some of last summer's peach wine chilling. Let's fortify ourselves with a glass and get it done.'

Betty fans herself with the book in question while Hazel fills two tall glasses with the golden wine. 'Do you think the title is significant? I mean *The Call of the Wild*? Do you think Tweezers felt the call?' she asks.

'I imagine so. He was facing a twelve-year sentence.'

Hazel sits down and pushes the piece of paper she's been working on across to Betty, who glances over it. Hazel's neat child-like lettering makes her eyes smart with tears.

'Does it make sense?' asks Hazel, sounding anxious.

'It's perfect,' says Betty, with a smile. 'Why don't I take over the magnifying glass and I'll tell you the letter and you can write it? Good practice for you too.'

Hazel nods and they set off, with Betty scouring each page, peering through the magnifying glass as she picks up the trail of pencil dots leading them to the treasure. As they work, she imagines Tweezers locked in his little cell (with some dreadful murderer or bank robber), sitting on his bunk while he painstakingly pencils in these dots, knowing that his days are numbered—

'Are you all right, Betty dear?' asks Hazel.

Betty dabs her cheeks with the back of her hand. 'I'm just sad for poor old Tweezers, locked up and knowing he's dying.'

Hazel agrees. 'I suppose he did lead a life of crime, so it's bound to end that way.'

Betty admits that's true. 'I wonder what led him down that path in the first place.'

'So many ways a man might fall into that life after the war,' says Hazel sympathetically. 'It's a wonder more men didn't.'

An hour later, they reach the end of the book, then fill in a few gaps and the task is finally complete. Betty reads it aloud:

'*Don't tell no one I kept something for later its not easy but I will try to help you find it remember we went there on the train after the bookie job and had that champagne at the Kings Arms and we walked down*

*the road a bit and seed delsdon road thats where it is walk along a bit,*
*about one mile, and see a big gum on the right its all bush look out for*
*the big gum its round there I don't know what its worth but I kept it*
*secret and you need to also.'*

'Well, Irene was right about the Kings Arms, so she probably knows more than she realises,' says Betty.

'I wouldn't count on that,' says Hazel with a smile.

Betty stares at the page, puzzled. 'He makes it sound like he's left her a tree.'

'Or something buried near the tree.'

Betty smiles. 'Ah yes, of course. I think we might have cracked it, Hazel.'

The setting sun blazes orange and scarlet through the kitchen window bathing them in a golden glow, like two heroines in the closing scenes of a film. Betty imagines a happy ending to this story in which they find the jewels and collect the reward from the grateful owner. She sees the last frame, a close-up on a sign hanging above a doorway: 'Bates and Dewsnap, Detective Agency'. In smaller letters below: 'All cases considered.'

Betty squirms with excitement at the prospect of telling Irene at lunchtime but, as luck would have it, Merl arrives first with Irene lagging after her.

'So what have you been up to?' asks Merl, unpacking her thermos and lunch.

'Nothing!' says Betty. 'Why?'

Merl glances over at her. 'It's a polite question, Betty. What is wrong with everyone around here? It's how people start conversations.'

Irene sits down and fishes her pipe out of the pocket of her cardigan. 'Says who?'

'People in society who understand the art of conversation,' says Merl.

Irene examines the contents of her pipe, then strikes a match and belches a filthy cloud of smoke. Betty doesn't complain, but she catches Irene's eye and raises her eyebrows several times, hoping to communicate their breakthrough.

Puffing away, Irene stares at her dead-eyed. 'Yer gunna ask me on a date, Betty? Yer not me type, sorry.'

Betty blushes. 'No, of course not. I just finished reading *The Call of the Wild*.' She articulates each word but still it doesn't sink in.

Merl sighs. 'I'm having trouble following this conversation. Oh, thank goodness, here comes a little sanity.'

Hazel greets everyone, but Betty can see straightaway that something's wrong. 'How's things at work, Hazel?'

'Where do I start?' Hazel sits down and opens her pack of sandwiches slowly before looking up. 'Dottie and Frankie met with the Café-bar rep this morning and they're planning a trial in the factory. Edith Stern overheard her telling Frankie that they need to "pitch" it correctly to the machinists.'

'What's that mean?' asks Irene.

'Oh! I know,' says Betty. 'At the fair when you pitch a ball to win a fluffy toy. You throw it and see what happens.'

'That's close, Betty,' says Merl, in her schoolteacher tone. 'But a better definition would be "hit the right note". They want to find a way to make it appealing.'

Quite honestly, Betty wouldn't care about Merl getting sacked, or Irene (who deserves to be sacked), but she would sacrifice herself to save Hazel's job. If someone so beloved by everyone in her firm can be sacked, then everybody is at risk. No one will be spared until the last tea lady disappears and people forget they ever existed. Like the dodo, which is only famous for being dead. In a blinding moment of insight, Betty can see the fate of tea ladies laid out before her.

'We are not going to be dodos,' she says.

Merl looks up from her egg and cress sandwich. 'I doubt we'll become extinct.'

'I'm not sure what you mean, Betty dear,' says Hazel.

Betty decides it's not worth explaining, especially with Merl and Irene ready to pounce on her. 'We have to make this strike big, so everyone knows about it.'

'Quite frankly, I can't see anyone getting too worked up about missing a cup of tea,' says Merl. 'It's not going to change management's mind.'

'Merl! Please stop. You're always the naysayer!' says Betty.

'I beg your pardon,' says Merl.

'Not granted,' says Betty huffily.

Irene snorts with laughter, coughing smoke over everyone.

'What about that Eileen Weston? I think we all liked the cut of her jib,' says Hazel. 'It would make a big difference if the union backed us.'

'They're all commies in there, yer know,' says Irene. 'Next thing yer'll be preaching with the reds.'

'If the communists can help us keep our jobs . . .' says Betty, even though she's a bit afraid of communists. Especially since they seem to like hiding out under people's beds.

'You know,' Merl begins thoughtfully, as she gets out her knitting. 'The dodo, since you brought it up, Betty, was a very simple trusting creature, one that didn't fight back. So, on reflection, you could be on to something. Complacency could be the end of us.'

'Thank you, Merl,' says Betty. 'We need the numbers. That's the problem.'

'I'll speak to Mr Kovac,' suggests Hazel. 'He delivers to dozens of tea ladies around town. I'm sure he'd be happy to spread the word.'

'What are you going to do, Irene?' asks Betty.

Irene takes a long thoughtful drag on her pipe. 'The usual. Bloody nuthin—' She pops her dentures out and sucks them back in again (still a little blue, Betty notices). 'I can tell some folk at the pub, I s'pose.'

'Actually, one of my neighbours works at the Department of Defence. They have a couple of dozen tea ladies there,' says Betty.

'I don't really associate with tea ladies,' says Merl.

'Lucky,' says Irene. 'Since yer won't be one soon.'

It seems that Merl has finally seen the light, because when Betty suggests they use the funds the Guild has raised to put an ad in the paper notifying tea ladies of the stop work meeting next week, she agrees without an argument.

For no apparent reason, Irene then proceeds to detail her recent bout of constipation. Halfway through this torturous account, Merl declares the conversation has reached rock-bottom, packs up her knitting and leaves in a huff.

'That's got rid of her,' says Irene.

'I'll bring you a bottle of my celery and prune wine,' offers Hazel, never one to be put off by the sordid details of Irene's digestive system.

'I was just getting to the high point of me story,' says Irene. 'It all came good this morning—'

'Glad to hear it,' interrupts Hazel.

'I was just trying to get rid of her Ladyship, so we can talk about me treasure.'

Betty hands her the piece of paper with the decoded message. Irene reads it, mouthing the words as she goes. 'Oh yeah, told yers it was the Kings Arms. Now what?'

'We need to get together with Mrs Li and Effie to work out a plan,' says Hazel.

Every time a meeting of the secret guild is called, Betty feels a shiver run through her body. She imagines a distant trumpeting, the bugle call to battle. She pictures an army of tea ladies tightening their pinnies and slipping on their rubber-soled shoes, ready to face danger with nothing more than a thermos of boiling water and a rolling pin to defend themselves. It brings tears of pride to her eyes to be a small part of the team. She shakes herself out of her reverie and gets up. 'I'll go and ring Effie from work.'

'Don't forget yer stink cushion,' Irene reminds her, giving it a nod.

'Thank you, Irene,' Betty sniffs. 'You know I'm prone to piles. And at least I don't bore everyone unnecessarily with details of my inner workings.'

For some reason, Irene finds this hilarious, cackling and coughing up smoke.

Betty tucks her cushion under her arm and stalks back to work, struggling to reclaim the vision of herself as a courageous and intrepid detective. She wishes she had been charged with a more challenging mission than a phone call, like following a suspect or placing a bug in a criminal mastermind's house, but she will call the secret guild to action, starting with Effie Finch.

# 21

# HAZEL MEETS THE ROBOT

For Hazel, the complex smells of the Chinese herbalist's shop have become synonymous with the activities of the secret guild, as Betty calls it. Stepping into the shop is like entering a different world, the air rich with unfamiliar smells, some sharp, others thick and cloying. These days, when they arrive, the men behind the counter glance up only briefly before returning their attention to their work.

In the cosy quiet of the back room, Hazel updates the others on their progress with Fred's coded message and Betty reads it out.

Irene tells them she now recalls they had their honeymoon in the Blue Mountains.

'Honeymoon?' echoes Betty, obviously finding it difficult to imagine this, but she nevertheless makes a note. 'And you didn't think of that earlier? It's not something you forget.'

'Fifty years ago, mate. I was seventeen, just a girl . . . Lost a bit of grey matter since then.' Irene gives a bark of laughter. 'Didn't have much to start with!'

'Would he go back after all this time to hide something?' asks Mrs Li doubtfully.

Hazel nods. 'It's a very long time ago. And why there?'

'He liked the place, I remember that much,' says Irene. 'Fred liked trees.'

'Everyone likes trees,' says Betty.

'Not that keen on them meself,' says Irene. 'But Fred . . . he loved trees.'

Effie speaks up. 'We need to do some reconnaissance. I'll drive us up there on Saturday, check the place out.'

'Not me,' says Irene.

'It's not happening without you, Irene,' says Effie.

Irene takes a swig from her flask and considers her options. 'How long will it take?'

'As long as it takes,' says Effie.

Not for the first time, Hazel's impressed by Effie's practical approach. She's just the person to keep Irene in line and get this mystery resolved.

'Not keen on creepy-crawlies neither,' adds Irene.

'Good heavens, Irene! Stop being such a sook!' says Betty.

'That's a joke coming from the world's biggest blubberer,' says Irene.

Betty sighs. 'I'll come with you.'

'I don't need yers looking after me, thanks very much,' says Irene irritably.

'I'm sorry I can't come,' says Hazel. 'I have a commitment on Saturday, but I'll be with you in spirit.'

'That's settled then,' says Effie. 'We'll leave at dawn on Saturday, back by sunset.'

'Dawn?' asks Betty but Irene doesn't argue, making do with a scowl.

'There's something else I'd like to bring to the group,' says Hazel.

'It's been on my mind for a while that there's something odd going on up at St Vincent's.'

'Is this to do with the convent?' asks Effie.

'It's more to do with Father Kelly, so I'm not sure. In fact . . .' She pauses before saying it out loud for the first time. 'I'm starting to be suspicious about Auntie Vera's death.'

Irene cackles with laughter. 'Yer think Kelly did her in?'

'I don't know. I'm not making any accusations, but Father Kelly has been behaving very strangely. The other day Mrs Mulligan and I ran into him with two visiting Catholic brothers, and I had the strongest feeling they're not who they say they are.' Hazel looks around at the others. 'My neighbour, young Maude, is now the priest's housekeeper and . . . that's why I'm particularly concerned.'

'How long has Father Kelly been at St Vincent's?' asks Mrs Li.

'Six months, I believe. Auntie Vera was with the previous priest for twenty years. When he died, Father Kelly came out from Ireland to replace him, and Auntie Vera stayed on.' Hazel pauses. 'These two brothers, Riley and O'Connell, seem to be living there but are not involved in the community, which is odd. Maude seems to think they have a lot of sway over Father Kelly. All of this makes me curious about what's really going on in that house.'

'I could organise a fire inspection of the presbytery, take a good look around,' suggests Effie. 'I often go along on the inspections.'

'They let the tea lady go on an official inspection?' asks Betty in disbelief.

Effie grins. 'Don't forget I was in the Women's Auxiliary Corps during the war. They don't let women into the fire service now, but I've got a lot more experience than some of the youngsters. The chief gets me to keep an eye out.'

Hazel smiles to herself at the thought of a strapping young fireman going off to an inspection with the tea lady along to supervise. Each of these women is very different but they're a surprisingly good combination. 'That's a start,' she says. 'I think we need to find out exactly who these men are, and why they're here.'

Jørn Utzon and his failed attempt to retain control of the Opera House project have been in the news all week. Hazel had watched the press announcement of his severing from the project on the television in Gibson's shop window, and her heart went out to this young man. His brilliant smile had lit up his face, but now he looks worried and worn out. She can only imagine the fierce arguments that have taken place behind closed doors. The Minister for Public Works, Davis Hughes, never misses an opportunity to reiterate his opinion that Utzon is an 'impractical dreamer' incapable of completing the project, but Hazel wonders how he plans to finish the building without a dream.

Assembling her trolley on a warm Friday morning, Hazel considers what might happen to Oscar. Up until now, his only concern has been for his friend and colleague. But if Utzon leaves the project and returns to Denmark, Oscar may well go with him. Either because his contract is cancelled, or he may feel he has to resign in solidarity.

When she spoke to him earlier in the week, he had a renewed sense of optimism, hoping the dispute could be resolved. There were plans for a protest in the streets around the site and he seemed to think that public opinion had swayed in support of Utzon. But if there is one thing Hazel has learned over the years, it's that people may appear to be surrounded by supporters but that can be misleading, especially when there are hidden political forces involved.

It was always a risk for her getting involved with a foreigner, she knew that. But Oscar has slowly but surely won her heart and saying goodbye to him will be difficult. She wonders if she should see him again or step away now. Before she has time to reach any conclusion, Edith Stern appears at the door of the kitchen.

'Edith? This is a nice surprise,' says Hazel, glancing up from her trolley.

'You'll change your mind when you hear what I have to say,' says Edith. 'Dottie left a note to say that you don't need to do the tea service in the factory this morning. They installed a Café-bar last night and a chap is coming to demonstrate to the girls during tea break today.'

Hazel is momentarily lost for words. Out of habit, her eyes skim the half-assembled trolley. 'That's very sudden,' she says finally. 'It would have been nice to give me some notice.'

'Everything happens overnight with Dottie. According to her, it's a trial.'

'I don't really understand the urgency. Anyway, let's go and watch this demonstration ourselves. We need to understand the competition,' suggests Hazel.

Edith nods. 'I feel awful about it. Just awful.'

Hazel smiles. 'It's not your fault, Edith. Save your energy for something you are guilty of.'

'Humph, where do I start?' says Edith dryly.

They walk down the hallway and in through the double doors of the factory as the buzzer goes for the break. The machinists stop their work and get to their feet, the sight of Hazel without her trolley immediately causing confusion.

'Hazel?' says Gloria, walking over. 'What's happening?'

'I think we're about to find out,' says Hazel.

The double doors swing open. Dottie appears, wearing a smart grey suit with a tight skirt and high heels. Her companion looks as if he would be more comfortable on a rugby field. Compressed into a maroon double-breasted suit, he has the wide grin of a salesman.

'Gather around, girls!' calls Dottie.

Hazel notices a table has been put against the wall near the bundy clock. Something the size of a car engine sits on it, covered in a tablecloth. The machinists move reluctantly towards Dottie as she beckons them forward.

'What the hell is the mad cow up to now?' Gloria murmurs. Lighting a cigarette, she blows a disdainful stream of smoke in Dottie's direction.

'An exciting announcement, girls,' says Dottie. 'Tea and coffee. Hot chocolate. Anytime you like. All day, every day. Let me introduce Mr Dexter.'

'What an attractive bunch of ladies!' Mr Dexter says, grinning at them. 'You lovely ladies are going to love this new machine that will make your lives so much easier. And you'll be pleased to know this is an all-Australian invention, now taking over the world.'

Dottie removes the cloth, revealing what looks like several metal boxes piled on top of one another. The largest is at the top, and below it is a row of handles, a slot for cups and a tray to catch spills. Looking it over, Hazel feels the cold hand of the future rest on her shoulder. She'd always been amused by the talk of robots taking over people's jobs. They had even joked about a robot delivering tea, which seemed preposterous, but here it is.

'This is a hot beverage dispenser, at your disposal all day,' explains Mr Dexter. 'No more dealing with the grumpy tea lady.

No more having to beg for another cuppa.' Despite the silence in the room, he chuckles at his own joke.

Dottie accidentally meets Hazel's eye and quickly glances away.

'Who would like to try the first hot beverage?' he asks, looking around. When there are no takers, he cries, 'Come on, ladies. This is a historic moment. In years to come you'll be boasting that you had the first ever hot beverage from this dispenser.'

Gloria steps forward, a cigarette dangling off her lip. 'I'll try it.'

Relieved, Mr Dexter demonstrates the various features, finally delivering a cup of instant coffee into her hand. 'Try it,' he urges. 'I think you'll be impressed.' Pointing to each dial, he continues. 'We have three options: coffee, powdered tea – the latest innovation – and hot chocolate.'

Gloria takes a sip. Looking puzzled, she takes another. 'I don't mean to be rude, but is this tea or coffee?'

Mr Dexter has a quick glance at the dials. 'Coffee, of course.'

'It tastes like tea *and* coffee.' Gloria hands the cup back to him. 'We'll stick with our grumpy tea lady, thanks all the same.'

A big laugh from all the machinists relieves the tension in the room, but Dottie is clearly not amused.

Undaunted, Mr Dexter continues. 'Girls, this machine is here on trial for a month. Once you get used to it, you'll see it's very convenient.'

'Do we still get tea breaks?' asks Gloria.

Glancing around, Dottie's self-assurance falters briefly. 'Yes, of course.'

Mr Dexter grins. 'Now you can help yourselves. No need to wait for the break.'

Raising a sceptical eyebrow, Gloria wanders back to her alcove without another word. Several machinists (darting apologetic looks at Hazel) try the Café-bar. The rest go back to their workstations without morning tea and start their machines.

Hazel and Edith slip back to the privacy of the kitchen.

'What can we do, Hazel?' asks Edith.

Hazel gives a sigh. 'Continue as usual for the moment. I feel terrible that they've all gone back to work without a cuppa. But if there is no other choice, they will all eventually come round to it.'

Edith nods. 'That's what Dottie's counting on. The only choices are *her* choices. Dottie the Dictator.'

Hazel glances at her watch and goes to the cupboard. 'Before I go upstairs, I'll just duck around the factory with the biscuit tin, keep everyone's spirits up.'

'I never thought I'd say this, but I think they deserve "upstairs biscuits" today,' says Edith.

## 22

# IRENE TAKES A TRIP

'Mrs Turnbuckle!'

Almost leaping out of her skin, Irene stamps her foot hard on the button of the vacuum cleaner and gives Miss Palmer her full attention. She watches her employer (in a lime green jacket and tight pants the same colour) stalk down the hallway towards her.

'We've discussed this already, Mrs Turnbuckle. You can't simply flick a dirty rag around and call it dusting. Polish is what we need. Polish as a verb.'

Irene has no idea what the silly woman is on about but accepts the can of Mr Sheen being waggled in her face and puts it in the front pocket of her pinny.

'Clean cloth. Spray, then wipe it down,' continues Miss Palmer, miming the action as if Irene doesn't understand English.

'Anything else?' Irene asks, keeping a polite smile pasted on her face.

Clearly impressed with Irene's dentures, Miss Palmer stares at them for a long moment. Then she frowns. 'And please do not hang around gossiping with my girls. And those expensive Cuban cigars are for the clientele – not you. Just do your job and stay out of sight.'

Irene nods. She'll cut back on the cigars but has no intention of giving up her chats with the girls; they've taken quite a shine to her. Miss Palmer's probably jealous.

'Be more invisible. That's part of your job. Be like the little elves that appear in the night to make shoes for the shoemaker.'

Irene wonders if Miss Palmer is on drugs but nods again anyway. 'I'll be the elves.'

'Thank you. More shine and less visibility,' says Madam, walking off.

Irene is in fact enjoying being invisible, more like a ghost than an elf, and congratulating herself every day on having scored free board in a luxury mansion. The only tiny thing she doesn't like is that her room in the attic only has one window, and it's in the ceiling. Ideally, she likes to clear her lungs with a healthy hoick out the window first thing. Other than that, the attic is ideal. It's hidden away and a good size. The bed takes up half the room and she's got the rest to chuck her stuff over. It smells a bit if she goes to work and forgets to empty her potty (worse if she leaves a number two sitting there in this heat), but it's cosy and she's very comfy there.

Even though Miss Palmer is very particular, Irene has a lot of respect for her. It might be an illegal business, but she runs it professionally. It's the thinking behind the whole operation and the shrewd cover of the secretarial school that impresses Irene more than anything. Easy to explain all the attractive young women coming and going through the front door, and no one's any the wiser about the visitors through the side entrance. Everyone knows it's a knocking shop, but the important thing is that it's not making the Vice Squad look bad. It's discreet.

Irene knew from the outset this was an upper-class establishment. The front parlour has been turned into a private bar where clients are offered drinks and can chat with the girls while they decide who to have it off with. Other brothels might have the ladies hanging around in negligees, but Miss Palmer's tarts wear fancy frocks or cocktail dresses and jewellery. It's more like a nightclub than the average knocking shop.

The house is empty when Irene cleans, so she's been able to have a good stickybeak around the rooms. Most of them are smallish with a big bed and a lot of fancy wallpaper covered in more bloody peacocks. Then there's the Royal Suite, which is twice the size of the others, with a four-poster bed and everything decked out in green and gold. It's like a bedroom in a castle, apart from the locked cupboard (which she took the liberty of opening), which holds the whips and handcuffs, as well as a studded dog's collar on a chain and various nasty-looking bits and pieces. If only she had a peep hole into this room – that'd be a laugh!

Halfway up the winding back stairs is a small window. Sitting in the dark, Irene has a decent view of the side gate and who comes in and out. In just a few days, she's already recognised the local mayor and two SP bookies. On Friday afternoon, before opening, Irene recognised a bloke from the Vice Squad who turned up to collect a nice fat envelope. There's long breaks between sightings, but it's worth the wait.

She's not keen on the cleaning side of things, dragging the vacuum cleaner up and down the carpeted stairs and along hallways and having to stop all the time to plug the thing in on each floor. Today's not the first telling off she's had from Miss Fussypants, who goes on as if she's expecting a Health Department raid. It's pretty obvious these blokes are not here to check the standards of hygiene.

But Madam is the boss and Irene doesn't want to get kicked out and end up back at that lousy boarding house.

On Saturday morning she sets her alarm and gets up early to make sure the place is done before Effie Finch picks her up. As Irene heaves the vacuum cleaner up the stairs, she thinks about how odd it'll be going back to the Blue Mountains decades after her honeymoon. She and Fred had a few good years before they went their own ways after he came back from the war. Got back together a couple of times. Plenty of other blokes in between. Poor ol' Fred. Would have been nice to see him before he carked it. At least he could have given her the message directly, instead of all this kerfuffle. On top of that, she wouldn't have to share the loot with the others and waste it on a bunch of no-hoper orphans.

Dawn, not being Irene's favourite time of day, turns out to be surprisingly nice. As she stands waiting on the street for her ride, there's a pinkish glow in the sky and little birds chirping. Hearing a roaring in the distance, she looks up the street to see an old green army jeep with no roof coming towards her, Effie in the driver's seat.

The jeep stops in a belch of smoke in front of Irene, and she gets into the passenger seat. She gives Effie's khaki overalls the once-over but decides to keep her opinion to herself.

'What a day!' Effie shouts over the crashing of gears and roar of the engine as they take off.

Irene shrugs. She's not keen on these cheerful conversations and is worried about losing her good hat. She squashes it down a bit tighter on her head and grips the sides of the seat. Effie drove fire engines back in the war, and you'd think they were going to a fire now the way she throws the jeep around corners. She gnashes through the gears like a getaway driver and the whole operation shakes and rattles. Irene's got her doubts as to whether this bucket of bolts will make it up to the mountains.

They pull up at Betty's house to find the silly goose standing outside in a pink and white frock and a big white sunhat with two daisies growing out of it. She has a basket, like someone off to the church fete. The look on her face at the sight of Effie's vehicle is priceless.

Irene gets out of the car to help Betty into the very small back seat and cops a scolding for her troubles.

'Irene! I can't believe you're wearing your slippers and your pinny! We're going to the countryside, for goodness sake!'

'I don't know why yer trussed up like a bloody . . . cream cake. Just get in, will yer?'

'Now, now, girls,' says Effie. 'We're on a mission. We need to watch out for each other and work as a team.'

Irene and Effie wait while Betty huffs and puffs her way into the back seat with her bottom in the air. Finally, she's right way up and they head off.

'I've got a map,' Betty shouts, leaning forward between them. 'A topographical map!' She pushes a large, crumpled map, covered in fine wavy lines and dots, into Irene's hands.

After staring at it for a moment, Irene feels sick and passes it back to Betty. The wind catches the flapping map and wraps it around Betty's face. She gives a scream and starts wrestling with the thing. A minute later it flies out the back of the car.

Irene watches it toss about before getting caught in a tree, hanging there like a broken kite. 'That's that then,' she says.

'Irene! You did that deliberately!' cries Betty. 'That cost me two dollars.'

'Don't worry. I have a compass!' bellows Effie over her shoulder. 'We'll be right!'

'Two dollars!' shrieks Betty.

Irene feels tired already. She reaches into the pocket of her pinny for her flask. It doesn't feel right in her grip. Too round. Taking it out, she discovers it's the can of Mr Sheen. She puts it back with a sigh. It's going to be a long day. There better be a pot of gold waiting up in those mountains. Bloody Fred.

## 23

# HAZEL GETS THE TINGLES

There's a damp freshness in the air as Hazel enters the grounds of the convent. The sprinklers have been on overnight and the garden is thriving despite weeks of heat. She looks across to the presbytery but there's no sign of Maude.

Sister Ruth waits at the long table in the library, a stack of books at her side. She looks up with a smile when Hazel arrives. 'I saw you chatting with Maude the other day. How's she getting on?'

Hazel's not sure how much to reveal. She sits down and takes a moment to gather herself. 'I think it's difficult for her, coming from such a big, noisy family to the quiet of the presbytery. She's been kept very busy with Father Kelly's guests.'

'Oh yes, they've been here a little while. I've only met them briefly. Normally visiting clergy come and inspect the convent, but perhaps they're too busy for the moment.'

'So they're quite recent arrivals?' asks Hazel, fishing for more detail.

'Just after Auntie Vera died, I think. It's good that Father Kelly has company right now. Apart from Maude, I mean.'

'I know what you mean, Sister. Maude couldn't hope to replace the counsel Auntie Vera offered the Father.'

Sister Ruth ponders this for a moment. 'Auntie Vera had been a priest's housekeeper for longer than Father Kelly had been a priest. Having a housekeeper without any experience has probably unsettled him. I suppose we didn't realise how dependent he was on her. He must miss her terribly. We all do.' She turns to the pile of books. 'I thought we could start one of these books and read a little bit each time you come.'

She passes Hazel the book from the top of the pile and picks up a wooden ruler, the sight of which makes Hazel flinch.

Sister Ruth looks horrified. 'Oh, I'm so sorry, Mrs Bates! I didn't think . . . I never use a ruler on the children, so I don't think of it as . . . well, a weapon. I promise you, I don't believe in corporal punishment. There are a few teachers here who don't strap the children, and I'm one of them.'

'Thank goodness for that,' says Hazel, feeling more shaken than she would have expected. 'I remember one particular teacher . . . I would go home with my knuckles bleeding and be in trouble with my mother. I tried so many times to explain that the words wouldn't stay still, dancing over the top of each other, but I suppose she thought that was just a child's silly excuses—'

'But it wasn't, Mrs Bates, not at all. This ruler is not for keeping children in line, it's for keeping words in line.'

Hazel takes it from her. She places it under the top line of text on the first page and slowly reads the words, sounding each one out as Sister Ruth has taught her. By the end of their session, she has read two whole pages and leaves the library exhausted but jubilant at the same time. Walking through the portico, looking forward to a cup of tea at home, Hazel sees Father Kelly coming towards her, head bowed as though deep in thought.

'Good morning, Father Kelly,' she says, as he draws close.

He looks up with a start. 'Good morning, Mrs Bates, isn't it? I didn't see you there . . . I was off in a world of my own, writing tomorrow's sermon in my head.' He gives a laugh, but behind his black-rimmed spectacles, his eyes are unsmiling. 'What a day our Lord has sent for us to enjoy. Nice to see you again and good day to you.' Without waiting for an answer, he strides off down the walkway and disappears into the convent building.

Hazel watches him leave, her ears tingling. Was he lying about writing the sermon in his head? If so, why bother saying it?

Oscar is waiting at Circular Quay when Hazel arrives on Sunday morning. He greets her with a kiss. She takes his arm, and they join the queue for the ferry. The harbour sparkles under a clear blue sky and there is an air of celebration onboard: children with towels looped around their necks, buckets and spades at the ready; mothers armed with picnic baskets; fathers carrying beach umbrellas. A perfect Sydney day for the beach.

They find a quiet spot on the southern side of the ferry for a view of the giant shells of the Opera House as they pass. Every time she sees it, Hazel is struck by the majesty of the building, the size and scale. More tiles have been laid on the shell structure and the building gleams in the sun.

Oscar takes her hand. 'There was a final meeting on Friday between Jørn and Hughes. It did not go so well.' He shakes his head. 'His only option to remain on the project is as a member of the design team with no control. This is unacceptable to him and so his resignation is final.'

'Oh dear. The ultimatum seems to have backfired.'

Oscar sighs. 'I think Jørn did exactly what this government wanted him to do. They understood that he would not agree to the contractors and materials being chosen by tender, where he would be forced to accept the lowest price. This building is not an office block, the cheapest materials are not always suitable. Unfortunately, while Jørn was away on holiday, the press began to turn against him. They don't have any good news, so they feast on bad news. The costs, the time and the belief that this building is indulgent.'

Hazel watches the white shells fade into the distance. 'It will be one of the most beautiful buildings in the world, Oscar.'

He gives a chuckle. 'You told me you are making jigsaws of the seven wonders of the world, so I know you are an authority in this area.'

Hazel laughs. 'Yes, I know a good building when I see it. When it's finished, they will make jigsaws of this building. And you'll be able to say you had a part in making it.'

'I hope so,' agrees Oscar, gazing into the distance.

Children run past, tripping over their feet. Parents call them to order. Small yachts skim along on the bright surface of the water. As Manly Beach comes into view, Hazel asks the question she doesn't want to ask. 'Will you have to go home?'

He sighs and leans over to kiss her forehead. 'I hope not. They may send all the Danes home with Jørn, but that would be foolish. The acoustics are one of the most important parts of the building. No matter how beautiful it is on the outside, the sound on the inside could be a disaster. I hope I will be kept on.' After a moment, he adds, 'If I cannot stay, perhaps you could come back to Denmark with me.'

Hazel laughs out loud in surprise. 'I don't think it will come to that!'

Oscar gives her his twinkling smile. 'Let's wait and see.'

# 24

# BETTY HEADS FOR THE HILLS

Betty has always wanted to go to the Blue Mountains (ideally not with Irene) and was keen to look her best for the outing. So it was disappointing to see Irene in her usual grubby get-up, and Effie looking ready to parachute into enemy territory. But now, thundering along in this open vehicle, there's no doubt in her mind that a headscarf would have been a better choice than the hat. The turbulence in the back seat (obviously designed with a small child in mind, not a full-bodied woman) is like being in the eye of a storm. She grips her hat with both hands. If it comes off, her set will be ruined. Her excellent map, which she studied in detail last night, is now lost to the wind. It's just fortunate it didn't get caught on someone's windscreen and cause a nasty accident. On top of all that, she baked some Melting Moments for the occasion and now the tin peeks temptingly out of her basket. If only she could let go of her hat.

As they head up the mountains, the twisting road makes her feel increasingly carsick. When she risks reaching for her antacids, the hat is peeled from her head and goes the way of the map. She twists around in her seat to see where it lands, the optimist in her hoping they might stop and pick it up on the way home. But, following its trajectory, she sees something that makes her forget the hat altogether.

'Effie! Effie!' Betty has to shout over the engine as it strains up the steep incline.

'How are you going back there?' Effie bellows.

'Don't turn around, but we're being followed!'

'Yer imagining it, Betty,' says Irene, half turning in her seat. 'Bloody hell. If it's not yer bloody ailments, it's somethink else.'

Betty leans forward between the front seats. 'When the map blew away, I just happened to see this car – and before you say anything, Irene, you know I have excellent observational skills – and I just turned around to see where my hat went and the same car is still behind us, almost an hour later.'

'Could be a coincidence,' says Effie. 'Only one road in and out.'

'But all the way from Surry Hills? I don't think so,' says Betty. 'Don't look round, Irene!'

'Betty, how else am I gunna see the bloody thing? Don't have eyes in the back of me head, yer know,' grumbles Irene.

'You don't need to. It's a dark blue Ford Fairlane. I can't read the number plate, it's too far away.'

Effie looks over at Irene (her eyes off the road a little too long for Betty's liking). 'You know it?' she asks. 'The Fairlane?'

'I seen one in Lisbon Street a couple of times. A couple of blokes sitting in it. Thought it might be Vice Squad. Plain-clothes coppers have Fairlanes.'

'The Vice Squad would not bother following us all the way up here,' says Effie.

'I don't know about that,' interjects Betty. 'Irene has quite a lot of vices.'

Effie finds this very funny and roars with laughter, much to Betty's annoyance.

'It could be Detective Pierce,' says Betty, desperate to turn around and look.

'Doubt it. Can't see Pierce putting in the effort,' shouts Irene.

Betty, exhausted from having to compete with the engine and crashing gears, has to agree. 'You're right. What if he's hired some thugs to knock us off?'

'Woah there!' says Effie. 'No one's going to knock us off. We're going to stop for a cuppa up a bit further and see what they do. Let's all keep calm and pretend we haven't noticed them.'

Ten minutes later, to Betty's great relief (her bladder is ready to pop), they pull off the road and stop outside a lovely little teashop. Effie turns off the ignition and, after a couple of shudders, the car falls silent. Out of the corner of her eye, Betty sees the Fairlane slow for a moment and then continue up the road.

'All that wind, my tinnitus is like an air-raid siren,' Betty tells the other two.

Neither take any notice or even pretend sympathy and Betty wishes Hazel was there to say the right thing about Betty's lost map and hat, her upset tummy and her ears driving her mad. But she's not, so Betty makes her way quickly to the restroom and, once that's out of the way, feels a little better about the situation. They sit at a small table near the window. There's a pretty view of hills and bushland and she feels calmed by nature. A waitress comes and takes their order for a pot of tea.

'Now, Betty,' says Effie. 'No one's planning to kill us, so forget that.'

Betty nods. After Hazel, Effie is the second most sensible person she knows. Betty gets out her notebook and writes that down to remind herself to forget that idea.

'If Pierce knows Fred has left something behind and thinks that you know the location of it, I'm surprised he hasn't brought you in for questioning. I hear you're living at 555 now.'

Irene nods. 'Safest place in the district.'

Effie looks doubtful. 'Not if another tart shop wants to put that Palmer woman out of business. I hope you've got a fire escape.'

'Irene's more likely to start a fire than be the victim of one,' explains Betty, and Irene agrees. Their tea arrives and Betty offers the others a Melting Moment from her tin. Irene takes two and lights a cigarette.

'If Pierce is watching you, he's probably expecting you to lead him to a safe deposit box,' says Effie.

Betty nibbles thoughtfully on her biscuit. 'Or a locker at the railway station.'

'There must be a good amount of cash for him to be interested,' muses Effie. 'And because it's a cold case, he's got time to chase it.'

Irene's quiet. In Betty's experience that means she has a devious plan of her own. 'What do you think, Irene?' she asks.

'Dunno,' Irene says with a shrug. 'As I said, Pierce could bring in the jewels and palm the cash. Or he could get rid of the jewels.'

Effie agrees. 'Anyway, if we see them again, we'll shake them off before we get close to the Kings Arms. Leave that to me.'

Effie's clearly enjoying herself and, as far as Betty is concerned, if anyone can get them out of this fix, it's her.

They buy a new tourist map at the teashop (which Effie pays for) and get back in the jeep. Irene nabs the front seat once more and Betty heroically resists the urge to squabble over it, vowing that Irene will not get it on the way home. Assuming they make it home.

After studying the map silently for a few minutes, Effie hands it to Irene and sets off, driving slowly. There aren't many places to pull off the road now and Betty expects to see the Fairlane around every corner. Sure enough, there it is parked at the lookout, looking towards the mountain view. Effie continues on for another mile or two, but when she spies a narrow road to their right, without warning, she swings off the main road and puts her foot down.

If Betty thought the back seat was uncomfortable before, it is so much worse on an unsealed road. Dust billows behind them. Betty wants to ask Effie to slow down but has her hankie pressed over her mouth for fear of choking. Sharp bits of gravel flick up from the wheels, stinging her arms. She tries squeezing herself down to half lie on the seat, only to be bounced about so badly she sits up again before she's sick. This awful experience continues for some time until they hit a smooth sealed surface again. They stop and look at the map and then off they go again. Eventually, Effie pulls onto the grass verge and noses the vehicle in behind some trees.

'This is Delsdon Road. The Kings Arms is about a mile up that way.' Effie jabs a thumb over her shoulder in the direction of the main road. 'So we should be close.'

All Betty wants to do right now is sink into a warm bubble bath and cry, but she gets out of the car, bruised and aching, dusts herself off and follows Effie and Irene.

Effie looks up and down the empty road. Nothing but bushland and a couple of houses in the distance in each direction. 'Fred said a mile down the road from the pub. Hard to gauge it exactly without driving it. You'd imagine he'd be pretty accurate with these estimates, being a safecracker and all. Irene, anything here seem at all familiar?'

Irene stares around her. 'There was a lot of trees, I remember that.'

Effie gives her an exasperated look. 'Anything else? Think, Irene.'

'We were pretty pissed . . . but I remember Fred liked all the nature.'

'Irene, try a bit harder, please,' says Betty. 'We've heard this before.'

'The cicadas . . . I remember an owl . . .' Irene says in a dreamy voice. 'White face.'

Betty sighs. 'I'm sure the owl has flown away by now so that's not helpful.'

'I don't know about that,' says Effie. 'Owls tend to stay in the same territory.'

'Let's walk down here a bit,' Betty suggests, pointing further down the road.

Her sandals are not designed for gravel roads, she now discovers. (Even Irene's slippers seem to be better suited to the terrain than these silly shoes.) But she plods along, uncomplaining, one foot in front of the other. Then she stops, noticing something. 'Irene, did you bring the stone?'

'Nah, Hazel's got it – why?'

'Look at the sides of the road. The stones are the same pinky-gold colour.'

This seems a heartening indication that they're on the right track, but Irene couldn't care less. She stops from time to time and stares at a tree, usually a gum tree. There's no shortage of them. Every size and shape with different trunks and coloured bark. Betty's hopes rise when Irene stares at one for an inordinate amount of time. But then she walks on.

After an hour or so of this, Irene says, 'Wouldn't have a clue. These bloody trees all look the same.'

'Irene!' cries Betty. 'That's not true. They're different types and sizes. Concentrate.'

'All right, clever clogs, you find the bloody thing then. Anyway, the one he's on about could've fallen down by now.'

Irene's hopeless in this state of mind. Exasperated, Betty swings around and snaps at her. 'I don't think so. Fred was away for five years, but that robbery was in 1960, so it must have been here then. These things live for hundreds of years. Look, that's a very big gum there,' she points out. 'Very big, and it's close to the road. That might have caught his eye.'

'Let's go and explore inland,' suggests Effie. 'I'd like to see that owl.'

Leaving the road, they walk through the long grass, which Betty imagines is riddled with snakes – and her in sandals. The sun is beating down on her head and she could kick herself for being so unprepared. She follows Effie's giant footsteps and Irene follows behind her, complaining that she doesn't like grass, let alone long grass.

They wander around, more like a grumpy queue at the post office than intrepid explorers. After what seems like hours, Betty spots something that looks like a hideaway kiddies might build in the bush, made of branches all woven together. She points it out to Effie and the queue moves to gather in front of it.

Bending down to look inside, Effie gets on her knees and pulls out a swag, or what's left of it. The thing's in tatters and an army of insects and giant cockroaches swarm out. Undeterred, Effie crawls inside the hut.

'Watch out for snakes!' calls Betty. 'And spiders. And bull ants.'

A few minutes later, Effie crawls out with a metal box under her arm and gets to her feet. 'Here we go. The big moment,' she says, setting it down on a fallen tree.

Betty giggles, her heart beating wildly. 'A treasure chest! Go on, Effie. Open it.'

'It's not locked,' says Irene suspiciously.

When Effie opens the lid they all bump heads in the rush to peer inside. She lifts out a copy of *White Fang*, a packet of tobacco and some rolling papers, a torch and a lighter.

'He was very keen on Jack London,' observes Effie, examining the book with interest.

'That tobacco will be stuffed,' says Irene.

Betty bubbles over with disappointment. 'Where are the jewels? I thought there'd be rubies and diamonds.'

Unfazed, Effie glances around at the bushland and suggests that maybe Fred just wanted Irene to enjoy the majesty of nature, since he obviously made a habit of coming up here. Irene, grumpier than ever, says she can enjoy the majesty of nature every time she goes to the dunny, she doesn't need to come all the way out here for it.

They walk back to the jeep in silence. Effie suggests a drink at the Kings Arms before they go home, and that cheers everyone up.

The hotel is quite nice, all polished timber and brass. There're only a couple of people inside and, even better, it's cool and clean. They can sit down and be perfectly still for a spell.

Betty insists she'll buy the drinks, since Effie is doing the driving. Standing at the bar, she feels crushed by fatigue and disappointment.

While she waits, she idly watches a man in his fifties help his elderly mother up and usher her gently to the door. The sight gives Betty a pang of a deeper disappointment that she doesn't have a son, or anyone to look after her when she's old and frail (which feels closer today). As the pair make their way out the front doors, Betty leans over, not wanting to lose sight of this heart-warming scene. The man helps the old lady down the front steps and into a dark blue Ford Fairlane parked out the front.

Betty stares at the car for a long moment and glances over her shoulder. Irene and Effie haven't noticed anything, and she plans to keep it that way.

## 25

# HAZEL MAKES A PROPOSAL

As Hazel waits for Mr Kovac to deliver the weekly tea and biscuits supplies, she looks up and down Zig Zag Lane with renewed affection. Many of the cobbles, badly repaired over the years, are broken in places. There are scattered scraps of fabric and cardboard boxes flattened by delivery vans, and a sparkling trail of sequins along the centre gutter. She has an overwhelming sense that a chapter in her life is ending, something she's felt before at different times. It's as though this life is slowly being pulled from her grasp. Sooner or later, it will be gone, and she wonders what she will do with her days.

When Mr Kovac arrives, he hops out of his van with his usual cheery smile, hair slicked neatly to one side and, as always, his shoes polished to a brilliant shine. They greet each other and remark on the heat while he opens the back doors of his van, gets out a trolley and stacks boxes onto it. He follows Hazel down the hallway, where she opens the door to the storeroom for him, as she has done hundreds of times before.

As he unloads the trolley, Hazel asks, 'Mr Kovac, have you heard about this new machine some places are putting in? The Café-bar?'

Mr Kovac says nothing for a moment. He slowly puts the last box down and turns to her. 'I have been asked to deliver the supplies for these machines. They seem to be catching on, I fear.'

'It's already underway here,' says Hazel. 'There's a machine installed in the factory.'

'I see. What do the ladies think about the quality of the tea and coffee? I think it is not good.' He steps out of the storeroom to allow Hazel to lock the door.

'Well, they don't like the taste, but they're not being given a choice,' says Hazel as they walk down the hall together. 'I've been taking them morning tea on the quiet – just to keep them going through to lunchtime.'

Out in the laneway, Mr Kovac lifts his trolley into the back of the van. 'In the office where my wife works, they have a canteen. Now the tea lady has gone, the staff have to go to the canteen for their tea. My wife said they spend most of their tea break standing in a queue.'

Hazel shakes her head. 'Not really an improvement in "productivity".'

'I don't want to deliver for these machines.' Mr Kovac gestures up the laneway. 'Mrs Turnbuckle, Mrs Dewsnap, Mrs Perlman, and many more lovely ladies, you are all friends to me. It will be a sad day if we lose these ladies who care for the workers.'

Hazel sighs. 'Mr Kovac, if you don't take the delivery job, then someone else will get that contract and it'll be too late for you. You have to think of your family and your business. Things are changing and we all need to think ahead.'

'Oi! Mate! Mrs Bates is not yer only customer!' comes a shrill voice from down the lane. 'Yer can't stand there yakking all day while the rest of us are waiting for yers.'

Very used to Irene's funny ways, Mr Kovac gives her a friendly wave. 'I'll be there in a moment, Mrs Turnbuckle.'

Hazel smiles. 'At least the tea machine doesn't shout at people.'

'But it does not give good advice either.'

'Actually, Mr Kovac, there is something you could do to help us,' says Hazel.

'Of course, Mrs Bates. Anything for you.'

After she's done a quick round in the factory, Hazel takes two cups of tea and a plate of biscuits into the old stockroom where Alice and Pixie have set themselves up at a long table. Alice is working on the new designs and Pixie is squinting at the stock sheets – which are not normally allowed to leave Accounts. Pixie accepts her tea with a tired smile. Alice gives Hazel a nod and turns back to her drawings.

Hazel looks from one to the other. 'Are you two getting any sleep?'

Pixie leans back in her chair. 'Sleep is for oldies,' she declares, taking a sip of tea. 'Sorry, Mrs Bates.'

Hazel laughs. 'You'll look like an oldie if you don't get more of it.'

'We could screen-print that on a T-shirt,' says Alice. 'Sleep When You're Old.'

'Hmm . . . you might regret that later in life,' suggests Hazel. 'When you're old, for example. To live to be old is a privilege, not an . . . affliction.'

The two young women exchange smiles, as if they know something she doesn't, reminding Hazel that she also believed she would always be young. It comes as a rude shock to everyone, it seems.

Pixie picks up the pile of stock sheets. 'Mr Levy is helping me learn all the tricky bits of the business. That's making me feel old.'

The door opens and they turn towards it in alarm. This reaction seems to have become a habit with everyone since Dottie started roaming the building. Fortunately, it's only Gloria with a box of fabric samples and trims. She dumps the box on the table, and she and Alice and Pixie look over cards of tiny pearls, diamantes, sequins and fabric samples. Alice places one of the fabric samples and a length of beading next to one of her designs and Hazel can immediately see the final garment: a sleeveless shift in pale-pink polished cotton with a high neckline, and a strip of pearl beading at the neck. The length is closer to the hip than the knee. Simple and modern, but daring at the same time.

While the three young ones discuss the design, Hazel pops back to the kitchen and brings Gloria a cup of coffee.

Gloria takes it from her with a sigh. 'Oh, Hazel, I appreciate this more than ever after tasting that dishwater from the machine. I'm sure upstairs will see sense at some point and get rid of that thing.'

'I wouldn't be so sure,' says Pixie. 'I overheard Dottie on the phone saying there's another machine going into Accounts next week. We need to do something. Before it's too late.'

Everyone nods emphatically, but then they turn back to the designs and the moment passes.

Hazel can't remember when she was in such a fluster. As soon as she gets home, she has a bath and washes her hair. Then it's upstairs to put clean sheets on the bed and make sure the room is tidy. Back downstairs to make sure the chicken à la king is doing what it should be doing. Into the front room to check it's still as tidy as when she checked it ten minutes earlier.

When Oscar arrives, she tries to appear calm but he's barely in

the door before he rests his hands on her shoulders and says, 'Something smells delicious, but when I said don't put yourself to trouble,
I did mean it. I am not a prince. Just a simple man.'

'Oh, it's really no trouble,' says Hazel.

Oscar touches his ear. 'I feel . . . what do you call it? A tingle?'

Hazel laughs and they walk down the hall to the kitchen. Oscar
puts a bottle of white wine on the table. Hazel hands him the cork-
screw and gets out two wineglasses.

'Shall we sit in the front room?' she asks.

Oscar shrugs. 'If you prefer, but I'm very comfortable here. It's
near the food and you – that's all I need.'

Hazel nods with a smile. She never knows what to make of
these charming comments, though her ears tell her they are quite
genuine.

They settle themselves at the table. Oscar tips his glass to hers
and she takes a sip of wine. Just as she starts to relax, she hears the
telltale click of the back gate and a moment later Maude appears.

'Mrs Bates!' she calls. 'Oh, sorry.' She stares at Oscar for a
second and turns her gaze to Hazel as if she hasn't seen him.

'Maude, this is my friend Mr Sorensen,' says Hazel. 'Maude
lives next door.'

'Ah, you must be the young woman Hazel told me about, who
is working for the priest.' Oscar stands and shakes Maude's hand.
'Pleased to meet you.'

Maude, who clearly has something on her mind, gives him a
curt nod. 'Mrs B, there's some funny things going on in the house.
I don't know what to make of them.'

'Sit down, dear. Can I get you some tea?'

'That's all right, thanks,' says Maude, pulling up a chair at the
table. 'This afternoon there was a phone call from Auntie Vera's

sister, who lives in Adelaide. She didn't come to the funeral because she's got some medical problem and she was in hospital for an operation. She told me all about it, but I've forgotten. Anyway, she wants Auntie Vera's personal things sent to her. Father Kelly and the brothers were all out as usual – I'll get to them in a minute – so we talked for quite a while. She told me that Auntie Vera called a few days before she died and asked if she could come and live with her. According to the sister, Auntie Vera wanted to leave Father Kelly urgently.'

'She wanted to give up her home and job, after all these years?' asks Hazel.

'Exactly,' says Maude. 'The sister said that Auntie Vera was in good health. Then three days after that call she died. Auntie Vera's sister thinks there should be an autopsy.'

Hazel and Oscar exchange glances.

'So, Auntie Vera didn't give her any details about why she was unhappy?' asks Hazel.

Maude shakes her head. 'She wouldn't say why, but she mentioned a brother . . . something about since the brother arrived things had changed. I don't know whether she was talking about Brother Riley or Brother O'Connell. Or both, since I don't like either of them. Anyhow, Auntie Vera said she'd tell her all about it when she got there. She was going to buy a train ticket that day and leave straightaway.'

'Very interesting,' says Hazel. 'And Auntie Vera's possessions?'

'Just her clothes and papers and some books and things. I cleared the stuff out of her room when I first arrived. It's all in a couple of boxes,' explains Maude.

'I expect Father Kelly would pay for those boxes to be shipped to her sister, but you have a good excuse to go through her things carefully when you pack them up. See if there is anything that might give us a clue to what happened in those few days.' Hazel pauses. 'You said there was something else going on?'

'One thing is their strange hours. They get up for morning Mass but other days they sleep until late. They go out in the evenings and then come back in the middle of the night and wake me up to make them food. Then they shut themselves in Father Kelly's office and talk, arguing by the sound of it, and drink until the early hours.'

'Do you have any idea what they're talking about?' asks Hazel.

'Not really, with the door shut it's all muffled. Also I don't want to get caught spying on them.'

'Maude, I'm worried about you being in that house. Something's not right there.'

'I've got to stay for the three months, that's what I agreed. Mam's not going to change her mind on that.'

Oscar clears his throat. 'This is not my business, but could you not explain all this to your mother?'

'I agree, Maude, it's worth a try. Your safety is more important than—'

'Mrs B, you don't understand. You're not a Catholic. Father Kelly is like God to her.'

Hazel has to admit that Maude is right. She doesn't understand at all.

'Don't worry, I'll be careful.' Reading Hazel's worried expression, Maude continues. 'I have a lock on my door.'

'I'll give you a call tomorrow and check on you,' says Hazel.

'All right,' says Maude, getting up. 'You know how to investigate things, Mrs B. I feel better knowing you're on the job.'

When she's gone, Oscar looks bemused. 'It seems that everyone brings their troubles to your door, Hazel.'

Hazel manages a smile. 'All part of being a tea lady, I'm afraid. It's a twenty-four-hour-a-day job. Now, I believe this chicken needs my attention.'

Over dinner they discuss Maude's revelations, exploring the possibilities, and Hazel can imagine that one day she might even tell Oscar about the secret guild. For the moment, though, it will remain a secret. The evening slips away and she's surprised to see it's nine o'clock and the long-awaited rain has arrived without her noticing.

'It is about time I went home,' says Oscar, rolling down his shirtsleeves and buttoning his cuffs in preparation.

After a moment of hesitation, Hazel allows the words she wants to say to rush out before she can second-guess herself. 'You're going to get soaked . . . would you like to stay, Oscar?'

He raises his eyebrows in surprise. 'Are you asking me . . .'

'Would you like to come upstairs?' Hazel confirms.

'Are you certain?' he asks. 'The neighbours . . .'

'It's the sixties, Oscar, things are changing. Besides, we don't need to worry about impropriety at our age. We're beyond all that.'

Oscar reaches across the table for her hand. 'I would like very much to come up the stairs. Thank you for inviting me, Hazel.'

The front door bangs closed, followed by footsteps along the hall. 'Sorry I'm so late, Mum. The traffic was ridiculous! I can't believe this rain!'

Norma bursts into the kitchen, an overnight bag in her hand.

Oscar quickly gets to his feet and offers his hand. 'Hello, I'm Oscar Sorensen, a friend of your mother's. You must be Norma.'

'Oh, the Opera House chap,' says Norma, shaking his hand. 'Good to meet you.' She turns to Hazel. 'Did you forget I was coming?'

'Not exactly,' ventures Hazel. 'I thought it was tomorrow night.'

'Oh, that's probably my fault. The date of the dinner changed. I must have forgotten to tell you.'

Oscar takes his jacket from the back of the chair. 'I was about to leave.'

'Sorry to barge in on you,' says Norma. She sits down and kicks off her shoes.

'Not at all. For myself, I'm glad we managed to meet.'

Hazel walks Oscar to the front door. 'I'm sorry about that,' she whispers. 'Another time, perhaps.'

'I will telephone you tomorrow,' says Oscar, and brushes a kiss on her lips.

As she walks back into the kitchen, Hazel can't decide if she is disappointed or relieved. At least she had the courage to make the move and offer the invitation.

In the kitchen, Norma leans against the sink, her arms folded. 'Are you sure you know what you're doing, Mum?'

'That remains to be seen,' says Hazel with a smile.

## 26

# IRENE MAKES A DEAL

When Irene arrives in the laneway at lunchtime, Merl is there alone and starts in straightaway with: 'I hear you went up to the Blue Mountains last weekend?'

'Where'd yer hear that?' Irene packs her pipe and watches Betty waddling up the lane, slow as an old tortoise.

Merl goes on. 'Seems odd that you never mentioned it on the Monday when I asked if you did anything interesting over the weekend.'

'Wouldn't call it *interesting*.' Irene lights the pipe and belches a satisfying cloud of smoke, further annoying Merl.

'Was there a purpose to this trip?'

Irene gets a Scotch Finger out of her pocket, picks the fluff off it and takes a bite. 'Nah.'

Merl mutters on but Irene ignores her. Finally, Betty arrives, plops her cushion on the wall and lets out a sigh. Merl buttonholes her right away. 'I hear you went along on this jaunt to the Blue Mountains last weekend?'

Betty gives Irene a cross look. 'Yes, we felt like a day out.'

'So you and Irene went on a day trip together to the Blue Mountains and didn't think to mention it. On the train?'

'No, we have a friend with a car,' says Betty.

'A friend with a car?' echoes Merl. 'A gentleman friend?'

Irene laughs. 'Yeah, he's got a Rolls and a flash uniform.'

'That I find hard to believe,' says Merl.

As soon as Hazel arrives, Merl starts in on her. 'Did you know about this trip to the Blue Mountains, Hazel? I assume you were invited.'

Hazel gets a vague look on her face, one of her little tricks Irene's seen many times. 'No, I was busy anyway.'

Merl's not giving up yet. 'Was there a purpose to this trip?'

Irene's getting fed up with all this. 'What's it to yers? We had a day out, so bloody what? Where'd yer hear it anyway?'

'A little birdy.' Merl wobbles her head importantly.

Irene inhales too much smoke and half chokes. 'From that dodgy son-in-law of yours?' she croaks.

'I beg your pardon. Are you referring to Detective Pierce? If so, I thoroughly object to the word "dodgy". And, anyway, why would he be interested?'

'Yeah, good question,' says Irene.

'Unless you're up to no good.' Merl purses her lips and gets out her knitting. 'I just thought there might have been a special reason for this trip. You might be . . . searching for something . . . for example.'

Irene does her best not to bite. 'Like what? Oh, yeah, I remember now, we murdered some fella and buried him out in the sticks.'

'Oh, Irene, please don't start rumours like that,' says Betty.

'Perhaps they were searching for the meaning of life?' suggests Hazel with a smile. 'Now, on to other matters. We have a second tea machine going into Accounts this week.'

Betty goes all pink and quiet; that usually means she's about to start blubbering.

Hazel pats her on the shoulder. 'It's not over yet, Betty dear. There's still some fight left in these old girls.'

'I just can't believe they're turning against us,' Betty says in her wobbly voice.

'That Dottie Karp is a piece of work,' says Merl. 'She's the one who started all this. Everything was fine until she put a spoke in the wheel.'

'I don't think we should take it personally,' says Hazel. 'No point in feeling sorry for ourselves, we're not the only ones going to suffer. But there's no doubt that the situation is becoming urgent.'

'Who gives a stuff about us?' asks Irene.

'Mr Kovac for one. He's agreed to spread the word about the stop work meeting coming up this week,' says Hazel. 'He sees a lot of tea ladies on his rounds. We might have more support than we think.'

'And we might not,' adds Irene.

Irene's quite keen on these secret guild meetings at the herb shop in Chinatown. It's like going to a criminal meeting but not so dicey. The stink of the place is something else, but she's getting used to it. Mrs Li, Effie, Hazel and Betty are all here tonight and Irene has to admit they're a cluey bunch. If they were doing something useful like robbing a bank or blackmailing someone, they'd be a crack team.

Betty arrives last, sweating with excitement and bursting with news.

'We've got a couple of issues to discuss this evening,' begins Hazel. 'The trip to the Blue Mountains was something of a dead end, it seems—'

Betty's hand shoots up. 'It wasn't . . . you'll never guess. Never!'

Irene sighs. 'Don't keep us in suspenders, mate.'

Betty looks around with a daft grin on her face. 'It wasn't jewels Fred left you. Or maybe it was, but they're likely long gone . . . We'll never know that now . . .'

'Spit it out, Bets,' says Effie.

Betty sobers up. 'I was thinking about it all last night and I wondered how come his little hut hasn't been pulled down while he's been locked up. It's so obvious when you think about it. It's the land! That's what he left. This afternoon I went to the Land Titles Office and did a search of the properties on that road. The land where he had his camp belonged to him.'

Hazel laughs. 'Fred bought himself a country estate.'

'Bloody Fred,' says Irene. 'I told yers he liked trees.'

'That's good news for you, Irene,' says Effie. 'Be worth a few thousand now.'

'What am I s'posed to do with it?'

'If it was bought with the proceeds of crime, it could be seized,' says Mrs Li.

Effie shrugs. 'They'd have to prove it, which would be difficult and probably more trouble than it's worth.'

Mrs Li looks doubtful. 'I'm sure they could stop you selling it while they investigate. And that could take years.'

'Which explains why he was so careful,' says Hazel.

'Exactly!' says Betty.

'You need to get it transferred into your name as his next of kin. Do you know a solicitor?' asks Mrs Li.

'Do I look like I know a solicitor?' Irene stops and thinks. 'Oh, yeah, I do.'

'Well, that is a triumph,' says Hazel. 'Congratulations to Betty for solving that mystery.' Hazel leads a round of applause, then turns to Irene. 'Fred wanted to leave you something and he went to a lot of trouble to make sure you got it. So good on Fred.'

'I s'pose,' Irene agrees. That's Hazel. Makes you feel guilty when you haven't done a thing. Cash or jewels would have been a lot easier. But she has to admit it's better than nothing.

Hazel continues. 'So now that case is off our books, we can turn all our attention to the situation at St Vincent's.'

Betty gets out her notebook and pen, ready to go.

'The plot is officially thickening over at the priest's house. Maude has spoken to Auntie Vera's sister, and it seems that a few days before she died, Auntie Vera was desperate to leave, and quickly. She mentioned problems with a "brother" who had arrived. There are two Catholic brothers living at the presbytery, Riley and O'Connell. From what Maude says, there is something odd going on and I wonder if it could be to do with the sale of the convent land.'

'How can we find out more about these fellows?' asks Betty.

Everyone goes quiet, thinking. Finally, Hazel says, 'Father Kelly mentioned they were down from Queensland, which I'm not sure is true. Maude seems to think they're recent arrivals from Ireland.'

'If they arrived in the last month or so, we could check the shipping passenger lists,' suggests Mrs Li.

'There's probably thousands of Rileys and O'Connells on ships coming out of Ireland,' says Effie.

Mrs Li considers this for a moment. 'Nevertheless, the entry cards have a lot of details about the passengers. Birthdate, where they were born, occupation et cetera.'

'It might be difficult to get access to passenger cards,' says Hazel. 'We don't really know what we're looking for. It seems they're close with Father Kelly. Perhaps if we knew the area of Ireland that he came from . . .'

Betty looks up from her notes and waves her pen. 'Leave it to me!'

Irene couldn't care less. She's lost interest in all this brother stuff. Her mind is now on the messy business of Fred's land and how to get rid of it.

Walking into the Thatched Pig, Irene congratulates herself on having settled her debt with Big G so she can come in here without fear. She finds Arthur Smith sitting up at the bar, exactly where she left him a few weeks ago. He looks pissed but perky.

She leans on the bar next to him. 'G'day, Arthur.'

'Ah, I knew today was going to be special,' says Arthur. 'I assume you're blinding me with that alarming azure smile because you want something?'

'Know anything about wills and things, property and whatnot?'

He turns back to his drink, no cocktail this time but a pint of beer. 'I'm not a conveyancer, if that's what you're suggesting.'

'Course not, yer a punter and a pisshead,' Irene points out.

'Touché.' Arthur lifts his glass in a toast to her. 'Will that be all, ma'am?'

Being built low to the ground, Irene's not keen on bar stools and it's a struggle to get onto the one beside Arthur. He watches her efforts with interest but no offer of help.

'That was like watching a rat crawl onto a sinking ship,' he remarks.

Irene leans towards him. 'Arthur, we're sort of mates, aren't we?'

'I reject that preposterous notion with three words: Most. Definitely. Not.'

'What if there was money in it for yer? Easy money?' Irene says quietly.

'I may be prepared to delete two of those words in that case.'

Irene's getting confused with all these words. 'Which ones?'

He gives her a look of pity. 'Most and not, obviously.'

'Right,' says Irene, trying to remember the third word.

Arthur lets out a long sigh. *I wasted time, now time doth waste me*. Make your point. Tell me what you want, Mrs Turnbuckle.'

'Call me Irene.'

'I prefer to keep this on a professional level if you don't mind, Mrs Turnbuckle.'

'As yer might recall, me hubby carked it. There's no will.'

'So just to clarify, this was Prisoner T56987, last known address Long Bay Gaol?'

Irene glances around to make sure no one's listening. 'That's the one. He owned some land. Need help to get me mitts on it and flog the thing.'

Arthur stares silently into his empty pint glass.

'Yer right?' Irene asks, giving him a prod.

'Just lacking lubrication,' he says.

If there is one thing Irene hates, it's buying drinks. Bloody waste of money. She catches the barmaid's eye and nods towards Arthur's empty glass, grudgingly sliding the coins over the counter.

Arthur comes to life like a puppet with a yank on his strings. 'And how would I, as a highly qualified barrister, be compensated for my time and expertise?'

'I thought yer was a judge,' says Irene.

'Briefly, but it's not the services of a judge you're requiring here. You'd be employing an over-qualified clerk to sort out probate and transfer of assets.'

'How about ten quid?' suggests Irene. 'I'm not doing the new money.'

Arthur gives her a shrewd look. 'How about a ten per cent success fee?'

'What's that mean?'

'It simply means that if I'm not able to complete the task, you pay nothing. If I can, you pay ten per cent of the sale price to me. In old or new money, it's the same.'

Irene spends a good minute trying to work out if he's getting the better of her. Giving up, she offers her hand. Ignoring it, he reaches for a bar mat and writes on the back. He passes it to her to sign and calls the barmaid over to witness her signature.

Irene's impressed. Very impressed. The fellow knows his paperwork.

## 27

# HAZEL HAS A RUDE AWAKENING

When Hazel arrives at St Vincent's on Saturday morning, Maude's waiting at the gate.

'I checked the presbytery daybook and there is no mention of the brothers before Auntie Vera died,' Maude says breathlessly. 'She normally put in lots of detail about priests and nuns who visited from other dioceses. If a parishioner visited, she would even note down what they had for afternoon tea, and whether it was in the garden or in the front parlour. But there's nothing.'

'All right, let me think about that,' says Hazel. 'How are you going with Auntie Vera's belongings?'

'I've packed it all up to ship and I rang her sister back to get the address. I didn't find a diary, but I did find a note she must have written when she got sick. It's a bit scribbly but . . . shall I read it for you?'

Hazel nods and Maude reads aloud: '*Something wrong . . . terrible headache. Can't think straight groggy confused. Sick three or four times can't remember. FK called the doctor. Told him not to. Wouldn't listen.*'

'Poor woman, that sounds very frightening. Father Kelly called the doctor against her wishes, but that makes sense if she was confused.'

'She might have thought it was just a funny turn,' suggests Maude, handing Hazel the note. 'She never wanted to have attention on her.'

'Perhaps you're right, but I wonder why she made notes. How are the residents in the house going?' Hazel asks.

'Much the same, but more . . . I don't know . . . rowdy?'

'Rowdy? In what way?'

'Loud, I suppose. Excited. I don't know, they're just not like I expected.'

'Father Kelly too?' asks Hazel.

'He tries to get them to quiet down. Then they get into an argument, and he shushes them. Brother Riley's the worst. He's not very holy at all.'

'It would be good to know exactly where the brothers came from, and when. It might help to know whereabouts in Ireland Father Kelly came from—'

'He's from Belfast,' says Maude.

'Oh, good. See if you can pick up any other clues about the brothers, and let me know.'

Maude agrees, a little brighter now she has a mission, and sets off back to the presbytery.

In the convent library, Sister Ruth is kind and patient throughout the lesson, but Hazel struggles to concentrate on the words that flutter across the page like butterflies.

'Never mind,' says Sister Ruth, closing the book after only half an hour. 'We all have good and bad days, so don't take it to heart, Mrs Bates.'

Hazel apologises and they agree to finish early. As she gets up to leave, Hazel notices the plans for the new orphanage taped up on the wall of the library and stops to look them over.

Sister Ruth joins her, pointing out the different areas: two dormitories, a dining room and kitchen and a living room with a fireplace. 'I think the fireplace is a nice idea,' she says. 'It will make the orphanage more like a home for the children. It's already started – I can show you if you like.'

Hazel says she'd love to see it and follows Sister Ruth out to the far side of the convent, where a large excavation is underway for the cellar, now with a foot of water at the base. Sister Ruth points out the surveyor's pegs and explains that the new building will be attached to the wall of the convent with an entry through to the main building.

'We do have a wealth of land and space here that can be shared with the needy,' she says. 'Some of the children's homes . . . well, we know they're not looking after the children well. In fact, some of these children are suffering horribly in places that are run like prisons. This would be a safe home. We will teach them skills to find work and, of course, make sure they can read and write.' Sister Ruth turns to Hazel with a smile. 'That's Father Kelly's vision: a safe house for the wellbeing of children. Our Lady of Hope gives hope to others.'

Hazel agrees that it is a noble vision but as she walks home, she doesn't know what to think. Father Kelly, who is apparently a saint, seems to be another person behind closed doors. And if that is true, how did Auntie Vera put up with him for six months? Hazel's best guess is that he is being controlled by the other two. And she wonders again about the wound on his head and how he got it.

*

It's still dark when Hazel is woken by the telephone early Sunday morning. She hurries down the stairs, not quite awake, to answer it.

'Hazel, I'm sorry to wake you. This is Oscar.'

'Oscar, has something happened?'

'Something quite beautiful is happening on the harbour and I thought you would enjoy seeing it. Would you like to come down here?' he asks. 'Now?'

Touched by his desire to share an experience with her, she agrees.

'Very good. I will call a taxi to pick you up.'

'A taxi? That's very extravagant. But if you're sure, I can be ready in a jiffy.'

Fifteen minutes later she's being driven though the sleeping city to Circular Quay. The light of dawn glows on the horizon, the Opera House is shrouded in white, and the harbour bridge has disappeared into the morning fog.

Oscar helps her out of the taxi with a beaming smile. 'We have some interesting work to do this morning.'

'I gather it's not making tea,' says Hazel, noticing several cases of equipment at his feet. 'But I brought a thermos anyway.'

Oscar laughs. 'You are always a step ahead of me. Now, let's walk to the water and watch or, perhaps more importantly, listen to the harbour in this wonderful fog. This I have hoped to hear for months!'

Today he has a key for the gate. Carrying her shopping bag and one of his cases, Hazel follows him. They skirt the building, passing the giant crates of construction materials, and pick their way through building debris until they reach the point where the base of the building meets the harbour and strands of mist float above dull silver water.

Oscar quickly assembles a dazzling variety of recording equipment with several microphones on stands that are wired to half-a-dozen meters. Hazel's curious to know what he plans to record that has him so excited, but doesn't interrupt him. Then comes the moment he has evidently been waiting for: the sound of the ferry foghorn.

Oscar, clearly thrilled, watches his equipment light up and makes rapid notes in an exercise book. The foghorn sounds again. He checks his watch and peers at his meters. The ferry continues on its path, the foghorn sounding at two-minute intervals, becoming ever distant as it disappears into the fog.

'Now for the big moment,' says Oscar, barely able to contain himself as he checks his watch for the tenth time.

When it comes, the sound reverberates across the harbour like a giant bassoon playing a low note, then a lower note again. Two tugboats accompany the white prow of a vast cruise liner as it emerges from the fog. Oscar crouches down in front of his recording equipment, making hurried notes as the ship glides slowly and regally past them and disappears into the white distance.

Standing up, he heaves a great sigh of satisfaction. He checks his equipment and his notes and systematically turns everything off. 'We can manufacture this sound, but it can never be exactly like the real thing,' he explains. 'I read the shipping news every day in the hope that a departing ship will coincide with this weather condition. Ideally, we would record from every part of the building. But this is a start. A perfect start to the day.'

Hazel asks how he will prevent a sound that loud entering the building.

'The theatres will be rooms within rooms, with air locks to insulate from this level of sound. Because, of course, this would be very distracting in your Mozart concert,' he explains as he packs up his equipment. 'What I am measuring here is the level of sound and the reverberation, the time it takes for the particles of sound to decay. Ah, I'm boring you.'

'Not at all,' says Hazel, enjoying his enthusiasm. 'But I expect you'd like that cup of tea now.'

Oscar laughs. 'I can think of nothing better.'

He snaps his cases closed and pulls up a couple of nearby crates. Dusting one off, he gestures to Hazel to take a seat. She removes the cup from the top of the thermos, hands it to him and pours his tea. She pours one for herself and they sit watching the skeins of fog swirling across the gleaming water as the sun bursts through and bathes them in a pink glow.

Hazel glances back at the building, like a giant Meccano set, all its insides visible. The ground around them is covered in debris and, among it, she notices several red, white and green Mintie wrappers. It seems an odd coincidence to see these here, and she wonders if someone working on the site broke into Mr Utzon's office and stole plans. Perhaps someone paid to help his enemies?

# 28

# THE SECRET GUILD GET TO WORK

Sitting at her dressing table, Betty holds a hankie over her face while she gives her hair a good lacquering to keep her new set in place. That done, she applies several layers of coral lipstick and a touch of blue eyeshadow. Everyone's wearing more make-up these days, even false eyelashes. Not suitable for older ladies, in her view, but things are changing, and you have to change with them whether you like it or not. There was a time when she would barely leave the house without a hat of some kind, but when Hazel gave up hats, Betty did too. One minute, you're not properly dressed without matching shoes, hat and handbag, then all of a sudden no one cares any more.

It's all part of this 'sexual revolution' the papers are on about. These days, if a girl can get herself on the contraceptive pill, she can be naughty and not get caught. When Betty was young, being a good girl was highly prized. Bad girls usually got caught out sooner or later, so people said. But, funnily enough, she sees those so-called bad girls around, married for decades with children and grandchildren. And here's Betty, the good girl, with no husband, no children or grandchildren. No one's fault. The stork was held up somewhere else. There's a lot of Catholics around here; they probably had the stork working overtime.

Staring at her reflection, Betty notices something. She leans forward, holding her own gaze. Her eyes, once bright blue (which she felt made her look a bit dippy), have faded to a greyish blue. Now they appear wise. Holding her head a little higher, she walks down to the Hollywood, where she finds Irene sitting at a table without a drink. Typical.

'Put yer neck out again, have yer?' asks Irene.

It's the perfect opportunity for Betty to demonstrate her newfound wisdom, but nothing comes to mind. 'Honestly, Irene, can't you at least buy one drink for yourself?' she snaps.

'Considering it. Gettin' bloody parched here.' Irene glances over at Shirley behind the bar. 'That one's toying with me emotions.'

When Hazel arrives a moment later, Irene's head cranks back in the direction of the bar. 'See what I mean? Can't bloody get here fast enough now youse've turned up.'

'Didn't notice you there, Mrs T,' says Shirley, unloading three shandies from her tray. 'Evening, Mrs B, Mrs D – no Mrs P? Oh, she's got another wedding coming up.'

'So many bloody weddings,' grumbles Irene. 'That lot must've all been married twice by now.'

'No divorces yet,' says Hazel. 'These days her grandchildren are tying the knot. Put these on my tab, thanks, Shirley.'

'We're just here for a quickie—' says Betty.

Irene grins. 'Speak for yerself.'

'A quick drink is what I'm referring to. We have business to attend to this evening.'

'Oh, la-di-dah,' says Shirley. 'Off to negotiate world peace, are we? Good luck.'

When Shirley goes back to the bar, Betty gets a filthy look from Irene.

'What did I do?' asks Betty.

'Yer tryna make people suspicious?'

Betty feels a hot blush creep up her neck. 'No, of course not.'

Irene leans close with her stale smoker's breath. 'Then stop big notin' yerself.'

'I just meant . . .' Betty doesn't know what she meant, or why she even brought it up.

'Yer always goin' on about being a bloody ace detective and blabbing to everyone.'

Unwelcome tears spring in Betty's eyes. She feels the light touch of Hazel's hand reminding her to take a deep breath. 'I didn't . . . All right, Irene. I will be more discreet in future.'

Hazel gives her a smile. 'I gather you've got some good info for us?'

Betty straightens up and takes a gulp of her drink. 'Yes, I do.'

'Hold on to it for a few more minutes. Let's wait until we meet the others,' says Hazel.

Betty nods and pulls herself together. They finish their drinks and walk down to Chinatown. The shop is quieter this evening, with only a couple of people waiting. Mrs Li and Effie are seated at the table in the back room, and tea has been prepared.

Once everyone's settled in, it's over to Betty. She gets out her notebook. 'Firstly, only one passenger ship, the *Lady Catherine*, has arrived here from Dublin since Christmas. I went through the passenger list very thoroughly. There was a Patrick Riley and Shaun O'Connell listed, both born in 1937.'

Hazel nods. 'That sounds about right. They're a fair bit younger than Father Kelly.'

'Both from Belfast,' continues Betty. 'And there's something else – the passenger list shows half-a-dozen men named Kelly, but I noticed there was a Michael Kelly, date of birth nineteenth of April, 1914. Also from Belfast.' Betty glances around to see if anyone else finds this pattern of numbers interesting, but apparently not. 'Isn't Father Kelly about that age – early fifties?'

'Yes,' agrees Hazel. 'Father Kelly's also from Belfast, but he's been here six months.'

Betty continues. 'O'Connell and Riley are single, and their occupations were listed as Catholic brothers. Kelly is a factory worker and married, but he didn't travel with his wife, it seems.'

'Those brothers wouldn't have nothing to do with the likes of a factory worker,' says Irene.

Effie agrees. 'Just a coincidence. As you said, there were plenty of Kellys onboard.'

'Out of interest, how did you get hold of the passenger list?' asks Mrs Li.

Betty, pleased at the opportunity to demonstrate her resourcefulness, explains how she came up with a story about a missing nephew and how distraught the family were. She exaggerates a tiny bit because, in fact, the clerk at the shipping office handed it over quite easily just to shut her up. 'The *Lady Catherine* docked on the fifth of January,' she concludes.

'Auntie Vera died on the tenth of January,' says Hazel. 'Interesting timing. We don't know when the brothers moved into the presbytery. They don't appear in the daybook, which is odd because, according to Maude, Auntie Vera kept scrupulous records of all the comings and goings.'

A thought occurs to Betty, goosebumps rising all over her body. 'You said Father Kelly hasn't been himself – all rattled and that.

What if these other two fellows arrived without invitation? What if they have something over him?'

'Maude said there's been a lot of arguing behind closed doors,' muses Hazel. 'I'm not sure where to go from here. We have the sister's suspicion that Auntie Vera's death was not from natural causes and two mysterious visitors, who are perhaps not what they seem.'

'What if these two men are not Catholic brothers at all?' asks Mrs Li.

'What if they're blackmailing him?' suggests Betty.

'So many possibilities,' says Hazel. 'Maude does seem to think Father Kelly is being controlled by these two, particularly Riley. You might be right, Betty. Perhaps they have some kind of hold over him. There has been some odd behaviour at the presbytery.'

'What sort of behaviour?' asks Mrs Li.

Hazel explains that the men go out at night and stay up late drinking. Betty, who has no idea what men of the cloth might do in their spare time, wonders if this is just normal.

'What if . . .' asks Betty, '. . . Auntie Vera got on the wrong side of these brothers? Or she found out they were blackmailing Father Kelly?'

'And they knocked her off,' says Irene.

'Yeah, but how did they get away with it?' asks Effie.

Mrs Li speaks up. 'One thing I know is that if Auntie Vera had died suddenly, the Coroner might have decided there needed to be an inquest. But if a doctor had been called out to the patient in the previous three months, then it's considered natural causes, unless there are suspicious circumstances. That would lead to an autopsy.'

'Kelly'd know that,' says Irene. 'He'd get called out for last rites.'

'So, for example, if you wanted to poison someone, you'd do it slowly, or at least in a couple of stages?' asks Hazel.

'Poison,' murmurs Betty, her tummy squirming as she writes it down.

'If you've read any Agatha Christie, you'll know there's the famous three: arsenic, cyanide and strychnine. They're not difficult to get—' says Effie.

'But they can be traced,' interrupts Mrs Li.

'They can, but only if there's an autopsy,' says Effie.

Irene nods. 'Easy to get yer hands on arsenic – rat poison, flypaper, weed killer.'

Mrs Li is not convinced. 'They all have signs that will show up. When a doctor does the death certificate, he'd notice. People are caught all the time for using rat poison.'

'Now, cyanide,' continues Effie, obviously enjoying this conversation. 'You can't kill someone slowly with that. It's pretty much instant. Few grains and boom, down you go. And strychnine, that's more difficult to administer. It tastes bitter and the effect is quite dramatic and usually within a couple of hours. So I think those two can be discounted as well.'

'Betty, remind us of the symptoms in Auntie Vera's note,' asks Hazel.

Betty refers to her notes. 'Headache . . . groggy . . . being sick . . . feeling sick.'

'It could be anything,' says Mrs Li, shaking her head.

Effie makes a note. 'I've got a few books on the subject. I'll look into it.'

Betty glances at her notebook again. 'I've got Lady Catherine, Patrick Riley and Shaun O'Connell . . . could be nasty . . . not in daybook . . . poison . . . blackmailing priests . . . Michael Kelly nineteenth April 1914 . . . all from Belfast.' She looks up. 'He's probably not relevant, but I'll leave him there for the moment.'

'I wonder about the sale of this land at the convent. Are you able to find out more about that, Betty?' asks Hazel. 'Maude mentioned some issue was getting Father Kelly upset. I'm not sure how we can follow that up.'

Irene, who has been quietly rolling a cigarette, looks up with a sly grin. 'About time I went to confession, I reckon.'

# 29

# TEA LADIES IN AN UPROAR

Hazel is woken by sunlight streaming into the bedroom. She turns to look at Oscar sleeping peacefully beside her. He wears his usual slight smile, his breathing even and calm. It seems this morning sun is lighting a shadowy corner of her life, the place she retreated to after her first husband, John, died and then again after Bob left.

When John died early in the war, Hazel had thought she would never get over it. But, with Norma only eleven, she had to think about making a living. To get herself through those dark days, she developed a habit of telling herself every morning that she was happy. She kept up that pretence for a long time (some days more difficult than others) and gradually it became true. Never more so than today. Gazing across at Oscar's kind and handsome face, his white hair fluffed up like a dandelion gone to seed, she feels a sense of contentment.

She slips out of bed, puts on her brunch coat, and goes downstairs to the kitchen. It's fortunate that Irene's no longer in residence and they have the house to themselves. No doubt the entire street knows Oscar stayed the night, but that doesn't bother Hazel the way it once might have. She makes tea and takes two cups back upstairs. She places one on his bedside table and pauses to open the doors onto the tiny balcony before slipping back into bed.

'Did you sleep well?' she asks, seeing he's awake.

'Better than I've slept in weeks,' he says, as he pushes himself up to sitting.

'You've had a lot on your mind.'

'I have.' Oscar sips his tea reflectively. 'The most difficult part has been having no control over what will happen. I'm not involved in the meetings and only have Jørn's version of what has been discussed. I understand his point of view, of course, but . . . you were right, Hazel. It began on the wrong foot.'

'We would say he shot himself in the foot,' says Hazel.

'And showed his hand?' suggests Oscar.

'Played into the hands of his rival, in fact.'

'All the hands and feet are in the game now, and I think there will be no winners,' says Oscar with a sigh. 'The people of Sydney will lose his genius, and he will have this unfinished business hanging above him. It's not only him, but there are also many more people directly affected – me, for example.'

'Surely the new regime will keep you on?'

'They will be suspicious of the people Jørn recruited from the far north. There are two Swedes and a Norwegian engineer as well.'

'That would be foolish, but . . .' Hazel gives a sigh. 'But there are a lot of egos involved, so I suppose anything could happen.'

'I fear everything may come falling down on us now. Even the Opera House itself,' Oscar concludes ominously.

Hazel turns to him in surprise. 'You're not serious?'

'There was a story in the newspaper this week. Some critics

of the building, they believe it is a failure and will be a "white elephant". I'm not certain what this means.'

'Something big and useless – expensive to keep,' explains Hazel.

'Exactly.' He gives a nod. 'They want to see it pulled down. There is also a proposal to build a casino there. They say that gambling is more popular in this state than opera.'

'That's no doubt true, but surely no one wants to build a temple to gambling?'

'You would be surprised. Now the enemies of the Opera House will come out from every corner to show themselves.' Oscar looks over at Hazel with a smile. 'We will deal with whatever happens, min skat.'

'Min skat?'

He leans over and gives her a kiss. 'My treasure.'

Hazel bats him away. 'You're too charming sometimes, Oscar Sorensen. You know I don't trust that.'

'What I know is that your ears are telling you this man is to be trusted. And this morning I will make you Danish porridge called øllebrød with the special bread and beer I have brought with me, and you will become a little bit Danish.'

Hazel arrives in the laneway at lunchtime to find Merl knitting aggressively, Irene smoking her pipe and Betty sobbing into her hankie. 'What on earth's happened?' she asks.

'They're putting a tea thing in at her place,' says Irene, nodding at Betty.

Betty dabs at her eyes with the handkerchief and blows her nose loudly. 'I was so brave when they told me, Hazel. I even made a little joke, even though I felt sick and . . . well, I had to run to the bathroom—'

'We don't need all the details of *that* episode, thank you,' interrupts Merl. 'I also have a delicate constitution, you know.'

'What was the joke?' asks Irene. 'We could do with a laugh.'

'It's not worth repeating,' says Betty miserably.

Hazel asks exactly what happened.

Betty blots her face. 'Same as your place. They said it's a trial, but once the staff are used to it, well . . . then I'll be replaced . . . by the machine.' She gives a sob and admirably attempts a brave smile.

'Klein's won't dispense with me, I'm quite certain of that,' says Merl. 'The lingerie industry expects a high standard of catering. The machine can't do that.'

Betty bursts out angrily. 'Just because you keep saying that doesn't make it true. You're kidding yourself, Merl! Lingerie is just a fancy word for undies and nighties! You're no different to the rest of us. You're dispensable!'

Merl glances at Betty over the top of her spectacles, needles flicking angrily. 'I can see you're upset, Betty, so I'll let that comment go.'

'You know that fella from Café-bar? Seen him before,' says Irene. 'He worked at the car yard on the corner near the brewery. He's been in and out of every firm along here.' She jabs in the direction of each of the buildings with the stem of her pipe. 'Empire, Farley's, Klein's and my place—'

'Just because he's been into Klein's doesn't mean that they're going to install the contraption,' argues Merl.

'We'll see,' says Irene, relighting her pipe and adding to the dark cloud hanging over them.

Betty blows her nose. 'I think I'll go back to work.'

'You haven't eaten your sandwiches, Betty dear,' says Hazel. 'And don't forget we have the Guild meeting to look forward to this evening. Mr Kovac has been spreading the word, so we could have quite a turnout.'

Betty nods despondently. She picks up her bag. 'I'm not hungry.'

'Never thought I'd hear those words come out of her gob,' remarks Irene, watching Betty walk back to work.

Merl sighs. 'I do think it will be very difficult for any of us to find other work . . . if this Café-bar business goes ahead.'

'Speak for yerself,' says Irene. 'I reckon I'll find something.'

'I expect criminal work is always easy to come by,' notes Merl with a sniff.

'Oh, well, if yer going to be fussy.'

'What's up, Hazel?' Leaning back in his chair, Doug Fysh stares at Hazel. 'We can't have the tea lady looking down in the mouth. Being cheerful is part of the job, haw haw haw.'

Hazel puts his tea and biscuits on his desk. 'It's just all this Café-bar business. It seems to be spreading to other companies around us.'

Doug dunks a biscuit and pops it in his mouth. 'I can't see it catching on.'

'Perhaps you're not looking properly,' says Hazel, a little more sharply than intended.

Doug gives her an injured look. 'Sorry, Hazel. I didn't mean to annoy you.'

Hazel manages a smile. 'Things change, there's not much we can do.'

'I for one will miss you, Hazel. We all will. End of an era.'

Hazel's bemused at how quickly he seems to have accepted the situation. 'Thanks for the thought, Doug.'

Pixie appears in the doorway. 'Oh, I thought Gloria might be up here.'

'Sadly not, but come on in, sweetheart,' says Doug. 'Hazel's all upset about this tea machine business.'

Pixie stares at Hazel. 'Oh, Mrs Bates, I've been so caught up planning our fashion parade—'

'We'll miss her, won't we?' says Doug.

'Miss her? The place will fall apart.' Pixie thinks for a moment. 'Don't give up yet. Let me think about it. There must be something we can do.' Heading out the door, she turns back and says, 'Mr Fysh, do you mind not calling me "sweetheart"? Pixie is fine or, if you want to be formal, Ms Karp is also fine.' She flashes him a smile and is gone.

Doug frowns at Hazel. 'Did she say "mizz"? What's that supposed to mean?'

'I'm not sure, but I assume it's a sort of neutral title for women, like mister.'

'That's ridiculous,' he scoffs. 'Women are either married or they're not. Miss, then Mrs. You can't be something in between.' He shakes his head despairingly. 'She's turning into a tough cookie, that one.'

'I notice we never call men tough cookies, or smart cookies,' muses Hazel. 'They're just tough and smart. Do you think the cookie part makes women sweet and more palatable?'

'Haw haw haw, don't you start turning into a women's libber, Hazel . . . Gawd help us!'

*Haw haw indeed*, thinks Hazel. But she says nothing, simply collects his cup and goes about her business.

\*

Hazel and Betty arrive at the Hollywood to find forty or more women already gathered in the bar.

'Evening, Mrs B, Mrs P,' calls Shirley, as they make their way to the bar. 'You'll have to make this a regular thing, very good for business.' However, in the time it takes to serve their drinks, the crowd doubles in size and the smile fades from her face. 'I better call for back-up,' she says, turning away to pick up the phone.

Hazel and Betty make their way through the crowd to find a quiet corner. The Italian women have enlisted at least a dozen others. Betty points out her neighbour, who has brought along a group of tea ladies from the Defence department. The bar is now full, with women spilling out onto the pavement.

Eileen Weston joins Hazel and Betty. 'Quite a crowd you've got here,' she says.

Hazel nods. 'Shows just how many tea ladies realise their jobs are under threat.'

Shirley hurries out from behind the bar to demonstrate how the microphone works and brings a chair for Hazel to stand on. The noise of chatting women fills the bar. Hazel wonders how on earth she got herself into this situation, speaking to such a large crowd.

Betty gives Hazel a steadying hand and, when she's standing on the chair, passes up the microphone. Hazel takes a calming breath. When her call for attention has little effect, Irene delivers a two-fingered whistle so loud that people visibly flinch and Hazel begins.

'We had no idea this many of you would come, so thank you. As you all know, we are facing a crisis that could see our jobs lost forever. We perform a valuable and unique role in caring for staff. Offices and factories will be emptier places without us. Management won't realise what they've lost until we're gone. Now is the time for us to act before it's too late.'

There are murmurs of agreement in the crowd. Hazel introduces Eileen and passes the microphone to her.

'Right now, tea ladies are at risk of redundancy because of automation,' says Eileen. 'One option is joining a union, but getting union support to strike may take months and let's not forget unions are run by men. If the union won't support a strike, you'd be talking about a wildcat strike.'

Irene calls out, 'What's the bloody point then?'

'That's what you need to decide as a co-operative,' says Eileen. 'You can organise a strike yourselves or join the union for support.'

An angry buzz of conversation swells through the room.

'I say we strike now,' calls a voice and a cheer goes up. There are more calls for a strike. A chant starts at the back and fills the room. 'Strike! Strike! Strike!'

Hazel takes back the microphone and asks, 'Who is in favour of an immediate strike?'

A forest of hands shoots up.

'How long for?' someone calls. Hazel recognises her as the woman who walked out of the previous meeting because her husband was on strike.

Hazel speaks up. 'We'll call a one-day strike to start. I think we should do it tomorrow while the iron's hot, or the kettle in our case.'

The room explodes with chatter.

Eileen puts her hand up for silence. 'We need a show of force. Normally a strike would have a picket line, but we all work in different buildings, so that's not an option. A rally would get the point across, though. A peaceful demonstration.'

Hazel takes over again. 'We'll meet in the park on Lisbon Street at 8 am tomorrow, bring everyone you can find—' There's so much noise and excitement in the room, Hazel is forced to raise her voice to be heard. 'Tea ladies, tomorrow we strike!' she cries.

A great cheer goes up, followed by a rush for the bar, and Hazel quickly gets down off the chair before she's knocked down.

'Who would have thought tea ladies would be so radical?' Eileen remarks. 'And so united. Normally these sorts of meetings start well and end in a rabble with brawling.'

Hazel smiles. 'The difference is a room full of mature, sensible women.'

Eileen laughs. 'Let me buy you a drink. I think something bubbly is in order.'

Hazel couldn't agree more.


An hour later, in the quiet of her kitchen, Hazel spreads out an old white sheet on the kitchen table. She glances again at the draft of the words on a piece of paper. Words she wrote herself. She's torn between pride in this achievement and fear of starting. Copying from her draft, she carefully paints the letters in bright blue poster paint: SAVE OUR TEA LADIES.

It feels like a milestone, the letters so firm and bright and hopeful.

## 30

# THE TEA LADIES CAUSE CHAOS

Irene is up at sparrow's fart vacuuming the halls and sloshing out the bathrooms. Now she's figured out how little she can do to keep Miss Palmer off her back, the job is not too difficult.

She unplugs the vacuum cleaner, coils up the power cord and shoves it back in the cupboard. She puts on her good hat and a slash of lipstick. Poking around under the bed for anything useful, she finds some knuckle dusters and lock-picking keys. She tucks them into her pinny pocket and sets off to the tea ladies' riot. What a day. She can't wait.

They're meeting at the scabby little park where all the deros sleep, but when Irene gets there, she can't even see the park for ladies: tall, short, chubby and skinny, of every age. Not just old ducks, young ones too. Some have even brought their tea trolleys along.

Overflowing the park, they gather along the pavement in Lisbon Street, holding up their signs and waving tea towels at passing cars.

That bolshie Eileen is there with a load of her commie mates, handing out pamphlets and directing the ladies to spread out along the pavement. Well, good luck to them. Irene's a capitalist land-owner now, so she won't be joining the reds any time soon.

There's Betty waving at her. Irene gives her a wave back. What the hell is the old chook wearing? Pink and more pink, with a big pink hat, and holding a sign: 'WE LOVE OUR TEA LADIES' painted in wobbly blue and surrounded by love hearts.

'What a turnout!' Betty screams. 'Can you believe it?!'

Irene has to admit she can't quite. There must be a couple of hundred people here, probably more. She spots Hazel, Effie, Mrs Li and Violet, as well as a few other familiar faces in the crowd.

Soon people start coming out of the nearby buildings. Empire Fashionwear is right opposite and those pretty little things they call the Queen Bees come tripping down the front stairs, followed by the factory girls and that mouthy supervisor, Gloria something, all led by the Karp girl, Pixie. The whole lot of them dressed like tarts in ridiculously short dresses. The grumpy secretary, Edith, and a dapper little fellow, the accountant, all cross the road to join them. She wouldn't be surprised to see Old Karp turn up next! No one from Irene's firm has bothered to come, ungrateful lot they are.

Behind her, a voice asks, 'Can I put this on your tab, Mrs T?' She turns to find Shirley grinning at her.

'Quite a turnout, in't it?' says Irene but the publican's already wandered off to talk to other patrons.

Looking across at the Empire building, a bright glint in the 3rd Floor window catches Irene's eye. Someone watching them with binoculars, that'll likely be Frankie Karp. There's a woman with blonde hair standing beside him. Dottie, the twit who started all this trouble in the first place. At the next window along, she can see old Mr Karp standing at the open window. Poor old bugger.

A dozen or so tea ladies, who Irene recalls as being Betty's mates from the Defence department, push their trolleys out, spreading out across the street to block the traffic. The old boilers are carrying chains and padlocks in their pinny pockets. They link their trolleys together and lock them up – right across the street! Lisbon is a busy thoroughfare and straightaway the traffic comes to a standstill, with drivers rubbernecking out their windows, shouting and honking their horns. Over the top of the noise and chaos, Irene hears sirens. It's getting better by the minute.

The spinning lights of two cop cars stop down the street, stuck in the traffic. A few minutes later, half-a-dozen uniformed coppers walk towards them. As they get closer, Irene can see these fellows are barely out of nappies, no match for an angry tea lady.

'Come on, ladies,' calls one of the fresh-faced cops. 'Let's move along.'

Betty starts singing 'We Shall Not Be Moved' and some of the old warblers join in. One of the Italian sheilas steps up to the copper and gives him a tongue-lashing so furious it makes him step back a pace, even though he probably didn't understand a word.

Irene's pretty sure there will be some arrests here today. She moves as far away as possible and lights her pipe to make the point she's not part of the spectacle. She manages one puff before some battleaxe wearing the same floral pinny as Irene tells her off for smoking and makes her put it out.

Now they're all belting out 'We Shall Overcome', with the churchy ones singing harmony over the top. This lot are having the time of their lives. What a bunch. It's enough to bring a tear to Irene's cynical eye.

Having no bloody idea what to do with a couple of hundred old biddies having a singsong, waving signs and stopping traffic in the middle of rush hour, the coppers stand around, probably waiting for braver cops to come. Before long, one turns up with a big pair of boltcutters. After a lot of mucking about, the Defence ladies are all handcuffed and marched off down the street to a chorus of booing by the crowd.

Irene grins to herself. Best thing that could've happened. That'll make the headlines. Glancing over at the Empire building, she sees Dottie downstairs in the entry foyer and watches her close the glass entry doors and lock them from the inside. Probably locked the back door as well. Irene decides to make herself useful unlocking all the doors so everyone can go back to work none the wiser. And, while there's no one around, she'll do a bit of tinkering with those tea contraptions.

## 31

# HAZEL GETS BAD NEWS

The day after the protest, Hazel is back in the downstairs kitchen at Empire Fashionwear as if nothing happened. The strike and demonstration got more attention than they had anticipated. Last night, she and Betty watched the television news in Gibson's shop window. There was a larger crowd of locals than usual, all keen to see Surry Hills on the news, and most were sympathetic to the cause, apart from an old drunk who kept insisting that the knacker's yard was the only place for them. The protest had been the first item up, showing an impressive number of women singing and waving their placards, and closing on the sobering sight of a dozen tea ladies being led away under arrest.

On her way to work today, Hazel picked up a couple of newspapers. The headlines read: 'Grannies Spit the Dummy' and 'Tea Ladies Out of Order'. She doesn't have time to read the content, but it seems the press are united in treating the strike as a joke. She's pleased to see a very flattering photograph of Betty holding her 'WE LOVE OUR TEA LADIES' sign. She'll be delighted.

The phone rings. 'Mr Karp would like to see you, Hazel,' says Edith Stern.

Hazel says she'll be right up. Expecting the worst, she slips off her pinny and hangs it on the back of the door. She takes the lift to the top floor and as she walks through Edith's office the two of them communicate their concerns without a word being spoken, and Hazel goes straight through to Mr Karp's office.

'Ah, Hazel. Close the door, could you, please?' says Mr Karp.

Sitting down in the visitor's chair, Hazel notices how small and elderly he seems these days. It's probably just a matter of time before the combined forces of Dottie and Frankie oust him and take over.

Mr Karp leans forward, his elbows on the desk, hands locked together. 'Hazel, yesterday's disruption was something this firm has never seen in twenty years of business. Our entire staff walking out without notice over, of all things, a cup of tea.' He pauses, staring at her over his glasses as if seeing her in a new light. 'I asked myself, how did it come to this? Is Hazel actually a quiet revolutionary? Has she put the staff up to this? But Pixie has assured me that you weren't behind our staff walk-out and, in fact, knew nothing about it. That was her initiative.'

Hazel nods. She has no idea where he's going with this and how it will end.

'It seems the prospect of losing our tea lady is so serious that the entire staff put their livelihoods at risk, without a moment's thought, to join the fray,' he continues.

'We're very grateful for their support,' murmurs Hazel, determined not to apologise.

Mr Karp continues as if he hasn't heard her. 'Apart from the problems this has caused the firm, it occurred to me that if I was . . . dispensed with, not one member of staff would down tools on my behalf. It seems you are the mortar that holds this firm together, not me.' He takes a deep breath and leans back in his chair. 'A sobering thought, as you can imagine. I had a sleepless night thinking about the legacy I want to leave here at Empire. What I'm about to tell you doesn't concern you directly, but I wanted to tell you anyway. I know you will keep it to yourself, as always.'

He gets up and walks up and down the room in an agitated way, hands behind his back. 'I'm the majority shareholder in the company with fifty-one per cent. Frankie and Dottie have the other forty-nine. The two of them have been pushing to make me the minority share-holder, but I've been holding out. Last night I thought about you tea ladies. Yours is a hopeless cause, but you still came out fighting. And I've decided to do the same.'

'Good for you, Mr Karp,' says Hazel, despite feeling disheart-ened by his harsh assessment of their cause.

'The fact is that the company is on the brink of either success or failure. The extravagance of these gowns in time and materials . . .' He shakes his head in disbelief. 'Frankie and Dottie tell me they can revive its fortunes, but I have my doubts with the wastage up from ten per cent to forty. I think you were right when you said Pixie is the future. So I've decided to retire, hand over the company to Frankie and Dottie to run. I don't have the energy to bring it back from the brink, but perhaps they do.'

Hazel can barely believe what he's saying. It seems like a terrible decision. 'What about Pixie and her—'

Mr Karp holds up his hand. He perches on the corner of the desk in front of her and says in a quiet voice, 'Mr Levy approached me a few weeks ago with the idea of making Mod Frocks into a separate limited company. At the time, I didn't want to break the firm up. But I've changed my mind. At this very moment my solicitor is preparing the paperwork and Pixie will have her own company, including her brand name and designs.'

When she came upstairs, all Hazel could think about was saving her job. She had expected him to fire her, but it seems she might have a reprieve for the moment. 'I think that's a wonderful plan, Mr Karp. Pixie will be pleased.'

'I'm glad you think so. I'm very pleased with it myself. Now, it must be almost teatime,' he says, with a wink.

Walking out of his office, Hazel breathes a sigh of relief. But, before she has a chance to speak to Edith, Dottie appears from Frankie's office and beckons her inside.

Frankie sits at his desk looking uncomfortable and sulky. Dottie stands to one side of him, as if posing for a family portrait. She doesn't offer Hazel a chair but leaves her standing like a naughty child.

'What a spectacle yesterday,' Dottie begins. 'You must be proud of yourself. A tea lady with the power to cause such disruption.'

Frankie shakes his head. 'You've done irreparable damage, Hazel. I know you didn't mean to, but you have. The shop steward from the Textile Workers' Union was there yesterday, and I found out this morning that all our machinists have signed up. We've always paid award wages and kept the union out, now overnight—'

'It wasn't my intention, I assure you,' says Hazel.

'Too late,' interrupts Dottie. 'The damage is done.'

No one says anything for a moment, then Frankie, in a weary voice, says the words she's been dreading. 'We have to let you go, Hazel. There's no choice. I'm sorry.'

'You don't need to apologise,' Dottie tells him. 'She's caused chaos, and we're left to clean up the mess.'

Frankie sighs. 'Dottie, she's been here a long time, have a heart.'

Hazel simply nods. 'I understand.'

'You can finish up today,' says Dottie. 'Before you cause more trouble.'

Frankie looks sorry for himself. 'Could you bring me a cup of tea and a couple of bikkies, please? Just one last time?'

Hazel looks from one to the other. What a pair they are. Frankie knows this is a mistake, but he's allowed himself to be steamrolled by Dottie to make his life easier.

'I'm sorry, but you'll have to get it yourself,' Hazel says, and walks out the door.

Sitting in the downstairs kitchen with a strong cup of tea and a Scotch Finger, Hazel has to face the reality of finishing up this afternoon and leaving Empire. She looks around the familiar room. How many hours has she spent in here over the years? Doug Fysh often refers to her kitchen as the firm's unofficial headquarters. Everyone knows her routine and where to find her for a private chat.

It's a generous size compared to some of the others. Betty's kitchen is small and dark and Irene's is not much bigger than a cupboard. Hazel has room for a table, a couple of chairs and her trolley, which makes preparation easy. She even has a second kitchen with an oven upstairs. She decides to bake scones for all the staff this afternoon, as a parting gift.

At lunchtime, she has to steel herself to walk up the lane and meet the others. She's later than usual so Betty and Merl have finished their sandwiches and, judging by the haze around her, Irene's on her third cigarette.

'Hazel, we were worried,' says Betty. 'We've just been talking about yesterday and what a triumph it was. I couldn't sleep. I was buzzing all night. Did you see the photo of me in the paper?'

Hazel nods. 'A lovely shot, Betty dear.'

'It's unfortunate those renegades got themselves arrested,' says Merl. 'Gives the general public quite the wrong impression of us.'

'Yeah? Whaddayah think got us on the front page?' says Irene. 'A bunch of ol' ducks singing's not gunna do it.'

'Are you all right, Hazel?' asks Betty.

Hazel looks around at them. 'I'm sorry to have to tell you, I've just been sacked by Dottie and Frankie.'

'Oh, Hazel,' says Betty, tears springing in her eyes.

'Their excuse is that the strike has made all the machinists sign up with the union and they're holding me responsible.'

'I'm very sorry to hear that,' says Merl, clearly unnerved. 'It won't be the same without you. The end of an era, you might say.'

'Yeah, and I'll be stuck with these two nitwits,' says Irene gloomily.

Merl gives an offended sniff. 'Nobody forces you to have lunch with us, Irene.'

'That's a point,' agrees Irene. 'I might go down the pub instead.'

Betty blows her nose. 'And buy yourself a drink? I can't see that happening.'

Irene grins. 'Yers can come with me.'

'Can I remind you we're still talking about poor Hazel?' says Betty. 'What are you going to do? Do you think Mr Karp might override their decision?'

'No, I don't,' says Hazel. 'There's going to be a few changes in the company. I'll try to find another job.'

They all fall silent again. Hazel unwraps her sandwiches, but her appetite has gone.

'Been collecting cockies,' announces Irene, out of the blue.

Betty frowns at her. 'Cockatoos or cockroaches? Also, why?'

'Cockroaches, yer dope. For the tea machines. I'll give yers a little bag and yer can take the top off the machine and pop 'em inside.'

'That's disgusting,' says Merl.

'I have a horror of cockroaches,' says Betty. 'I don't even like saying the word.'

Irene looks offended. 'Suit yerself. I've put in a bit of work on this, yer know.'

'I suppose it's worth a try,' agrees Betty. 'As long as I don't have to look at the creatures. You're not going to charge me for them, are you?'

With only a moment's hesitation while she weighs up that idea, Irene says, 'Yers can have 'em for free. This time.'

While sabotage is not Hazel's style, and it's too late for her anyway, everyone needs to fight this in their own way. She feels an overwhelming sadness at the loss of these lunchtime gatherings. Irene winding Merl up and ribbing Betty, the baking, the squabbling, and the gossip. She will miss it all.

The afternoon brings more sadness as she says goodbye to each of the staff. The scones do little to cheer people up. There are tears and hugs and outrage on every floor. Even the Rosenbaum sisters get a little weepy. Thinking about it, Hazel is almost certain that Mr Karp knew she was about to be sacked. He was just relieved that he didn't have to do it.

At the end of the day, she leaves her kitchen spotless, packs up her personal items and walks home with the heaviest of hearts.

# 32

# IRENE HAS A SIGHTING

One of the many things Irene likes about living at 555 is having her own outside bog where she can sit and smoke and reflect to her heart's content. Inside the house there are two very swanky bathrooms she gets to clean every day. They're not to her taste, both tiled in sickly pink with a maroon basin and bath. The outdoor lav has been converted to flush (Miss Palmer wouldn't want the dunny man barging through the back gate) and that's luxury enough. With the yard to herself at night, Irene can sit with the door open, smoking and looking up at the stars. What a life!

Tonight she's thinking about Fred's land and what to do with it when Arthur Smith finishes mucking about with all the paperwork. She spares a thought for poor ol' Fred and what was going through his head when he bought that bit of scrub in the middle of bloody nowhere. Not a bad idea if he was hiding some loot. She wonders about how much it might be worth and what she'll do with the money. The unwelcome words 'a fool and her money are soon parted' keep popping up in her head – even worse, in Merl's voice.

Her thoughts are interrupted by the sound of clients arriving. She tiptoes out of the dunny for a stickybeak. The side entry to the building is guarded by a dodgy-looking bloke, all trussed up in a suit, who calls himself the doorman. He lets the punters in through the locked gate, then they walk along a short path and up a couple of steps into the building. The whole operation is shielded from Irene's view by a high paling fence that divides the side path and the backyard. However, she has taken it on herself to poke out a knot in that fence, giving herself a peephole. It's not ideal, but she gets a decent glimpse as they pass.

Now, crouched in the dark, she sees two shadowy figures coming through. As the door opens and light spills outside, she recognises both these blokes. Before the door has even been locked behind them, Irene's out the back gate, hurrying as fast as her sore ribs allow down to Hazel's.

Every light in Glade Street is off when she knocks on Hazel's door. No answer. She waits a few minutes and tries again. She pulls out her hatpin and a minute later is standing in Hazel's hallway.

'Hazel!' she shouts upstairs. 'It's me!'

She's about to charge up the stairs when Hazel appears, pulling on a dressing-gown. 'Irene? What time is it?'

'Yer not gunna believe who I just saw. I can't believe it meself. Couldn't believe me own eyes!'

Hazel sits down on the stairs. 'Who did you see?'

'Those two so-called brothers!' Irene's expecting some reaction from Hazel, who's still half-asleep. 'Riley and O'Connell – just now at 555!'

'Are you quite sure, Irene?'

'Saw 'em clear as anything. Only for a second, mind, but it was them all right.'

'Come into the kitchen. I'll put the kettle on,' says Hazel, getting up.

Irene follows her down to the kitchen, makes herself comfy and waits for the tea. It's just like old times, apart from the new toaster sitting on the bench.

'No Father Kelly?' asks Hazel.

'Nup, just that Riley with his curly top and the big lug, O'Connell.'

'There's something we're missing here.' Hazel sits down with her tea and hands Irene a cup. 'How much do we really know about Father Kelly? You said were going to confession . . .'

'Yep, didn't have much to confess.' Irene sees a doubtful look on Hazel's face. 'Managed to come up with one or two things.'

'And? How did Father Kelly seem to you?'

Irene shrugs. 'Just gimme the usual Hail Marys.' She thinks for a minute. 'Don't think he was really listening. When I came out, the other two was hanging around waiting for him. That's the only time I seen them.'

Hazel sits, thinking quietly. After a while, she gets up and opens the pantry. Irene can already taste that malt whiskey about to come her way. Her smile fades at the sight of a packet of Milk Arrowroot placed in front of her.

'We need to call an urgent meeting at the herb shop,' says Hazel. 'Now I'm really worried about Maude. This puts a new complexion on the whole business.'

After work, Irene heads down to the Thatched Pig to check on her inheritance. Turning the corner into the street, she runs straight into Detective Pierce, Merl's dodgy son-in-law, leaning against a wall, smoking. Like he's waiting for her.

'Mrs Turnbuckle, you're in a fine old hurry,' he says, moving into her path.

'Whaddyah want?' Irene tries to duck around him, but he blocks her way.

'There's word going around that you've come into some money.'

'All lies. Can yer move?'

He blows a smoke ring and watches it disappear. 'I understand your late husband left something—'

'Where'd yer get that idea?' Irene asks.

'Mrs Turnbuckle, anything your criminal husband left is the proceeds of crime, and you need to turn it over. There's plenty of charges we can bring against you, receipt and sale of stolen transistors, among others. So let's make this easy.'

'I got nothing. Bloody police harassment of an old lady. I got a lawyer, yer know.'

'Very impressive,' says Pierce. 'Don't waste my time.'

'Listen, mate, you're the one wasting *my* time. Yer got bloody nothing. So arrest me or bugger off.'

In a surprise move, he jams his hands under her armpits, lifts her clear off her feet and yanks her into the laneway beside the pub. Next thing she knows, she's slammed against the wall. He has one hand around her throat and a threatening fist hovering in front of her face.

'Listen, you old bag, I'm tired of your nonsense. I can make life very difficult for you.'

'Yer already are,' croaks Irene. 'Geroffme!'

A man appears at the back door of the pub. 'What's going on here?'

Pierce lets her drop, and she stumbles against the wall. Her ribs are killing her. This not being a conversation she wants to continue, she legs it around the corner and into the Thatched Pig.

Irene straightens up her hat and climbs onto the bar stool beside Arthur Smith. He's got his mitt clamped around a glass of gin or vodka. Or water. Unlikely.

'Ah, the incomparable Mrs Turnbuckle. I thought I'd be seeing you in the not too distant.'

'Here I am in close up and full technicolour,' says Irene, beckoning the barmaid over. 'Another gin for yer?'

'These reoccurring bouts of generosity are disconcerting to say the least,' says Arthur.

'Meaning?' asks Irene.

'Never mind. This clear liquid you see before you is in fact H2O,' he says.

Irene turns to the barmaid. 'Whiskey and ginger ale for me and H2O for the gentleman, ta, love.'

'Help yourself,' says the barmaid, pushing a water jug along the bar towards them.

'Hang on, yer sitting in a bar drinking water?' asks Irene.

'For the moment,' says Arthur. 'Did you bring your marriage certificate?'

'Right here.' Irene gets the document out of her pinny and puts it in front of him.

He flicks it open with the tips of his fingers, as if it's infected with leprosy or typhoid. 'I'm not even going to ask where this has been stored. It's fortunate it's legible.'

'Yeah, got left out in the rain a couple a times,' says Irene.

Arthur reads it. 'So you weren't cohabiting but never divorced?'

'We're Catholics, mate. No divorce. Besides, he was away at the war, then in and out the big house. Listen, mate, that copper Pierce is after me. Giving me grief. Tried to bloody throttle me. Someone told him something. Dunno who.' Irene looks around the pub and notices Big G in his usual corner. His eyes meet hers and he looks away. Pierce must've put the bounce on him, threatened to fit him up with something serious. Irene decides to let it go. He owes her now.

'The constabulary are your problem, not mine. I'm sure you have plenty of experience in the area, driving getaway cars and so forth. My job is relatively straightforward,' says Arthur. 'Once probate is granted, the asset can be transferred to the next of kin. That's you, and I can facilitate that.'

'Good. Then can yer sell it for me?'

'I'm a barrister, not a real estate agent.'

'Whaddayah reckon it's worth?' asks Irene, knocking back her drink.

Arthur stares at her for a long moment. 'Let me pluck a figure from the air. Fifteen hundred dollars.'

Irene nearly falls off her stool. 'What's that in the old money?'

'About half,' says Arthur.

'Oh, bloody hell. Doesn't sound half as good. Go on, why don't yer have a proper drink? Cheer yerself up. Yer not yerself when yer not talking in riddles.'

Arthur stares into his glass of water. '*The instruments of darkness tell us truths*,' he murmurs.

'Good try, but anyone can see yer heart's not in it, mate.'

Arthur turns to the barmaid, raising one finger.

'That didn't last long,' says the barmaid, pouring a finger of whiskey into a glass and placing it in from of him.

'We have to start somewhere. Now, Mrs Turnbuckle, how are you planning to fritter that amount of money away once it's in your greasy little paws?'

Irene's not keen on the greasy paw business, but she has given the question some thought. 'Was thinking new slippers. Put a bit on the dogs. Wouldn't mind a telly for me room.'

'You wouldn't think to put some aside for your old age?'

'This is me old age. I need to spend it quick before I cark it.'

Arthur stares at her for a long while. 'As a matter of fact, I went up to the mountains to see your little piece of paradise.'

'Did yer now?' Irene stares at him. 'Why'd yer do that?'

'I have a proposal for you. One that would provide an income for you to fritter immediately while, at the same time, preserving your asset indefinitely, in case of some future catastrophe. My proposal would also serve to keep the asset hidden. Just in case it was purchased with ill-gotten gains.'

Irene has no idea what he's talking about. 'Go on then, let's hear it. But make it snappy, I've got things to do.'

'What a busy life you lead, Mrs Turnbuckle,' he says. 'I'll be brief then.'

# 33

# THE SECRET GUILD GET SERIOUS

Hazel has managed to convince the other ladies to allow Detective Dibble to attend their meeting at the herb shop this evening. As usual, he looks bemused at the sight of Hazel, Betty, Irene, Mrs Li and Effie huddled around the table. But his attitude has changed. Where he once treated them as interfering and misguided, he now regards them with respect.

'So Mrs Perlman's not part of this breakaway group, I gather?' he asks, pulling a chair up to the table.

'No,' says Hazel. 'Nothing against her personally, but we can't risk a certain detective with his own agenda getting involved.'

'Very wise,' Dibble says. He gives Mrs Li a curious look. Hazel wonders if he recognises her as the tea lady from his days at the Surry Hills Police Station before he moved to Special Branch. But if he does, he decides to ignore it. 'Now, what have you got for me, ladies?'

'Strange occurrences at the St Vincent's church presbytery,' explains Hazel. 'We'll give you a quick overview and then we can get into the details.'

Dibble nods and takes out his notebook.

'It all started, or at least we think so, when the priest's house-keeper, known as Auntie Vera, died quite suddenly—'

Dibble glances up from his notebook. 'When you say "suddenly", are you saying in suspicious circumstances?'

'It didn't seem so at the time,' says Hazel. 'She'd had stomach pains and the doctor had been called out a day or so earlier. But she died the day after making a call to her sister saying she wanted to leave the presbytery urgently.'

'We think she could have been poisoned,' adds Effie. 'Probably arsenic.'

Dibble looks sceptical. 'Hmm . . . Go on.'

Hazel explains that Maude had been pressured by her mother to take the housekeeper job and had found the habits of the three men unusual. He listens as she describes their odd behaviour, but it's not until Irene tells him about seeing Riley and O'Connell at 555 that they get his full attention.

'You're absolutely certain, Mrs Turnbuckle? It was definitely them?'

'Wit'out a doubt,' says Irene, grinning at her Irish accent.

'There are plenty of Irishmen in Sydney,' says Dibble.

'When I did me confession with Father Kelly, I got a good squiz at these blokes. One of 'em has a curly top and the other's a big tall bloke. It was them.'

Dibble refers to his notes. 'So they arrived on a ship coming from Dublin.'

Betty hands him a slip of paper. 'The addresses they gave were in Belfast.'

Dibble frowns. 'Belfast?' He looks around at each of them. 'Righto, I'm taking this very seriously.' He turns to Irene. 'So you're a parishioner at St Vincent's?'

'Been going there all me life,' says Irene.

'Has there ever been any indication that Father Kelly could be involved with Irish dissidents, anything in his sermons or any odd comments?'

'Dissawhat?' asks Irene.

'Anti-British, for example,' he says.

'We're all anti-British, mate,' says Irene. 'What's yer point?'

'I'm talking about Irish nationalists, loyalists . . . IRA,' says Dibble.

Irene shakes her head. 'Nah, Father Kelly's a decent sort. He's not gunna be throwing petrol bombs at people. Yer on the wrong track there.'

'It's possible that he's under pressure from these other two,' suggests Dibble.

Hazel nods. 'Several people have mentioned that Father Kelly hasn't been himself since Auntie Vera died, which coincides with the arrival of these other two fellows.'

Betty puts her hand up urgently. 'They could be holding a gun to his ribs!'

'That's something they do in films,' says Effie dismissively.

'They might have something on him but,' adds Irene. 'Blackmail.'

Dibble clears his throat authoritatively. 'All right, I need full descriptions of the men and the street address of the presbytery. I'll get an application before a magistrate first thing tomorrow to install a listening device. With any luck we can get the place wired within the next twenty-four hours. They'll send a technician from Special Branch to install it. He'll be disguised as something like an inspector from the Water Board. Ideally Maude gives him access at a time when these fellows are out, so as not to arouse any suspicion. In the meantime, be very careful and if you're able to contact Maude discreetly, make sure she's on her guard. Now, I know you never take any notice when I say this, but don't take any risks. If these people are who I suspect they could be, they're extremely dangerous. Utterly ruthless.'

When Dibble's gone, Hazel says, 'Twenty-four hours seems like a very long time in a house with ruthless, dangerous men. We need to come up with some excuse to get Maude out of there.'

'I was thinking the same thing,' agrees Betty.

Irene disagrees. 'One thing yer don't wanna do is alert them to something going on. Could put the girl and Father Kelly in danger.'

Effie agrees with Irene. Mrs Li is undecided. 'If she was my daughter . . . but then, what if Auntie Vera cottoned on to what was going on and they murdered her? I can see what Irene's saying, we could be putting Maude in danger.'

In the end, they agree to put their trust in Detective Dibble. As they part ways, it's obvious to Hazel they're all just as worried as she is about Maude. If anything happens, there's no one to help the girl.

It's almost 9 pm by the time Hazel gets home. She sits down at the card table in the front room with a glass of rhubarb wine, hoping it will calm her so she can think more clearly. But her imagination is working overtime and the jigsaw is adding to the muddle. She goes to the phone, calls the Bellevue Hotel and asks to be put through to Mr Sorensen's room. A moment later, his soothing voice comes on the line.

'This is a good surprise,' he says. 'I was reading an excellent book called *Physical Vibrations of the Natural World* – fascinating. But you did not telephone to discuss my reading matter.'

'I'd love to hear about it some other time,' says Hazel. She explains her concerns about Maude's safety. 'I just don't know what we can do to protect her. I'm so worried about her.'

'Hmm . . . what is the time now? It will only take me a few minutes to construct such a thing as the police have and I can be at your house within the hour.'

'Such a thing as the police have?' asks Hazel.

'I believe they call this device a bug. I will be with you soon,' he says, and hangs up.

True to his word, just before ten, Hazel hears a taxi pull up outside and opens her front door to find Oscar and his briefcase on the step. 'Now, min skat, how will our plan work?' he asks, as they walk into the kitchen.

Hazel sits down at the table. 'I've been thinking about that. Explain to me what's needed with your device.'

Oscar sits down opposite and opens his briefcase. The recording device, with headphones attached, takes up most of the space inside. He gets out a tiny device with wires dangling from it. 'This is a little microphone. I have made something similar to what the police call a wire. Maude can wear it and we will be able to listen to any conversation within her range.'

'I'm going to telephone Maude and ask her to come over now,' says Hazel.

Oscar nods. 'Excellent. I will put the kettle on.'

Hazel goes into the hall and calls the presbytery. Maude sounds half asleep, but when Hazel explains she's put her back out and needs help up the stairs, she says she's on her way. Fifteen minutes later she flies in the back door to find Oscar and Hazel sitting at the kitchen table drinking tea.

'What are you two playing at?' Maude asks breathlessly.

Hazel suggests she sits down, and Maude falls into a chair, still panting.

'I don't want to frighten you, but I am concerned about what's going on at the presbytery and I have discussed it with Detective Dibble,' Hazel says.

Maude frowns. 'Really? All right.'

Hazel continues. 'He's so concerned he's planning to set up a bug in the house tomorrow, but in the meantime, Mr Sorensen has made one, so we can keep watch on you.'

Maude nods. 'I think they're getting ready to go somewhere. They've been packing their suitcases.'

'Do you think O'Connell and Riley have something over Father Kelly?' asks Hazel.

Maude considers this for a moment. 'I reckon they do. He's sort of nervy, jittery.'

'I see. I want you to be very careful, Maude. Don't take any risks, and make sure you lock your bedroom door,' says Hazel.

Oscar explains how the listening device works and, while he sets up the receiving end of the arrangement, Hazel helps Maude pin the microphone to her brassiere. They test the microphone in different parts of the house and walk down the road to test it from a distance.

Half an hour later, Maude is on her way back to the presbytery and Hazel is on the phone calling for reinforcements to work shifts throughout the night.

## 34

# TROUBLE BREWS AT THE PRIEST'S HOUSE

Betty floats in a state of limbo. In her bones, she knows they're onto something big and Dibble was clearly alarmed. As she sits in her quiet little flat, waiting for the old lady upstairs to get out of the bathroom, the most exciting thing to look forward to is the woosh of bathwater draining down the pipes.

Then, from one minute to the next, everything changes – she gets a call to action!

She can barely contain herself as she rips out her rollers with abandon (in case she's in the newspapers *again*), ties a scarf over her head, throws on a light jacket and hurries out the door without even bothering to look in the mirror.

As instructed by Hazel, Betty hurries around to 555 to attempt to contact Irene. It's an awkward situation when you can't knock on someone's door or ring them on the telephone, but there are probably plenty more disadvantages to living in a brothel that Betty doesn't know about.

She knows that Irene likes to spend time in the outdoor lavatory (which she talks about glowingly), but how to contact her there is another matter. In the end, Betty decides to take a chance and stands in the back lane throwing pebbles over the wall, occasionally hitting the tin roof of either the lavatory or the washhouse.

Before long the back gate opens and Irene's scrawny head pops out. 'When I get yer bloody kids I'll bang yer heads together and yer won't sit down for a week.'

'Irene, it's me,' says Betty, stepping out of the shadows.

'Betty? Whaddayah want? Can't it wait?'

'No, Hazel wants us all around at hers now. Pronto.' Betty likes the little foreign touch she added there, like a secret code.

'All right. See yer there,' says Irene, and disappears.

Instead of calling out her traditional 'coo-ee', this evening Betty arrives in Hazel's kitchen by stealth, catching Hazel and Mr Sorensen by surprise. He has made himself at home, no tie, top buttons undone, and his shirtsleeves rolled up. There's an open briefcase full of dials and wires on the table and he's wearing headphones connected to it.

'Thank you for coming so quickly, Betty dear,' says Hazel. 'We're going to take it in shifts so there are always two people on duty, one listening and the other to keep them awake and get help if necessary.'

Betty feels her tummy do a thrilling somersault and (worried what might come next) manufactures a hearty cough, then feels bad when Hazel looks concerned and fetches her a glass of water.

Irene arrives, grumbling about her evening (spent in the lavatory!) being ruined but cheers up at the sight of the handsome Dane. She sits down opposite him with a lopsided grin, like an old dog eyeing off a bone. 'Nobody said there'd be blokes involved,' she says, giving him a wink.

Fortunately, Mr Sorensen has headphones on and most likely can't hear her.

Hazel explains the plan for the evening. 'I suggest we take turns during the night and then Mr Sorensen and I can continue tomorrow while you're at work. We'll keep it up until the police take over and we know Maude is safe.'

'It's almost midnight. It'll probably be quiet until morning now,' suggests Betty.

'If Maude says they're packing up, they could get out the door early, or anytime,' Irene points out.

Hazel agrees. 'We need to give it our full attention throughout the night.'

Betty and Irene take the first shift while Oscar and Hazel go upstairs to rest. Betty's curious to know whether they are resting in the same room – in the same bed! Could there be shenanigans going on right above her head? Or perhaps he's in Irene's old room? It's really none of her business, though it is a little bit her business because Hazel is her best friend. She'd really like to know, but there is nothing upstairs apart from the two bedrooms, so it's not as though she could pretend to be passing and happen to peek in. Not that she wants to, of course. But it would be good to know the lie of the land, so to speak.

'Off in one of yer dreams, mate?' says Irene, pulling off the headphones. 'Here, you stick these things on. They're giving me a bloody headache.'

Betty reluctantly puts the headphones on. She listens to Maude snoring (a sweet little pipping sound) and watches Irene searching through Hazel's cupboard.

'I bet that Sorryson bloke's drunk all the good stuff,' says Irene, as she drags a chair over and pokes into the back of the cupboard. 'It's gonna be a long night without a decent drink.'

Betty ignores her to concentrate. This is her first technical surveillance role, and she wants to do a good job. She wonders how she looks with these headphones on – quite important, she would imagine. Realising she still has her headscarf on, she removes the headphones and the scarf.

Irene has given up on the kitchen cupboard and gone off down the hallway, muttering about the cleaning cupboard. Hard to know what goes on in her head, and Betty instructs her not to make any noise because she needs her concentration. It's only a minute or two at most before Betty gets the headphones back on, but something has changed.

Maude's voice. 'Get off me! What are you doing? Stop!'

It's only now the full realisation that this is one-way communication sinks in for Betty. She calls out to Irene, not daring to take the headphones off again, even for a second.

A man's voice tells Maude to calm down and do as she's told. Then it's Maude again, telling someone to get away from her. There's a shriek, then silence. Muffled sounds of male voices. A man saying he'd said to leave the girl to the last.

Betty calls out, 'Irene! Irene!'

Irene appears in the doorway. 'What?' she asks irritably.

Betty points frantically at the earphones, then upstairs, afraid to speak for missing something. 'Get Hazel!'

Irene stamps down the hall and shouts up the stairs.

Betty concentrates harder, listening for the slightest sound. A man's voice, his words muddy and indistinct. The voice again: 'We'll deal with her later.'

When Hazel and Mr Sorensen appear, Betty leaps to her feet and hands him the headphones. 'They've got her! They're going to deal with her!' she cries.

Mr Sorensen, listening intently, nods. 'Two or three men arguing. Different tones but too distant from the microphone to understand what they are saying.'

Hazel turns pale. 'I'll call Detective Dibble. If you hear where they're going, shout out,' she says, hurrying off to the phone.

Betty watches Mr Sorensen's worried expression and feels horribly responsible for the situation getting out of hand. She takes a breath and gets a grip on her wobbly self. She hears Hazel hang up and make another quick call. A moment later, Hazel's back in the kitchen.

'He wasn't very happy about us bugging the place. He wants us to stay here. He'll send someone over there.'

'Bugger that,' says Irene.

'I agree,' says Hazel. 'I also called Mrs Li and she'll call Effie. Let's go.'

Mr Sorensen gets to his feet. 'I'll come with you.'

Hazel puts her hand on his shoulder. 'Oscar, this could be dangerous. You stay here. We'll handle it.'

'We're tea ladies,' Betty explains. 'We're used to this sort of thing.'

These words make her feel strong and capable. She puts her head-scarf on, ties it firmly under her chin and follows Hazel and Irene out the door. They practically jog all the way and arrive at the side gate to the convent just as Mrs Li and Effie appear out of the darkness.

The five of them gather on the pavement. Betty's knees tremble uncontrollably as she glances around hopefully for signs of the police. She wonders if Special Branch use marked cars or plain ones. The street is empty of any sort of car, so it's not relevant.

'I suggest we fan out. Try to stay in the shadows,' says Hazel, indicating the different directions. 'Betty, you go with Mrs Li and look around the church. See if there's a car down the side. Irene and Effie, we'll go over to the presbytery and see what we can find. We might need you to get us inside the house, Irene.'

Secretly relieved not to be venturing into the priest's house with those dangerous dissidents, Betty follows Mrs Li. The carpark is empty but, as they edge their way along the side of the church, Betty can see the back end of a car (a Morris Minor, judging by the shape) parked behind the church and wonders if Maude is in it.

As she and Mrs Li creep along silently in the dark, Betty's thoughts are with Hazel in the house with who knows what. She almost screams when Mrs Li grabs her arm and signals her to be silent (which she was anyway before she was given such a fright).

Mrs Li jabs her finger towards the back of the church. Betty peers into the darkness (her night vision's not the best), noticing little spots of light like fireflies fluttering around. They must be going into the church because they disappear and then reappear. Blackness, then spots of light. People rushing back and forth with torches.

Betty follows Mrs Li. Staying close to the wall of the church, they shelter behind the buttresses before moving to another section of wall. The full moon casts a bright bluish light, making ominous black shadows. Closer and closer they creep. Betty wishes Hazel was here. She doesn't have the same confidence in Mrs Li in this frightening situation. She's so scared it's all she can do not to wet herself. If only she'd thought to have a wee before they left!

The torches gather in one place. Betty can hear the men speaking in low voices. In the torchlight she can see the object of their attention is a wheelbarrow. Curious time to be gardening. She wonders if it's some old Catholic tradition to do with the equinox or the moon – or are they the same thing? They do have their mysterious ways.

Edging closer, concealed by the last buttress, it seems at first the wheelbarrow is piled high with earth. Then one of the men folds something soft on top and she realises it's full of blankets. So that's what they're up to! Stealing blankets from the nuns and the little orphans.

'Go slow,' says a gruff voice. 'Pack them tight as you can. Don't let 'em move.'

Another man uses a very bad word and says they could be blown from here to kingdom come. 'No shame in dying a martyr,' says the gruff one.

The other man argues that 'there's enough down there already', so why do they need to take this lot? It's too dangerous moving it.

The gruff fellow tells him to shut up. 'Get going, will yer? Where's the bags, Curly?'

Curly mumbles something that makes the gruff one steaming mad.

'Of course we're not coming back here!' he says. 'Did I not say that to yer? Now get 'em, will ya? We'll meet you out at the road. Be quick.'

One of the torches moves off towards the presbytery and by the light of another, Betty can see one of the men packing the blankets in the boot of the Morris.

Mrs Li turns to Betty and whispers, 'What should we do? Follow them or . . .?'

'We need to warn the others and work out what to do,' says Betty firmly.

## 35

# HAZEL FINDS A VITAL CLUE

As they approach the darkened house, Hazel is torn between immediate concern for Maude and worry that her decision to go in before the police could put others in danger. She took the precaution of bringing a torch and now tightens her grip on it.

The three women skirt the building, keeping low, pausing to peek in each window. The house appears to be empty. No lights on anywhere. Effie tries the back door and, finding it unlocked, they enter the house.

As they move quietly from room to room, Hazel's heart thuds so loudly it's a wonder the others can't hear it. Perhaps their own hearts are thumping too – Effie's at least. Irene is likely enjoying herself.

They arrive back in the kitchen having established that the house is empty. No priests. No Maude.

'Buggers have gone,' says Irene. 'Get the lights on.'

'No,' says Effie quickly. 'They could be still in the grounds. Let's look around outside—' She stops at the sound of footsteps; someone thumping along the back path. A moment later, before they can move, a man bursts in through the kitchen door.

Quick as a flash, Irene leaps at him. In the dark, Hazel can't make out what's happening but sees his hands fly to his face and hears a scream of pain. The man reels around the kitchen, hands over his eyes, shouting that he's been blinded and swearing furiously.

Effie grabs a heavy frypan sitting on the stove and, while he's still confused, whacks him over the back of the head. He falls to his knees with a groan and flops on the floor.

Hazel shines her torch on the man's face to reveal Brother Riley, out cold, wearing workman's clothes and what seems to be a balaclava pushed down around his neck.

Irene and Effie waste no time. Ripping up several tea towels, they tie Riley's hands and feet together.

Hazel looks over to see Betty's frightened face at the window and beckons her inside.

'We saw them,' Betty says breathlessly, arriving in the kitchen with Mrs Li close behind. 'They're going somewhere in a car with a wheelbarrow. Stealing the little orphans' blankets!' She stares at the unconscious man on the floor. 'This one came back for the bags.'

'They must have Maude with them,' says Hazel.

'She wasn't with them,' says Mrs Li. 'Or we didn't see her, anyway. Although she could have been in that car – we couldn't get close enough.'

'How were they taking a wheelbarrow in a car?' asks Effie.

Mrs Li clarifies. 'They were unloading something from it into the car.'

'You're quite sure it was blankets in the wheelbarrow?' asks Hazel.

'Mounds of blankets,' confirms Betty. 'We could see in the torchlight—'

'That doesn't make sense,' interrupts Mrs Li. 'The one in charge kept telling the other to be careful, go slowly.'

'Explosives,' says Effie. 'They're moving explosives.'

'What do you mean?' asks Hazel.

'Betty said there were mounds of blankets. Blankets packed around dynamite or gelignite.'

Betty gives a gasp. 'One of them said they could be blown to kingdom come.'

'And the other one said he'd die a martyr,' adds Mrs Li grimly.

Hazel nods. 'What if Detective Dibble's right and they're IRA?'

'We need to stay well clear of them,' says Effie. 'They could blow up the whole convent, and the nuns with it.'

'What if they come for this one?' asks Betty, pointing at Riley.

'I'm ready for 'em,' says Irene. She pulls something out of her pinny and gives it a shake. 'Brought me mate Mr Sheen along.'

A blinding beam of light shines in Hazel's eyes. She almost drops her torch in fright. A man's voice commands, 'Stay where you are! Hands on your head!'

Hazel puts her hands on her head and the others follow. The kitchen light flicks on to reveal two bulky policemen in uniform. Detective Dibble steps out from behind them. 'I told you ladies to stay home and let us handle this.'

'Maude's disappeared,' says Hazel, letting her arms drop. 'Was there a car parked near the church?'

Dibble shakes his head. 'No car, just a wheelbarrow.' He gestures for the two policemen to search the house.

'They've gone,' says Hazel. 'They've taken Maude.'

Dibble looks down at Riley's prostrate body, his hands and feet tied together. 'Who's this gentleman?'

'This is Brother Riley. They must have panicked and gone without him. We need to go after them,' says Hazel.

'We think they had explosives in that wheelbarrow,' says Effie. 'Now in the car.'

'The car was a green Morris Minor, but unfortunately it was too dark to read the rego,' says Betty.

'Any idea where they might have gone?' asks Dibble. 'Any hint at all in their conversation?'

Hazel asks him to wait while she goes into the hallway and calls her home number.

Oscar answers immediately. 'I cannot hear Maude talking,' he says. 'I hear two men and a car engine. Not a new car, quite old. Judging by the distance from her microphone, I think Maude is behind them, in the back seat or on the floor. They argue but the sound is not clear. One man tells the other to drive carefully. The other tells him to shut up. And so it goes in this way.'

Hazel thanks him and hurries back to the kitchen to convey this to Dibble.

One of the policemen is crouched down, going through Riley's pockets. He gets out various bits and pieces and lays them out on the kitchen table: a lighter, the stub of a pencil, cigarette butts and a handful of Mintie wrappers.

'I know exactly where they've gone,' says Hazel.

Dibble nods. 'Right. Mrs Bates, come with me. The rest of you, *stay right here.*'


In an unmarked police car, they race through the quiet streets of the city to Circular Quay. From the back seat, Hazel leans forward between Dibble and the driver while she explains how Mr Utzon's office had been broken into and she'd noticed a Mintie wrapper on the floor of his office, and later several others on the construction site. 'Now here's Riley with half-a-dozen wrappers in his pocket. It's too much of a coincidence.'

Dibble agrees. He gets on the two-way radio and it crackles back and forth as he reports his suspicions, gives a description of the car and two men and requests urgent back-up.

As they approach the Opera House, the building looks fragile in the grey dawn, despite its armour of concrete and steel. It reminds Hazel of an illustration in her encyclopaedia of a prehistoric dinosaur skeleton. It crosses her mind that it would take a lot more than a wheelbarrow load of dynamite to bring a building this size down.

The driver pulls over on the approach road to the quay, a safe distance from the site. Other police cars pull up behind them and the two men get out, leaving Hazel alone.

Listening to the two-way, Hazel gathers the Morris has managed to get through the gates and is hidden among the workers' cars parked on the site. She feels dizzy with fear at the thought of Maude trapped and isolated with those men – who may well decide to martyr themselves and take her with them. All she knows about the IRA is that they are extremists who have no mercy when it comes to sacrificing innocent bystanders.

The shriek of a siren is followed by a voice booming over a loud-speaker, instructing the workers who live on site to leave everything behind and immediately evacuate on foot towards the Botanical Gardens on the eastern side. No cars are permitted to leave. The gates have been locked and the men must not go to their cars under any circumstances.

Dibble slips back into the passenger seat and issues further instructions on the two-way. He turns to look over his shoulder at Hazel. 'About a month ago, a demolition firm in Tempe had a break-in and a large quantity of gelignite was stolen. We don't know how much – probably under-reported because it wasn't stored correctly or securely. As far as we knew, the only active terrorists in Australia right now were the Croatian Revolutionary Brotherhood group. The IRA has never had a presence here. Since we spoke the other day, I've been in touch with British intelligence. It seems that the IRA are making moves to take their cause internationally. Possibly even here.'

'Blowing up the Opera House won't get them any sympathy,' says Hazel.

'It *would* get international attention. They're not going to blow up a building this size with a wheelbarrow load of explosives, but they could do some structural damage.'

'Don't the IRA use car bombs?'

Dibble is silent for a moment. 'They do, and sometimes they use a proxy to drive the car to the location.'

His words seem to hang in the air. The radio crackles. A siren shrieks.

'Maude can't drive,' says Hazel. After a moment she adds, 'Betty and Mrs Li overheard one of the men saying there was "enough down there already" – there must be more explosives somewhere.'

Dibble thinks for a moment. 'It's a big area with plenty of places to hide bombs, if they planted them earlier.' He pauses, thinking. 'But there's a high risk of them igniting with all the construction work going on. The question is how would they set them off?'

He gets out of the car and walks back to talk to the other police.

Hazel sits, watching the stream of men amble past the quay, going against instructions as they walk towards the city, smoking and grumbling among themselves. They have no idea why they are being evacuated. Several stop to watch police boats gathering on the harbour, fanning out at a safe distance, and an army helicopter that arrives to hover overhead.

To her horror, she sees Brother O'Connell walk past. He's dressed in workmen's clothes, but his size makes him stand out among the crowd.

Hazel gets out of the car and hurries over to where Dibble stands talking to other police. In the minute it takes her to get his attention and describe the man, O'Connell has disappeared into the crowd, marshalled and hurried along by the police.

'I need to find a phone,' says Hazel and walks away quickly before Dibble can stop her. Staff arriving for work are being evacuated from the Unilever office building on the quay. Hazel walks into the foyer of the building, where there's a reception desk but no receptionist. The switchboard is nothing like the one Hazel worked on many years ago, but the principle is the same. She picks up the receiver, opens a line and calls her home number.

Oscar answers. 'I have just now telephoned the police. The men have gone, but Maude is still in a car. She is talking but it is difficult to understand. She has a handcuff to the steering wheel. She says there is a bomb in the car.'

'We're at the Opera House site. Come down. Bring your equipment. Ask for Detective Dibble. Hurry!'

'I will arrive soon,' says Oscar and hangs up.

Hazel walks out of the building in a daze. There are more police than ever. She walks over to where Dibble stands.

'She's alone in the car,' Hazel tells him. 'With the explosives.'

Dibble nods. He leans into the police car and relays this through the two-way.

With the area cleared, there's an unnatural silence and stillness. The Opera House glows white and violet in the clear morning light, a sleeping beauty unaware of the drama playing out around her. But, for Hazel, the tension in the air is almost unbearable and she tries desperately to think of what she can possibly do to save Maude.

## 36

## IRENE PUTS HER FEET UP

Irene can't remember when she had such a bloody good time. There's a telly at the presbytery, Irish whiskey in the cupboard and currant cake in the tin. Not only that, but plenty of company to watch the drama down at the Opera House. They're now calling it a siege. It's all fuzzy in black and white and filmed from a distance, but apart from that, nearly as good as being there.

Betty, Effie and Mrs Li sit in a row on the couch, drinking tea while they share their worries and stare at the telly. It's a shame they can't break up the news with an episode or two of *The Flintstones* – be nice to watch it in comfort instead of standing outside a shop.

'They're bringing in the army, by the looks of it,' says Effie.

Irene's pretty sure that will liven things up; they might have a rocket launcher or something. But she has a comfy armchair and a footstool, and she's not worried about the situation because if anyone can handle a siege, it's Hazel Bates. And how often do you get to watch a show with someone you know in it?

Betty, on the other hand, seems very worried. She gets up and paces around the room, and peers out the window, probably thinking there's going to be more bombers coming their way (doubtful given there's coppers crawling all over the place now, looking for God knows what). Then she walks over and stands gawping at a calendar on the wall with a photo of two kittens playing with a pink ball of wool. Just the sort of thing Betty loves. Odds are she'll be blubbering in a minute.

The television fellow, on board a boat in the harbour (one of many by the looks of it), reports: 'It's believed that this IRA group has been establishing itself in Sydney over the past six months. It's possible there is a plan to blow up Sydney's new Opera House in what is perhaps the most dramatic publicity stunt in the history of this terrorist group, well known for their violent activism.'

'Six months,' says Effie. 'That's interesting.'

Mrs Li nods. 'The exact length of time Father Kelly's been here.'

'You know, that's very strange,' says Betty, more interested in the kittens than the Opera House being blown to smithereens. 'Someone's made a note, probably Auntie Vera. It's Father Kelly's birthday next month.' Betty takes the calendar off the wall and turns to stare at the others. 'On the nineteenth of April.'

'Yer gunna bake him a cake?' asks Irene, not taking her eyes off the screen in case she misses Hazel's appearance. She chuckles to herself. 'He'll need a metal file to get through them prison bars.'

Betty taps the page. 'Remember? The passenger list showed Michael Kelly's birthdate as the nineteenth of April.'

Irene shrugs. 'Coincidence. Same birthday, but it doesn't mean they were born the same year.'

Now Mrs Li and Effie go over to look at the calendar in Betty's hand, all three of them staring at the thing as if it's going to magically give them an answer.

'I see what you're saying,' says Mrs Li. 'But it still doesn't make sense. Let's say Father Kelly and this Michael Kelly are related . . . where's the other one?'

Effie nods. 'Be a big coincidence if another bloke named Kelly happened to have the same birthday.'

'There's gotta be bloody thousands of Kellys,' says Irene. 'There's only so many days . . .' She pauses to think how many days in a year.

'Three hundred and sixty-five,' says Betty, reading her mind. 'What are the odds?'

'Are yers agreeing with me, or what?' asks Irene.

Betty sits down on the sofa. 'What I'm saying, Irene, is what if there are two Father Kellys? Or two men named Kelly, at least. What if the one you think is Father Kelly is not Father Kelly at all? Think about it. All the odd behaviour Maude's told us about, and Auntie Vera mentioned a brother, but what if she was talking about an actual brother?'

The others continue to discuss it, but as far as Irene's concerned, it's all getting too confusing. She switches her attention back to the telly, not wanting to miss seeing someone getting shot or blown to pieces.

The announcer warns people not to go down to the waterfront. 'It's believed that a young woman, who cannot be named at this point, is in extreme danger, and it is beholden to the public to stay well away from the site. The public are hampering the police effort to resolve the crisis.'

'Oh no, Maude!' says Betty, her face crumpling. 'I wish we could do something!'

'Mate. Hazel's down there,' says Irene. 'She won't let anything happen to Maude.'

Effie gives Irene a doubtful look. 'I think even Hazel might be out of her depth here.'

Irene shakes her head. 'O ye of little faith.'

# 37

# HAZEL RECEIVES A STRANGE PROPOSAL

Hazel's relieved to see that Oscar has been allowed through the police barrier. She introduces him to Detective Dibble, and they hurry across to the office building where Oscar can set up his equipment. In the empty foyer, he opens his briefcase on a desk and reveals his recording device.

Dibble raises his eyebrows but says nothing, putting on the offered headset. After a moment he says, 'She's singing. Brave girl.' Taking off the headset, he hands it back to Oscar.

'What are you going to do?' asks Hazel. 'Time's running out.'

'I'm aware of that,' says Dibble. 'The bomb squad are setting up now.'

'If she's handcuffed to the steering wheel, we need to get in and free her,' says Hazel.

'We can't risk anyone getting that close to the vehicle,' he says. 'We have to wait.'

'Every minute she's in there the risk is higher.'

'Mrs Bates, you need to trust us to handle the situation.'

'Let me go in,' she says. 'Get me the equipment and I'll go.'

Dibble shakes his head in disbelief. 'Don't be ridiculous.'

'Maude has her whole life ahead of her. It's a risk I'm prepared to take,' Hazel argues.

'Absolutely not. Can you hear anything else, Mr Sorensen?'

Oscar shakes his head. 'She talks to herself very quietly. I cannot hear the words.'

Hazel suspects that Maude is praying, and she hopes it offers her some comfort. Despite Mrs Mulligan branding her a heathen, Hazel keeps an open mind on spiritual matters and takes a moment to offer up a silent prayer herself.

Dibble heads back to join the police cordon, asking Hazel to report to him if they hear anything useful. She watches Oscar, all his concentration focused on listening. Restless, she walks over to stand in the doorway, wishing there was something she could do. She's never felt so useless.

A moment later, an explosion shakes the ground under her feet. Black smoke and flames erupt from among the cars inside the site. A sob tears itself from her throat as she runs out of the building and down towards the site. A police officer catches her by the arm and holds her back. She stands, helplessly watching black smoke billowing from the carpark.

The smell of burning rubber fills the air. The fire engine waiting nearby starts its siren and edges down the street to the gates, but there's a delay while the gates are unlocked. A moment later there's another explosion, followed by the sound of shattering glass and bright red flames leaping in the air.

The wire mesh gates are pulled wide open and the fire engine edges its way inside. Within minutes, the firefighters release the hoses and train jets of water over the cars. The black smoke turns to grey, rolling like a thick fog.

The policeman holding Hazel loosens his grip. She breaks free and heads for the gates, but Dibble appears from nowhere and intercepts her.

'I'm sorry, Mrs Bates,' he says in a choked voice. 'There was nothing we could do. If you'd gone in there, you would have gone too. I'm sorry. Very sorry.'

Hazel watches the billowing clouds of smoke, trying to comprehend what just happened. It's not possible. It can't be possible.

Dibble puts a protective arm around her shoulder and leads her away. 'You need to stay well back. There could be further explosions, other cars could catch fire.'

Numb to everything around her, Hazel allows herself to be moved along. She sees Oscar hurrying down the street towards them. She hears the clanging of the fire engine and feels Dibble's kindly hand on her shoulder. None of it makes sense. She can't let go of the hope that Maude somehow escaped the blast, even though she knows it's impossible.

Oscar arrives by her side and takes her in his arms. Her heart is so broken, the pain is unbearable. 'Come, min skat,' he murmurs. 'I will take you home.'

As they walk away, Hazel hears shouting. She turns to see half-a-dozen police moving towards the open gates. She watches as the ambulance on stand-by switches on its flashing lights and nudges its way through the police cordon. Oscar and Hazel wait in silence, neither daring to speculate on what might be happening.

It's difficult to see what's going on, but the ambulance stops outside the gates and the back doors are opened. After some minutes, Hazel spots one of the firemen assisting a woman, blackened and limping, through the gates to the waiting ambulance.

Hazel can't believe what she's seeing. Now the tears come. Tears of relief.


Hazel should be exhausted but she's never felt more awake. The room at Special Branch police headquarters gives nothing away about the location. The walls are painted cream, carpet brown, furniture brown. The outside world looks hazy through frosted glass.

She glances at Oscar seated beside her with an apologetic smile. How on earth did he get roped into all this? Under the table, he takes her hand and holds it lightly on his knee.

Maude has been checked over by a doctor and brought straight to police headquarters. It seems she was already out of the vehicle when the explosion occurred. She was sent flying by the impact of the blast and hit by debris. Her cuts have been treated but she's still blackened by the oily smoke. The clean-up will have to wait. The crisis is far from over.

Within minutes of the bombing, the IRA had made a call to ABC radio claiming responsibility, with the threat that this was a taste of what was to come if their demands were not met within twenty-four hours. On their way here, Detective Dibble had divulged this information but not the nature of those demands, only telling them that both Interpol and British intelligence were now involved in the negotiations.

Hazel, Oscar and Maude have been instructed to wait in silence until the Special Branch team are present. A young policewoman brings them strong cups of tea and slices of Vegemite toast. Oscar sniffs the toast suspiciously and gives his piece to Maude, who wolfs it down. Finally, Dibble arrives with a senior detective introduced as Inspector Whitlock. They're also joined by the female police officer, now acting as a stenographer.

'Let's hear from Maude first,' says Dibble. 'Tell us everything.'

Maude takes a sip of tea. 'I didn't know what was happening at first. Two of them came into my room and grabbed me. Then I was chucked in the back of the car. Father Kelly said I had to drive, but I told them I don't have any idea how to drive a car so they started arguing and Brother O'Connell said, "We'll dump her."'

Maude pauses and gathers herself. 'They had a key for the gates at the Opera House. When we were inside, they both got out and fiddled around in the boot, starting the bomb. I could hear it ticking from the back seat. They dragged me out and stuck me in the driver's seat. They handcuffed me to the steering wheel and tied a hankie around my mouth.

'I had my right hand free, though, and I managed to undo the gag. I had a couple of hairpins in my hair. The first one I dropped on the floor, so then there was just the one. I knew I didn't have much time, but I tried to stay calm and not think about that. I pulled the rubber end off of the hairpin with my teeth and jiggled it around in the lock. Mrs Turnbuckle showed me how to do that.'

Whitlock turns to Dibble with a quizzical look.

'One of the tea ladies,' explains Dibble. 'Go on, Maude.'

'She showed me how different locks work, and also that you have to keep at it, not just give up. I've been practising a bit,' she adds.

Dibble asks her to go right back to the beginning and give them everything she can think of, no detail too small. Maude explains how she ended up in the job, her disappointment with Father Kelly's attitude and the rudeness of the other two men. 'I liked Father Kelly, before. He was kind and polite. But in the house he treated me like a servant.'

'You were a servant,' Whitlock points out. 'That's what a house-keeper is.'

'That's not what I thought, at the start. I thought it was an honourable job to care for His Reverence.' Maude glances at Hazel. 'Like being a tea lady, but more holy . . . Anyway, it wasn't only that. I thought Father Kelly was very devout. These other two were not. They're like the drongos my dad drinks with at the pub.' She pauses. 'Hang on a minute, are they actual brothers?'

'We're still gathering intelligence on them,' Whitlock tells her. 'Did you ever hear them discuss these terrorist plans or any hint of this sort of activity?'

Maude shakes her head. 'They were sort of sneaky and if I was around, they'd sometimes talk in Irish, so I couldn't understand them. They'd be locked away in Father Kelly's office a lot. I thought it was all church business. There's a lot of politics in the church – I remember Auntie Vera saying that. Anyway, I was flat out keeping them fed and staying out of their way, to be truthful.' She recounts the conversation with Auntie Vera's sister and how Hazel had become suspicious, which led to Maude wearing a microphone.

When she has finished her account, Whitlock turns to Hazel and asks about her involvement. Hazel explains that she had known Auntie Vera and visited the convent regularly. She had met Father Kelly on a couple of occasions.

Whitlock suggests that, as a parishioner, wouldn't she already be familiar with Father Kelly?

'I'm not a parishioner.' Hazel pauses, hoping to avoid this conversation, but then plunges in. 'One of the nuns there works with adults who suffer from word blindness, which is known as dyslexia. I'm there learning to read and write.'

Hazel can see from Dibble's expression this comes as a surprise, but he says nothing.

'I see. What was the first indication that something wasn't right?' Whitlock asks.

Hazel describes noticing Father Kelly's injury on her first meeting. Her sense that he was being untruthful about the identity of Riley and O'Connell. Later there were the reports from Maude, and her concerns about the girl's safety.

'So how did you get involved in all this, Mr Sorensen?' asks Dibble, turning to Oscar.

'Mrs Bates telephoned me last night. She told me the police planned to put a listening device into the house. It would take one day, perhaps longer, and she was worried about Miss Mulligan.'

'What reason did Mrs Bates give for her concerns?' asks Whitlock.

Oscar frowns. 'Miss Mulligan is a young woman alone in a house with suspicious men. I understood there was reason to worry. This is why I offered to make a temporary listening device.'

'You happened to have one with you?' asks Whitlock in a sceptical tone. 'A foreign national with this sort of equipment is as much a concern to us as these men. Particularly when you're using it to illegally record people.'

Oscar explains calmly that he is not from an enemy country but from the friendly nation of Denmark and employed as a senior acoustic consultant on the Opera House project. This is his profession. 'I do not work with this type of device, but I have the expertise and the equipment to assemble one easily. This is what I did for Mrs Bates.'

Whitlock stares at Oscar as if he doesn't believe a word. 'Why would you take the risk, knowing it was illegal and could get you deported?'

Oscar shrugs philosophically. 'I'm making . . . I believe the term is "brownie points".'

'I don't understand,' says Whitlock.

'In the hope that Mrs Bates will agree to marry me,' explains Oscar.

Despite the seriousness of the situation, or perhaps because of it, Hazel sputters with laughter. 'Oscar, come on, be serious.'

'I believe he is serious,' says Dibble. 'But we're getting off track here.'

'I agree,' says Whitlock. 'We'll look into this illegal recording issue at a later time.'

Hazel loses her patience. 'Maude is here with us, and safe, thank God. If we hadn't known what was going on in that house last night, things would be very different this morning. Very different indeed.'

With a grudging nod of agreement, Whitlock says, 'We're finished with you for the moment, Mr Sorensen, you may go. Don't leave the country without our say-so.'

Oscar gives a respectful nod and, with a quick smile in Hazel's direction, allows himself to be ushered out the door by the policewoman.

Whitlock turns to Maude and Hazel. 'Think carefully, ladies. Kelly and O'Connell are still on the loose. We have to track these men down before the deadline expires.' He pauses, perhaps wondering how much to reveal. 'The threat is so severe that every railway station in the city is being shut down and all the buildings within a mile of the foreshore are being evacuated.'

'Miss Mulligan, it's likely that you know more than you think,' says Dibble. 'Not just their identities, but other information that might lead us somewhere.'

Maude shakes her head. 'I'm pretty sure I told you everything I know.'

'You might have seen something that didn't make sense at the time,' suggests Dibble.

'None of it made sense, but I've never lived with a priest before so I didn't know what to expect.'

A silence falls on the room. Dibble flicks through his notebook. He looks up at Maude. 'In the search this morning, there were a lot of dry-cleaning dockets in one of the kitchen drawers.'

Maude nods. 'I have to keep all receipts for the bookkeeper. I never knew anyone to have so much dry-cleaning as those so-called priests. Practically every day sending me off with a package of clothes for cleaning and then bringing another package back. One thing at a time. It seemed silly.'

Dibble looks puzzled. 'Where is this drycleaners?'

'In the city, on Macquarie Street. There's plenty of drycleaners closer but Father Kelly said this was a special holy one.'

'Did the drycleaner say anything to you—' begins Dibble.

'Macquarie Street, near St James Station?' interrupts Hazel.

Maude nods. 'On the other side of the street.'

Hazel turns to Whitlock and Dibble. 'There are tunnels under Macquarie Street. They run from St James Station all the way down to Circular Quay and . . . the Opera House.'

'Unused tunnels?' asks Whitlock with a frown.

Hazel nods. 'Yes, they were built at the same time as the stations for future railway lines. I noticed a plan in Mr Utzon's office showing where they run. I'm sure if you spoke to someone on the railways—'

Dibble and Whitlock are already getting to their feet. 'No time for that. Do you remember the plan? Can you show us?' asks Dibble.

'I think so,' says Hazel, with some trepidation.

Dibble turns to the policewoman. 'Make sure Miss Mulligan gets home safely.'

'Let's put a watch on her, just to be sure,' calls Whitlock, as he heads for the door. 'For her own safety.'

## 38

# HAZEL GOES UNDERGROUND

For the second time today, Hazel finds herself in a police car racing through the streets. Dibble drives while Whitlock barks orders into the two-way to expand the evacuation beyond a mile, clear the entire area around St James Station, and dispatch the bomb squad immediately.

Within minutes, the whine of sirens fills the air. By the time they reach the station, the area is being cordoned off by police and shoppers on Elizabeth Street are being herded through hastily erected barricades.

Hazel gets out of the vehicle with Dibble and Whitlock, and they enter the station against the flow of confused passengers being hurriedly ushered out by police. She quickly finds the green door on the lower platform that Mr Utzon had mentioned. Dibble steps forward to examine the lock to find it's already been broken into, and the door swings open.

A crowd of police have begun to gather around them. Whitlock orders most of the uniformed police to stay outside the station, with only four officers and the bomb squad, led by Dibble, to enter the tunnel. Whitlock will stay above ground with the command centre.

Dibble looks over at Hazel. 'Are you sure you remember where to go?'

Hazel closes her eyes for a moment and pictures the plan she saw that day. She clearly recalls that one tunnel led south to the bomb shelters built during the war and the other towards Circular Quay. Gradually she begins to see the image quite clearly in her mind. She nods and, stepping through the doorway, begins descending the stairs.

Plunged into darkness, with only the police torches to light the way, they take the stairs deep underground to an abandoned platform. Once they climb down to where the track would have run, things get more difficult. The tunnel is damp and airless, the air thick with the smell of mould and rot. Dozens of rats scurry away in their path. In places, the group are forced to push through dangling tendrils of tree roots. The curved walls are slick with seepage from above and Hazel's shoes are soon soaked by puddles of water up to her ankles.

She remembers Mr Utzon saying there was no access from that end, so it seems likely that anything to find will be at the dead end of this tunnel. She has to force herself not to think about being trapped in here with a pile of explosives.

After ten minutes or so, they come to an intersection of two tunnels; one sweeps off to the right and the other to the left. Hazel stops and pictures the map in her mind.

'That one goes off towards the eastern suburbs,' she says, pointing to the right fork. 'We continue down this way.'

On they go. Now the water is halfway up her shins, and rats are swimming around them. It's not just water dripping from the ceiling but small creatures she can't see, but she brushes them off quickly, imagining they're cockroaches or small lizards.

Another ten or fifteen minutes pass. One of the many torches bouncing along behind her flashes the length of the tunnel and she glimpses what looks like a solid wall at the end.

'Are you all right?' asks Dibble, wading along beside her.

'Yes,' says Hazel. 'Is that a dead end ahead?'

Dibble trains his torch straight down the tunnel. 'Yes, looks like it. The two-way doesn't work down here, so we're on our own.'

'Apart from half a dozen police behind us,' says Hazel.

'Oh, yes, I forgot about them. Thanks for reminding me.' He gives a gruff laugh, and Hazel hears the fear in his voice.

'Are you all right?' she asks.

'I don't like the dark,' he says. 'Claustrophobia.'

Hazel moves a little closer and takes his arm. 'We're nearly there.'

'That's not a comforting thought, Mrs Bates.'

'These fellows must be very dedicated to come all the way through here to deliver their explosives,' she remarks.

'Fanatics,' says Dibble. 'Martyrs. Who knows what goes on in their heads? They probably get a kick out of this.' He turns to the troop following them. 'Let's just stop here. Bomb disposal go first. Uniforms wait until we know what we're dealing with.'

The four-man bomb disposal squad in their heavy padded uniforms move ahead. It's clear to Hazel that if something goes wrong, a bit of padding will be useless. In the case of an explosion, the tunnel itself will collapse.

In silence, they watch the disposal men wade slowly to the end of the tunnel. There's a long tense wait while they inspect whatever they find there. Finally, one lone officer comes back towards them. The police gather as he approaches.

'There's roughly six hundred pounds of jelly,' he tells them. 'We're defusing the detonator and then we can move it out in small batches.'

'Six hundred pounds?' says Dibble.

The man nods. 'It's hard to tell exactly what's above us, but I'd say we're fairly central to the construction. It'd blow the ground out from under it. There's no timer. It was set for remote detonation, so they can't be too far away.' He looks up into the dark arches overhead as if imagining what's above. 'Better you boys – and lady – go back up. We'll handle it from here.'

Flooded with relief, Hazel barely notices the discomfort of the walk back to the station, but the final ascent up the long staircase almost finishes her off.

Whitlock is pacing the corridor as they come through the door. When Dibble reports back their findings, Whitlock allows himself a smile of satisfaction. 'We've just arrested Kelly and O'Connell as well as three other suspects at the drycleaning place. Took them completely by surprise.' He turns to Hazel. 'Mrs Bates, I don't know what to say . . . Without your help . . .' He gazes at her as if seeing her properly for the first time. Noticing her soaked feet, he adds, 'At the very least, we owe you a new pair of shoes.'

'Thank you and thank goodness . . .' Hazel pauses. There are so many things she's thankful for but, now, overcome with exhaustion, she decides to leave it at that.

'Just another day in the life of a tea lady, eh?' says Dibble with a wink.

## 39

# BETTY ATTENDS A DEBRIEF

Betty has read the papers every day, morning and afternoon. In the evenings, she's the first one outside Gibson's, ready and waiting for the news to start. There's been such a crowd lately they've had to put bigger speakers out the front of the shop. The terrorist threat to the Opera House has been in the headlines every day. The whole country has been enthralled as the revelations keep on coming. Maude Mulligan is a heroine who managed a Houdini-like escape. Another citizen, who prefers to remain anonymous, led to the discovery of a bomb under the Opera House. More than a dozen IRA terrorists are now in custody. What people don't know is that it was Betty's sharp eye that alerted police to another aspect of the case.

Today Betty's at police headquarters to go over all the evidence. Hazel, Mrs Li, Irene, Effie and Maude are all present, as well as Detective Dibble, Inspector Whitlock and a young policewoman who delivered tea and six biscuits. The meeting room is rather dull. Betty had hoped for a wall of criminal photos and lists connected by pieces of string but it's a bland room with a big table and not enough biscuits for everyone (which is exactly what happens when there's no tea lady in charge).

Dibble looks around at each of them with a serious expression. 'I take my hat off to you ladies, history could have been made in a very different way without your intervention. There are still many loose ends, but we will get to the bottom of them eventually. We need to ensure we have every tiny detail of evidence documented. That's why we're here today.' He pauses and glances at Inspector Whitlock.

The inspector clears his throat. 'Following the tip-off from Mrs Dewsnap concerning Michael Kelly and a hunch from Mrs Bates, we have now recovered the body of the real Father Kelly from the building excavations on the church grounds.' He looks over at Betty. 'Mrs Dewsnap's report of the coincidence of the birthdates led to the knowledge that the man you knew to be Father Kelly was, in fact, his twin brother Michael, an active member of the IRA. We can't be sure when the substitution took place, but it seems immediately prior to the death of the housekeeper.'

'So I never met the real Father Kelly,' says Hazel. 'That explains a great deal.'

Betty looks around the table at the sombre faces. It's a lot to take in on top of everything else. No one knows what to expect any more. She wonders if one of the three terrorists will confess. They'd all be riddled with guilt. Complicated Catholic guilt.

Dibble looks at his notes. 'What we know from the Kelly family in Belfast is that Michael has been heavily involved with the IRA for some years, but they were not aware he had left Ireland, let alone that he was in Australia.'

Whitlock takes up the story. 'We have managed to get some information from one of the suspects, so we know that the IRA, worried their cause was losing traction, decided that bombing a well-known public building would get worldwide attention. Someone came up with the idea of the Opera House – already in the news. From there a plan developed to kidnap Father Kelly so Michael Kelly could take his place and Riley and O'Connell pose as Catholic brothers, giving the group a perfect cover and freedom to move around. Mrs Bates mentioned that the person we now know to be Michael Kelly had a wound on his head. Forensics have found blood on a communion plate in the church and on the altar. It seems that the kidnapping went wrong when Father Kelly put up a fight. He may have been killed accidentally, that we don't know yet.' He turns to Maude. 'What we do know is that the drycleaning business was a front and Miss Mulligan was unwittingly delivering and collecting messages and plans concealed in the clothes. That's where we arrested Michael Kelly and O'Connell, and three other men.'

'Why drycleaning?' asks Effie.

Dibble shrugs. 'The premises were chosen for their proximity to the tunnels. It's just an agency, no equipment.'

'There were enough explosives packed in the tunnels, right under the foundations of the Opera House, to do irreparable damage to the building,' says Whitlock.

'What about Auntie Vera?' asks Hazel. 'She must have cottoned on to what was happening. She would have quickly picked up that Michael Kelly was an imposter.'

Dibble shakes his head. 'At this stage we don't know. All three deny any involvement in her death, but we believe it's no coincidence that she died suddenly around the same time as Father Kelly was murdered. Unfortunately we will now have to exhume her body for an autopsy.' He glances down at his notes. 'I think that covers it. We're still piecing it together. All we now need from you ladies is any further detail that might help with our investigation.'

Hazel suggests they interview Sister Ruth. 'This may be a separate issue altogether, but the church sold part of their land to finance the building of the orphanage—'

'Yes,' interrupts Maude. 'I heard the fake Father on the phone about it, arguing with someone . . . I think it was someone at the bank.'

Dibble and Whitlock exchange glances. 'Perhaps they were trying to access the funds, build up the coffers,' says Whitlock. 'We'll look into that.'

Maude hands over the contact details of Auntie Vera's sister. Betty provides the passenger details she copied at the shipping office. Irene suggests they search the gardening shed behind the convent for poisons.

As they leave the police headquarters to go their own ways, it occurs to Betty that being involved with a Special Branch terrorist investigation is all in a day's work for her now. It's as much a part of her life as making tea, but far more exciting.

# 40

# HAZEL'S DILEMMA

With everything else that's been happening, Hazel has barely had time to think about Oscar's oddly timed proposal. She's been wed twice. The first marriage was happy and fruitful until the war intervened. The second one also made her very happy until she discovered a deception at the heart of it. After that, she felt she couldn't trust her judgement.

She has become very fond of Oscar and when he goes back to Denmark (as she has no doubt he will) she will miss him terribly. Had he made the proposal at a time when she still had a job, it would have been an immediate no. But now she has no job and has begun to wonder if she will ever have another one, given that she's not the only tea lady out of work. So, she has given it some consideration.

She's found ways to keep herself busy, but it takes some effort. After the years spent talking to people all day long and being involved in their daily lives, it's lonely being at home on her own. The empty days stretch out ahead.

Now, as she walks through the Botanic Gardens with Oscar, towards their favourite bench overlooking the harbour, she asks if his comments at police headquarters were serious.

'We Danes have an excellent sense of humour, but we do not joke about these things,' he says. 'It was not the most romantic location, but a good story for us to tell in the future.' He pauses. 'If we have a future.'

'Oh, Oscar, I'm very touched. With everything that's happening . . .'

'Of course. You must take your time.'

When they're settled, he continues. 'The end of the project has come. It is finished for our team. It may be that a new agreement is reached later, but . . . I think not. There have been too many meetings, too many arguments. It is like an angry divorce. I think the government will be happy to see the end of the foreigners and start with a new team. It has been decided we will leave this week.'

'I'm so sorry to hear that, Oscar.' The thought of never seeing him again makes her feel wretched. 'In that case, I owe you an answer to your proposal,' she says.

Oscar smiles, the light catching the gold frames of his glasses. 'I think I know your answer,' he says. 'I understand. Denmark is a long way from your world.'

Hazel nods. 'Much as I will miss you, to never see my family or friends again would be the end of the world to me.'

Oscar takes her hands in his. 'You can always know there is a Danish gentleman who is happy to hear from you and will send you an airplane ticket to this far away land if you ever wish for it.'

'I will keep that in mind, thank you.'

He puts his arm around her, and she leans her head on his shoulder for a moment. 'Perhaps you'll come back one day.'

'Perhaps,' he says quietly. 'I came to Australia last year to make the acoustics of this building the best in the world. I never expected to be thrown from the project or that Jørn would leave it unfinished.' He shakes his head and gives a laugh. 'But I also never expected to help save it from being destroyed. Or that I would meet someone who captured my heart. The unexpected things in life are often the best.'

Hazel agrees. 'I will miss you, Oscar.'

'And I will miss you, min skat.'

With that conversation out of the way, they sit in silence, hand in hand, and watch the afternoon shadows pattern the lawns and light dance on the water. Around them families begin to pack up picnic rugs and shepherd their children towards home. But Oscar and Hazel stay on, stretching out these last moments together.


Monday mornings in particular continue to be difficult for Hazel. She considers calling Norma, but she'll be busy with her day. Betty is at work, as are Irene and Merl. She feels compelled to get on with something – but what? She could go to the corner shop and buy a newspaper. She's reasonably confident she could read the classified ads now. There must be a job she can do.

Impossible as it seems, an hour after this thought, she's still sitting at the kitchen table, pinned to the chair by indecision. It's a relief when she hears a knock on the door; even if it's only the milkman with his bill, she'll be happy to see him.

As it happens, she finds Detective Dibble on the doorstep.

'Come in, Detective.' She gestures down the hall. 'Go straight through. I was just about to make a pot of tea.'

'I won't take up too much of your time,' he says.

She follows him down to the kitchen. 'Time is something I have a surplus of right now,' she says, putting on the kettle. 'Do sit down.'

'I stopped in to see you at work, and they told me you'd left the place.' He peers into the offered cake tin and takes a piece of shortbread.

Hazel leans on the bench while she waits for the kettle to boil. 'Not by choice, I assure you. I've been replaced by a machine.'

'I see. One of those Café things, I presume. So, bringing the city to a halt didn't save the day in the end?'

Hazel smiles. 'Not for me. But perhaps for others. I heard the ladies who chained themselves up got off with a warning.'

Dibble shrugs. 'Probably unlikely to reoffend.'

Hazel pours boiling water into the teapot. 'I don't know about that. They seemed to be enjoying themselves enormously.'

Dibble helps himself to another piece of shortbread. Glancing across at Hazel, he taps his ring finger. 'No diamond, I see.'

Hazel smiles. 'No. I decided against it in the end.'

'He's a clever chap, but I hear it's cold over there,' he says. 'And a long way away.'

'Exactly. How are you going with the investigation? Do we have any answers about Auntie Vera yet? She's been on my mind.'

'That's what I came to tell you,' says Dibble, taking the cup of tea from her. 'The autopsy showed traces of ethylene glycol in her system. Forensics have been through the gardening shed and Riley's fingerprints were found on a container of anti-freeze, which contains the chemical. So he's been charged with her murder. All three were involved with Father Kelly's kidnap plot but insist his death was an accident – so we will see.'

Hazel sighs. 'Poor Auntie Vera, what a tragic end. She was so loved in the community. Has her sister been told?'

'I've done that myself. She was very . . .' He pauses to find the right word. '. . . thankful that we had got to the bottom of it.

She knew something was wrong. We've also discovered from the bank that Michael Kelly did attempt to access the funds set aside for the orphanage building but he ran into a problem. The cheques needed three signatures: Father Kelly's, the bishop's and Mother Superior's. Not easy to forge all three and get away with it, so he cooked up some story to try and talk the bank into accepting one signatory – without luck.'

'They must have realised that attempting to get the money could draw attention and possibly wreck their plot for the Opera House,' says Hazel.

'These terrorist groups are always desperate for funds, so it must have been very tempting to make a grab for the money.' Dibble finishes his tea and pushes back his chair. 'Thanks for the tea, Mrs Bates. By the way, I believe Maude Mulligan has applied to join the police force.'

Hazel sits back in surprise. 'Has she now? You must have been an inspiration to her.'

Dibble laughs. 'One of us was. Maybe you could consider doing a bit of work for us yourself? Special ops?'

Hazel chuckles. 'I'll stick to my amateur status, thank you. Less paperwork.'

He stares at her thoughtfully. 'Is that because of the reading business?'

Hazel considers his question. It's been a protective habit to briskly dismiss anything that risks exposure, but is that something she needs to reconsider now she's on her way to reading? 'Possibly,' she concedes. 'I'm not quite there yet.'

'There are ways around it, and I'd be happy to help you out.'

'That's very kind of you.' Hazel gives him a hard look. 'Are you serious?'

Dibble nods. 'I've discussed it with Inspector Whitlock. You have the perfect cover, as we already know. We wouldn't put you in any dangerous situations, obviously.'

Hazel brushes his concerns aside. 'I can take care of myself, Detective.'

Dibble laughs. 'So you can.' He gets up to go. 'Think about it.'

Hazel stands at the front door and watches him drive away. She still has her lessons with Sister Ruth and there's plenty of time to practise, so no excuses not to continue to improve. It occurs to her that she could push herself a little harder by joining the library, and feels a rush of pleasure at the thought.

Mrs Mulligan pops her head out from next door. 'Penny for 'em, Hazel.'

'Oh, I was miles away. How are you going, Mrs Mulligan?'

'I can't bear to think of it. Our dear Auntie Vera being resurrected, so to speak. Terrible, disturbing the dead like that.'

'Yes, an unfortunate necessity,' murmurs Hazel.

'Why do you think they did it? Auntie Vera was kindness itself. How could anyone find it in their selves to murder her?'

'She was very close to Father Kelly. Something must have aroused her suspicions. We may know more when the case goes to court.'

'And poor Father Kelly, spare me days! It's unbelievable! I had my suspicions, you know. He was looking a bit scrawny – him the brother, not the real Father. I did notice his sermons had gone downhill.' She glances at Hazel guiltily. 'Not real suspicions, of course, or I wouldn't have sent Maude there. The funeral is this week with high-up church people coming from all over. We will pray for his soul in the afterlife, poor man.'

'I hear Maude is joining the police force,' says Hazel.

'Not a job for a girl, in my opinion.' Mrs Mulligan hesitates. 'Not much I can say after all that's gone on, I just have to accept it. Quite frankly, I can't see any man wanting to marry a copper, but that's her funeral.'

Hazel smiles. 'Much better than an actual funeral though, isn't it?'

Mrs Mulligan nods. 'It is that.'

## 41

# IRENE TAKES STOCK

What a bunch, thinks Irene. Three old chooks sitting in a row on the wall. Irene smoking while Merl and Betty eat their sandwiches. It's not the same without Hazel, though there's nothing to stop her coming down. She doesn't have much else to do. But Betty reckons Hazel doesn't want to hang around the laneway now she doesn't work here. Fair enough.

The thing is, Hazel always kept the peace. Now Irene has to watch what she says in case the other two get riled up with no one to calm them down. Takes the fun out of lunchtime. That said, she decides to risk a little light stirring. 'I don't reckon yer should be eating fish paste with yer problem, Betty.'

Betty doesn't bite but Merl does. 'It's not actually fish, you know.' (Only the hundredth time she's said that.)

'What is it then?' asks Irene.

Still nothing from Betty, munching away in silence.

'Essence of fish,' says Merl, after some thought.

'Yer mean like the smell of it? Still fish.' Irene coughs up a cloud of smoke. 'Dunno why yer keep saying that. It's not pig or cow. It's fish.'

'Do we have to talk about this?' asks Betty, folding up her lunch wrap.

Irene gives her a comforting pat on the shoulder and gets a dirty look for her troubles.

'Betty, yer can't sit around sulking all day because Hazel's gone.'

'For your information, Irene, I'm not sulking, I'm sad. It's a normal human emotion. I thought with the success of the strike, Hazel's job would be saved but it got her sacked. I feel partly responsible, if you must know.'

Merl stops attacking her knitting and looks up. 'Betty, the reason Hazel was dismissed was to do with what's going on in that firm. Old Mr Karp has retired, and Dottie and Frankie are in charge.' She has a little chuckle. 'My boss said it might as well be Abbott and Costello running the place.'

That makes Betty smile. 'You may be right. Perhaps it was only a matter of time. They used our rally as an excuse. I just hope Hazel finds something else nearby.'

'Of course she will,' says Merl. 'Hazel always falls on her feet.'

'I heard Violet's lost her job,' Betty says with a sigh. 'I feel bad about putting those dreadful insects in our machine, but it did do the trick. They've sent it back.'

Having saved Betty's job, Irene feels free to light another smoke. Privately, she wonders if Hazel is meant for bigger things. It was quite a surprise to hear that Hazel couldn't read. Thinking back, she was always asking Irene to read things (even though Irene's not keen on reading herself) and making the excuse that she'd lost her glasses. Takes some doing to cover that up your whole life. Hazel's a shrewd one, all right.

Merl starts in on Irene. 'Is that a new hat, Irene? And new slippers too, I see. Come into some money, have you?'

'Bloody rolling in it, mate. Got me job and no rent. Might even buy meself a new cardie.' Glancing down at the scorch marks up her sleeves, Irene remembers Hazel gave this cardigan to her. 'Nah, this one'll do me.'

The truth is Irene's got more money than she ever thought possible. That dopey legal eagle has arranged to rent Fred's land off her. One of his lawyer mates towed an old caravan up there for him and he plans to go bush for a few years, put some distance between him and the gee-gees. Good luck to him. Suits her, she's happy at Miss Palmer's. There's plenty of company and interesting things going on. Her list is growing by the day; she'll have dirt on half the city soon. If she sold that land she could buy a little flat, but that'd attract the wrong sort of attention and, anyway, she doesn't fancy being stuck somewhere on her lonesome, wiping down benches and paying rates. All that responsibility. She's got new slippers, a new hat and a few spare bob to put on the dogs of a Friday. It's all worked out for the best.

'So, Hazel's gentleman friend . . .' Merl pauses her knitting to raise a questioning eyebrow.

'He's gone home,' says Betty. 'Another thing for Hazel to be sad about.'

Merl gives a grunt. 'Hazel's really getting a bit long in the tooth for—'

'You're never too old to fall in love,' says Betty, annoyed. 'He was a very nice fellow, and clever too. He worked on the Opera House – he's an acoustics engineer.'

Merl doesn't miss a beat. 'Well, all I can say is thank goodness they've sent all those Scandinavians, with their airy-fairy ideas, back to where they came from. We never should have got them involved in the first place. Now we can get some practical Aussie know-how on the job and get the blasted thing finished.'

Irene has no idea what this Scandiwhatsit is about. She thought the bloke was from Denmark. She's about to correct Merl when she notices Betty's getting steamed up.

'Let's get our army of tea ladies on the job, eh?' says Irene, giving her a nudge. 'We'd get the bloody thing done in a week.'

That makes Betty giggle. 'And have a good singsong while we're at it.'

Even Merl smiles at the thought. 'Not a bad idea,' she says. Packing up her knitting, she gets up. 'Back to the grindstone, I suppose.'

'See you at the Hollywood tonight?' asks Betty.

Merl nods. 'I'll be there.'

# 42

# THE END OF THE DAY

Hazel sits at the card table in her front room, adding the last few pieces to the Hanging Gardens of Babylon. With so much time on her hands, it's all come together quickly.

'Coo-ee! Hazel, where are you?'

'In here, Betty dear,' Hazel calls back.

Betty comes in and sits down on the sofa. 'There's no rush to get to the Hollywood this evening. You're probably feeling a bit down with "you know who" leaving, on top of everything else.'

Hazel still feels a pang every time she thinks of Oscar, which is more often than she'd like. He has promised to write, and she will too – another reason to keep practising. Perhaps he will come back one day. But despite her heartache, she has no regrets. Every moment with him was a pleasure.

She puts the last piece in place. 'There, all done.' She gazes at it for a moment then, picking up the box, scrapes the jigsaw into it and puts on the lid. She looks up at Betty. 'I'm all right, dear. Please don't worry about me.'

'I was wondering, if Empire offered your job back—'

'I don't think you can go back, dear,' interrupts Hazel. 'My time there is finished. I need to wait and see what's in store for me next.'

'It's not the same at lunchtimes,' Betty says glumly. 'I'm so used to seeing you every day.' She manages to put on a brave face. 'I suppose I'll get used to it in time.'

'I've been thinking about that. I need to rent the upstairs room out. I think you and I could rub along well together in this little house . . .'

Betty gives a gasp. 'Oh, Hazel! There's nothing I would love more than that. I will be the best lodger ever, I promise.'

Hazel laughs. 'The last one did set a high standard, but I'm sure you can surpass it.'

Betty gives a dismissive huff. 'That won't be difficult.'

'I had an interesting visit from Detective Dibble yesterday.'

Betty's eyes light up. 'Oh, yes?'

Hazel tells her about the results of the autopsy and Riley being charged with Auntie Vera's murder.

'Cold-blooded killers,' says Betty. 'That could have been Maude too if not for us.'

'Speaking of which, Detective Dibble suggested there could be an opportunity for me to work on an operation with him, so I'll need to try even harder with my reading and writing.'

Betty clasps her hands to her chest. 'I'll help you! We can work on it together.'

'Wonderful, that's settled then,' says Hazel with a smile. 'I'll just pop up and get my glad rags on, and then we'll be off.'

Upstairs, Hazel slips into her favourite summer dress, adds a little lipstick and runs a comb through her hair. As she and Betty walk down to the Hollywood, the heat of the day lingers like a warm embrace. People sit out on their front steps, some drinking from bottles of beer as they chat to neighbours and passers-by. Children squat in semi-circles on the pavement playing marbles or knucklebones. Stray dogs lie on the road, worn out by the long hot day. Neighbours greet Hazel and Betty, left and right, and they stop now and then to chat.

As they approach the welcoming lights of the Hollywood Hotel, a little later than expected, Betty links her arm in Hazel's. 'I'm so glad you didn't go to Denmark, Hazel.'

Hazel gives her arm a squeeze. 'Me too.'

Hazel knows that Irene will be waiting for someone to buy her a drink, Merl will be knitting and fretting about them being late, Effie will be halfway through her first pint and Shirley will pour their shandies as soon as they walk through the door. Some things don't change. One day they will, but for now, these are the constants, and Hazel is deeply grateful for them.

# ACKNOWLEDGEMENTS

In 2004, I signed my first contract with Penguin Books for my novel *The Olive Sisters*. The publication of my debut was the realisation of a lifetime dream and its success beyond all expectation. Over the past two decades, Penguin Random House has published seven more of my novels, and there are many people to thank for their contributions and support. At the top of that list is my publisher, Ali Watts. As well as offering her valuable insights that make every book better, she has championed my work throughout the years with unwavering enthusiasm and has been a joy to work with.

The wonderful success of *The Tea Ladies* series is due to the combined efforts of a brilliant team at Penguin Random House. Many thanks to my dream editor, Amanda Martin, who takes every detail as seriously as I do; designer Debra Billson for her sparkling signature covers; proofreader Sonja Heijn, whose forensic reading unearths hidden errors; and publicist extraordinaire Bella Arnott-Hoare, who is tireless in her endeavours.

Thanks also for the support of Julie Burland, Holly Toohey, Rebekah Chereshsky, Sarah McDuling, Janine Brown and her sales team, and Veronica Eze and the rest of the audio team. Special thanks to Zoe Carides, whose voice brings the tea ladies to life in the audiobook.

To the booksellers who hand-sold and personally recommended *The Tea Ladies* to their customers – thank you!

And thanks to you, my readers, for taking the time to enjoy my books and recommend them to your friends. In a world where we are badgered to buy things at every turn, good old-fashioned word-of-mouth carries more weight than ever.

Special thanks to Rosy Browell, Acoustic Engineer, and Laurence Burgess, former NSW detective, who provided their invaluable expertise for *The Cryptic Clue*.

Thank you to the early readers for your insightful feedback: Billie Trinder, Samantha Roughley, Dorothea Gallacher, Nada Sinclair, Rosemary Puddy, Meg Dunn, Meredith D'Alton, Rosemary Perry, Joe Harrison and Diana Qian.

Thank you to Elliot Lindsay, historian and archaeologist, who runs true crime walking tours of inner Sydney through his company Murders Most Foul – these tours have been a regular source of inspiration for me.

I am forever grateful for the support of my wonderful children and their partners, Tula Wynyard, Joyce Cheng, Milan Wynyard, Hayley Farrell, Darren and Tonia Gittins, my grandchildren Claudia, Ollie and Chelsie, and my sister, Kim Hampson.

This book was written on unceded Wurundjeri Country. I acknowledge the First Nations people as the custodians of this land, and pay my respects to Elders past, present and emerging.

# BOOK CLUB QUESTIONS

1. How did *The Cryptic Clue* compare with the first book in the series, *The Tea Ladies*?
2. The tea ladies believe 'there's more to the job than just serving up tea and bickies'. In which ways do they prove this to be true?
3. Did you enjoy being transported back in time to the sixties, and did the historic events in the book bring back any memories for you?
4. Which character is your favourite, and why?
5. What do you think about the friendships between the characters, and how important do you think these relationships are for women?
6. Do you think the Café-bar was a good sign of progress?
7. The Tea Ladies Guild fights to protect something they believe to be 'irreplaceable'. Which other jobs that became redundant are now sorely missed?
8. What do you see the tea ladies getting up to in the next book in the series?

9. Why do you think the cosy crime genre is so popular now, and what other authors do you enjoy?

10. Have you read other books by Amanda Hampson, and which is your favourite?

# The Tea Ladies

THEY KEEP
EVERYONE'S
SECRETS...
UNTIL THERE'S
A MURDER

Amanda
Hampson

'A total joy!'
JOANNA NELL

'I couldn't put it down.'
THE ABC BOOK CLUB

'Sheer delight.'
*COUNTRY STYLE*

*They keep everyone's secrets, until there's a murder ...*

Sydney, 1965: After a chance encounter with a stranger, tea ladies Hazel, Betty and Irene become accidental sleuths, stumbling into a world of ruthless crooks and racketeers in search of a young woman believed to be in danger.

In the meantime, Hazel's job at Empire Fashionwear is in jeopardy. The firm has turned out the same frocks and blouses for the past twenty years and when the mini-skirt bursts onto the scene, it rocks the rag trade to its foundations. War breaks out between departments and it falls to Hazel, the quiet diplomat, to broker peace and save the firm.

When there is a murder in the building, the tea ladies draw on their wider network and put themselves in danger as they piece together clues that connect the murder to a nearby arson and a kidnapping. But if there's one thing tea ladies can handle, it's hot water.

'*The Tea Ladies* is a total joy! With her ear for dialogue and eye for authentic detail, Amanda Hampson has created a refreshing take on a murder mystery that is both wickedly funny and highly entertaining.'
Joanna Nell

THE
OLIVE
Sisters

AMANDA HAMPSON

The
FRENCH
Perfumer

AMANDA HAMPSON

THE
Yellow
VILLA

AMANDA HAMPSON

Sixty
SUMMERS

AMANDA HAMPSON

LOVEBIRDS

AMANDA HAMPSON

# Discover a
# new favourite

Visit **penguin.com.au/readmore**

To learn more, please visit
www.amandahampson.com